_____

EDWARD LEE

_____

JOHN SHIRLEY

_____

JOHN EVERSON

_____

BRIAN KEENE

_____

CHARLEE JACOB

_____

L.H. MAYNARD

_____

M.P.N. SIMS

_____

GERARD HOUARNER

_____

BRYAN SMITH

_____

GAK

INFERNALLY YOURS

This edition of
INFERNALLY YOURS
is limited to 450
signed & numbered copies.
This is number:

Infernally Yours

Yours

Edited & Illustrated
by Gak

Necro Publications

2009

FIRST HARDCOVER EDITION

INFERNALLY YOURS: A TRIBUTE TO EDWARD LEE'S INFERNAL WORLD
© 2009 by Necro Publications

cover & interior art © 2009 by GAK

"Foreword"   © 2009 Edward Lee
"The Senary"   © 2009 Edward Lee
"Head-Hunted"   © 2009 John Shirley
"Then Shall the Reign of Lucifer End..."   © 2009 John Everson
"Shunned"   © 2009 Charlee Jacob
"Demonlee Devilish"   © 2009 L.H. Maynard & M.P.N. Sims
"Baby Nukes in Hell"   © 2009 Gerard Houarner
"Hell Ain't a Bad Place To Be"   © 2009 Bryan Smith
"The House of Ushers"   © 2009 Brian Keene

book design & typesetting:
David G. Barnett

limited edition hardcover
ISBN: 978-1-889186-83-2

INFERNALLY YOURS
is also available in a 26-copy
deluxe lettered edition hardcover

assistant editors
John Everson, C. Dennis Moore

a Necro Publications book
www.necropublications.com

For the city of New York. Because if Hell exists on Earth its an island called Manhattan.

—GAK

Thank you to: Wendy Brewer, Dave Barnett, Don D'Auria, Tim McGinnis, GAK, Bob Strauss, Jason Byars, William Patrick, Thomas Deja, Christine Morgan, John Everson, Charlee Jacob, Brian Keene, John Shirley, Gerard and Linda, Bryan Smith, Maynard & Sims; Chris Casmedes, William D. Gagliani, Jeff Burk, Ken Arneson, Bob & Jaime Taylor, Megan Dipo, Wetbones, Killa Klep, asimmons, Liquidnoose, Harvester, Jack Staynes, corpsegrinder, darvis, darkthrone, bellamorte, splatterhead, maladar, patronick, infnlfolowr, worldspawn, Rob Johns, jonah, thereptilians, GNFNR, mpd1958, The Yak, Jdamen, sassydog, horrormike, vladcain, flahorrorwriter, Kerri.

I must also acknowledge authors S.T. Joshi, Darrell Schweitzer, and Anthony Pearsall for their various quintessential non-fiction works regarding H.P. Lovecraft.

—Edward Lee.

FOREWORD

S ending oneself to Hell on purpose might propose a curious psychological speculation, but as a writer of mass-market paperbacks and, in particular, hardcore small-press horror, I'm quite used to a virtual avalanche of such speculations from fans and critics alike; indeed, I often wonder myself as to my obsession with the Domain of the Devil. I suppose it initially involved putting myself in Lucifer's shoes. What's the most logical way to create a domain whose purpose is to exist in polar opposition to Heaven? Perhaps my creation of the Mephistopolis might be one of them; besides, it makes sense for Hell to evolve right alongside of good ole Human Civilization. And if that's the case…I wonder how Heaven has evolved too (Wait a minute! There's an idea for a novel!) Fans of my "Infernal" mythos have a tendency to ask me if I actually believe in the existence of Hell myself. The answer is yes! And since I'm also a horror writer, I suppose it's my job to imagine some aspects of my beliefs—be they metaphoric or concrete—and infuse them into my work. I'll begin this hopefully not-too-boring preamble by first including a wee foreword I wrote for my paperback publisher's website upon the release of my third "Infernal" novel HOUSE INFERNAL:

"TO HELL AND BACK…THREE TIMES

FOREWORD

Let's hope that not many people can say the most exciting thing that ever happened to them was HELL. Don't get me wrong; I hope I never have to go there, but having lucked out enough to become a horror novelist, I can't think of anything more thrilling than re-inventing the Mythology of Hell and then taking readers on guided tours. I'm no Dante, but let's face it, he wrote the *Inferno* in 1310. It's time for a tune-up, I'd say, and I'm taking it upon myself to be the mechanic. And forget about what you've read in the Bible; things have changed a lot in Hell. Look at the human race, for example. We've gone from being a bunch of dirty savages rubbing sticks together to a sanitized social order that cooks Lean Cuisines in microwaves. Now THAT'S evolution, right? Well, Hell's evolved too, my friends. It's no longer a smoking sulphur pit. It's a great big bad-ass city. And it's no longer full of boring demons with pitchforks and pointed tails. It's full of Grand Dukes and Hierarchal Succubi, and Warlocks and Bio-Wizards, and Emaciation Squads and Municipal Mutilation Zones, and Agonicity instead of electricity. On Earth we've got science and democracy, but in Hell we've got sorcery and demonocracy. Here we've got genetic engineering, but there we've got Hexegenic engineering. Slag-faced Ushers and 9-foot-tall Golems made of cursed clay serve as police, while warped-headed demons dredge body parts from lakes of blood and Octo-Vultures fly high into a black-mooned sky. Here we've got San Francisco's Chinatown, New York's Upper West Side, London's Piccadilly, and San Antonio's Riverwalk, but Hell's got Rot-Port, Osiris Heights, Tepesville, and Satan Park. In *City Infernal* and, next, *Infernal Angel*, I took great creative joy in venturing characters just like me and you through the various nooks and crannies of this endless city called the Mephistopolis. See, it's a city that never ends, just as human endeavor never ends. In fact, if anything, infernal endeavor is even more exciting. Who needs Lake Michigan when you've got the Sea of Cagliostro? If you think the Four Seasons is something, wait till you see the BTK Motel. Anyone can sell hamburgers from a street vendor cart, but only in

EDWARD LEE

Hell can you get *man*burgers. I'm happy to say that both *City Infernal* and *Infernal Angel* were successful enough to go into multiple printings, and have current active film options as well as translations in several other countries; and I'm even more happy to tell you that writing *House Infernal*, my third installment of the City Infernal Mythos, proved the most enthralling experience of my career. Of course, you have to wonder about a guy who keeps going back to Hell—all I can say is I'm delighted to have you along for the ride."

There. But I feel the verbose need—regarding this project in general, and my contribution in particular—to jack my jaws a bit more because, well, I REALLY DIG the book you're now holding in your hands. *Infernally Yours* is the result of an inquiry a while back from horror artist extraordinaire GAK. (It just occurred to me that though I've known the guy for years, I don't know what his real name is...) GAK is one of my favorite artists, and I was duly flattered when he proposed a project in which a handful of veteran horror writers contribute stories based on my mythos. So, thank you, GAK, for devising this project, and for the wonderfully unique artwork which you purveyed.

In such an exciting circumstance, I have no reservations about other writers—especially writers I like a lot—playing with my creative "toys"; indeed, the premise couldn't have been more invigorating—and in the light of that fact, I found myself quite *creatively* invigorated about my own contribution. It gave me the opportunity to re-explore my stomping grounds of three previous mass-market novels, but it also gave me the chance to execute a work without any strictures at all. For years, a contingent of my hardcore fans have been asking me: "When are you going to write a Mephistopolis story that's hardcore?" Well... Here it is. And I'm very happy with it. But, far more important than that, I must aver that I couldn't be more flattered nor honored by the squad of writers who have chosen to contribute to this anthology—for sure some of the finest horror scribes to ever tell a tale. To you all, I extend my utmost thanks. I hope you all had as much fun with your inclusions as I did with mine.

FOREWORD

Lastly and ultimately, I must thank *you* as well—the reader. It is your interest and enthusiasm in my Infernal world that made this project possible.

Edward Lee
St. Pete Beach, Florida
April 30, 2008

THE SENARY

EDWARD LEE

PROLOGUE

Six minutes after he officially died, Slydes found himself standing agog on a street corner like none he'd ever seen. He stood as he had in life: broad-shouldered, tall, dark dirty hair and a bushy black beard. Blue jeans and workboots, and his favorite T-shirt stretched tight over his beer belly; it read ST. PETE BEACH - A QUIET LITTLE DRINKING TOWN WITH A FISHING PROBLEM. Slydes was a redneck, tried and true, a shitkicker. A *bad ass*. He'd seen a lot of—for lack of more elegant phraseology—fucked-up shit in his day, but now... Now...

This?

The wind screamed. Winged mites swarmed in the humid air and splotched red when he swatted them against his brawny forearms. *What...kind of city is this?* the horrid question occurred to him when his gaze was dragged upward. Dim, drear-windowed skyscrapers seemed a mile high and leaned this way and that at such extreme angles, he thought they might topple at any moment. Twisted faces that couldn't possibly be Human peered out of many of the narrow panes, while other panes were either broken out or spattered with blood. The sky visible between each building appeared to be red, and there was a black sickle moon hanging between two of them. Slydes blinked.

THE SENARY

A dream, it had to be. It was this notion that he first entertained. His Condemnation only minutes old, he couldn't remember much. He couldn't remember where he was born, for instance, he couldn't remember his age, nor could he remember his last name. Indeed, Slydes couldn't even remember dying.

But die he had, and for a lifetime of wincingly outrageous sins and wickedness, he'd been Damned to Hell.

So here he was.

A nightmare, that's all, he convinced himself. A red sky? Office buildings leaning over at sixty degree angles? And—

SWOOSH

A black bat with a six-foot wingspan and a vaguely Human face glided by just over his head. Slydes felt a stinking gust, then recoiled when the impossible animal shat on his head.

"Fucker!" Slydes yelled.

The bat—actually a Hexegenically created Crossbreed of one of several genera known as *Revoltus Chiropterus*—looked over its leathery shoulder and smiled.

"Welcome to Hell," it croaked.

Slydes stared after the words more than the creature itself. *Hell,* he thought quite obliquely. *I'm not really in—*

WELCOME TO ST. PUTRADA CIRCLE, HELL'S NEWEST FISTULATION & TRANSVERSION PREFECT, the sign severed his thoughts.

Slydes could only stare at the sign as the splat of monstrous guano ran down the sides of his face.

Hell's Newest...WHAT?

At the corner another sign blinked DON'T WALK, and then a rush of pedestrians crossed the street. Slydes just kept staring...

He didn't know *what* they were at first: People? Monsters? Combinations of both? A slim couple held hands as they strode by, flesh rotting from their limbs and faces. Several impish children wove through the crowd, with fangs like a dog's and eyes as big and as red

18

as apples. A Werewolf in a business suit and briefcase passed next, and after that a fat clown with a hatchet in its face. To Slydes, the clown bid, "Hi, how are ya?"

Slydes could not respond.

If anything, the street was worse. Cars that looked more like small steam engines chugged by on spoked wheels, a smokestack up front gusted black-yellow soot and vapor. Carriages and buggies rolled by as well, hauled along not by horses but by things *like* horses, whose flesh hung in dripping tatters. One carriage was occupied by a woman with skin green as pond scum who wore a tiara of gallstones and a dress made from tendons meticulously woven together. She fanned herself with a webbed, severed hand. In another carriage rode a creature that could've been a pile of snot somehow shaped into Human form. Then came a haulage wagon of some sort, powered by six harnessed beasts with festering carnation-pink skin pocked with white blisters; Slydes thought hideously of skinned sheep when they bleated and spat foamy sputum. A man perched behind them cracked a long, barbed whip—or...perhaps *man* wasn't quite right. He wore a wool cloak and banded leggings like a shepherd of the old days, yet atop his anvil-shaped head grew a brow of horns. The whip cracked and cracked, and the bleating rose to a mad clamor. Slydes looked one more time and noticed that, like the bat, these bald "sheep" had faces grimly tainted by Human features.

"Oh my God, I am in some shit," Slydes stammered. Things were starting to click in his head, and with each click came more and more fear. Did a tear actually form in his eye? "I-I-I," he blubbered. "I don't think this is a dream..."

"It's not," sounded a voice that was somehow raspy and feminine simultaneously. The woman who approached him was nude, and yet—he thought at first—checker-boarded. Slydes squinted at her impressive physique, and then recalled women with similar physiques whom he'd raped and sometimes even murdered without vacillation. But *this* woman?

THE SENARY

Every square inch of her skin was crisply darkened by black tattoos of upside-down crosses. Even her face, around which shimmered long platinum blond hair.

"Slydes, right?" she asked. "My name's Andeen, and I'm your Orientation Directress. You may not even realize this yet, but you're what's known as an Entrant."

"Entrant," Slydes murmured.

"And, no, this isn't a dream. You should be so lucky. This is all real. Over time your memory will re-form."

Before Slydes could mutter a question, his gaze snapped to another passerby: another impressively figured nude woman. Her arms, legs, abdomen, and face were but one colossal psoriatic outbreak. Only the breasts and pubis were without blemish.

"Rash lines," remarked Andeen. "In the Living World you have tan lines, here we have rash lines."

Slydes' gaze snapped back to the tattooed woman. "Here…as in…"

"As in Hell. You're dead, and for your worldly sins, you've been Condemned." Her slender shoulders shrugged. "Forever."

Slydes began to grow faint.

She grabbed his hand and tugged. "Come on, Slydes. We gotta get you out of this Prefect. It's really fucked up here," and then she tugged him down the street a ways and ducked into an alley. "We'll lay low awhile, and try to get you someplace where your ass won't be grass."

"I-I," Slydes blubbered. "I don't understand."

"Trust me, there's no good place in Hell, but there are places that are worse than others. Like this place, St. Purtrada Circle. You must've been a real scumbag to be Rematerialized *here*. Yes, sir, a real humdinger of a shitty person."

"I don't understand!" Slydes now sobbed outright.

"A Prefect is like a small District. And this one happens to be a Fistulation and Surgical Transversion Prefect. I'll keep an eye out for Abduction Squads. They'll Transvert anybody here, Humans and

20

Hellborn alike, but Humans are the desired target. The Surgery Centers pay the most for Humans."

Slydes looked cross-eyed at her.

"The short version. Every Prefect, District, or Town has to have an active mode of punishment, while there are some areas, known as Punitaries, that exist *solely* for punishment. But anyway, this Prefect uses Fistulatic Surgery to conform to the Punishment Ordinances. Fistula is Latin; it means 'communication between,' and Transversion is, like, re-routing things. That's what they do here—they re-route your insides."

Even though Slydes didn't have a *clue* what she was talking about, he stammered, "Whuh-whuh-*why?*"

Andeen smirked. "Because it's perverse and disgusting...the way it's *supposed* to be. This isn't Romper Room, Slydes. This is Hell, and Hell is hardcore. Eternal torment, suffering, and abhorrence is the name of the game. It pleases Lucifer, therefore, it's Public Law." She smirked more sharply this time. "Look, go over to that public wash basin and wash the bat shit out of your hair. It's grossing me out."

Dazed, Slydes noted the elevated stone basin only feet from the alley mouth. He dunked his head in the water, agitated the rank guano out of his hair, then seized up and jerked his head out when he realized what he was washing in.

"That's not water! That's piss!"

"Get used to it," Andeen said. "Unless you're a Grand Duke or an Archlock, you'll never get *near* fresh water. Only other way is to distill it yourself out of the blood of what you kill."

Revolted, Slydes flapped the piss off his face, then noticed lower basins erected intermittently along the smoky street. "What are those things? They look like—"

"Oh, the commodes. It's another Public Law. In this Prefect, it's mandatory that everyone urinate, defecate, and give birth in public."

Slydes' bearded jaw dropped.

"And there," Andeen pointed, "across the street. There're the various Surgery Suites."

Slydes' crossed eyes scanned the signs over each transom...

RECTO-URINARY TRANSVERSION

URETHRAL-ESOPHAGEAL REVERSAL

UTERO-RECTAL FISTULA

And many, many more.

Andeen's evilly tattooed hand pulled him back into the alley. "And look, there's an Abduction Squad. The clay men are called Golems. They're like state employees, public works, police, security, stuff like that..."

Slydes watched with a cheek to the edge of the alley wall as a troop of gray-brown things shaped like men thudded down the sidewalk, each shoving along a handcuffed Human, Demon, or Hybrid. The Golems were nine feet tall, and walked in formation. Then they all stopped at the same time, and marched their prisoners into various Surgery Suites.

"And like I said, the State pays more money for Humans, so that's why we gotta get you out of the Prefect."

Slydes whipped his face back around, and repeated, helplessly now, "I don't understand..."

"Once you've seen what goes on here...you will. Oh, and check out this chick."

Slydes watched as a morose-faced nude woman who appeared to be half-Human and half-Troll staggered toward one of the street commodes. She leaned over, parted her buttocks, and began to urinate out of her anus, and when she was done, she turned around, squatted, then began to wince. Slydes winced right along with her as they watched the incredulous act. Long trails of feces slowly squeezed out of her vagina and dropped into the commode.

"See?" Andeen asked. "Oh, wow, and check this out! Here comes a Uteral-oral Fistulation..."

A woman in a bloody smock labored down the street. She was

covered with red-rimmed white scales…and obviously quite pregnant. She held a scaled hand to her bloated belly, and when she could walk no longer she stopped, leaned over, and—

SPLAT!

—out gushed a slew of amniotic water from her mouth. She maintained the uncomfortable position, and as her belly began to tremor, her jaw came unhinged. Her throat began to impossibly swell, and as her stomach shrunk in size, a squalling, demonic fetus slid hugely out of her mouth and flapped to the pavement.

"How's that for the spectacle of childbirth?" Andeen jested. "Pregnancy is a big deal in Hell, Slydes. If Lucifer had his way, every single female lifeform here would be pregnant at all times. You see, the more babies, the more food, fuel, and fodder for Lucifer's whimsy."

Slydes leaned against the wall, moaning, "No, no, no…"

"Yes, yes, yes, my friend. And if you think *that* was bad, get a load of this guy. Remember what I said about pregnancy?"

Slydes' gaze involuntarily veered back to the street. This time, a Human man stumbled along. He wore a "wife-beater" T-shirt and stained boxer shorts dotted with Boston Red Sox insignias. If anything, though, his stomach looked even more bloated than the woman who'd just delivered a devilish baby through her mouth.

Slydes stammered further, in utter dread, "He's not—he's not—he's not—"

"Pregnant?" Andeen smiled darkly. "Male pregnancy is a fairly new breakthrough here, Slydes. And you can bet it tickles Lucifer pink. Teratologic Surgeons can actually transplant Hybrid wombs into *male* Humans and Demons. It's a trip. Watch."

Slydes watched.

Grimacing, the bloated man stepped out of his boxers and squatted. Amid boisterous grunts and wails, his rectum slowly dilated, then—

He shrieked.

—out poured a gush of what looked like squirming hairless puppies, with tiny webbed paws and little horns in their heads.

"Ah," Andeen observed, "a brood of Ghor-Hounds. Pretty rowdy, huh?"

"Rowdy!" Slydes bellowed. "This is FUCKED UP! That guy just pumped a litter of PUPPIES out his ASS!"

"Yeah. And watch what he does now…"

Gravid stomach gone now, the exhausted man abandoned his litter on the sidewalk and trudged over to one of the street commodes. *What, he's gonna take a piss?* Slydes wondered when the man poised an understandably shriveled penis over the commode.

The answer to his question, however, would be a most indubitable *No*.

Now the man's cheeks billowed. He began to grunt.

And his penis…began to swell.

"Ahhhh," he eventually moaned as the penis, next, began to disgorge firm stools. Quite a number of them squeezed out and dropped into the commode. When he was finished, he pulled his boxers back on, and at the same time caught Slydes staring agape at him.

"What's the matter, buddy? You act like you never saw a guy take a shit through his dick before."

"In case you're wondering," his hostess said, "the procedure that guy underwent is called a Recto-Urethral Fistulation…"

Slydes reeled. When he could regain some modicum of sense, he glared back at Andeen, and howled, "This is impossible! Women can't have *babies* out their mouths! Their mouths aren't *big* enough! And men can't shit *turds* through their cocks! Their *peeholes* aren't *wide* enough! It's IMPOSSIBLE!"

Andeen seemed amused by Slydes' crude rant. "You'll learn soon enough that in Hell…*anything* is possible. Now come on."

Dizzied, aghast, Slydes trudged after her. She walked fast, her high breasts bouncing, her flawless rump jiggling with each stride. "Once I get you out of this Prefect and on one of the Interways, you'll be a lot safer. Believe me, you don't want to hang out here." She grinned over her shoulder. "You're damn lucky I'm an *honest* Orientation Directress, Slydes."

"Huh?"

"There are a lot of dishonest ones. They'd tip off an Abduction Squad and turn you in—for money, of course."

"Huh?"

"Just come on. I know, you're confused right now, and you can't remember much. Eventually it'll all sink in, and you'll be all right."

Slydes sorely doubted that he would ever be All Right, not in Hell. But he did feel some gratitude toward Andeen for endeavoring to get him out of the abominable Prefect. *Anywhere, anywhere,* his thoughts pleaded. *Take me anywhere because no matter how bad the next place is, it can't be as bad as this...*

"Here's the shortcut out, and don't worry about the gate," she said. She lifted something from beneath her tongue. "I have the key."

Thank God... Slydes followed the lithe woman down another reeking alley whose end terminated in a chain link gate closed by an antiquated lock. When Andeen finnicked with the key, rust sifted from the keyhole.

That thing better open, Slydes fretted.

"I guess the hardest thing to get used to for a Human in Hell is, well, the insignificance. Know what I mean?"

"Huh?" Slydes said.

"No matter what we were in the Living World, no matter how strong, how beautiful, how rich, how *important*...in Hell we're nothing; in fact, we're less than nothing." She giggled, still jiggling the key. "We're like those non-characters in the beginning of a novel—I guess it's called the prologue?—where we don't really have a purpose like a regular character. Follow me, Slydes?"

"Uh, no. Ain't much for readin'."

Andeen shrugged. "We don't do anything for the plot or anything for the *meaning* of the book. Seriously. In Hell, a Human is like one of those sub-characters that only exists to introduce the reader to the setting…"

Slydes was getting pissed. "I don't know what'cher talkin' about! Just open that fuckin' lock so we can get out of here!"

She giggled but then frowned. "Damn. This bugger's tough. Check the alley entrance, will you—"

"All riiiiiiiii—" but when Slydes looked behind him he shrieked. Proceeding slowly down the alley was a congregation of the short, dog-faced imp-like things he'd seen chicanering previously on the street. They grinned as they moved forward, fangs glinting.

Slydes tugged Andeen's arm like a child tugging its mother's. "Luh-luh-look!"

Andeen's tattooed brow rose when she glanced down the alley. "Shit. Broodren. They're demonic kids and they're *all* homicidal. The little fuckers have gangs everywhere—"

"Open the lock!"

She played with the key most vigorously, nervous herself now. "They'll haul our guts out to sell to a Diviner, then they'll fuck and eat what's left…"

"Hurry!" Slydes wailed.

Suddenly the pack of Broodren broke all at once into a sprint, cackling.

When they were just yards away—

CLACK!

—the lock opened. Slydes peed his jeans as Andeen dragged him to the other side. She managed to re-lock the gate just as several Brooden pounced on it, their dirty taloned fingers and toes hooked over the chain links.

"Jesus! We barely made it!"

Andeen sighed, wiped her brow with her forearm. "Tell me about it, man."

"What now?" Slydes looked down a stained brick corridor that seemed to dogleg to the left. "How do we get out?"

"Around the corner," Andeen said.

They trotted on, turned the corner, and—

"Holy motherfuckin' SHIT!" Slydes yelled when two stout, gray-brown forearms wrapped about his barrel chest and hoisted him in the air. Tall shadows circled round in total silence.

Slydes screamed till his throat turned raw.

"One thing you need to know about Hell," Andeen chuckled, "is that *trust* does not exist."

Five blank-faced Golems stood round Slydes now, and it was in the arms of a sixth that he was now captive.

One of them handed Andeen a stack of bills. "Thanks, buddy. This guy's a *real* piece of work. He deserves what he's getting," and then she winked at Slydes and pointed up to another transom. It read: DIGESTIVE TRACT REVERSAL SUITE.

"For the rest of eternity, Slydes," she intoned through a sultry grin. "You'll be eating through your ass and shitting out your mouth."

"Noooooooooooooo!" Slydes shrieked.

The Golems trooped toward the door, Slydes kicking and screaming, all to no avail.

"Welcome to Hell," Andeen bid the parting words.

Slydes' screams silenced when the Suite door slammed shut, and Andeen traipsed off, greedily counting the stack of crisp bills. Each bill had the number 100 in each corner, but it was not the portrait of Benjamin Franklin that graced each one, it was the face of Adolf Hitler.

(I)

Six words drifted across his mind when he entered the bar:

A whore is a deep ditch...

It was a line from *Proverbs,* one of many which warned men of the power of lust. Foster had actually studied the Bible, with great zeal, but that was a long time ago.

THE SENARY

Six tiny cracks could be seen in the long bar mirror, but why would Foster count them? *Obsessive-compulsive?* he wondered.

No. Just someone with no better way to occupy his time. *Like this bar,* he thought. *Some bar. It's a dumpster that serves beer...and full of white trash.*

So...what does that make me?

His reflection in the mirror looked like that of a bus bum. Unkempt, hair in need of cutting, eyes open wider than they should be as if used to looking for something that wasn't there. The bar was simply called LOUNGE; that's what the tacky neon said outside. When he looked down the long dark room, he counted only six customers—three men, three women—then he noticed they were all smoking. Tendrils of the smoke hung motionless in the establishment's open space, like slivers of ghosts. Foster didn't smoke himself. He'd never even tried because he recalled a childhood sermon: "Your body is a gift from God, and any gift from God is a temple of God. When we inhale cigarette smoke into our bodies, it's the same as throwing rocks through the stained-glass windows of this very church. Desecration..."

Hence, Foster never lit up. He did drink, however, and not once did he consider that the same minister who'd given the smoking sermon had never added alcohol to his list of substances that desecrated one's God-given body, nor that said minister had died years later of cirrhosis.

"I ain't kiddin' ya," one redneck with a Fu Manchu affirmed to another redneck with a bald head. "I know it was the same ho' who ripped me off a year or so ago. But she was so fucked up on Beans the bitch didn't even remember me!"

"What'chew do?" asked the bald one.

"Jacked her out's what I did—"

"Bullshit."

"Think so?" Fu Manchu pulled out a blackjack, jiggled it, then put it back in his pocket. "Jacked her out right in the car, and took her cash but ya know what? All the bitch had on her was six bucks!"

The bald one looked suspicious over his Black Velvet and Coke. "But I suppose you fucked her, too, huh? Unconscious?"

"Thought about it, but once I got her panties off, her gash stunk up the car fierce. Killed my wood, ya know? So's instead I pulled into a back lot near the old K-Mart, dragged her out the car, and tore off her top."

The bald one frowned. "That's it?"

"Gimme a break! I pulled my pants down and dropped a big ol' Cleveland Steamer right smack dab between her hooters."

By now the bald one could take no more. "Man, I don't believe a word you say. Why you tellin' me all this jive?"

"Buy me a drink if I prove it?"

The bald one laughed. "Sure, but you *can't* prove it."

Fu Manchu flipped open his cellphone. "I love these camera phones, man." He showed the tiny screen to the bald one, who immediately slumped and ordered the guy a drink.

A real high-brow crew tonight, Foster thought. What made him cringe, though, was an unquenchable desire to see the screen himself. *Just one sin after another...*

One of the women—a middle-aged blond—had drifted over to the cigarette machine. Very tan, in a clinging maroon T-shirt and cut-off jeans. She'd knotted the T-shirt to reveal an abdomen whose most obvious trait was an accordion of stretchmarks. Lots of eyeshadow. Veiny hands. *Too weathered,* Foster judged.

"Hi, honey," she said in a Marlboro-rough voice and as she headed back to her stool, her hand slid along Foster's back. "Come on over, if ya want. I mean, you know what this place is all about, right?" but before Foster could even dream up an answer she was already back in her seat.

Indeed, Foster did know what the place was all about—that's why he was here. Prostitution that was not quite the bottom of the barrel. He could afford little more. His conscience squirmed amid his blooming sin. Obviously she'd struck out with the other men in the bar. *Yeah, but the weathered ones know what to do...*

29

THE SENARY

"Another beer?" asked the barkeep, a ramshackle rube with a circular patch on his gas station shirt that read BARNEY.

"Yes, please."

The keep leaned over, as if to relay a confidence. He had shaggy hair, and a pock on his cheek that looked like a bullet scar, and he was probably sixty. "Don't worry, it's all cool. I know you ain't a cop."

"What?" Foster questioned, dismayed.

The keep grinned. "I seen you around. Seen you walkin' into the dirty book store a time or two—"

Terrific, Foster thought.

"And since you been sittin' here since about—what?" The keep looked at his watch. "Six?"

"Yeah, that's about when I came in."

"I figure you must know what the Lounge is all about—" He jerked his eyes down toward the old blond. "Like she done said."

Foster's chest felt tight. "I—uh—" One of several TV's showed a baseball game. "I'm just in to watch the game."

"Sure, sure," the keep chuckled. He pulled out another bottle of beer and set it down next to five empties. Foster paid for each beer one at a time, for in establishments such as this, tabs were never run.

"I kind'a look the other way, got no problem with what a gal feels she has to do for money—" Then the keep winked. "As long as there's a cut for me. You wanna fuck one in the bathroom or get a blowjob—that's cool. Just make sure you slide me a ten first, ya hear?"

"Uh, uh—sure," Foster blabbered.

"Ya been here a while now so I thought maybe ya didn't know the deal." The keep winked again. "But now ya do."

"Uh, thanks for filling me in…"

The keep leaned over again. "But as for Thelma over there—"

"Who?"

"The blond."

Foster glanced over, and suddenly found that the woman's burgeoning bosom possibly nullified her beat looks. "What about her?"

30

"She's been around the block more times than the mailman, get it? Just some neighborly advice. She fucks like a champ but if you make any deals with *her*...wrap it—if ya catch my drift."

Foster flinched when a toothy grin floated just to the right side of his face. It was Fu Manchu. "Wrap it? Shit, man. Thelma's pussy is *toxic*. She's got stuff up there that can melt a triple-Trojan like one'a them Listerine breath strips." He elbowed Foster. "You fuck her? Put a scuba foot on your pecker," and then he and the barkeep broke out in laughter.

Foster couldn't have been more uncomfortable. "Thanks, uh, thanks for the pointers, guys."

Foster gazed up at the TV. Tampa Bay led New York six to nothing, but the sound was down. He glanced aside, pretending to be looking for someone. Two more women—younger but nearly as weathered as Thelma—sat apart at the far end, one brunette with a ludicrous mullet and a shirt that read DO ME TILL I PUKE. The other, a rusty redhead, wore a T-shirt that claimed NO GAG REFLEX. *Well, here they are,* Foster thought. *So what am I doing? When am I going to make a move?*

Another TV hung just above the brunette's head, also silent: a dashing evangelist in a huge stadium. Foster could read the Closed Caption blocks as the revivalist's mouth moved.

WHEN YOU STRIVE TO NOT SIN, WHEN YOU MAKE THAT *EFFORT*, GOD HOLDS YOU IN SPECIAL *FAVOR*. GOD PUTS HIS SHIELD OF PROTECTION OVER YOU. SO TO *STAY* IN GOD'S FAVOR, WE MUST *ALWAYS* STRIVE TO NOT SIN. WE MUST DO EVERYTHING WE POSSIBLY CAN TO RESIST THE TEMPTATIONS THAT LUCIFER THROWS BEFORE US...

Foster's eyes lowered—in shame. *No shield of protection for me today,* he thought to his beer. *But I DO try, I DO...* He believed he was a good person...but tainted. Too often he felt lashed between horses: one horse was God, the other the Devil, and lately the Devil seemed to be winning most of the tugs. It was all sin, it was all lust.

It was everywhere.

THE SENARY

I know I shouldn't be here but I'm staying anyway, he realized. *I'm here to pick up a hooker…and that's what I'm going to do because I'm not strong enough to walk out…*

He did good deeds. He felt he had true compassion. He gave to charities, he gave to the homeless—even though he was poor himself, he *did* try. He believed in God, and he could only pray that God's mercy was as everlasting as the Bible claimed.

AND MANY OF YOU MIGHT BE THINKING RIGHT THIS SECOND, "BUT PASTOR JOHNNY, I'M A GOOD PERSON, I GO TO CHURCH, AND I TRULY DO STRIVE TO NOT SIN…AND I'M TRULY SORRY WHEN I *DO* SIN…LIKE LAST WEEK WHEN I WENT TO THAT PORNO STORE, OR THE WEEK BEFORE THAT TEEN SEX WEBSITE, OR THE WEEK BEFORE THAT WHEN I PICKED UP THAT PROSTITUTE…

Foster stared.

IT'S NOT SUPPOSED TO BE EASY, MY FRIENDS, AND LET ME TELL YOU SOMETHING. IT WASN'T EASY FOR JESUS, EITHER.

His soul felt stained black. *He's talking about me.*

AND SOMETIMES WE WANT TO *CHALLENGE* GOD, WE WANT TO SAY TO HIM "GOD, YOU'VE GIVEN ME THESE DESIRES BUT TELL ME IT'S A SIN TO ACT ON THEM. WHY? IT'S NOT FAIR!" The evangelist seemed to look directly at Foster. BUT HERE'S WHY IT *IS* FAIR, AND PLEASE, MY DEAR FRIENDS, *LISTEN* TO ME. IT'S FAIR BECAUSE GOD SO LOVED THE WORLD THAT HE GAVE HIS ONLY BEGOTTEN SON…

Foster felt sick. Were his palms sweating? He couldn't keep his eyes off NO GAG REFLEX. *All I have to do is slip the keep a ten and go over there…* The other one, with the mullet, looked not half-bad as well (except for the mullet). Had she tweaked her nipples? They stuck out against the DO ME shirt like bullet casings.

She looked right at Foster—in the same way the evangelist had—and mouthed, *Blow job?*

EDWARD LEE

MOST OF THE TIME, FRIENDS, BEING A GOOD PERSON ISN'T GOOD ENOUGH. WE SIN AND THEN DO GOOD WORKS BECAUSE WE THINK ONE GOOD THING CANCELS OUT THE BAD, BUT DON'T BE DECEIVED BY THIS. DON'T BE A *CRUMMY PERSON* BY PURSUING YOUR TEMPTATIONS. DON'T LIVE A CHUMP-CHANGE LIFE. WE TEND TO SIN IN SECRET, BECAUSE NOBODY CAN SEE. HUSBANDS, YOU THINK THAT NOBODY SEES YOU WHEN YOU WALK INTO THAT PORNO STORE, OR SLIP INTO THAT MASSAGE PARLOR. YOUR WIFE CAN'T *SEE* YOU WHEN YOU'RE DRI-VING DOWN THAT DARK ROAD AFTER WORK TO LOOK FOR A STREETWALKER. AND WIVES? YOU THINK THAT NOBODY SEES YOU WHEN YOU SNEAK INTO THE BATHROOM TO DO THAT LINE OF COCAINE. NOBODY SEES YOU WHEN YOU CHEAT ON YOUR HUSBAND WITH YOUR OFFICE MANAGER. BUT HEAR ME, FRIENDS. GOD *DOES* SEE YOU...

Foster was percolating now, his penis half-erect just from the con-templation, even as the evangelist's silent words haunted him. Now DO ME was standing next to GAG REFLEX, whispering. Every image of carnality steamed in Foster's mind.

GOD LOVES US *ALL*, HE WANTS *ALL OF US* TO JOIN HIM SOMEDAY IN THE FIRMAMENT OF HEAVEN, BUT THE TRUTH, MY FRIENDS, IS THAT MOST OF US WON'T GET THERE BECAUSE MOST OF US DON'T TRY *HARD ENOUGH* TO RESIST THE DESIRE TO SIN. AND SOME OF YOU MIGHT WANT TO SAY TO ME, "PASTOR JOHNNY? IF GOD REALLY LOVES ME, THEN HOW CAN HE SLAM HEAVEN'S DOOR IN MY FACE FOR ACTING ON THE DESIRES THAT HE GAVE ME?" BUT I SAY TO YOU, *JESUS* WAS SUBJECTED TO THE *SAME* TEMPTATIONS THAT WE ARE BUT HE *NEVER* SINNED, SO IN THE LIGHT OF THAT TRUTH, WHEN YOU DON'T TRY HARD ENOUGH TO TURN YOUR BACK ON THOSE TEMPTATIONS, IT'S NOT GOD WHO'S SLAMMING THE DOOR IN YOUR FACE. IT'S YOU.

THE SENARY

Foster tore his eyes off the TV, then groaned to himself. DO ME and GAG REFLEX were gone—

Damn it, he thought. *They must've split—*

He almost yelped as several hands played across his back. DO ME pressed in on one side, GAG the other. Cheap perfume and shampoo suddenly intoxicated him.

"Hey, there," GAG said. She began to rub his back where he sat, her breasts pressing. "My name's Sylvia."

"My name's Jeanie," said the other. "What's yours?"

Foster couldn't resist. "How about...John?"

The two women looked at each other, stalled, then laughed aloud.

"I like this guy!" said GAG. "And we were wondering..."

"Yeah," said DO ME. Her hand rubbed his chest, and when the keep disappeared in back, she smoothly rubbed his crotch. "Ever had a double-blowjob?"

Foster was taken aback. "Uh, well—"

GAG's breath smelled like Juicy Fruit. "Ask anyone. Me'n Jeanie do the best double-headers. We know all the right stuff guys like—"

Foster opened his mouth...

"You know, tongue your balls, play with your asshole," added DO ME.

"And we'll both pull our shirts up so ya can come on our tits." They both shot Foster a quick flash of their breasts. Four pink, plucked nipples looked back at him. Foster got drunk just from the sight. A sideglance showed him Fu Manchu and the bald guy both grinning at him, and nodding approval.

The T-shirts came back down when the keep returned. GAG's lips touched his ear when she whispered, "And it's only fifty bucks each, plus ya gotta give the—"

"Ten to the bartender," Foster finally said something coherent. "Yes." He felt flushed, prickly. His penis oozed in his pants. He looked in his wallet. "I only have sixty dollars on me. Is there—"

"An ATM?" DO ME finished his question. "At the bank—"

34

"—right across the street," the other hot, wet whisper brushed his ear. "You could be back in five minutes."

Foster felt disconnected from himself when he stood up. "I'll...be right back..."

GAG gave his buttocks a squeeze when Foster rushed out. He crossed the parking lot with a drone in his head. Darkness had arrived like an oil spill; the old sodium lights painted glowing yellow lines across the cracked asphalt. His anticipation revved his heart; he could picture what would soon follow: himself standing in a seamy bathroom with his pants down while the two woman knelt and took turns swallowing his erection. He would look down and see their sullied yet awesome breasts bare and dark-nippled in the seedy light. *Oh, God...* He quick-stepped past a dollar store, then crossed the street to the bank. Six people stood in line before him at the ATM, mostly half-broken rednecks or old people. *Come on, come on,* he thought, tapping his foot. When he glanced across the street, he saw GAG and DO ME watching him through the glass door. *With my luck someone else'll pick them up while I'm waiting in this FUCKING LINE!*

Finally Foster got his turn and withdrew five twenties. He grimaced at the receipt where it read AVAILABLE BALANCE: $6.00.

"Jesus," he sputtered, and then he stood there for a time, spacing out. *Put the money back in the fucking bank and go home!* his alter-ego yelled out him. *Look at yourself! You're a scumbag! You're a whoremonger!*

But he could, couldn't he? He looked at the cash. He could re-deposit it right now, save it for the things he needed rather than wasting it on seamy lust. But—

Instead he put it in his pocket and left the machine. *My life is a pile of shit,* he realized, *and I don't even care...*

On his way back his mind was clogged with more delectable images: puckered nipples, feminine fingers tightly caging his testicles as wet lips tight as an o-ring roved up and down his shaft, and lastly the worm-fat plumes of sperm lying across proffered white-trash breasts. It was the imagery, he knew, that had stifled his otherwise endless guilt into non-existence. Even as the block letters flashed behind his eyes—DON'T BE A *CRUMMY PERSON* BY PURSUING YOUR TEMPTATIONS. DON'T LIVE A CHUMP-CHANGE LIFE—Foster couldn't see them.

The drone dragged him on. He had no awareness of making the mental decision to stop, but when he realized he had, he found himself several yards from the dollar store where a skinny woman in a dirty sundress and lanky hair was having a conniption at the front door. A pair of skinny little kids with dead eyes stood next to her. "Fuckin' bullshit! I can't fuckin' believe it!" she was yelling at herself. "It's not supposed to be this fuckin' hard!"

Foster hated confrontations. He wanted to move on, to the tacky delights that awaited. Instead, he said, "Is something wrong?"

"Yeah! *Everything's* wrong! I got two fuckin' kids to feed so I go in there to buy food"—she held up a plastic card with an American flag on it—"and the machine says my food credits are all used up. My fuckin' husband maxed the card out before he split yesterday. Instead of paying the power bill, he spent the money on crack, then he maxes out the card and leaves town! Fucker leaves me with two kids and no food, and even if I *had* food, I can't cook it 'cos I got no power, so I gotta buy Pop Tarts and canned spaghetti, but I can't even buy *that* 'cos my fuckin' piece of shit husband MAXED OUT MY CARD!"

The woman looked close to a psychotic break. Meanwhile, her two children looked up at Foster, stared a moment, then looked away.

The woman's eyes were red now. "Mister, could you give me five or ten bucks? Please? This shit's fuckin' killin' me."

"I—" Foster began but didn't finish.

"My fuckin' food card doesn't renew till the sixth—that's over a week from now. I'll have to feed these kids garbage till then."

"I—" but Foster thought, *I could give her twenty bucks and still have plenty for the whores...*

"Aw, fuck it!" she wailed. "You guys are all the same! Don't wanna help anybody. Ya think I'm gonna buy *drugs* with the money. Shit! Does it look like I'm tryin' to buy drugs!"

"I—"

The woman shoved both of the kids. "Come on, we're going home..."

"Wait," Foster said. She turned and glared at him. Foster took everything out of his wallet and gave it to her. "This should help," he said.

She looked cockeyed at the hundred and sixty dollars. "Aw, fuck, man! Thanks! You saved our asses!" She yelled at the kids. "Come on, you little crumb-snatchers! In the store! They close in ten minutes!"

Foster watched blankly as she pushed her kids back into the store. The woman fully entered, but then stuck her shabby head back out.

"Hey, man." She smiled. "God bless you."

Somehow I doubt that He will, Foster thought. "Goodnight."

He turned and headed down the sidewalk. Behind him, from the bar, DO ME and GAG screamed at him.

"What did you DO?"

"You ASSHOLE!"

"Scumbag lyin' chump motherfucker!"

Foster looked at them in the doorway and shrugged. Then he walked home, feeling lousier than he'd ever felt in his life.

(II)

Foster slept in fits, and when he finally awoke, he cursed when he saw the clock. It was six p.m. *How the FUCK could I have slept all that time!* He cursed further when he recalled last night's goings-on. Had passing up the prostitutes in order to help a poor woman *really* been a good deed? *Or was it just guilt?*

He thought it must be the latter, for he felt awful. He was broke now, and his oyster-shucking job probably wouldn't re-open till the fall. At least his bills were paid for the month, and he had enough food to get by for a while. But still...

This sucks.

He frowned out the window, to see gloom and drizzle.

Dread seized him when he went to the mailbox. *Probably some bill I forgot about,* he shuddered, *which I won't be able to pay because I gave ALL MY MONEY away last night...*

Junk mail. It astonished him: not one but three offers for low car insurance. Foster hadn't owned a car in a decade. The next was a catalogue from Omaha Steaks. *Yeah, I'll be ordering from them soon.* Then more junk mail, from a contractor offering the lowest prices in town for basement waterproofing. Foster's shabby apartment didn't have a basement.

The last letter was a notice from his landlord: his rent had just risen sixty dollars per month. *Those FUCKERS!* his thoughts tiraded. *Those skinflint, money-grubbing FUCKERS!*

He whirled when a knock resounded at the door.

Oh, for pity's sake... It had to be somebody selling something. No one else *ever* knocked on Foster's door.

"Look, whatever it is you're selling," he preempted when he jerked the door open, "I'm flat-broke—" but the rest was severed when he looked at his caller.

An attractive but blank-faced woman stood without. The cause of Foster's jolt was her attire: a long black surplice and, of all things, a Roman collar. *A female minister?* he hazarded. *Must be asking for donations—* He could've laughed. *Lady, you picked the WRONG door to knock on today!*

Her blond hair had been pulled back; her eyes were an odd dull-blue. She was in her forties but striking: shapely, ample bosomed. A stout wooden cross hung about her neck.

"Are you Morley Foster?" the woman asked in the driest tone.

"Yes but, look, I'm not interested in—"

"My name is Deaconess Wilson." She stared as she spoke, as if on tranquilizers.

"I'm sorry...Deaconess, but I don't have any money—"

"I'm here to tell you that you've won the Senary," she said.

Foster stalled. "The *what?*"

She handed him a 9x6 manila envelope. "May I...come in, Mr. Foster?"

Foster winced. "I'd rather you didn't." He looked at the envelope. "What is this?"

"It...would be easier if I told you inside..."

Oh, for pity's sake! He stepped back. *It's some scam, or some donation thing—Jesus!* "All right, but just for a minute. I'm very busy," he lied.

She entered slowly, as if unsure of her footing. Foster closed the door. "Now what's this? I've won the *what?*"

She turned and stood perfectly still. It occurred to Foster now that whenever she spoke, she seemed to falter, as if either she didn't know what to say or she was resisting something.

"The Senary," she said in that low monotone. "It's like...a lottery."

"Well I never signed up for any *Senary,* and I never bought a ticket."

"You don't have to. All you have to...do is be born." She blinked. "I've been instructed to inform you that you're the eleventh person to win the Senary. Ever. In all of history."

"Oh, you're with one of those apocalyptic religious sects—"

"No, no." The Deaconess ground her teeth. "I'm just...the messenger, so to speak." Then she flinched and shook her head. "I'm—I'm...not sure what I'm supposed to say..."

Crazy, Foster thought, a little scared now. *Mental patient with some religious delusion. Probably just escaped from a hospital.*

She groaned. "You see, every...six hundred...and sixty-six...years, someone wins the Senary. This...time it's...you."

THE SENARY

She reminded Foster of a faulty robot, experiencing minor short circuits. Several times her hands rose up, then lowered. She'd shrug one shoulder for no reason, wince off to one side, flinch, raise a foot then put it back down. And again he had the impression that some aspect of her volition was resisting an unbidden impulse when her hands struggled to rise again.

Shaking, they stopped at the top button of her surplice. Then, as if palsied, her fingers began to unfasten the buttons.

Her words faltered. "Sssssss—atan fell from Heaven in 5318 B.C. The ffffffffff—irst Senary was held in 4652 B.C. It was wuh-wuh-won by a Cycladean coppersmith named Ahkazm."

Crazy. Pure-ass crazy, Foster knew now. Yet, he didn't throw her out. Instead he just stood…and watched.

Watched her completely unbutton the surplice, skim it off along with the Roman collar and cross. She jittered a bit when she faced Foster more resolutely, as if to display her total nakedness to him.

Holy shit. Look at the BODY on her…

"Listen," he finally forced himself to say. "You're going to have to—"

The image of her body stunned him. Her torso was a perfect hour-glass of flesh; high, full breasts; flat stomach and wide hips. Her skin shone in perfect, proverbial alabaster white.

Foster's eyes inched lower, to her pubis, where his speechless gaze was hijacked by a plenteous triangle of bronze fur. Within the fur, the tiniest pink twist could be seen.

This Deaconess is a full-tilt brick shit-house…

"I-I-I," she faltered. The dull blue of her eyes seemed to implore him. "I've been instructed…to tell you that you kuh-kuh-can sodomize me if you sssssso…desire, or fuh-fuh-fuh…fuck my tits. It'sssss part of winning the Senary." She seemed to gag. "You get to fffff-uck the messenger…they said to say." Then she turned, quite robotically—showing an awesome rump— and foraged through some old cupboards.

EDWARD LEE

"*They* said?" Foster questioned. "Who's *they?*"

"A Class III Machinator and his Spotter," she told him, still rummaging. "They're Bio-Wizards. They work in a Channeling Fortress in the Emetic District. They're mmmmmm-achinating me. That's why...I'm acting errrrrrr-atically. They're manipulating my...will," and then she bent over, to search a lower cabinet.

Holy moly! When she'd bent, the action only amplified the magnificence of her rump. At the bottom of the buttocks' cleft, a minute blond dovetail showed, along with the pink twist. "What are you looking for?" he finally asked.

"Ah. Here." She straightened, holding a bottle of Vigo olive oil. She stood awkwardly then, and began smoothing palmfuls of the oil over her body. Foster stared, stupefied.

What am I going to do? he thought. *I've got a buck naked deaconess with a body like Raquel Welch in* Fantastic Voyage *lubing herself up with my Vigo. This is insane. SHE'S insane.*

She sat up on the dowdy kitchen table and lay back, continuing to spread the oil. Her skin glimmered almost too intensely to focus on for long. "They t-t-told me you'd liked thissssss."

"Well." Foster had to confess. "They're right."

"I-I-I'm chaste, by the way—I have...to tell you that too." Now her hands were re-oiling her breasts and belly. "It's a prerequisite. Any Senarial Messenger mmmmm-ust be virginal, as well as a Guh-Guh-Guh-Godly person." She pulled her knees back, then splashed some oil right on her anus. A pinky delved in and out. "Wouldn't you llll-like...to put yourrrrr puh-puh-puh-penis right in here?"

Foster stared at the question as much as the gleaming spectacle. Simply *thinking* about doing it seemed more luxurious than anything he'd ever fathomed. But—

Am I really going to fuck a crazy deaconess in the ass?

"Or-or-or...here," she said, now pressing the perfect breasts together, to highlight the slippery valley. "You can t-t-tit fuck me, too. Just nuh-nuh-not my pussy... I mmmmmust remain chaste."

41

The action of her hands, in tandem with the shining, perfect skin, nearly hypnotized Foster. It seemed as though she were *wearing* a magnifying glass out in the sun; that's how brightly she gleamed. His arousal became uncomfortable in his pants. *This woman's off the deep end. I need to get her out of here.* Yet every time he resolved to tell her to leave, the image of her body grew more intense, silencing him, *commanding* him to watch.

Now her hands massaged the oil into the abundant triangle, which began to shine like spun gold. She drew her knees even closer to her cheeks to display it all for him: the flawless fissure. Next, her hands slipped beneath and spread the buttocks more deliberately, elucidating the anus.

Even her asshole is beautiful, Foster thought.

Then she simply lay still, waiting.

"You-you-you-you're allowed to," she droned.

Foster reeled, staring. He rubbed his crotch, imagining the absolute extravagance…

"No," Foster blurted, cursing himself. *I want to, damn it, but…it's just not right.* "Just get out. I'm not interested."

"Oh," she responded. "Okay," and then she dully put her raiments back on, adjusting the white collar. She shambled to the sink to soap and wash her hands.

For fuck's sake. What is going ON?

Foster looked on, mute, as she ground her teeth a few more times, winced, then headed for the door.

"You're-you're under no obligation, by the way," she said, her back to him. "I'm-I'm-I'm sssss-supposed to tell you that, and muh-muh-make it clear."

"What is this Senary shit!" Foster barked.

"But if you're…interested… Fuh-fuh-follow the instructions," she feebled, and then she walked out of the apartment, leaving Foster dumb-struck, painfully aroused, and smelling olive oil.

Did any of that really happen? he asked himself. He stared at the closed door for five full minutes. Perhaps he'd dreamed it, perhaps he was sleeping. He pinched himself hard and frowned. *But if you're interested...follow the instructions.*

Only then did he realize he was still holding the envelope she'd initially given him.

He opened it and pulled out, first, a plain sheet of paper on which had been floridly handwritten:

YOU HAVE WON THE SENARY. ALL WILL BE EXPLAINED IF YOU CHOOSE TO PROCEED. SHOULD YOU DECIDE THAT YOU ARE INTERESTED, CARRY ON TO THE FOLLOWING ADDRESS AFTER SUNDOWN WITHIN THE NEXT SIX DAYS.

An unfamiliar address—24651 Central—was written below, which he believed was somewhere in the downtown area. Foster read what remained.

YOU ARE UNDER NO OBLIGATION TO ACCEPT, AND WHETHER YOU DO OR NOT, YOU MAY KEEP THE REMU-NERATION.

Remuner—

Foster dug back into the envelope and discovered *another* envelope.

It felt fat.

He tore it open and found—

Holy SHIT!

—six thousand dollars in crisp and apparently brand-new $100 bills. The bills were oddly bundled, however, in paper-clipped divisions of six.

THE SENARY

(III)

After sundown within the next six days, the words rolled around his head like dice. Foster walked down the side road toward the glittering lights and hot-rod-and-motorcycle traffic of the main drag. The money hadn't vanished yet, and neither had the olive oil sheen on his kitchen table, so by midnight he had no choice but to believe that the entire incident was not a dream-product.

He walked into the QWIK-MART, a ubiquitous 7-Eleven clone that was stuck between a pizza place and a Thai restaurant. The only person Foster knew well enough to dare call a friend worked the night shifts here. One could never see inside due to the literal wallpapering of the front glass with poster-sized advertisements: mostly LatinoAmerica! phone cards and the state lottery. PLAY TO WIN! one poster assaulted him. *Doesn't everybody?* Foster figured. *Does anybody play to LOSE?* but then he caught himself staring.

Lottery, he thought. *Senary.* Then: *It's like…a lottery,* he recalled the naked deaconess. *But how could I win when I never played? I never bought a ticket, never got my numbers.* When he nudged the thought behind him and edged into the store, an irritating cowbell rang.

No customers occupied the disheveled and poorly stocked store. A rat looked up from the hot dog rotisserie, then darted into the gap between the wall and counter. *I pity the rat that eats one of those hot dogs,* Foster commiserated. He frowned around the establishment. No customers, true, and no Randal.

A door clicked, then came the snap of flip-flops. Foster's brow shot up when a skanky young woman in frayed cut-offs and a faded but overflowing bikini top snapped out of the rear hall. Her sloppy breasts were huge, swaying as though the top's cups were hammocks, and no doubt most of their distention could be attributed to the fact that their scroungy owner had to be eight-plus-months pregnant. The tanned, veiny belly stretched tight as an overblown balloon around a popped out navel like someone's pinkie-toe. *That's not a bun in the oven,* Foster thought. *It's a fuckin' Pepperidge Farm warehouse.* But he saw women such as this all too frequently. A prostitute even lower on the social rungs than the women he'd nearly solicited last night. These drug-addict urchins were the flotsam of the local streets.

"Is, uh, Randal around?"

She frowned back, neglecting to answer. She kept her lips tightly closed, and began looking around the store. Foster immediately got the impression that she had a mouthful of something and was desperate to find a place to expectorate.

When she found no convenient wastebasket—

splap...

—she bowed her head by a carousel of Herr's brand potato chips and released a wincingly large volume of sperm from her mouth.

"*Fuck,* I hate that taste," she sputtered.

Foster attempted to repeat his query, "Is, uh—"

"I don't know the asshole's name, buddy," she snapped. She yanked off several bags of chips, attacked a Mrs. Freshly's snack cake rack, paused, then darted behind the service counter and grabbed a carton of Marlboros. "The tightwad poo-putt motherfucker's in back," and then the cowbell clanged and she flip-flopped briskly out, milk-sodden breasts tossing as if they sought to rock their way out of the top. Foster was surprised he couldn't actually hear them slosh.

The sidewall was hung with black velvet paintings of either Elvis, Jeff Gordon, or Christ. *Christ,* he thought. The Jesus paintings were cheapest. Randal appeared next, looking displeased. "Oh, hey, man. They say there's no such thing as bad head but you know what? They're wrong."

"The Yale grad just left, none too happy."

"'Cos I talked her down to fifteen." Randal shook his head—a shaggy head and an atrocious Taliban-like beard. "Guess I get what I pay for. She kept raking my Johnson with her teeth, and her teeth were all cracked. I'll probably get fuckin' AIDS."

"She did leave you a present, though," and Foster pointed to the splat of sperm.

Randal's nostrils flared, an indignant bull. "That *bitch!* She spat my nut on the *floor?*"

"And then promptly relieved you of some chips, snack cakes, and one carton of Marlboros."

"That *bitch!* That *pregnant* bitch!" Randal raged further. "Walks in here with a belly full of white trash and rips *me* off? Shit, if that trick baby ain't stillborn, I hope it's got flippers." He clattered with a mop and bucket. "Got to clean this up before some junkie, bum, ex-con, or all of the above walks in here, sees it, then slips on purpose. Then the redneck scum sues the store for ten million bucks and wins."

Wow, and I thought I was cynical, Foster thought. He watched Randal haphazardly mop up the expectorant, then roll the bucket back down the hall.

"So how's the shucking business?" Randal asked and brazenly scratched his crotch.

"So good Crabby Dick's laid me off again," Foster lamented. "Shitty year for oysters. Everything they ship from Louisiana's still got worms from Katrina."

"Wow, that really *shucks,* man," and Randal laughed. "Get it?"

Foster groaned.

Randal poured two coffees, but the brew looked like squid ink. "Believe it or not, I got a *dynamite* crack ho' last night."

"Yeah?"

"Yeah. Twenty bucks. Ever had a Saran Wrap job?"

"A *what?*"

"Seriously. I'd never heard of it." Randal pulled a bag of jerky off a rack, slit it slightly with a boxcutter, and withdrew a slice. Then he scotch-taped the hole and put it back on the rack. "Christ, even the lowest crack ho' charges eighty-ninety bucks to suck your asshole."

Foster rolled his eyes. "That's…rough work."

EDWARD LEE

"But not with Saran Wrap," Randal enthused, pointing to an opened Saran Wrap box below the counter. He carefully glued the box closed, then put it back on the shelf. "But this crackhead last night? She tells me all about it. You take a sheet of Saran Wrap and press it against your ass, then kind of wedge up into your butt crack." As Randal explicated, he straightened his hand into karate-chop form. "Then she sucks your asshole through the Saran Wrap while she's giving you a reach-around. Only twenty bucks, no lie, and I swear to God you can't tell the difference."

"I don't know that it's necessary to swear to *God* about something like that."

Randal guffawed. "It's a killer nut. You ought to try it."

"Doubtful," Foster said.

Randal grinned. "Aw, don't give me that shit, man. You've done some ho'ing in your time, you *told* me you have."

"Yeah, but not for a long while," Foster affirmed but neglected to mention how close he'd come last night. "Most of those girls are drug-addicts. When you solicit them for sex, you're helping them remain in an environment of degradation and misery."

"For fuck's sake," Randal sputtered.

"If you give them money for drugs in exchange for action, it's the same as if *you're* buying the drugs yourself. It all goes to the same place, the same evil. Besides, hookers *and* johns offend God."

"Here we go with *this* shit again." Randal grabbed a broom and whisked it around the store, half-assed. "If there was a God, then there'd *be* no drug addiction, so then there'd be no girls offering to suck the snot out of your rod for money."

Foster frowned. "I think God is about free will, Randal. It's about the *choice*. Does one choose to do drugs or does one choose not to?"

"Bulldick," Randal said. "You're not a bad guy—I mean, you're definitely not as much of an asshole as me—so how come God let you get shit-canned from your oyster-shucking job?"

47

Foster sniffed the coffee but wasn't sure if he should take a sip. "God's got nothing to do with it," but then he decided to drop the subject. He felt hypocritical enough, and only just now was he admitting to himself what he'd likely do tonight if the money the Deaconess gave him turned out to be genuine...

"Furthermore," Randal went on, "if there was a God, the Yankees wouldn't be thirteen games behind Boston. If God's a Red Sox fan, He can kiss my ass." Randal paused with his broom. "Oh, look, I know we're friends and all...but don't bother applying here. We ain't hiring."

"I couldn't work here," Foster said, his lips black after one sip of the coffee. "Not with coffee like this. But I would like to ask a favor..."

"Fuck no, man. Get out of my store." Randal hooted. "Relax! I'm kidding," but then his eyes darted. "Damn, I forgot." He opened the glass door on the rotisserie, then spat on the hot dogs.

"What the hell!"

Randal smirked. "Those fuckin' things are two bucks a pack wholesale. But if you spit on 'em every hour, they last longer. Only people who buy 'em are the bums and illegals. Big deal. Besides, the heat kills the germs."

Foster didn't know what to say.

"So what's this pain in the ass favor?"

Foster didn't like to lie but in this circumstance—*A nude deaconess?*—he could surmise no other option. "I found a $100 bill today but, I don't know—it feels funny."

"Funny?" Randal questioned. "As in fake?"

"Well, yeah, I guess. It's, like, brand-new. But I've seen you check bills here with the funky pen..."

"Anything for a friend," Randal got it. "You want to make sure it's not funny money before you try to spend it."

"Exactly."

Behind the counter, Randal produced a fat black pen whose body read SMARTCASH - COUNTERFEIT DETECTION MARKER. Foster gave him one of the ultra-crisp bills.

"I get a twenty-percent commission if it's real, right?" Randal posed, holding the uncapped marker.

Anything for a friend, my ass, Foster realized. "Yeah, sure."

Randal nodded. He rubbed the bill between his fingers. "Wow, that *is* new." He grinned up. "You sure you're not printing these up in your pad?"

"With what? My oyster board?"

Randal chuckled. He drew a quick notch on the bill, then gave the iodine-saturated ink time to dry.

It's fake, Foster knew. *It's got to be fake. It's just some scam I haven't figured out yet.* Six grand landing in his lap out of the blue like this? *Too good to be true.*

Randal shrugged, deposited the bill in the register and gave Foster eighty dollars back. "It's real."

"You're kidding me..."

"It's as real as my coffee is bad."

"*That's* real."

"I'm gonna get another Saran Wrap job with my end," Randal said. "What'cha gonna spend the rest on?"

Foster wavered, suddenly hard-pressed to conceal his exuberance. *It's fucking real! Now I won't get kicked out of my apartment!* "I don't know," he said, thoughts drifting.

He could go back to the Lounge, where in all likelihood he'd be able to find DO ME and GAG...

Two redneck construction workers came in and each purchased a hot dog. Foster cringed. "Smells like...cum in here," one commented to the other as they left.

"They got that right," Randal said. "I should've asked them how my spit tastes."

"That's pretty revolting, man."

The bell rung. "You wanna talk about *revolting?* Check this homeless scumbag out," Randal said.

A malodorous man who surely weighed four hundred pounds

squeezed through the door. He mumbled to himself, his lips like mini-bratwursts on the huge, greasy face. A rim of long gray-black hair (with flecks of garbage in it) half-circumscribed the bald, dirt-smudged head. Stained orange sweatpants clung to elephantine legs, and for a shirt he wore a reeking yellow raincoat. He seemed to jabber something like, "It was Peter Lawford and Bobby," and "Would somebody please cut off my head?"

Jesus, Foster thought. *The poor bastard. Totally destitute and probably schizophrenic.* It seemed there were more and more of these lost souls.

Randal cut Foster a snide grin. "So we're all children of God, huh? Well if so, then God's got a *shitload* of fucked up kids."

"It doesn't involve God at all," Foster answered, unfazed. "Humanity exists in error, ever since Eve bit the apple. God gave us the brains and the wherewithal to help people like this guy, with medical technology and compassion. But we have to *choose* to have the grace to do it." Foster reached in his pocket.

"Don't you *dare* give that walking garbage can money," Randal ordered. "The shit-smelling fucker rips me off all the time." He rapped a baseball bat against the counter, and yelled at the man, "Get the fuck out of here! I've got you on tape ripping off Wing Dings and Yoo Hoos three nights in a row."

The man looked back, wobbling. His phlegmatic voice fluttered. "The fuckin' LBJ, I saw him pull his dick out at the barbeque."

"Take your crazy ass *out* of here!" Randal yelled, and CLACKED! the bat again. "Otherwise I call the cops *after* I joggle that piss-sponge you've got for a brain!"

"Fucker," the voice rattled back, then he hitched and released a trumpet-blast of colonic gas.

"Aw, Jesus! You're a fuckin' animal! How can somebody homeless weigh *that* much? You shoplift five thousand calories a day?"

Foster's eyes teared from the sudden waft.

"You're a fucker!" the man warbled back.

Randal waved the bat. "I'm *killin'* ya if you don't GET OUT!"

The huge man shimmied in place, then leaned over, stuck his fingers down his throat and—

"No! Don't!"

—urped up what had to be a gallon of vomit. It hit the floor like a bucket of barley and vegetable soup.

"Holy shit!" Randal came around the counter with the bat, but Foster grabbed him.

"Just let him go, man. He's fucked up, he can't help it."

Randal fumed, but by now the man had already wobbled out of the store. He looked at the splatter of vomit on the floor and nearly keeled over.

"Yeah, he can't help it—shit."

"It's called compassion, man," Foster said, gagging at the smell.

"Fine, smart guy. Ready to walk it like you talk it?"

"How's that?"

"Now you can have some compassion for *me*." Randal threw Foster a mop. "And help me clean this shit up."

Foster laughed and said, "Sure."

(IV)

That night Foster was heckled by a stew of awful dreams. He heard a wind that sounded like screams. Words seemed to fly in the air as if abstract birds: "DON'T BE A CRUMMY PERSON!" and "I SAW HIM PULL HIS DICK OUT AT THE BARBEQUE," and "WALKS IN HERE WITH A BELLY FULL OF WHITE TRASH AND RIPS *ME* OFF?" and "I'M HERE TO TELL YOU THAT YOU'VE WON THE SENARY."

He dreamed of writhing sexual pleasure as GAG and DO ME knelt topless before him, each of their mouths taking turns suckling his penis. "Come on our tits, baby," one of them cooed but when Foster obliged, it was not sperm that he ejaculated but something as black as the Qwik-Mart's coffee. Then DO ME said, "You know. I never could figure why they call it a blow job. I mean, you suck it, you don't *blow* into it." "Hmm," uttered GAG. "Let's try," and then she took Foster's flaccid, black-ink-dripping penis back into her mouth and began to blow. When Foster's scrotum began to inflate, DO ME laughed. Foster himself, however, did not laugh. GAG kept blowing as the scrotum kept inflating, and when it had swollen to the size of a medicine ball— POP!—it erupted. DO ME and GAG cackled like witches, but now they both had vampire fangs. Next, the dream showed him a Polanski-like tracking shot which began with, well, Polanski himself feeling up a thirteen-year-old in a hot tub, and then the point of view soared into, of all places, a bowling alley, where the outrageously pregnant prostitute from the Qwik-Mart was performing fellatio on a team of blue-collar rednecks in orange bowling shirts. She spat the product of each orgasm into an empty paper cup and when she was done, she drank it all and said, "*Fuck,* I hate that taste," and then all the rednecks applauded. They began to hoot all the more when she inexplicably stepped out of her shorts and walked bare-bottomed down the lane. Her huge breasts swayed nearly enough to knock her off balance when she leaned over and moved the head pin out several feet, and then she spat on the head of the pin and squatted on it. "Ugh, ugh," she grunted, biting her lower lip. She'd worked the top of the pin into her vulva and began to squat down harder. Eventually one of the rednecks yelled, "What the *hail* you doin', girl?" but she just grimaced back and said, "Tryin' ta break my water, asshole. I gotta get this hunka shit out of me," and now that Polanski dream-camera moves off; it's picking up speed as it absurdly changes tenses; it seems to want to leave the alley but first skims past a long glass case where one would expect to find bowling trophies but, lo, the case is full of bottles of Vigo brand olive oil. The point of view swerves next, then dives, until it hovers over a table on which lay Randal who flops helpless there as several nude women (with horns in their heads) chat calmly while they wrap him

EDWARD LEE

from head to foot in Saran Wrap. The only area of his body left
exposed is his nose, presumably as an airway. One woman says,
"Okay, let him in," while two more, plump breasts jiggling, open a
door and admit the terribly obese homeless bum from the Qwik-Mart.
"Let 'er rip, buddy," another woman says. "It was that fuckin' Peter
Lawford and Bobby that did it," he jabbers and peels down his filthy
orange sweatpants over a hairy, rash-pinkened buttocks that may have
been a full yard across. He hunkers down and, in colonic gusts, defe-
cates very wetly into the bucket until it is full to the brim with diarrhea.
"Good job," someone compliments, and in no time Randal's ankles are
noosed and the women pulley him up and then slowly lower his head
into the atrocious bucket, and next the "camera" caroms off to a
strange smoking street tinted in weird light where hunched workmen
labor in silence as they build a house but as the point of view draws
closer, it becomes discernible that the workmen aren't using bricks to
build the house, they're using human heads, and then, next, the camera
shoots upward, rocketlike, and only plunges after an exceedingly long
period of time until it fires through a stained-glass window and stops
in the chancel of a church where six horned demons that look like
skeletons covered with raw chicken skin cavort within a circle of
brown ashes and stinking candles. A woman lies naked on the floor,
her arms and legs lashed wide. One demon studies a scroll of yellowed
paper, or perhaps skin, while the other five amuse themselves by
fondling the squirming woman. A lipless mouth full of pus sucks at the
fur-rimmed flesh between the woman's legs. The first looks up from
the scroll and orders, "The Benumbment Spell has taken effect. The
Inscriptions must begin," but the entity's voice sounds echoic and like
gravel being poured from a dump-truck. On command, each of the
remaining things dip long, jointy fingers into what looks like a mortar.
The fingers come away brown. "Anoint her," speaks the primary
demon. "Make her despoilment rich. It nourishes the Flux..." With
their sullied fingertips, the demons begin to write on the woman's lux-
uriant, nude body, and in the midst of the dream, Foster's psyche

53

becomes active, and he wonders, *What was that stuff in the cup? It's not…SHIT, is it?* but the query is stifled when he sees exactly *what* the demons are inscribing: a multitude of sixes. "Good, good," the first demon approves. "The anointing is sufficient." The voice crackles and grinds. "We must discorporate shortly. Light the Subservience Ash," and then it begins to intone words in some unknown language. Before the dream veers away, the woman's face is finally revealed: Deaconess Wilson. The point of view blurs fast as a bullet, then stops dead.

It shows, simply, an old stained wall, with a large hole in it. From the hole eddy words in an accent like someone from New England: "…stretched out my fingers and touched a cold and unyielding surface of polished glass."

That's when Foster woke up.

What a pile of shit for a dream! his thoughts squalled. The recollections disgusted him. He dragged himself up, showered, then nearly howled when he looked at the clock.

Six p.m.

I slept the whole day away AGAIN!

He searched the cupboards for something to eat but found nothing—just a bottle of Vigo olive oil. *Great…* Then he stared at the kitchen table, noticing the envelope full of money and the handwritten notice that he'd won the "Senary." *At least that part wasn't a dream.* A self-satisfaction arrived when he remembered that he'd come straight home last night, tempted as he may have been to mosey into the Lounge in search of GAG and DO ME. *But I didn't. I didn't do it, even with all this money.*

Did that make him a better person in God's eyes? He wondered. *Don't be a crummy person*, the evangelist's words kept side-swiping him. But when he looked at the money envelope again…

Maybe it's time to see what this Senary business is all about…

《《 — 》》

Two winos shared the bus shelter with him. A third man, who looked normal, must've been possessed by some syndrome like Tourette's. He looked right at Foster and spouted, "Cock fuck big dick big vibrator hairy big pussy asshole bitch shit lick aw fuck motherfucker I stepped in fuckin' gum."

And a good day to you too, Foster thought. The shelter's plastic windows shuddered when the bus pulled up. Foster took the first seat, while the winos neglected to get on. *Maybe they're...dead,* he considered, looking out the window at them. They remained sidled over in the shelter, drooling. The Tourette's man went all the way to the back, then the bus jerked away.

The Senary, Foster contemplated. *What the hell is it?* He looked at the announcement, with the address and instructions.

...CARRY ON TO THE FOLLOWING ADDRESS AFTER SUNDOWN WITHIN THE NEXT SIX DAYS...

It had only been one day, and a glance to the horizon showed him he still had several hours before sundown. A copy of the *Tampa Bay Times* sat on his seat; Foster picked it up, began to thumb through. One article enthused over the new governor's bid to build a "biomass" electric plant; the plant ran on natural gas derived from elephant grass and dog feces. Then Foster spotted this:

FEMALE PASTOR DISAPPEARS

The article went on to disclose that Andrea Wilson, 40, a well-regarded deaconess at the Grace Unitarian Church of St. Petersburg, seemingly disappeared from her post several days ago. She gave no notice of resignation, nor notice of taking leave.

It's her, Foster thought when he looked at the accompanying picture, the blond hair conservatively pulled back, the strongly angled but attractive face, and the Roman collar.

"She's such a wonderful person," quoted a woman who regularly attended the church. "She's so inspiring, so full of faith. And she's simply not the type of person to leave and not tell anyone where she went."

I know where she went yesterday, came Foster's dreadful thought. *My apartment, to tell me I've won a contest called the Senary, and then strip nude and rub herself down with my olive oil...*

He wondered if he should call the police and tell them that he'd seen the missing woman, but... *No. What on earth could I say?*

He squinted at the next, shorter article which reported that a grave had been vandalized late last night at Carver Forest Memorial Cemetery, and the very instant Foster read the information, he glanced out the window to discover that the bus was cruising by a long, overgrown cemetery. The sign at a fenced entrance read CARVER FOREST. *Uncanny*, he thought. The spotty article went on to reveal that the grave vandalized had been that of a four-month-old infant who'd been murdered last spring.

Jesus. What a world...

Foster closed the paper when he saw his stop nearing. Had he turned the page he would've seen a grimmer article about the discovery of a dead newborn baby found in a recycle bin last night. Foster pulled the cord. "Thank you, driver," he said, and the driver, in turn, frowned. The Tourette's man railed from the back of the bus just as Foster stepped off: "Hairy big pussy jack off big fuckin' vibrator in the bitch's ass motherfucker shit on a motherfuckin' stick asshole dick wad chump cock suck six," and then the doors flapped closed.

Foster turned as the bus pulled away. *Did he say six?* He squinted after the disappearing bus, and saw the Tourette's man give him the finger through the back window.

He walked down Central, shirking at loud cars and motorcycles. He'd already memorized the street address (24651) because he didn't want to be consulting his wallet in this neck of the woods. The area was mostly ghetto, small saltbox houses in various disrepair. *Maybe this isn't such a good idea,* he considered when he noticed stragglers obviously selling drugs only blocks deeper off the road. Burned up yards fronted most of the little houses; piles of junk sat like tee-pees amid trashed cars. *So much for urban renewal...*

He sensed more than saw a figure behind him.

"Yo!" came a girl's voice.

Foster turned, not quite at ease. A black girl in tight knee jeans and a zebra striped tube-top boldly approached him. Her dark skin gleamed over robust curves.

"How's, uh, how's it going?" Foster bumbled.

"I'll suck the nut right out your white dick, man, for twenty-five bucks," she spoke right up.

"No, really, I—"

"Bullshit, man." She stood haughtily, hand on a cocked hip. "I knows a john when I see one, and *you* a john. Come on, pussy or mouth, I got both. You wanna fuck, I kin tell."

"No, really—"

"Yeah, you white guys're all cheap motherfuckers. Awright, twenty bucks for a blow'n I'll swallow the nut. You fuckin' guys love it when the girl swallow the nut."

Only now did Foster fully realize how out of place he was. "I'm...not interested. I'm just trying to find an address."

The gleam of her white teeth matched that of her skin. "Shee-it. You lookin' for the Larken House, I know. Lotta folks always lookin' for it. 24651, right?"

Foster was astonished. "Well, yes."

"Folks been walkin' by it since it happened."

"Since...*what* happened?"

"Don't'choo watch the news?" She adjusted her tube-top. "Couple, three months ago, a brother named Larken, work construction, he cut off his ole lady's head when he found out the baby she had a couple months 'fore that were from another dude. Cut her head off in the house, then walk right down this street and stick it on the antenna of the dude's car 'cos, see, he hadda old car that had one'a them old fashioned antennas on it. Then Larken come back the house and cut the *baby's* head off, and he microwave it. Some say he fuck the headless wife on the kitchen table too but I dunno. Then he hang hisself. Said he had his cock out when he step off the chair." She looked at him. "Fucked up house, man."

Foster felt perplexed. "So that's why people walk by it? Because it's…infamous?"

"Yeah, man. 'cos, sometime, they say, you kin see Larken in there, hangin' by his neck. Sometimes you hear the baby cryin'."

A HAUNTED house. Terrific, Foster thought. "Most of these houses don't seem to have addresses, even the ones that are obviously lived in."

"Shee-it, sure. They take the numbers off so the pigs get confused," she said. "You gimme twenty dollars'n I show you where the house is."

"I'd be much obliged." Foster slipped a twenty from his pocket and gave it to her.

She grinned, stuffing the bill into her top, and pointed to the small, boarded up house right in front of him.

"That's it? For real?"

"'Fo' real, man."

At first Foster thought he was being taken but when he peered over the door, he noticed a black metal number 6 but also the ghosts of numbers that had fallen, or been taken off, a 2 and a 4 to the left, and a 5 and a 1 to the right.

"Thank you," he said but the girl was already walking away.

Foster peered at the squat house. It looked in better repair than many of the others on the street, even with its windows boarded over. Clapboard siding, fairly faded, portico over gravel where a garage should be, one level save for an awned attic. Screen door with a ripped screen.

What should I do, now that I'm here? he quizzed himself. Was he really going to break into a house where murders had occurred? And what if there were homeless bums inside, or addicts? *Am I REALLY going to do this?*

But then he thought: *The Senary…*

The instructions, however, mentioned after sundown. Foster still had about an hour, he thought. *I'll get something to eat and think this over.*

He jaywalked to a Church's Chicken. Six patrons stood in line, and five of them appeared to be African-American prostitutes. When his turn came, an Hispanic woman with half of one ear missing asked if she could help him.

Foster ordered the Number Six special: three wings, a biscuit, and a drink. *There's that number six again,* he reckoned. Just as he would sit down with his food, one of the prostitutes, a scarily thin woman with huge eyes and pigtails, slipped beside him, and whispered, "Gimme a wing." Foster did, then she whispered lower, "I'll suck the nut right out your white dick, man, for twenty-five bucks."

What, is that the patented line around here? Foster politely informed her that he had no interest in her proposal, and edged quickly out of the restaurant.

God, those are good! he thought, scarfing his remaining wings and biscuit as he walked down the street. He still had time to kill, but he didn't want to get killed himself as sundown approached. He walked down Central a ways, trying to look inconspicuous and knowing he wasn't doing a very good job. Sirens rose and fell in the distance, and then he jumped a bit at either a faraway gunshot or back-fire. *Hurry up, sundown,* he thought, and patted his wallet to make sure it was still there, then the other pocket where he'd slipped a slim flashlight. At the corner a dark hulk loomed, and then a shadow covered Foster: the shadow of a cross cast by the sinking sun. *A church,* he noticed next of the drab, pile-like edifice. For no apparent reason he stopped to study it. The sign read: GRACE UNITARIAN CHURCH OF ST. PETERSBURG, but a smaller sign in magic marker added, CLOSED UNTIL FURTHER NOTICE.

This is the Deaconess' church! came the jolting thought.

An old building of streaked gray stone. High, double-lancet windows framed mosaics of stained glass that looked black, and drought

THE SENARY

had killed most of the ivy that crawled up the walls. Foster was surprised to find the large front door unlocked, and even more surprised by his lack of hesitancy in entering. Fading sun tinted the nave with reddish light; as he approached his nostrils flared at a smell like urine and something more revolting. He passed empty pews, crossed the chancel. Several apsidal rooms arched behind the altar, two empty but on the floor of one he found, oddly, a coping saw. Foster ran his fingers along the thin blade and found them tacky. Could it be blood? *No, no, that's ridiculous,* he felt sure. It was probably tar or something, resin, maybe. Nevertheless, the saw irked him and he stepped quickly out.

Tires crunching over gravel alerted him; he hustled to a rear window in the dressing room where, in fading light, he saw a black car pulling out.

What would I have done if it was pulling IN?

And who might be driving it?

Probably just smoochers, he resolved. Or, in this area? A drug deal.

A draped baptistry stood to his right. Did he hear something? Foster put an eye to the gap in the scarlet drapes, and seized up.

"Yeah, yeah, fuck," a man with his pants down huffed. He was in his fifties, graying hair on the sides of a bald pate, and he wore a dress shirt and tie. His cheeks billowed in the obvious exertion of frenetic masturbation. He stood before another man who was on his knees—a fetid, homeless bum. Foster could swear he saw flies buzzing around the bum's horrifically sweat-stained ball cap. Six inches of dirty beard jutted from his chin; he knelt with his head jacked back, toothless mouth strained open below closed eyes.

The ludicrous masturbator's hand blurred; he was nearly stomping up and down to reach his climax. Finally, "Yeah, yeah, there, eat it, eat it," he panted as several small loops of sperm popped from his corona into the bum's mouth.

Foster pulled the curtain back. "This is a church, for God's sake!"

The corpulent client's face turned sheet-white. "Shit! Shit shit

60

shit!" he shrieked. He yanked his over-large slacks up and barreled out of the baptistry, stumbled down the nave and banged through the front door.

The bum raged. "You fucker, man!" Spittle and, evidently, sperm flew from his chapped lips. "That was my trick, man! He was gonna pay me twenty bucks! I ought to kill you, man!"

Foster stepped back, not nearly as afraid as he'd expect himself to be. "Relax," he kept his cool. "I was just looking around. Here." He handed the bum a $20 bill.

The bum turned instantly exuberant. "Cool, thanks. Gimme another twenty and I'll do you too."

"No. No, thanks," Foster said, realizing now that the man's beard was one of the scariest things he'd ever seen. "Who *are* you?"

"Forbes," said the bum.

"*Forbes?* So...Forbes, this is where you...do...business? A church?"

When the bum scratched his beard, dandruff fell like salt from a shaker. "Aw, Deaconess Wilson, she's cool. Let's me sleep here at night as long as I'm out by five in the morning." Now he lifted the liner out of the baptismal font and drank the water in it. "I feel bad 'cos, see, she sleeps upstairs and sometimes I sneak up there and watch her take showers and shit. She's got the best tits—"

I know, Foster thought.

"—and this big gorgeous fur-burger on her, man. *Blond.* And I just can't help it. I see *that* all wet and shiny in the shower, I just *gotta* beat off. Shit." He grinned, showing spermy gums. "Guess I'll probably go to Hell, huh?"

"They say only God can judge," Foster said lamely.

The bum scratched his ass. "She gives me canned food a lot too, makes me feel even guiltier. I guess I'm just a shit. It sucks when ya have to eat your own nut just for the calories, ya know? You ever eat your own nut when ya beat off?"

"Uh, no," Foster confessed.

"Yeah, man, when you're homeless ya gotta do it 'cos there's, like, a couple hundred calories per load, lotta protein, I heard. There was times when that and the johns comin' in my mouth were the only things keepin' me from starvin'."

Foster was speechless.

"But what're *you* doin' here, man? You a friend of Deaconess Wilson?"

Finally a topic of conversation he could take part in. "Not really, but I did meet her once. Do you know where she is?"

The bum reached down into the front of his rotten jeans and scratched. It sounded like sandpaper. "Disappeared, they say but...I don't know about that." He pulled his hand out and sniffed it. "See, when I'm sleepin' in here at night, sometimes I think I hear her coming in. I can hear her car."

"A black car?"

"Yeah. Old black car."

Interesting. "I just saw a black car pulling out of the lot behind the church."

"Shit! Really?" The bum scampered past Foster, leaving dizzying B.O. in his wake. "Ain't there now," he said, peering out the window.

"Maybe she'll be back," Foster contemplated. "Or maybe it wasn't her." He eyed the bum. "Say, did she ever mention a strange word to you? The word *Senary?*"

The bum was only half-listening. "Naw, never heard no word like that." He picked his nose and nonchalantly ate what his finger brought out.

What am I DOING here? Foster asked himself.

The window was turning dark, and at once the bum seemed edgy. "Shit, it's sundown—"

Sundown, Foster repeated.

"—and I gotta get out."

"But I thought you said you slept here."

"Yeah but I ain't gonna do that no more," the bum said, and shuffled back toward the chancel. "Every night since the Deaconess been gone, I have me these really scary dreams."

Foster didn't know what compelled him to ask, "What...dreams?"

The bum's eyes looked cloudy. "Aw, weird, sick shit, man, like in some city where the sky's red and there's smoke comin' out of the sewer grates on every street, and black things flyin' in the air and other things crawling up and down these buildings that are, like, a mile high, and people gettin' their guts hauled out their asses and these big gray *things* bustin' girls wide open with their cocks and eatin' their faces off their heads and drownin' kids in barrels'a cum and playin' catch with babies on pitchforks'n shit. And a house, man. A house made of heads..."

Foster stared.

"—and, fuck, last week, right before Deaconess Wilson disappeared, I was sleepin' in the pews and dreamed that these *monsters* were fuckin' with her, and reading all this evil shit like Latin or something."

"Monsters?"

"Yeah, man. Like, just skin-covered bones and horns in their heads. Had teeth like nails made of glass. They hadda bunch of candles burinin' in a circle and layin' inside the circle was Deaconess Wilson with no clothes on, man. These monsters are fuckin' with her, like suckin' her tits and feelin' her 'n fingerin' her and shit, and one of 'em suckin' her cunt, and then, then—" Now the bum looked sickened in the recollection. "They started writin' on her, man. They're *writin'* on her, with *shit,* but it wasn't just any ole shit—it was *Satan's* shit. Somehow I knew that in the dream."

Foster was getting unnerved. He didn't believe in shared delusions or shared nightmares. But...

The bum started toward the front door, but kept talking. "And last night, fuck. I dreamed I seen the Deaconess walkin' around here buck naked with her big tits and bush stickin' out, but ya know what she was carryin'?"

"Whuh—what?" Foster grated.

THE SENARY

"A coffin, man." He kept walking, his voice echoed in the nave. "But it was like a *little* coffin. Like a *baby's*. So, shit on that, ya know? I ain't sleepin' here no more 'cos this place gives me fucked up dreams." Rotten sneakers scuffed as the bum pushed open the front door and left.

Jesus, Foster thought in the fading light.

He had every intention of following the bum out, but for some reason his steps took him not toward the door but to the left, along the sides of the pews. He shined his flashlight beneath one, caught a breath in his chest, then knelt.

A shovel had been stashed there. Foster fingered the earth on the blade and found it—

Fresh…

There was also a pair of work gloves on the floor, that appeared soiled but recently purchased.

What the hell is this?

Stashed under the last pew in the farthest corner was a coffin.

A *little* coffin. Like a baby's.

Foster left the church so fast he didn't even close the door behind him.

(V)

The sun had sunk quickly, like something trying to escape. Foster looked up and down the street to find it oddly vacant. The drab house-front peered back at him as if with disdain. *The Larken House,* he thought. *A MURDER house.*

Of course, Foster didn't believe that a *house* could influence people by the things that had happened in it. *A HOUSE can't have power…* But maybe *belief* was the power. Could a person's *conception* of terrible events create the influence?

Foster wasn't sure why he would even consider such a thing. It simply occurred to him.

EDWARD LEE

He traversed the weed-cracked front path, surprised by his boldness, and opened the screen door. *No way the door's unlocked,* he predicted. *That would be senseless.* The oddest door knocker faced him. It had been mounted on the old door's center stile, an oval of tarnished bronze depicting a morose half-formed face. Just two eyes, no mouth, no other features. The notion made Foster shiver:

I knock on the door and Larken answers...

"Here goes," he muttered. He grabbed the knob and turned it. The door opened.

An unqualified odor assailed him when once inside. Not garbage or excrement or urine but just something faintly...*foul.* Foster snapped on his flashlight, panned it around the empty living room. His stomach sunk when he discerned brown footprints tracked over the threadbare carpet. *Old blood,* he reasoned. *From the murder night.* The compulsion to leave couldn't have been more pronounced but, *I have to stay,* he ordered himself. *I have to find out what this is all about.* He followed the footprints to a begrimed kitchen and was sickened worse when he saw great brown shapes of more dried blood all over the linoleum floor. The footprints proceeded to the microwave. *Larken must've killed his wife and the baby in here.* He eyed the kitchen table and gulped. In the corner stood a chair, directly under a water pipe. *And that's where he hanged himself...*

Then Foster froze at a sound: a quick *snap!*

A cigarette lighter?

That's what it reminded him of. His heart hammered. This was crazy and he knew it. An abandoned house in *this* neighborhood? *Vagrants, addicts, or gang-members...*

Yet he didn't leave.

He turned the flashlight off and walked down a shabby side-hall toward the sound. He paused and, sure enough, in a dark bedroom he detected what could only be the flicker of a cigarette lighter. In addition, he heard an accompanying sound, like someone inhaling with desperation.

THE SENARY

I could be killed…so why don't I leave? Foster had no answer to this logical question. When he took a step forward, the floor creaked.

His heart nearly stopped when a woman's voice shot out of the dark. "Oh, good, you're back. I'm in here," and then the lighter flicked again but this time to light a candle.

In the bloom of light, Foster couldn't believe his eyes. A woman sat on a mattressless box-spring, holding a crack pipe. A white woman, with dark lank hair, wearing a bikini top and cutoff shorts. The hostile face glared at him.

"Shit, you're not her," she complained. "Who the," but then she squinted. "Wait a minute, I fuckin' remember you…"

Indeed, and Foster remembered her. It was the pregnant prostitute he'd seen in the Qwik-Mart last night. It didn't take him long to realize why she looked different.

She was no longer pregnant.

"Yes," Foster droned. "At the store. And I…see that you've had your baby."

She maintained her glare. The huge breasts hung satcheled in the faded top. Her exposed midriff below the top looked corrugated now trowled. All she said was, "Fuck. What the fuck are you doing here? Are you with that woman?"

That woman, Foster's brain ticked. "Do you mean…a blond woman in a black gown? A white collar?"

The whore idly fingered groovelike stretchmarks on her belly. "Yeah, like what a fuckin' priest wears, but it's a chick, not a guy."

There was no lust at all in Foster's mind as he looked at the woman. She calmly lit the pipe, inhaled deeply, then collapsed against the wall. Her expression turned to a mask of oblivion.

"What is this woman to you? Deaconess Wilson?" Foster actually raised his voice.

The whore slipped up the stuffed bikini top to cover a great half-circle of nipple. "She paid me six fuckin' hundred bucks, that's what."

Foster was dismayed. *And I got six thousand.* "So, you've won the Senary, as well?"

"I don't know what the fuck you're talking about. All I know is what I'm supposed to do."

"And what was that? What *did* you do, for the six hundred?"

She shrugged. "Dug up a grave. Think I give a shit?"

Foster stared in the flickering light, thinking of the article. "Was it...a child's grave?"

"Yeah, man. A baby's. She said the baby was murdered in this house, had its head cut off. She said she needed the head."

Confusion circled round Foster's like a feisty crow. "But...what happened to *your* baby? You were pregnant last night."

"I shit the kid out behind the Qwik-Mart," she said, pressing another piece of crack into the pipe. "Fuckin' mess. I dropped it in one of those blue bins the recycling trucks pick up, then I split. Couple hours later, I met *her.*"

"And she—"

"Paid me six hundred bucks to dig up the grave." She sucked off the pipe and chuckled. "Kind'a weird, you know? An hour after I dump my own baby, this chick pays me to dig up somebody *else's* baby. Ain't that a trip?"

"Yeah," Foster uttered. "A trip..."

"She waited for me in her car. Didn't even take as long as you'd think, and the coffin was tiny, barely weighed anything. They always say six feet under, right? But this was like two, three. So I put the coffin in the back of her car, and she drives me downtown...and gave me six hundred bucks. Said she'd give me another six hundred if I showed up tonight. Said she needed me, said she needed my milk."

"Your *milk?* What on earth for?"

She shrugged again, and re-loaded the pipe. "Said 'cos I was lactating. You think I care?" She held up a baggie full of pieces of crack. "I mean, *look* at all this rock, man. And when she lays another six hundred on me tonight? I won't have to suck another dick for a month. Fuck, I hate it. Crack doesn't leave a woman with any choice. You have to suck ten dirty dicks a day at least, just to keep up your jones. Think about that, buddy. Ten dicks a day. It's like letting guys blow their nose in your mouth for money. Every time I see another dick in my face I wanna cut my throat but I know that if I do..." She jiggled the bag of crack. "I'll never be able to get high again."

Foster frowned. "Deaconess Wilson told me I won a contest of some sort, and told me to meet her here. Where the hell is she?"

"Right here," answered a silhouette in the doorway.

Foster grimaced from the shock. "God *damn!* Don't sneak up on people like that!"

The female minister stepped forward into the candle light. Her face appeared either blank or simply content and her blue eyes, which struck Foster as dull yesterday, seemed narrow and keen now. She wore the same black surplice and white collar.

"How irregular for you to take God's name in vain," she said.

"You scared the shit out of me," he objected. "Now what's all this about? And furthermore, what are *you* all about?"

She glanced at the prostitute, who was re-lighting her pipe.

"What I'm all about, Mr. Foster," the deaconess began, "is failure. You, on the other hand, are about success. I envy you—" Her voice hushed. "And I honor you."

"That makes no sense. I should leave."

"That is your prerogative, it has been all along. Didn't I make it clear that you are under no obligation?"

"Yeah, but—"

"And now you want answers. First, answers about me."

"You got that right. A bum living in your church had the same dream as me. I read an article in the paper about a baby's grave dug up, and it turns out this girl over here is the one who did the digging. And a half hour ago I see the fuckin' coffin stuck beneath the pews at *your* church."

"It's all part of the science—"

Foster's anger roiled. "The *science?*"

EDWARD LEE

"You'll understand more should you choose to proceed far enough to speak to the Trustee."

Foster opened his mouth to object further, paused, then decided not to.

Her eyes appeared like cool blue embers. "Do you choose to proceed?"

"Yes," Foster said.

"Then follow me." The deaconess touched the prostitute's shoulder. "Come along. You bring the candles," and then she raised a plastic bag which depended from an object about the size of a softball. "I'll bring the head."

«« — »»

The echoes of her words trailed behind her like a banner as they mounted the dark stairs. "The attic is the best place, for the power of its ambience. The cliché—do you understand? The sheer *weight* of the idea?"

"No, I *don't* understand," Foster said, the whore behind him.

"The same as the house itself, and what happened in the house. The house has become what's known as a Bleed-Point, while certain things from the *history* of the house serve as functional Totems. They're Power Relics."

Certain things, Foster wondered. *She means the head...* "What did you mean when you called yourself a failure but I'm a success?"

He could see the woman nod ahead of him. "You're on one end of the Fulcrum, I'm on the other—the *bad* end, I'm afraid."

"The Fulcrum, huh?" Foster complained.

"I was solicited because I was solicitable. My ebbing faith made me ripe for the Machinators. But you? You're actually the opposite. It's the desire of the powers I now serve that you make the *choice*. My rewards are minuscule compared to the rewards you will receive should you accept this incalculable prize."

69

THE SENARY

Great, Foster thought.

The stairs raised them into a long, dusty attic. Even after dusk, it was stiflingly hot. The prostitute began lighting candles from a bag she'd carried up, and in the growing light, Foster saw that the attic was essentially empty, save for a couple of lawn chairs and a couple of boxes. The deaconess went to the back wall, then paced off six steps toward the room's center. There, she placed one of the chairs.

"This is where you will sit."

From a darker corner, then, she pulled out—

Whoa! Foster thought, alarmed.

—a brand-new pick ax.

"And this is how we will access the Trustee."

"What are you *talking* about?" Foster whined.

The Deaconess smiled. She removed her Roman collar and started to unbutton her surplice. "Remove your clothes, dear," she said to the prostitute. "We must show our God-given bodies unclothed, to curry favor from our lord."

The prostitute smirked. "I want my fuckin' money first. You said you'd give me another six hundred."

The bills were produced like a card trick, and handed over.

"Curry favor from your *lord?*" Foster questioned. "Somehow I don't think you mean the Lord God."

"Our Lord Lucifer," the Deaconess said. "Certainly, you've already guessed that."

"Yeah, sure. But the thing I want to know is how did those skinny demons manage to get a hold of your Lord Lucifer's *shit* to write sixes on your body?"

The Deaconess popped out more buttons. "It's a process known as Object Transposition, a very new occult science. It's sub-dimensional. The demons—and the excrement itself, by the way—were only corporeal for the duration of the Rite. Six minutes. But six minutes were enough," and then she dropped the surplice to the floor, to stand splendidly nude in the candlelight.

Foster tried not to gawp at the robust physique. "You seem different today. Yesterday you were all fidgety."

She went behind the prostitute to untie her faded bikini top. When the garment dropped, buoyant breasts came unloosed, with large irregular nipples that looked like plops of chewed beef.

"That's because I've acclimated to the entails of the Machination Link. And I'm not resisting it anymore. I've accepted it, the beginning of my glorious demise. I'm being *machinated,* you see—by a trained Channeler and a high-echelon Archlock who operate out of a Telethesy Unit at the De Rais Academy." She smiled. "Think of it as puppeteering—from Hell. Only now my own soul has amalgamated with the process."

Foster stared.

"Oh, and Mr. Foster? You'll need to remove your clothes as well."

Foster winced. "I'm not taking off my *clothes,* for God's sake."

"For Lucifer's, not God's. It's all part of the protocol, I'm afraid. You must be as naked as Adam when he stalked out of the Garden."

What am I doing? came the thought as he began to strip. At least being nude would make the heat more tolerable. The Deaconess and the whore were already shining with sweat.

Now the Deaconess was inspecting the prostitute's heavy breasts, twilling the meaty nipples with her fingers. "Let's see here now," she murmured. Milk sprayed out at once. "Yes, good, so *full,*" and then the Deaconess tasted a wet fingertip. "Ah. Soiled. Perfect." Next her hand stroked up and down the recently deflated belly, whose stretchmarks now looked like a irrigation ditches. An abundant sprawl of black pubic hair sat clumped between the whore's legs. The Deaconess ran her fingers through it, fascinated. "So how many babies have come out of here, hmm?"

"Six, seven—fuck, I don't know," the prostitute said, disconcerted.

"And you left them *all* to die?"

"Yeah. Fuck it. The world's a bunch'a shit anyway. Who wants to bring kids up with all this shit goin' on? Besides, I make more money when I'm pregnant."

"Really? How interesting."

"Sure. Kink tricks, you know? Lotta guys out there go nuts for knocked up streetwalkers. They pay more. So I pocket the cash, and when it's time, I pop the kid out in an alley somewhere and walk away."

"Perfect," whispered the Deaconess.

Foster felt sick.

BAM! BAM! BAM!

Foster *and* the prostitute jumped at the start. The sound of impact shook the house. When Foster cleared his confusion, he noticed the Deaconess—

BAM!

—driving the pick-ax point with gusto into the wall. After a dozenish strikes, she'd managed to tear out a hole about the diameter of a dinner plate, roughly four feet from the floor.

Foster peered out the hole, which showed the moonlit backyard. Then he re-faced the Deaconess.

"I ask you once more, Mr. Foster. Do you wish to proceed?"

Foster could feel the sweat pouring out of him. "Yes."

"I thought you would," and now she had the plastic bag again, and reached in. Foster grimaced before she even extracted the contents: the rotten head of a baby.

The small face had dried to a rictus. But then Foster noticed something even worse. The *top* of the head was missing.

The Deaconess threw the head through the hole in the wall, where it landed, bouncing, in the backyard.

"But I thought—"

"That I needed it for a ritual of some sort?" the gleaming woman finished. The nipples on the high breasts stood out as if she were sexually frantic. "Not the head itself. This. The skullcap," and from the bag she produced just that: the top of the infant's skull, which had

EDWARD LEE

obviously been sawn off. At once Foster recalled the smudged coping saw at the church.

She's really been busy.

"The brains had already putrefied"; she showed him the inside of the empty dome. Then she raised her brow at the prostitute. "I'm afraid the newborn of our friend here wouldn't do. It hadn't lived long enough to be touched by Original Sin. It had to be *this* baby, from *this* house."

"And what did you *call* this house, earlier?" Foster asked.

"A Bleed-Point," she said, her bare, flat stomach glistening. Droplets of sweat beaded in her pubic mound, like clear little jewels. "Think of it as a sieve."

"A hole between here and Hell?" Foster figured.

"Yes, but only a semi-dimensional hole. A viewport, so to speak."

So if I look through this hole, I see Hell? but when he did it was still just the mangy backyard in view. He paused and narrowed his eyes, to glimpse a raccoon waddling away with what was left of the baby head.

Jesus…

"Come on, I gotta crack it up," griped the prostitute, scratching at imaginary bugs on her stomach. "When can I go?"

"Be patient," the Deaconess assured, then her eyes returned to Foster's. "You're still under no obligation. You can still leave."

Foster churned in place. *Haven't I seen enough?* Now he was genuinely beginning to want to get away from all this.

"But why not continue? You can even say no *after* you've taken the tour."

The tour…

She smiled thinly over the exorbitant breasts. "And I can assure you, it's *quite* a tour."

"Let's continue," the words clicked in his throat.

"A venturous man, and a wise one…"

Really? Foster wondered. *I'm standing naked in a ghetto house with a deaconess and a crackwhore for some—some Satanic purpose. What,*

73

though? A *tour?* What could that mean? Foster thought of himself as a Christian, however flawed, however abject and tainted by the world and his weakness. But why would he want to go on a tour of Hell?

The house creaked. The veil of candlelight wavering on the attic walls seemed to darken…

"Over here now, my dear," the Deaconess said, positioning the prostitute on her knees behind Foster.

"What the fuck's this all about?" she protested.

The Deaconess touched her shoulder. "It's about you earning your money. To put it simply, what I need you to do now is suck his ass."

Foster's eyes shot wide.

"Bull-fuckin'-shit!" The prostitute sprang back up. "I don't do rim-jobs for cheap. That second six hundred bucks was for some shit you said about needing my milk. You didn't say anything about ass-sucking—"

Six more $100 bills were thrust into the prostitute's face. She rolled her eyes. "Jesus, lady. For this much money I'll suck a *mile* of ass."

"Good. You'll need to do it for as long as I say, while I do my own tending," and then she drifted back around. "He needs to be stimulated till he can't see straight." Now her grin looked vulpine, and her hands ran down Foster's wet chest. "He needs to be *titillated* till he's fit to *burst*. He needs to be *bursting* with sperm."

Madness, Foster thought.

Behind him, the prostitute muttered, "Well, here goes nothing," and then thumbed his buttocks open and with no hesitance whatsoever began to lave her tongue back and forth over his anus. Each time she alternated between licking and sucking, Foster felt as though he were standing on a high wire. She paused a moment to pluck an ass hair from her teeth. "It's never a picnic but at least he took a shower first. Lotta fuckin' johns don't. Can ya believe it? I mean, is that fuckin' rude or what? If a guy's gonna pay a girl to suck his *ass,* you think he'd at least *wash* it first. But, no, not most of these scumbags. Serious."

EDWARD LEE

The Deaconess scowled. "Just…be quiet and do as you've been told, please."

The whore shrugged, then continued.

Foster didn't hear any of it; he was too bewildered. Now the Deaconess urged herself right up against him. He cringed in place as the large, slippery breasts slid over his skin. The confusion cleared his mind until all he could contemplate was lust. She bowed his head down, placed a nipple in his mouth, and whispered, "Suck…"

Foster did so, uncomprehending. The nipple swelled in his mouth to the size of a bon-bon; meanwhile, her hand played over his stomach, then slid to his genitals. Fingers teased him, not overtly, but only traceably. In only seconds his penis had erected between their two bellies.

"Harder now," she told him, and switched nipples.

It seemed the harder he sucked the nipple, the harder the prostitute sucked his rectum; the sensation was unreckonable. He was sucking so obsessively that sometimes he forgot to breathe, which caused him to break, gasp, and then begin sucking again. Her hand played with the back of his head, as a mother's might. Foster had to wrap his arms around her to keep from falling.

The Deaconess chuckled in his ear. "They were definitely right when they told me you were a tit-man."

They, Foster thought, but kept sucking.

This went on for minutes and minutes; Foster was cross-eyed when she pulled her breasts away and then actually looked at her watch.

"You're…*timing* this?" came the nearly delirious query.

"Oh, yes."

He managed a frown, even with the voracious sensations at the cleft of his rump. "Let me guess. Sixty-six minutes?"

"Of course," she whispered, "Only thirty-four to go now. Try to enjoy every one of them. The more excited you are, and the more seed you produce, the more positive the conduction."

75

"The conduction," he groaned. He thought for sure that the Deaconess would immediately begin to fellate him. His penis felt *strained.* It felt like a spring about to break. But instead of admitting it into her mouth she began to—

This is outrageous action!

—suck his testicles. Foster swayed, moaning. *Balls in one mouth, ass in the other,* came the crude thought. *This is like a porn movie.* Occasionally, she'd expel his balls, then slide her tongue down the nerve-charged perineum. The effort caused her to crane her head back as far as it would go, until her tongue would actually meet with the prostitute's. *Randal will never believe this,* Foster managed to think. *I don't even know if I believe it…*

The desire to climax was excruciating. It seemed that his cock, his anus, and his heart all beat at an identical—and frantic—pace. *If I don't come soon, I'm gonna croak,* he thought, but each time he tried to grab his penis, the Deaconess snatched it away.

"No, no, not yet. It's not time."

Finally the suction at his ass abated. "Hey, speaking of time, lady, I ain't sucking this guy's ass all night."

"Just a few more minutes," the Deaconess said after checking her watch. "Use your finger now, but slowly."

Foster went up on his tiptoes when a spitty pinky slipped into his anus. *You gotta be shitting me…* When he looked down he saw clear thread of drool depending from the corona all the way to the floor. But—

The Deaconess had kneed briefly away, and returned.

Where did she—

She came back, but seemed intent on her watch. Foster felt brainless now, his body nothing but an arrangement of frantic sexual nerves beginning to short-circuit. Then—

"Now, now," she snapped abruptly and took Foster's erection into her mouth. Her lips stroked over it at a mad speed; Foster was reeling, and then his climax occurred like an ash-can going off. The Deaconess mewled as Foster felt his sperm belt into her mouth. His rectum squirmed with each mad spasm, and the spasms seemed to go on and on. *Shit shit shit shit shit shit!* he thought as he came, and when he was finally finished, he fell over.

The orgasm had dizzied him. The prostitute crawled to a corner, muttering, wiping her mouth with her forearm. When Foster looked again, the Deaconess was spitting his copious ejaculation into the baby's skullcap. It looked like a mouthful of thin yogurt.

"This really is some fucked up shit," the prostitute remarked, but then the Deaconess was briskly approaching her.

"Up, up! Quickly."

"Hey!" the prostitute squealed when the other woman's hand grabbed her hair and lifted.

"The sperm must be covered without delay—"

The Deaconess held the top of the baby's skull beneath one of the prostitute's sodden breasts, and with her fingers she began to urgently milk the nipple. The white fluid sprayed out at first, then began to dribble. "As much as possible. Help me."

The prostitute looked disgusted when she girded the breast with her hands and squeezed. The extra pressure trebled the volume of milk coming out. When the lactation began to peter out, the process was switched over to the other breast.

Jesus, she's got as much as a cow, Foster regarded.

"Good, good," the Deaconess murmured, transfixed. By the time the second breast had been exhausted, the skullcap was nearly full. "Now…"

Foster stared, and so did the prostitute. The Deaconess stood firmly with her legs parted. She lowered the skullcap to her crotch.

What's she going to do? Piss in it now? Foster wondered.

But, alas…

The prostitute shrieked, and even Foster yelled aloud in his stupefaction. A tiny glint showed him what the Deaconess had produced: a razor blade which she immediately slipped right up the middle of her clitoris.

Instead of screaming herself, she moaned in what could only be ecstasy.

THE SENARY

"Lady, you're fuckin' cracked!" spat the prostitute. Foster looked away but something kept dragging his eyes back to the event. Two fingers were kneading the split clitoris, squeezing out blood. The blood ran right into the skullcap.

"There," she celebrated when she was done. Between the sperm, the milk, and the blood, now the skullcap was topped off.

"Can I *go* now?" the prostitute asked.

"Bring me that box," the Deaconess said, "and remove the stand, then, yes, you may be on your way." She held the skullcap ever so carefully, so not to spill its macabre contents, while the sickened whore dragged a cardboard box to the room's center, then removed a Sterno stand.

Foster thought, *Why do I think we're NOT going to be cooking a Chinese Pu-Pu Platter?*

"Set the stand immediately below the hole in the wall, please."

The prostitute's pallid breasts depended as she leaned to do so. She glared at the Deaconess, half in derision and half in nausea. "Look, I know that I'm one of the most fucked up people to ever be born but, shit, lady. This shit here? It's even more fucked up than me."

"Go with the blessing of the Morning Star," the Deaconess said with a great pumpkin grin. "Take your money and your drugs and your hatred and despair, and give thanks as you revel in your curse. Spread your degradation in the glory of his name, sell your body to the lustful, and indulge yourself in reverence to him. Have *more* babies to leave to die in gutters, and spread *more* disease, and continue to let yourself be used as a reservoir of filth and an altar for every offense against God..."

The prostitute stared.

"One day, you will receive a wondrous reward..."

The prostitute raked up her clothes, then barged out of the room, and thunked down the stairs. A moment later, Foster heard the front door slam.

The Deaconess looked at Foster. "Do you wish to continue?"

"Yes."

"Good." She smiled over the skullcap. "Let's begin..."

Foster sat mute in the chair as he watched her. It didn't surprise him when she placed the skullcap atop the Sterno stand, though he couldn't imagine why. From the box she also withdrew the strangest of objects: a foot-long cutting of ordinary garden hose.

A match flared as she bent to light the Sterno.

"Bubble-bubble, toil and trouble?" he misquoted *Macbeth.*

"These are powerful cabalistic components, Mr. Foster." The bleeding between her legs had ceased, leaving her pubic hair matted crimson and the insides of her toned thighs streaked. "What you need to know is that in Hell, ideas are objects, notions are material, symbols are tangible *things* wielded as tools or burned as fuel, and the waste of lust is the Devil's *favorite* tool. Symbols of fecundity and creation when turned to waste become occult energy."

"Milk, sperm? Come on," Foster challenged.

"Yes! What a great spoiler of God's intent. Mother's milk but from the teat of a mother who *murders* her babies. And sperm, sacred by God's gift of procreation, but sullied when spilled deliberately outside of the womb—a harrowing offense. And now...blood... The blood of the chaste, virginity upheld to honor the chastity of Christ, and then spoiled for this atrocious ministration to bid the glorious and unholy power of Lucifer."

Foster looked perplexed at the skullcap sitting above the flame, and then he looked into the hole in the wall.

Just nighttime outside.

"Don't get it."

"You will, once you really *see.*" Her naked body gleamed, not merely from the profuse sweating but from excitement. The candlelight crawled. "It's all science, or I should say sorcery, which serves as science in Lucifer's domain. What we're doing here is called an Ethereal Viewing. I told you, this house is a Bleed-Point; the horrors that occurred here have bruised the skin between the Living World and Hell. This rite will eventually *nick* that bruise enough that you'll actually be able to see the Trustee, and converse with him, too."

"The Trustee," Foster muttered. "A demon?"

"Possibly. I'm not sure. But *I* won't be able to see him. Only you."

"Why?"

Two perfect drops of sweat dripped off the tips of her nipples. "Because *you're* the person who's won the Senary. There's not much more I need to say to prepare you." She stood behind him and errantly rubbed his shoulders. "Just sit and wait...and reflect on the fact that *very few* people ever receive an opportunity such as this."

Foster jerked his head back. "But why? Why me? And *don't* say it's because I won the Senary!"

"Just be patient."

"So...what? When all that crap in the baby skull starts to boil, the hole in the wall becomes a window to Hell? I'm supposed to believe that?"

Her fingers glided hard over his sweat-slick shoulders, then slid forward to rub his pectorals. "That's as good a way of putting it as any. Upon boiling, the steam that rises off the Elixir will trigger the Conduction. You'll have exactly six minutes to listen to the Trustee, ask any questions you have, and then accept or reject the offer. And even if you accept, which I pray you'll do, you're under no obligation. Nothing becomes binding unless you say yes upon completion of the tour."

Those words bothered him more, perhaps, than anything else tonight. *The tour...* There was something potent about them. Even when he *thought* the words, they seemed to echo as if they were called down from a mountain precipice.

But then more thoughts dripped. "This is a pact with the Devil, you mean."

"Not a pact. A gift. One thing to keep in mind. The Devil doesn't *need* to offer contracts for souls very often these days. Think about that..."

Foster's eyes narrowed.

Then he heard the faintest bubbling. The contents of the skullcap—the Elixir—was boiling.

"It's time," she whispered and stepped away. "Look at the hole in the wall...and prepare to meet the Trustee."

Foster tensed in his seat, squinting. The teeming night was all that continued to look back at him from the hole. The steam wafting off the skullcap was nearly non-existent. *How the hell can*—but after a single blink...

The hole changed.

In that blink the hole's ragged boundary of sheetrock and shingles had metamorphosed into something like ragged flaps of what he would only think of as organ meat. Foster leaned forward, focused.

My God...

What he looked at now was a room, or at least a room of sorts. *Is that... No, it couldn't be,* he thought, because the room's walls appeared to be composed of sheets of what looked like butcher's waste (intestines, sinew, bone-chips, and fat) which had all somehow been frozen into configuration. Amid all this sat a splintery wooden table on which had been placed...

That's a fucking typewriter! Foster realized, and he could even read the manufacturer: Remington. Atop a shelf in the rear, more odd objects could be seen: a package of Williams Shaving Soap, a square tin of Mavis talcum powder, and an empty can of Heinz Beans. Foster meant to glance behind him, to question the Deaconess, but her hands firmly pressed his temples.

"Don't take your eyes off the Egress," she said.

When Foster refocused on the hole...a man stepped into view. *The Trustee...*

It was a very gaunt, stoop-shouldered man who looked back at Foster. "There you are, at last," he said in a squeaky accent that sounded like New England. He had close-cropped hair shiny with tonic and a vaguely receding hairline to show a vast forehead, which gave the man an instant air of learnedness. He wore a well-fitting but threadbare and very faded blue suit, a white dress shirt, and narrow tie with light- and dark-gray stripes. Small, round spectacles. His jaw seemed prominent as though he suffered from a malocclusion. The only thing about him that wasn't normal was the pallor of his face. It was as white and shiny as snow just beginning to melt but marbled ever so faintly with a bruised blue.

The man sat down at the rickety table. He paused momentarily to frown at the typewriter, then his eyes—which were bright in spite of the death-pallor—looked directly at Foster.

"I presume the Senarial Messenger has apprized you of the fact that we're subject to a considerable time constraint, the equivalent in your world of six minutes. So we must be concise and, above all, declarative," the man said. "My name is Howard, and I bear the curious title of this term's 'Trustee to the Office of The Senary,' and I'm speaking to you from a Scrivenry at the Seaton Hall of Automatic Writers. It's located in a quite malodorous prefect dubiously known as the Offal District..." Abruptly, then, he smirked. "Are you able to hear me, sir?"

Foster's mouth hung open for a time, but he eventually managed to say, "Yes..."

"Splendid. It's my infernal pleasure to tell you that you've won the Senary—"

"What's the Senary?" Foster blurted.

"Denotatively? From the Latin *senarius*: anything of or relating to the number *six*. But here we're only concerned with its *con*notation. The Senary is a drawing, in a sense, but those eligible are not random. Aspects of your own...resolve present the most pertinent considerations. Let me reiterate, we must be expeditious, and as I have no way of discerning that constant unit of measure known as time, your colleague will alert you when one minute remains. Do you understand?"

"No."

"That is immaterial. You've been invited to partake in a—"

"A tour of Hell?" Foster interrupted.

"Quite right. Only a smattering of persons, in all of Human history, have received this lauded opportunity. Indeed, you're one of a privileged lot. It is guaranteed that no harm will come to your physical body, nor your Auric Substance, should you choose to proceed. You will be returned, intact, to make your final decision. At the end, in other words, you'll be free to return to your normal life, should you so choose. But I can say to you, sir, that in 6,660 years...no Senary winner has ever elected to *not* accept the prize."

Foster could think of nothing to say, save for, "I-I-I..."

This man, Howard, held up a warning finger. "We mustn't be frivolous with verbosity, sir—I can only presume that time is growing short, so without further delay, I must show you the Containment Orb," and then he reached beneath the table and brought something up—something on a stick.

"Huh?" Foster uttered.

The object on the stick, about the size of a basketball, looked brown, mottled, and, somehow, organic. A twist at the top reminded Foster of a pumpkin's clipped stem, and in the middle of the bizarre thing was a half-inch hole. Howard pointed to the hole. "The intake bung is here, as you can perceive—"

"But, what *is* that thing? It looks like a brown *pumpkin.*"

"Hell's rendering, you might say—in specificity, the *Feotidemonis Vulgaris,* commonly referred to as a Snot-Gourd. It's been eviscerated completely, of course, and disenchanted by Archlocks, so to serve as your Auric Carrier. And—" Howard swivelled the peculiar fruit on the stick, to reveal its other side—

"Holy shit!" Foster exclaimed.

A semblance of a face existed on the other side of the *thing.* Two eyeballs had been sunk into the pulp; below that, a large, pointed snout as of some oversized rodent had been affixed. Also a pair of fleshy lips, and lastly, two ears, though the ears were maroon and pointed.

THE SENARY

A Jack-o-Lantern from Hell, Foster thought, but just as he began his next question, the Deaconess tapped him from behind. "Tell the Trustee there's only one minute left."

Foster bumbled, "Uh, uh, I'm supposed to tell you—"

"So I've gathered," Howard said, still holding up the hideous brown fruit with a face. "By now, it's my hope that you can cogitate the entails of what awaits; hence, I ask you, sir... Do you choose to proceed?"

Foster blinked. *No obligation,* his thoughts raced. *Guaranteed that no harm can come to me, that I'll be returned intact...*

"I ask once more, sir. Do you choose to proceed?"

"Yes!" Foster whispered.

Howard seemed to smile, however thinly. "A wise choice. I look forward to our coming discourse. Tell the Senarial Messenger I'm at the ready," and then Howard stood up and came round the table. He turned the Snot-Gourd back around and held the side with the hole in it up to the hole in the wall...

The Deaconess looked longingly at Foster. "Do you have...any idea how privileged you are?"

A tour...in Hell. He wiped his face off in his hands. "I don't even know how to answer that. Oh, and the guy says he's ready."

"Can you still see the Auric Carrier?"

Foster looked back up. In the opening the appalling fruit remained, showing the hole cut in it. "Yeah. It's a...fucked up pumpkin, and there's a hole in it. He called it a Snot-Gourd."

"Hmm, all right..."

"But he's blocking the hole in the wall with it. Don't I crawl through the hole?"

"Oh, no. Nothing solid can move from here to there, and vice-versa."

"Then how—"

"Remember, nothing *solid.* Be careful; make sure the end of the hose doesn't actually *touch* the intake opening in the gourd. Try to keep it a few millimeters away—"

84

Foster shot her a funky look. "What?"

"It's your *breath* that will be transferred from here to there," the Deaconess explained. "On this side, it's just breath, but on *that* side..." and before Foster could even plead for more information, the Deaconess got him out of the seat and urged him closer to the wall. In her hand now she held the short length of garden hose, one end of which she moved toward his mouth.

His eyes flicked to the bubbling skullcap. "No way I'm drinking that crap!"

"Of course not. You *breathe* it—the fumes."

When Foster's lips parted to object further, she placed the hose in his mouth.

"It's time, Mr. Foster. I'll be waiting for you when you come back." She pressed his shoulders with her hand, to gesture him to lean over. She held the other end of the hose into the faint steam coming off the Elixir. "Now. Count to six, then Inhale once very deeply and hold it..."

Foster's lips tightening around the hose. *I can't believe I'm going to do this...*and then in his mind he counted to six and took a hard suck on the hose.

The warm air tasted meaty somehow in his mouth. The fumes made his lungs feel glittery.

"Keep holding it," he was instructed, then the other end of the hose was placed in his hand. "Now, once you've lined the end up...exhale as hard as you can."

Foster's cheeks bloated. Very carefully he manipulated the end of the hose to fit over the hole in the gourd—

—and exhaled.

Foster's soul left his body, and he collapsed to the floor.

THE SENARY

(VI)

Your name is Morley Foster and you've just won the Senary. Your soul has been turned into gas and squeezed into Hell through a hole in the wall.

And here you are...

Regaining consciousness reminds you of the time you got your wisdom teeth pulled at the dentist's. You're a balloon under water that has just risen to break the surface. First, senses, then awareness, then memory. The only difference is, that time you awoke into your physical body, but now...

I don't have one, you think in an oddly calm realization.

There's a faint noise, something echoic like water dripping in a subterranean grotto. Your eyes open in increments but only register scarlet murk, just as another sensation registers: rocking back and forth and up and down as if in a car with too much suspension. Your vision struggles for detail as the dripping fades, to be replaced by a steady metallic clattering along with a *hiss.*

Then your vision snaps into perfect, even surreal, focus.

The macabre lips on the Snot-Gourd scream.

You're in a vehicle of some kind, which idles down a street whose surface is chunks of wet bone, split ankles and elbows, and other odds and ends of meaty gristle. "How's that for your first glimpse of the Offal District?" comes the familiar New England accent. "My own reaction was much the same, but of course, that's why they *call* it the Offal District. It's constructed primarily with surplus scraps from the Pulping Stations: less-edible organs, joints, bits of bone."

You look up and scream again when you realize exactly what you're looking at: a very black sickle moon hanging in a scarlet sky.

The attempt to move your arms and legs comes reflexively, then you remember, *My body's back in the house with the Deaconess, but my consciousness...is in the pumpkin...*

Your cue-ball-sized eyes blink. *I'm in Hell...*

"The Senarial Sciences here are impressively successful," Howard tells you, sitting off to the left. He cranes around and looks into Foster's eyes as if looking into a fish bowl. "I trust your senses are in proper working order?"

"I...think so," you reply through the brutish, demonic lips.

"Your Auric Carrier is quite the top of the line." Now Howard is cleaning his round spectacles with his shirttail. "You have the mouth of a Howler-Demon, the eyes of an Ocularus, the nose of a Blood-Mole, and the ears of a City Imp. Each represents a superlative. We want you to perceive everything with the greatest acuity.

"But, but—"

"Just relax, sir—if that possibility exists—and give your psyche time to acclimatize to the new environs, as well as the new vessel for your soul. There's no rush—answers to all your questions will be furnished. Just relax...and behold."

You try to nod. *Look around? Jesus...* First, you focus on your immediate surroundings. You appear to be sitting in the elevated rear seat of a long automobile—that is, not actually sitting since you no longer possessed a rump; instead your Auric Carrier has been mounted on a stick in this queer backseat. The clattering vehicle reminds you of pictures you've seen of cars from the 1920s, spoke-wheeled and long-hooded monstrosities like Duesenbergs and Packards. Yet no hood actually forms the vehicle's front end; instead there's a long iron cylinder showing bolts at its seams, and a petite pipe where one would expect a hood ornament. It's from this valve that steam hisses out. Howard talks as if he can detect your thoughts. "It's a steam-car, the latest design, an Archimedes Model 6. It burns sulphur, not coal—Hell never enjoyed a Carboniferous Period." The car rocks over more chunks of butcher's waste. "The sulphur heats the blood and other organic waste in the boiler; steam is produced and, hence, mobility. Nothing like the motors of my day, I'm afraid, though I never liked them. Awful, soot- and smoke-belching contraptions. But this suffices more than, say, a buggy drawn by an Emaciation Squad."

You don't understand how your head—the Snot-Gourd—can turn upon the command of your will. *I'm just a fuckin' fruit on a stick!* Nevertheless, it does, and now that you're getting used to it you find the courage to look upon the more distant surroundings with greater scrutiny.

The street *stinks,* and then you spot a globed pole that names the street: GUT-CAN LANE. Mottled storefronts whose bricks contain swirls of innards pass on either side. You notice more signs:

SCYTHER'S
PAYCHECKS NOT CASHED
THYMUS GRINDER'S
TOE-CHEESE COLLECTOR.

A chalkboard before a café boasts the day's specials: BROILED BOWEL WITH CHIVES and BEER-BATTERED SHIT-FISH.

When the steam-car clamorously turns through a red light—Abattoir Blvd.—you detect buildings that appear residential, like festering, squat townhouses whose walls are impossibly raised as preformed sheets of innards.

"I don't believe this place," you finally say. "Everything's made of…guts."

"Construction techniques differ greatly here from the Living World; where you utilize chemistry, physics, electrical engineering, we utilize Alchemy, Sorcerial Technology, *Agonitical* Engineering."

"But how can they make…guts and bone chunks…*hold together?*"

"Gorgonization, Mr. Foster," Howard replies and points past the vehicle's rim. "*Your* masons pour cement into molds and allow it to dry, ours pour *slaughterhouse residuum* and Gorgonize it with Hex-Clones of the Medusa's head."

You see what you can only guess are demonic construction workers emptying hoppers of butcher's waste into various sheet- and brick-molds. After which several cloaked figures with purplish auras walk slowly past the molds bearing severed heads on stakes. Each severed head has living snakes for hair. The horned construction workers are careful to look away from the process. Hoods are then placed over the Gorgon heads, then the molds are lifted, revealing solid bricks and wall-boards fully hardened.

Fuck, you think. *And everything here is made of it...*

"Fascinating, eh?" Howard remarks as the car rattles on. "At any rate, untold Districts exist in Hell, to compose an endless city called the Mephistopolis. Lucifer prefers diversity to uniformity; therefore each District, Prefect, or Zone features its own decorative motif. You'll see more as we venture on."

Beyond, though, you have the impression of losing your breath when you see what sits beneath the blood-red sky. It's a panorama of evil, leaning skyscrapers which stretch on as far as you can see.

"Hell is a city," Howard explains, "which I didn't find all that surprising myself. Why wouldn't it be? More and more the Living World is becoming metropolitan, so why shouldn't Hell follow suit? Progress is relative, and so is evolvement, I suppose. Lucifer has seen to it that Hell progresses in step with Human civilization. It's only the *direction* of the steps that are antithetical. It provides for a rich environment, and more so in this District than most others," and then Howard's nose crinkles at an awful smell that reminds you of the dumpster at the restaurant where you sometimes work. "It's just that the smell is *appalling,* not to mention the clamor—a babel of filth and noise, a breeding pot of cheapness and vulgarity. This horror-imbrued place reminds me of New York City in 1924. Ugh! I hope you've never had the misfortune of visiting there, Mr. Foster."

You try to frown again but then think of something. "Hey. How do you know my name? I didn't tell it to you back when we were doing the hole-in-the-wall thing."

"An Osmotic Incantation apprised me of everything about you. *Every aspect.* It's necessary, and part of my duties in this little sidejob of mine as the Trustee for the Office of the Senary."

"Sidejob? But didn't you say something about being a writer? That you worked in the Hall of Writers?"

"The *Seaton* Hall of *Automatic* Writers," Howard corrects. "One of many, but my facility devotes itself entirely to the writing of fiction. This is my forte; my job, since my Damnation, is to produce copy—novels, novellas, stories—which a select group of Wizards known as Trance Channelers then communicate to fiction writers in the Living World via the process of Automatic Writing and Slate Chalking. It's Lucifer's way of influencing worldly art forms so, quite wisely, he picks the most qualified of the Human Damned for the task."

A writer, you think, *in Hell?* "So...before you came...here, you were a writer too?"

"Indeed I was, sir, a writer of weird tales, and it's been conveyed to me that my work has since risen to considerable acclaim. Just my luck, eh? *Posthumous* acclaim—now I know how Poe felt."

"When did you die?"

"March 15, 1937—the Ides. Fitting that I should expire on the celebration day of the Mother Goddess Cybele. I penned a tale concerning that once but—drat!—my memory fails me. Something about rats... The Rats in the...House? The Rats in the...Tower?" Howard shakes his pale head. "Such are the pitfalls of Damnation. You're not allowed to remember anything gratifying. But it was some ballyhoo called Bright's Disease that killed me—shrunk my kidneys down to walnuts—oh, and cancer of the colon. Too much coffee and soda crackers, I can only presume. It's no wonder 'The Evil Clergyman' wasn't very good." As Howard straightens his tie, he appraises the orb of your head with something hopeful in his eyes. "Are you a reader, sir? Perhaps you've heard of me," and then he tells you his full name.

You strain your memory, picturing a beaten paperback with a foamy-green face and glass shards pushing through the head. "Oh, yeah! You're the guy who wrote 'The Shuttered Room!' Man, I *loved* that story!"

Howard's bluish-white pallor turns pink as he stares, vibrating in his spring-loaded seat. Then he hangs his head over the side of the open-topped vehicle and throws up.

"Are you, are you all right?" you ask.

Howard regains his composure, slumping. "Sir, I can tell you with incontrovertible authority that I most certainly did *not* write 'The Shuttered Room.'"

"Oh, sorry. You know, I could've sworn that your name was on it."

Questions upon questions still bubble up in your gourd-head, but they all stall by every glimpse you take of the nefarious street. *Panels* of guts raised like sheet-rock, *cinderblocks* of such butcher's waste form walls, sidewalks, and even entire buildings. You turn as you drive past.

"And in the event that you're wondering," Howard mentions, "you're able to traverse the Snot-Gourd by means of a Psychic-Servo motor. Your impulses engage the gears."

You hadn't thought about that, nor about how the steam-car itself is even being maneuvered. "Is it some kind of black magic that's driving the car?"

"Not at all, and my apologies for failing to introduce you to our driver." Howard leans forward and pulls back a webbed canopy before them, which reveals a hidden driver's compartment whose bow-tie-shaped steering wheel is surrounded by knobbed levers. Seated just behind the wheel is—

Holy SMOKES! you think.

—a stunningly beautiful nude woman. Hourglass curves rise up to grapefruit-sized breasts which offer nipples distending like overlarge Hershey's Kisses. By any sexist standard, she's perfect in every way...save for one anomaly.

She's made of clay.

"She has no name," Howard explains. "She's a Golemess. Dis-Enchanted riverbed clay is what she's made of. Her male counterpart—Golems—are quite larger, while these female versions are manufactured more petitely, and to be sexually provocative."

The wet, grayish clay shines—indeed—as if a centerfold has been air-brushed. Her hair, however—on her head as well as between her fabulously toned legs—bear sculptor's marks.

A Golemess, huh? you think. *That's pretty hot for a piece of clay...*

"Quite a comely monster," Howard says, "though my detractors could hardly conceive of me making such an observation, I suppose. They said I was homosexual, for goodness sake, in spite of my having *married* a woman! Regrettably, though, love is quite temporary, and I'll admit, her pocketbook was impressive to a poor artist such as myself. But, more dread luck—barely a year after we were wed, she was dismissed from her lucrative position! We had to move into a *detestable* rooming house in Brooklyn; one could scarcely distinguish between the tenants and the rodents! And forty dollars a month the slum barons charged!"

You hardly hear Howard's odd aside of petulance, in favor of scrutinizing the Golemess' impeccable features. *A brick shithouse...and you could literally build one out of her.*

"Pardon my digression," Howard says. "It's just that I have so much rancor now—a sin, of course: wrath—but still..." Howard seems dejected. "I can scarcely believe that Seabury Quinn was the name of the day while I foundered on considerably lower tiers. Gad! Have you ever read his work? Let's hope not. As for the Golemess, you may be wondering if it's sexually *functional*, which I can happily or unhappily asseverate. Quite a lot in Hell is, for reasons that need not be expounded upon. The common veils of empiricism are no less prevalent here than in the Living World. So, too, are the notions of invidiousness. I was an atheist but hardly a *bad* sort, yet here I am. The circumstances which led to my Damnation are barely even explicable. You, on the other hand, are in quite another circumstance, hmm?"

EDWARD LEE

Your pumpkin-face frowns; at least you are getting the knack of it now. But you barely understand your fussy tour guide. "So what *is* my circumstance?"

Howard grimaces over a bump and another waft of organic stench. "Miasmal! Ah, but to respond to your legitimate query, you, Mr. Foster, are spiritually teetering on the—how shall I phrase it?— the plus-side of the Fulcrum..."

Your furry brow arches. *The Fulcrum*... The Deaconess had said something similar, hadn't she?

The steam-car, at last, pulls off the chunky pavement as the Golemess turns the wheel. A sign floats past: TOLL BOOTH AHEAD. You can't keep your thoughts straight.

"I just don't get it. The Fulcrum?"

"Think of the apothecarist's triple-beam balance," Howard tells you, "where the weights on one side are Godly acts, and on the other side, *un*Godly acts. Very recently, I'm told, you have tipped the scale on the side of Salvation."

"Howard, I don't know what you're talking about."

"In spite of your fairly outrageous accrual of sins, you've managed to counter-balance them by approximately 101 percent. It's that extra one percent—you see—that has enabled you to win the Senary. You've tried with much diligence to lead a life that acknowledges God, and yet along the way, you've sinned mightily, but in each and every case that you pursue an occasion of sin, you're truly sorry and you make every effort to repent. It's your own volition, Mr. Foster, your own—and I emphasize—your own free will. That notion alone—free will—provides the summation of it all."

The steam of your soul feels hot in confusion. "Free will? A triple-beam balance? A hundred and *one* percent?"

"Your excursion several nights ago? The Scriptures state quite interestingly that 'a whore is a deep ditch.'"

The line rings a bell in your bizarre head. *Those two hookers at the Lounge the other night*... "You don't mean—"

"You had decided in your heart that you would partake in the delights of two ladies of the night? You even willingly ventured to procure the necessary funds, yet, at the last moment you decided to bestow those funds upon someone else, someone in grievous need…"

The redneck woman with the two kids at the Dollar General! you remember.

"And what you hitherto purveyed was what God perceived as a true act of charity, so said St. Luke 'Whosoever has two coats must share with one who has none…'"

Your jaw, however awkwardly, drops. "I gave the money to the poor woman instead of the two bar whores…"

"Indeed," Howard says, half-smiling. "And that gesture suffices as the one percent which carries you over to God's grace. Allow me to convey it this way: if you were to die right now, your soul would ascend to the Kingdom of Heaven, where you would live in the Glory of God, forever."

You feel a vast echo in your psyche.

When Howard taps the shapely clay shoulder of the Golemess, the steam-car stops, and he looks right at you, probably for effect.

"Lucifer wants that one percent, Mr. Foster, and he's willing to pay *exorbitantly* for it…"

Your head seems to quiver. "I—"

"Of course, it's much to take in, and it's our good fortune that our previous time constraint no longer exists, so put your multitudinous questions aside for a bit, and enjoy the ride…"

You take the advice as the car clatters on, though you have to admit, there's not much to enjoy. You seem to be leaving the Offal District through an archway in a great fortress-like wall of hardened organic waste via blocks the size of minibuses. Next comes a road of crushed sulphur, which grinds grittily beneath the car's narrow tires. "Here a toll, there a toll, everywhere a toll," Howard complains as they idle up to a shack whose single occupant is a man with a face axed down the middle.

"Toll," the attendant somehow utters.

Howard hands him a canvas sack that contains something the size of a melon. The toll-taker peeks in, nods, then waves them on.

"What was in the bag?" you have to ask.

"The gonad of an immature Spermatagoyle. They sell them to wealthy culinarists and executive chefs who carefully extract the seminiferous tubules. It's a favorite dish of Grand Dukes, Barons, and the higher Nobiliary, for it's the closest thing you'll ever get to spaghetti in Hell." Howard's brow raises. "But I suppose you're a bit of a culinarist yourself. It's my understanding that you are an oysterman, yes?"

"I shuck oysters in a redneck tourist trap," you append.

"Ah, the fruits of the sea. I grew up in a veritable *nexus* of shellfish and crustaceans. Oysters as large as your open hand, and lobsters the size of infants." Then Howard's face seems to corrugate in aggravation. "And wouldn't you know it? My iodine allergy prevented me from being able to eat *any of it!*"

Poor guy, you think.

"And you never attended university for lack of funding," Howard states the dim truth. "I can commiserate. It was understandably forecast that I would surely take up studies at Brown University, but—curse Pegana—my shattered nerves—thanks to a borisome mother off her rocker—foreclosed the possibility of my even graduating Hope Street High School. Lo, I would never be a university man…"

This guy really gets off track, you think. "Where are we going?"

"The Humanus Viaduct, which runs from the Dermas District to Corpus Peak, crossing the Styx."

DERMABURG, reads a skin-toned sign that floats by.

Howard gestures the sign. "This District is made of—as you may have ascertained—skin," and as Howard speaks the words, your Ocularus eyes remain peeled on the new surroundings. Rowhouses and squat buildings line the fleshy street, all covered by variously colored cuttings of skin. Some seem papered with dermal sheets as impeccable as the skin of the Deaconess, while other edifices suffer from acne and other outbreaks. The car, then, turns right at a perspiry intersection. You glimpse the sign: FASCIA BLVD.

"A whole town made of skin?"

"These days, the majority of it is Hexegenically Engineered, save for the loftier real estate here, south of town, where *natural* epidermis is procured. Oh, there's a City Flensing Crew now..."

You notice the activities on one corner, where a troop of beastly, slug-skinned things with horns, talons, and terrifying musculatures prepare themselves around a row of Humans pilloried nude. Cuts are made at the back of each victim's neck, taloned fingers slide in, and then the entire "body suit" of epidermis is sloughed off, leaving the victim skinless from the neck down.

You wince as the beasts go right down the line.

"The attendants are called Ushers, a long-time pure-breed that serve as government workers and police," Howard explains. "Human skin is much more valuable."

"Ushers," you murmur. "So they...peel the skin off and then—"

"Stretch it over wall-frames," and then Howard points again.

At the opposing corner, workmen congregate at a corner unit (more of the hunched, imp-like creatures) to evidently build an addition. But when two of them raise a wall-frame, you see that long, banded-together bones comprise each strut rather than two-by-fours. After the frame has been erected, other workmen stretch skin over it.

As for the pilloried "victims," you see that they're actually willing participants; when released—skinless now—an Usher hands them some money, then sends them on their way.

"Lucifer prefers Hell's denizens to *choose* to sell their skin, rather than merely taking it," Howard says.

"They *sell* their own skin?"

"For narcotics. The Department of Addictions has devised delights that make de Quincey's opiates and Poe's liquor seem paltry. Few can rehabilitate themselves, but when they do, they're forced into a Retoxification Center."

You watch the skinless queues trudge to a nearby fleshy alley, where an over-coated Imp in sunglasses waits to sell them various bags of cryptic powders. When one Human woman—who'd been attractive before her flensing—failed to produce sufficient funds, the Imp said, "A blowjob or an ovary. You know the prices, lady," and then he parts his overcoat to sport a large maroon penis covered with barnacles. "Fuck that," she says, then sits down, crosses her ankles behind her neck, and sticks a hand into her sex.

You don't watch the rest.

The Golemess turns onto another road called Scleraderma Street, where some of the structures have hair growing on their roofs; others have collapsed to ramshackle piles from some dermatological disease; one has broken out into shingles, another is covered with warts.

And on another corner, you glimpse another sign: SKINAPLEX.

"What the hell's that?"

"The motion picture show? They're rather similar here as in the Living World. And perhaps you'll be satisfied to know that Fritz Lang and D.W. Griffith are *still* honing their art."

Now you can see the marquee, complete with blinking lights: TRIPLE FEATURE! THE SIX COMMANDMENTS - WITHERING HEIGHTS - ALL DOGS GO TO HELL

"Can we get out of here?" you plead. "I've had enough of skin-town."

Howard chuckles. "Save for the revolting B.O., it's actually one of the more sedate Districts. You'll be happy to know, however, that we're merely passing through."

The last row of houses, you notice, are actually sweating. As you pass the District gates, more glaze-eyed denizens straggle in and head to the pillories.

Now the road rises through a yellow fog so thick, you can't make out the endless scarlet sky. "So now it's the…"

"The Humanus Viaduct. It begins at an elevation of 666 cubits, and provides a spectacular view. Lucifer wants you to be fully aware of the *immensity* of the Mephistopolis..."

Lucifer wants me..., your thoughts stall.

"He hopes that you'll want to return."

Now your monstrous lips actually laugh. "Fat chance of that! So far I've seen a town made of *guts* and a town made of *skin!* What, he thinks I want to move in?"

"The *immensity,* Mr. Foster, and in that immensity you'll consider the value to someone of your very *privileged* status."

"I still don't understand what you—"

Howard holds up a pale hand. "Later, Mr. Foster. There's still much more for you to see..."

The car chugs ever upward, and in the fog, you can swear you catch glimpses of horrid, stretched faces showing fangs.

"Gremlins," Howard specifies. "Wretched little things. They live in fog, swamp-gas, and clouds, and even are said to have cities in the higher noctilucent formations."

You spy more fangs snapping in a split second. "But-but-but—"

"Nothing can do us harm, so you needn't fear, Mr. Foster." Past the buxom driver's shoulder, Howard points to a trinket of some kind dangling from the rearview mirror: a small metal kewpie of a robed man holding a staff in one hand and an upside-down baby in the other. The pewtery detail implies that the baby's throat had been slit, and its blood is trickling into a bucket. "We're protected by the St. Exsanguinatius Medallion. It's quite a potent Totem."

Great, you think.

The car lumbers on, and Howard slouches back and begins to idly hum a tune, which seems aggravatingly familiar. In time, the name comes to you: "Yes, We Have No Bananas."

Finally, the fog expels the steam-car onto a high, rough-hewn mountain pass. You yell out loud when you peer over the side and see less than an inch of the cliff-road's surface sticking out past the outer side of the tire. "There's no fuckin' safety rails!" you shout.

Howard frowns. "That would hardly be logical in Hell, Mr. Foster. Now, if you'll put your consternation aside, I'll welcome you to one of our attractions here: Corpus Peak. Corpus Peak is a man-made—er, pardon me—a Demon-made mountain. It is composed, in fact, of exactly one billion demon-corpses..."

When the words finally register, you grind your teeth and peer once again over the side, and in a few moments it's the image that begins to register, however grimly. The vast side of the "mountain" sweeps down hundreds of feet, and in it, you notice the rigor-mortis'd cadavers of demons.

"A-a-a *mountain* of dead demons?"

"That's correct. The first billion Hellborn, in fact, to die under Lucifer's initial scourge when he took over. All manner of demonic species: Imps, Trolls, Gargoyles, Griffins, Ghouls, Incubi, Succubi— everything. The Morning Star wanted his first monument to be sym-bolic. 'Serve me or die.' He liked it so much that he ordered the highest eschelon Bio-Wizards to put a Pristinization Hex on the entire mountain. The corpses, in other words, will never decompose."

You keep staring at the twisted faces and limbs of the mountain-side. *Jesus, kind of makes the Hoover Dam look like Tinker Toys.*

"And below," Howard adds, "The abyssal River Styx."

Only then do you let your vision span out, to a ghastly, twisting waterway of black ooze marbled with something red. *"What* is it called?"

"The Styx!" Howard exclaims. "It's the most renowned river in all of mythology! Surely you've read Homer!"

"Uh, no, I don't think so. But I do remember a *band* called Styx." You try to shrug. "Never got into them."

"Whatever has the world come to?"

The noxious river is so distant you can't see details but you can make out tiny things like boats floating on the putrid surface as well as swarming, dark shapes beneath. Every so often, some colossal *thing* breaks the surface, swallows a boat in its pestiferous maw, then resubmerges.

THE SENARY

You're grateful for the distraction of still another sign: THE DEPARTMENT OF PASSES AND BYWAYS UNWELCOMES YOU TO THE HUMANUS VIADUCT. You envisioned yourself gulping when you get a good look at this "bridge" which stretches miles from the top of the corpse-mountain, across the appalling river, to a black polygonal structure sitting atop another mountain (this one of pinkish rock). The sights are spectacular in their own horrific way, yet your thoughts can only dread what must be to come.

The bridge—this Humanus Viaduct—is scarcely ten feet wide and consists of objects like railroad ties lashed together, one after another—thousands of them—which all comprise the spans of the bridge. A meager rope-rail can be seen stretching on either side.

"We're not driving the car over that, are we?" you object.

"Why, of course, we are," Howard says. "The view is thrilling, and it's crucial that you be thrilled."

"Fuck that shit, man! That bridge looks like something in a fuckin' Tarzan movie! It'll never hold us!"

"Mr. Foster, please, don't worry yourself. Naturally the viaduct has been charged by various Levitation Spells."

You try to feel reassured. He can see the rickety bridge sway in a sudden hot gust, and as the car rises to the gatehouse, your vantage-point rises as well. Now you can see the surface of the links.

And all at once, you don't need to be told why it's called the *Humanus* Viaduct.

Atop the links of railroad ties exist a virtual carpet of naked human beings, who have all been lashed together as well. All these people, thousands upon thousands—form the actual driving surface of the bridge.

You can only stare when you rattle through the gatehouse and pull in. The Golemess robotically shifts the vehicle into a lower gear, then you lurch forward.

"We're driving on *people,* for God's sake!" In a panic you look down. "And they're still alive!"

"Indeed, they are. Hell exists, in general, as a domain of all conceivable horror, where every ideology functions as an offense against God. But in particular, it's a domain of punishment. Hence, the 'human asphalt' beneath us."

They chug onward, narrow tires rolling over bellies, throats, faces, and shins. You watch the faces grimace and wail. "How come they don't die?"

"They're the Human Damned—who *cannot* die. That's why they call it Damnation; it's eternal. Only Demons and Hybrids can die here, for they have no souls. But as for the Human Damned, their bodies are nearly as eternal as their spirits. When your soul is delivered to Hell, you receive what we call a Spirit Body that's identical to the body you lived in on Earth. Only total destruction can 'kill' a Spirit Body, in which case the soul is spirited into the Hellborn lifeform with the closest propinquity. It could slip into something as large as a Demonculus, something as commonplace as an Imp, or something as minuscule as a Pus-Aphid."

Men bellow, women shriek, as the steam-car rocks on. Ribcages crack and sink inward, bones snap.

Yet in spite of the horror you're witnessing, more questions spin in your mind. "Great, but I don't have a 'Spirit Body.' I have a fuckin' *pumpkin*—"

"Please, Mr. Foster, profanity is so uncouth."

"—so what happens if this pumpkin or Snot-Gourd or whatever gets destroyed?"

"An astute question but immaterial. Should your Auric Carrier be subject to mishap, your Etheric Tether would simply drag your soul back to your physical body at the Larken House. But I say immaterial since you are not, as yet, one of the Human Damned."

As yet, you consider. *I'm not Damned...but they WANT me to be?*

The Viaduct sways back and forth as the car lumbers ahead. In the middle—with already several miles behind them—the bridge dips so severely that you feel certain it will break from the vehicle's weight.

THE SENARY

Levitation Spell, my ass. But soon enough, you begin to ascend again, that queer black shape drawing closer. You think of a pyramid with a flat top.

"So what's with the pyramid-looking thing? A rest-stop, I hope."

"A pyramid? Really, Mr. Foster, you must've studied your geometry with the same zeal you studied Homer. It's not a pyramid, it's a trisoctahedron: a quadrilateral polygon bearing no parallel sides, also referred to as a trapezohedron. Lucifer is very much enamored of polygons, because in Hell, geometry is thoroughly non-Euclidian. Planes and the angles at which they exist serve as a heady occult brew. I wrote of such stuff and wonder now from whence the ideas arrived."

Howard seems to be trying to recollect something. "Gad, I do hope my Shining Trapezohedron in 'Haunter of the Dark' was born of my own creativity and not that of some sheepshank scrivener in Hell," and suddenly a look of utter dread comes to his marbled face. "What a cosmic outrage that would be."

You still don't know what he's talking about, but in an attempt to divert your attention from the staggering height, you offer, "Maybe it was Lucifer's idea, and *he's* the one who piped it into your head."

"Impossible," Howard quickly replies. "Fallen Angels, though essentially immortal, are completely estranged from creativity and imagination. Every idea, every occult equation and sorcerial theorem, every ghastly erection of architecture and even every invention of social disorder—it all comes from a single source: the Human Damned."

This is getting too deep for me, you consider. Your pumpkin-head reels—or it would have, if it could. Now you think of ski lifts carrying skiers to the peaks, only there's no snow here, just craggy rock pink as the inside of a cheek. As you near the black polygon, you discern that it's about the size of Randal's Qwik-Mart. Just when it appears that the steam-car would drive directly into the polished black side of the thing, an opening forms: a lopsided triangle that stretches from the size of a Dorito to an aperture sizeable enough to admit the car.

EDWARD LEE

Well, that was nifty...I guess. Relief washes over your psyche; the Humanus Viaduct is at last behind you. *But now what?*

"Welcome to the Cahooey Turnstile," Howard says, "a superior mode of entertaining your tour. The process saves us from driving for thousands of miles."

"What do you mean, turnstile?" you counter. "You mean like in a subway?"

"Think, instead, of an occult revolving door."

A revolving door...to where?

The aperture closes silently behind, leaving you to peer around the unevenly walled room of smooth black planes. It looks like something born of science-fiction, save for the sputtering torches which light the chamber. Then—

Shit!

A shadow moves. When the Golemess shuts down the steam-car, you see the hulking shape approach: a sinewy Demon with meat cleavers for hands and a helmet fashioned from the jaws of some outrageous beast. Below the forward rim of teeth like Indian arrowheads, two tiny eyes bulge, and there are two rimmed holes for nostrils but no mouth. No ears can be seen either but only plugs of lead which seem to fill two holes where the ears *should* be. Some manner of cured hide covered with plates make up the Demon's armor. Reddish-brown muscles throb when it regards the car.

"What the FUCK is that?"

Howard continues to frown at your profanity. "The Keeper of the Turnstile, Mr. Foster—an Imperial Truncator, of the genus *Bellicosus Silere*. It can't hear or speak; it can only observe and *act*. The Imperial Conditioning is self-evident; note the spread jaws of a Ghor-Hound which suffice for the helmet."

You notice it, all right, but don't like the way it approaches the car.

"Should the Truncator entertain even a single anti-Luciferic thought? Those jaws slam shut and bite off the top of its head."

Hardcore, you think. "And its job is to—"

THE SENARY

"Anyone or thing who enters the Turnstile without authority," Howard says, "will be diced into bits, tittles, and orts."

Just as the sentinel's cleaver-like hands raise, the Golemess lithely leaves the car and shows it a sheet of yellowed vellum. The Conscript nods, steps back, yet oddly beckons the Golemess with one of its cleavers. In the torchlight, you wince at the stark beauty of the clay-made creature, the flawless curves, the high tumescent breasts and jutting gray-plug nipples. The Golemess follows the Demon to a cozy corner, and drops to its knees.

"What's that all about?"

"It's customary for authorized guests to give succor to the Sentinel," Howard says with some relief. "Another toll, so to speak. I can only thank the Fates that this particular Truncator is of the *heterosexual* variety."

You get the gist as you watch the Golemess unbutton a front flap on the Demon's armor, revealing its penis, if it could be called that.

"You gotta be shitting me!" you exclaim. "That's its *dick?*"

Howard sees fit to not respond.

The limp shaft of the Truncator's penis looks like six red arteries grouped together, perhaps as thin as six foot-long lengths of aquarium tube. You wince worse at the scrotum, which looks more like a cluster of Concord grapes, but even more appalling is the Demon's glans: a pink, lopsided sphere of shining flesh at the end of the corded shaft, tennis-ball-sized, with not one but half a dozen urethral ducts.

You look away when the Golemess takes the "tennis ball" into her mouth.

Howard grabs the stick on which your head is affixed and climbs out of the car.

"So...what now?"

"Time to charge the Turnstile," Howard says. "It's quite a fascinating apparatus which harnesses cabalistic energy lines that exist in the Hex-Flux—Hell's version of electromagnetics—and effects what we refer to as Spatial Displacement—one of Lucifer's favorite cos-

mological sciences," and with that—which you understand none of—
Howard approaches a black-plane wall. There, you see a circle of
engraved notches; at each notch there's a small geometric etching.

"So this is a revolving door through space and time?"

"Just space," Howard corrects. "There is no time in Hell. The use
of this facility will give you the opportunity to see a variety of the
Mephistopolis' landmarks, which we hope will impress you."

Impress me, you ponder, *enough to stay? Is that what he's talking
about?*

Howard touches one of the etchings, then—

A great, nearly electronic hum fills the black room.

How do you like that jazz? you think.

The configuration increases in size until it's as large as a typical
doorway. Yet a sheet of black static is all you see beyond the
threshold. That's all you see, but what you hear is something else alto-
gether:

Screams.

"Shall we go, Mr. Foster?" Howard asks, holding your head-stick
like an umbrella.

You feel stunned, half by curiosity and half by dread. "What about
the Golemess? Shouldn't she go with us?"

Howard veers the stick aside, to show you the corner. The
Truncator's macabre penis has erected now, the thin artery-like tubes
rigid, pulsing, and the bizarre, multi-holed corona glazed. Now it
looks like a ball on a stick, which the Truncator eagerly admits into
the Golemess' mouth and slides all the way down her throat.

"As you can observe, Mr. Foster. The Golemess is…detained."

"Oh."

Howard smiles and adjusts his spectacles. He steps through the
uneven doorway of black static and takes you through…

Even though you don't have a stomach, a nauseous sensation rises
up. Stepping through the egress feels like stepping off a high window
ledge; you expect a deadly impact but none arrive. Instead you hear a

105

crackling that sounds more organic than electric. Fear seals your eyes and you scream, plummeting...

"We haven't fallen even a millimeter, Mr. Foster," Howard chuckles. "It's merely the nature of the concentrated Flux we've just traversed."

Your head feels overly buoyant when you open your eyes. You leave them open only long enough to see that you are on a cacophonic street clogged with monsters, steam-cars, and carriages drawn by horned horses that look leprous. Flies the size of finches buzz around sundry corpse-piles on corners, a sign stuck in each pile: RECYCLE BY FEDERAL ORDER. You notice the sidewalk as well as the walls of most buildings are made of roughly crushed bones and teeth hardened within pale mortar. One storefront window boasts TORSOS: HUMAN & HELLBORN — ON SALE, and another window has been streaked on the inside with blood: OUT OF BUSINESS.

The sheer noise prevents you from ordering your thoughts: the clang of metal, the sound of hammer to stone, shouts—"Come back with my ears, you Imp fuck!"—vehicular horns which sound more like the brays of tortured animals.

"Pandemonium in sound and vision," Howard says, wending down the stained sidewalk with your head-stick in his hand. "Take the opportunity to look around."

This is the mistake.

As far as "looking around" goes, there's nothing to see save for horror and revulsion. In no time, you find that when you dare look at something, your psyche is arrested by some adrenalin-packed inner-scream—perhaps the sound of your soul rebelling at the wrongness of this place.

A city, a city, you keep thinking in a panic. *Hell is a city...*

You can only look for a second at a time, in grueling snatches that demand an alternating surcease. Each "snatch" shows you something either horrific or impossible:

—blood-streaked skyscrapers rising higher than any building you've ever seen, each leaning this way or that. When one collapses in the distance, before the churning blood-red sky, hundreds leap off corroded balconies with wizened shrieks—

—street gutters gushing with lumpy muck over which dilapidated Demons and Humans—obviously homeless—hunt for tidbits, while packs of cackling Broodren—Hell's children—stalk through the sidewalk horde hunting for the elderly or the defenseless to quickly eviscerate so to make off with their organs—

—Arachni-Watchers, like spiders the size of box turtles, crawling up walls and across high ledges. A cluster of eyeballs form the body, ever watching from all directions for citizen behavior in violation of current Luciferic Laws. Psychic nerve-sacs at the body's core immediately transmit real-time Hectographs of infractions to the nearest Constabulary Stations—

—streets, gutters, and alleyways aswarm with indigenous vermin such as Bapho-Rats, Caco-Roaches, Brick-Mites, and Corpusculars, all hunting for the unsuspecting to infect, to ensile with larva, or to eat—

—shapely She-Demons—some brown, some black, some spotted—chatting inanely behind a salon window as trained Trolls paint their horns and administer pedicures with their teeth—

—sewer grates belching flame, while beneath the iron grills faces strain, screaming, charred fingers wriggling in the gaps. Over some grates more Brooden roast severed feet on sticks—

—hot-air balloons floating in and out of soot-colored clouds overhead, each suspending iron-bolted baskets from which dog-faced Conscripts dump buckets of infectious waste, molten gold, or Gargoylic Acid onto the masses below. The skin of the warped balloons reads SATANIC NOBEL GAS FLEET—

—more storefront windows passing by. LIVE SEX WITH THE DEAD SHOW! LIVE PULPING SHOW! LIVE EYE-SUCKING SHOW! LIVE HALVING SHOW! and when you peer into this latter window, you glimpse destitute Demons and Halfbreeds being drawn slowly across tables fitted with band-saws, while spectators applaud from rows of theater-like chairs—

THE SENARY

—and Broodren, Broodren, and more Broodren—the hooligans of Hell—shifting stealthily through the throng with eyes bright and fangs sharp, absconding with whatever they can tear away from passersby: purses, wallets, skin, pudenda. One Broodren runs off with half of a Troll's face, only to be palmed flat into the sidewalk by a vigilant Golem—

—and a final dizzying scan of the noxious city's skyline: a sea of smoke, sinking rooftops, and screams; endless rot-encrusted buildings atilt; mile after mile of crackling powerlines dipping from rusted towers decorated by corpses hanging from gibbets; evil winged things gliding through the mephitic air, forever and ever—

—and ever and ever…

…and then the "snatches" end.

"Of course, acclimation takes awhile," Howard mentions. "But you'll scarcely take in anything with your eyes closed most of the time."

You're too afraid to take in another glimpse; it's all too tumultuous because you know that every impossibility here is utterly real. You open your eyes, then, to slits, careful…

"Here's something you'll find interesting…" Howard approaches a business establishment with a saloon-style swing-door as an entrance. The sign reads: LOODY'S MAMMIFERON TAPROOM.

"Taproom!" you exclaim. "Beer?"

"Regrettably not, Mr. Foster. Kegs of lager aren't on the offering, just kegs—so to speak—of milk."

"Milk?"

"Mammiferons…"

You enter the narrow bar. Various Demons and Humans sit about slate tables sipping from crude metal cups.

Howard points to the craggy brick wall behind the bar-top. There is, indeed, a row of "taps" as one would expect in a beer hall but…

Are those…TITS? you ask yourself.

"Mammiferons," Howard repeats. "They're Hexegenically manufactured; particularized genes are spliced and then enspelled, for the desired result."

All you can do is stare.

Six carriages of flesh hang along the wall, each sporting two bulbous breasts as large as basketballs. Veins pulse beneath the stretched, translucent skin. At first you think they must be torsos of preposterously endowed Human women but then you recall what Howard said about their "manufacture." Betwixt each pair of breasts there seems to be an organic "chute" of some sort, and each rimmed chute yawns open as if in wait for something.

"It's a wall of tits!" you have no choice but to object.

"The Mammiferons exist to produce milk in these more upscale taprooms."

The metal gird that surrounds each enormous nipple reminds you of the connector on a car battery, and affixed to the top of each gird is a tap.

You watch as a shockingly attractive werewolf yanks down on a tap and fills a cup for a demonic customer.

"The barkeeps are Lycanymphs," Howard elucidates. "Erotopathic female werewolves, oh, and look," and then he points to one of the organic chutes between one of the pairs...

The bar-janitor—some manner of ridge-browed Troll—lackadaisically drops a shovelful of sloppy refuse into the chute. The chute closes, pauses, then *gulps*.

"They're brainless," Howard goes on. "You can think of Mammiferons as living beverage dispensers. Miss?" he asks of the furred attendant. "A cup of the vintage, if you will."

The voluptuous She-Wolf holds a metal cup beneath one of the massive teats, works the tap, and fills it up with slimy off-white milk.

"All we need do is feed them garbage and they produce milk for eons..." Howard smiles at the cup. "I must have some sustenance, lest exhaustion supervene the necessary ambling to come." Howard drinks the cup of dense milk. "Such a treat!"

Yet all you can do is gawp at the row of preposterous, sodden breasts on the wall.

THE SENARY

Hell really is a fucked up place...

The feisty werewolf pours more drafts from the papillic taps.

"Howard?" you ask. "Can we get out of here? This is too fucked up for me."

"As you wish." Howard takes you back out to the hectic street. "I suspect we'll be rephasing soon; I haven't been counting—"

"Counting *what?*"

"My steps. The Turnstile is programmed to rephase our location every six hundred and sixty-six steps—"

"I never would've guessed," you groan.

"Don't scoff, Mr. Foster. The Imperfect Number is quite a powerful force of Nether-Energy. As God proclaimed seven to be the *perfect* number He unwittingly empowered the *imperfection* of one digit lower. Lucifer *embraces* it. In fact, when God cast his Once Favorite off the Twelfth Gate of Heaven, Lucifer, the Morning Star, plummeted in the configuration of the number six. Through that number, in one manner or other, all occult science is activated—the *Senarial* Science. You're about to behold more examples."

You suddenly grimace as the crackling black fuzz of the Turnstile shreds the sights before you. You feel the pressure drop, and again that feeling of falling recurs to the point that you wail, when—

PUNITARY FILLING STATION #5096 - HUMANS ONLY, the next sign reads. NEXT LEFT.

You shake off the vertigo to find yourself being walked into a compound supervised by figures in police-like garb. Every six of the figures is joined by a hooded monk with an aura of luminous black mist. "The Constabularies are the Federal police," Howard says. "They're mostly Human-Demon Hybrids who undergo extensive training and Spirit Manipulation. And the hooded gents are Bio-Wizards, in the event of, shall we say, civil disobedience."

As usual, you're duly confused. "But that sign said *filling* station, but I don't see any cars. They have gas here?"

Howard ruefully shakes his head no, and carries you farther...

"It's a *human* filling station, Mr. Foster. Another demonstration of Lucifer's execration for the Human Damned," and then Howard gestures a prison-wagon being drawn in by more unnameable horned beasts. Within the wagon's iron bars, you can't help but see the group of naked Humans. They're either pleading for mercy, or down on their knees in desperate prayer.

"This Cove tends to Humans who have the audacity to continue to pray to God. It should go without saying: Lucifer does not approve of such behavior..." Now Howard points upward to a high water tower but when you look at it, you do a double-take.

The tower reads URINE ONLY.

"Every urinal in the District empties into that collection tank. It's 66,666 gallons, by the way."

You're already getting sick in the contemplation; then your eyes follow several pipes leading from the tower's base to six objects that appear almost identical to gasoline pumps in the Living World.

Six at a time, then, Humans from the prison wagon—male and female alike—are strapped to gurneys and rolled before the pumps.

You feel your spirit paling as you watch...

Equally identical nozzles are brandished by Imp attendants. "Fill 'em up!" a Constable shouts, and then the Imps part the jaws and legs of the Humans and insert the nozzles down their throats and into their anuses. The handles are depressed, and bells begin to ring for each gallon dispensed.

The Human prisoners are promptly *filled*.

"Next!" shouts the Constable. "Keep 'em moving!"

"Exactly six gallons are pumped into each captive," Howard adds.

The gurneys are moved off, to be replaced by more. Of the Humans already filled, their abdomens *bloat*. More Imps move now, holding objects that look like blow torches but when the triggers are pulled, mist, not flame, shoot out. The mist is applied across the mouths and anuses of the captives, and before your own eyes, their lips and excretory orifices are impossibly sealed shut.

THE SENARY

Howard explains further, in his piping accent, "You see, Lucifer wants them *filled*. And what they're filled with—the urine of Hell—must remain contained; hence, the Flesh Welders. A gasified pontica dust provides the occult mist which seals them shut. This way, the urine can never be voided."

Gagging, you watch more. The captives, now swollen as if pregnant, are roughed off the gurneys and shooed out of the camp, their mouths and rectums "welded" shut forever.

Then your eyes steal back to the hideous pumps where the next deposition of unfortunates are being filled. Each gallon dings a bell, abdomens quickly distend, then they're sealed with the welder and moved on. A stolid efficiency.

"Why?" you rail. "This makes no sense! Why are they FILLING PEOPLE WITH PISS?!"

Howard shrugs off your alarm. "Because the very notion pleases Lucifer. He quite simply thrills at the idea—he likes for his detractors to be *filled*. Wombs, bellies, bowels. By your abhorrence, I take that you'd prefer *not* to see the Excrement Pumps at the next compound?"

"Get me out of here!" you shriek.

"Fill 'em up!" the Constab yells again, and as Howard hastens you out, that steady ding-ding-ding of the pumps follows...

A mental fog veils your vision as Howard ambles away. You pass several Agonicity Transformers which each contain a Human dangling from a trestle by his or her wrists. Wires threaded through tiny holes drilled in their skulls coil upward to sizzling capacitors. Constabs heave pitchers of boiling water on each "power element," and the resultant rush of agony fires the pain center of the brain which is then converted to occult energy and dumped into the local power grid. "Power without surcease," you think you hear Howard comment, "made possible by the immortality of the Human Damned. It's curious to ponder, eh? When God made the Human soul immortal, did He ever even conceive that some of those He condemned to Damnation would be utilized by his Nemesis as inexhaustible generators? Likely not!" More smaller compounds pass by and you can't help but notice the signs: BONE-MELTERS, FACE RIVETERS, BROODREN KILN, PENECTOMIST. The compounds are interestingly arranged throughout the Reservation, each intersected by quaint walkways, and it's along these walkways that you notice chatty groups of well-dressed Demons and Hierarchals traipsing along. They stop by each compound and peer in with dark smiles, some fanning themselves, others looking more closely with objects like opera glasses. Finally your curiosity pushes past your abhorrence and you propose: "All these Demons on the walkways... They don't work here, do they? They look more like—"

"Spectators?" Howard says. "Indeed. Because they are. Punishment Reservations such as the State Punitaries prioritize not only punishment but also commerce. The societal upper crust is urged to patronize these areas. They pay admittance. In Hell, punishment exists as sport, and such places as this serve equally as amusement parks."

"Oooo's" and "Ahhhh's" resounded around the next bend where the sign read: ROASTERY - BETS TAKEN. Several Coves stretched out in a line, while revolting spectators clamored to buy tickets printed with various numbers from small huts before each exhibit. *Roastery?* you wonder but can already smell something. "Step right up, folks," a ghoulish barker announces before the first Cove. "Let's watch and see which one of these despicable anti-Satanic insurgents can last the longest with a head-cooking," and then you notice three grim-faced Imps lashed to iron chairs facing the audience. Horned attendants busy themselves at a large circular oven in which a considerable pile of small stones are heated till they are red-hot. Chain mail sacks are then filled with the stones and carried over with tongs. Atop the head of each Imp a sack is lain, sitting much like a hot water bottle. Spectators watch in hushed fascination as each Imp's face billows and then they begin to let rip with soul-searing howls. Eventually, of course, their heads cook, but the one who screams the longest is the winner. Bets are taken more excitedly at the next Cove where demonic *mouths* are filled with the scorching stones and held shut by unfeeling Golems. Worse was the last Cove, where three stunningly attractive Succubi have been hung upside-down by their ankles, legs widely spread, and vaginas opened with retractors. It was into their vaginal barrels that more of the red-hot stones are deposited. For efficiency's sake, a Golem with something akin to a bore-cleaner for a cannon stands by and packs down each allotment of rocks. The first Succubi's eyes immediately pop out from the jolt of pain, and the second heaves so hard her bones are heard snapping. The third merely shudders and screams, smoke jetting from her mouth. When the screams treble in intensity, nearby glass shatters.

"The winner!" revels the attendant.

"This is what rich people in Hell do for fun?" you object. "They bet to see which one lives the longest? Jesus Christ!"

Howard winces at the name. "I will add, Mr. Foster, that the art of wagering was invented by *Humans*..."

"Then why aren't *Humans* beings tortured here, too?"

"These particular Coves function to judicially torture only the Hellborn, Mr. Foster. All of the victims here have been convicted of terrorist activity or traitorous thoughts via a Psychical Sciences Center. But soon enough it'll be my pleasure to introduce you to a facility for very *select* Humans only."

You finally put the Roastery behind you, the revel of bettors fading in the background. "I don't want to see anymore," you say, drained. "None of it makes sense. Head-cooking? Filling monsters' vaginas with hot rocks? Pumping *piss* into people? It's hideous."

"Well, certainly you understand that this is the intention in the Mephistopolis, Mr. Foster. Notions expressly *not* hideous are conspicuously bereft." Howard carries you through a gate exit manned by Ushers. Beyond this gatehouse steam-trucks empty hoppers of dead Hellborn onto conveyor belts which carry the piles into a warehouse marked, MUNICIPAL PULPING STATION #95,605.

Your vaporous mind feels like dead meat as the Turnstile's black magic sizzles before your eyes, and next—

"Perhaps you'll be pleased by the present change of scenery," Howard remarks. "Welcome to Shylock Square, a government-accredited Shopping District for Hell's most privileged and monetarily endowed. And the thoroughfare we're traversing now is the most recent addition."

When the black static dissipates you espy a street not unlike those in the Living World—save for the scarlet sky and black moon above—which is lined by fancy shops, cafes, and the like. Well-dressed She-Demons and creatures in business suits window-shop along the crowded lane. The street sign at the corner reads HELMSLEY BLVD.

"It can be likened to the Park Avenue of Hell," Howard adds. "Here you will see the city's most posh, most elite, and most upper crust—indeed, demimondes extra ordinaire..."

Window signs pass by: DEMONSWEAR BY MARQUETTE, FINE HUMAN LEATHER, THE HARRY TRUMAN HAT SHOP - ONLY THE FINEST MERCURY USED, CUSTOM PORTRAITS BY GUSTAV DORE. It takes a moment for your vertigo to drift off, then you peer into a window stenciled HAND-COUCH MASSAGE and see a shapely, greenish skinned She-Demon stretched nude on a couch made of severed hands. The hands meticulously knead every muscle in her body while a servant Imp stands by with a tray of refreshments. ELITE APPAREL FOR DEMONIC WOMEN reads the next window, and hanging on Human mannequins made of salt are an array of Tongue-Skirts, Lip-Sweaters, and Hand-Bras, and next— MATTRESS RETAILERS - PROCRUSTEAN BEDS—where an unfortunate female Troll, knob-faced and high-breasted, is forced to demonstrate before a group of more chatty She-Demons. Blades slam down to sever the creature's feet the instant she lay down; and next— COSMETIC AND DENTAL TERATOLOGY—where an attractive Human Concubine sits tensed in a chair while a Warlock extracts her teeth and replaces them with baby toes.

"And this is how rich people in Hell live it up?" you ask, revolted.

Howard seems surprised by the tenor of your remark. "Mr. Foster, the clients on this self-same street are among the most favored and most advantaged in the city. Barons and Blood Princes, Dukes and Archdukes, Viceroys and Chevaliers, and their superlative concubines—She-Demons and Fellatitrines, Erototesses and Succubi, Sex-Imps and Vulvatagoyles. The men possessed with the most *power* are always followed by women with the most desirability. What they merely *wear*, Mr. Foster, bespeaks their sheer social status," and that's when you take closer note of just what some of these ritzy monsters are wearing—

Good God!

One curvaceous She-Demon taps down the sidewalk in Bone-Sandals, wearing a bra whose cups are Human faces, while the monstrous woman's hot pants seem to be composed of stitched-together eyeballs. The eyeballs look at you when she prances by. Hand-Bras and Tongue-Skirts are prevalent as well but then a vivacious bluish-skinned Succubus turns the corner dressed in an entire bodysuit of tongues. You groan when you see that each and every tongue is alive. Through another window you steal a glance at a sleek and perfect bosomed Imp as she tries on a teddy made of shellacked bat wings, while yet another Succubus tries on negligee made from various scalps. In a Surgical Salon next door, a fussy She-Imp appraises her own round rump in a mirror and complains to an attendant, "My ass is too big. I want hers!" and then points to one of several Human women standing on display. A man in a white smock says "A fine choice, Miss," and promptly slices both buttocks off the Human who is held down on a cutting board by a Golem. The smocked man—presumably the cosmetic surgeon—hefts each buttock in his hands and says, "Come along to the surgery suite, Miss. I'll have these transplanted in a jiffy," and if that's not enough, your senses stall when a bell rings and then a crystalline door opens—fancily labeled COSMETIC GRAFTING—and out steps a petitely horned and very lusty She-Demon. Onto every square inch of her skin a nipple has been grafted. She seems delighted with the service and enthuses to Howard, "Oh, my husband, the Grand Duke Desalvo, has such a fetish for nipples, I just *know* he'll love this!"

"Charming," Howard compliments, then back to you, he continues, "Indeed, Mr. Foster. Hell's most exclusive are what you are beholding now. No indulgence, no luxury is deprived of this select group. In fact, there is only one class of inhabitant *more* favored, and that would be the members of the Privilato Class."

You offer Howard a funky look. "The Privilat—"

"And, look! There's one now!" Howard says and excitedly points upward.

An odd groaning sound ensues and fifty feet above the street, you notice something that can only be described as a wavering hole in the sky, approximately ten feet in diameter. A bizarre fluid-like green light rims the hole and within stands a long-haired Human man wearing clothes fashioned entirely from sparkling jewels. His face appears ordinary, yet it is set in the widest grin, and then you see that even his teeth are exorbitant jewels. On his forehead is a fancy Gothic mark: the letter P. *Hmm*, you think. *What's with that guy?* but what you notice even more profoundly are the man's companions, six of the most beautiful naked women you've ever seen.

"No wonder the guy's smiling," you mention. "Check out the drop-dead gorgeous chicks he's with."

"And they'll be with him *in aeternum*, Mr. Foster, or until he wearies of them in which case they'll be replaced by more. The women are known as Soubrettes—the very pinnacle of sexual servitor. Inhuman Growth Hormones are occultized and injected, to augment their most desirable body parts, and they're trained quite exhaustively in the Sexual Arts. The technology they're flying about town in is called a Nectoport."

You stare incredulous at the spectacle—literally a hole in the sky, or a portal that's *moving*. The oozing green light about the rim throbs. "What the...*hell* is it?"

"Hell's answer to flying carpets, you could say," Howard chuckled. "Did you know that I read *The Thousand and One Nights* when I was but a lad of eight years? Oh...of course you wouldn't know that. Nevertheless, a Nectoport is quite obviously a mode of transportation…as well as a very exclusive one. With only very rare exceptions, they're only to be operated by either the Constabulary, the Satanic Military, or the highest members of the Governmental Demonocracy."

"Oh, so that guy with all the hot Demon chicks is in the government or army?"

"I said, Mr. Foster only *very rare* exceptions. Nectoports are able to constrict great distances by reprocessing psychic energy from the Torturian Complexes. Sorcerers trained at the De Rais Labs devised the unique method. It's possible for a Nectoport to travel a thousand miles of Hell's terrain without the occupants ever really leaving their debarkation point. Do you comprehend me?"

"No," you emphatically state.

"It's neither here nor there. But to elucidate, the Privilatos are entitled to unlimited Nectoport usage, due to their staggering rank."

You shake your gourd-head in more confusion. "Okay, so the guy's not in the government, he's not a cop, and he's not in the military but he's super-privileged?"

"Precisely."

"Okay. *Why?*"

Howard beamed through his pallored face. "Mr. Foster, I'm absolutely delighted that you've made the inquiry…"

As Howard talks, your eyes flick to the Nectoport. The crush of sexy Soubrettes are cooing in the Privilato's ear, feeling him up with deft hands. Several take turns fellating the strange, jeweled man, or offering their awesome breasts to his mouth.

"—the gentleman's name is Dowski Swikaj, formerly a friar from Guzow, Poland—"

But as Howard goes on to answer your question, you continue to stare upward. The Nectoport hovers closer now, and the razor-sharp vision afforded you by your Ocularus eyes scrutinize each of the jeweled man's nude consorts. Several are Human, and their sexual enhancements are obvious, as though every aspect of what men find desirable in women has been accelerated tenfold, while the others, however demonic, are just as outrageously desirous in spite of genes that make them technically monsters. One, an auburn-haired Fellatitrine, has four full breasts on each side of her supple physique, yet each nipple is a puckered mouth, while the mouth on her orb-eyed face is a hairless and perfectly cloven vagina. Next to her stands a sultry Vulvatagoyle, with skin the hue of chalk but shining to a gleam as if lacquered. Wide hips and a flawless flat belly entice further staring, and then you notice the veritable *cluster* of vaginas packed between her coltish legs. Each vagina seems to be that of another life-form, and they all *throb* in excitement. Her navel, too, is a vulva—more petite—while another vagina exists in each armpit, and yet another where her anus should be. Lastly, a lissome Lycanymph—even more stunning than the barkeep at the Taproom—coddles the Privilato. She's covered with the finest red hair beneath which a perfect human physique can be seen. Gorged teats the size of baby pacifiers stick out from marvelously sloped breasts, and she grins fang-mouthed as her furred hands slip beneath her master's sparkling trousers.

An uproar rises from the street as the Nectoport lowers to the bone-hewn pavement. *It's landing,* you think. The Privilato stands hands on hips within the Port's green-glowing oval, looking upon the ritzy crowd of uptown Demons in a way that reminds you of an old picture of Mussolini looking down into the town square from a stone balcony. The crowd in the street hoots and hollers, the females in particular nearly apoplectic with enthusiasm. "Privilato!" a corroded chorus rises. "Privilato!"

"Oh, dear," Howard frowns. "He and his entourage are coming out," and then he takes you back to an alley. "I'm just not attuned to boisterous crowds, never have been. Indeed, New York was stifling enough but this—this *elephantiasis* of non-humanity exceeds my demarcation of tolerance."

You barely hear him, squinting at the loud rabble. For some reason you can't figure, this jeweled man—this *Privilato*—intrigues you. The glowing rim of the Nectoport's aperture dilates, and before the Privilato can step out—

"Holy shit," you mutter.

"All Privilatos, too, enjoy a fulltime detachment of bodyguards. Note the Conscripts from the lauded Diocletian Brigade."

From the Nectoport, two formations of said Conscripts dispatch. Some wield swords, others brandish mallets whose heads are the size of 55-gallon drums. Plated suits of Hexed armor adorn each troop, while their shell-like helms possess only slits to look through. The crowd's uproar turns chaotic; then a horn blares, and one of the Conscripts raises a large, hollowed out horn to his mouth like a loud-speaker. "Attention, all elite of Hell. A Privilato wishes to debark. Do not encroach upon the exclusion perimeter," and then more Conscripts run lengths of barbed chain from the Nectoport's mouth to the door of one of the shops on the street.

"The Privilato is about to step into your midst! Bow down and pay reverence to our esteemed favorite of Lucifer!" blasts the horn.

Most of the crowd falls to its knees, though many females in the audience can't control themselves when the Privilato finally emerges onto the street. One shapely She-Demon in a gown of bone-needle mesh leans over the barbed cordon, reaching out with a manicured hand. "Privilato! I'm honored by your presence! Please! Let me touch you!" but once she inclines herself over the chain—

SWOOSH!

—a great curved sword flashes and cuts her in half at the waist.

But the crowd continues to surge forward. You actually groan to yourself when two more Conscripts unroll a red carpet before the Privilato's jeweled feet.

You gotta be shitting me…

"Back! Back!" warns the loudspeaker. "Disperse now and let the Privilato enjoy a refreshment in peace!"

The Privilato comes forth, his robust concubines trailing behind. The crowd roars louder which only doubles your perplexity. You look at the jeweled man and notice that, save for the jewels, there is nothing extraordinary about him. His long hair sifts around a bland, unenlivened face. His eyes look dull. Nevertheless he offers the crowd a smile and when he waves at them the uproar rises further.

Finally you object: "This guy's acting like David Lee Roth. What's the big deal?"

Howard doesn't answer but instead shoulders through the crowd toward the storefront. "You'll be interested in seeing this, Mr. Foster. One of Hell's greatest delicacies. We'll have to settle for watching through the window, of course."

Hell's greatest delicacy?

"Behold the ultimate indulgence, Mr. Foster. One snifter carries a monetary value of one million Hellnotes." Howard sputters. "And to think I fed myself for 30 cents a day on Heinz Beans and old cheese from the Mayflower Store."

The sign on the window reads: FETAL APERITIFS.

Now the crowd watches in awe as the Privilato approaches, his busty consorts in tow.

"Let me suck you off!" comes the crude plea from a vampiric admirer.

The Soubrettes grimace at her, then one—the Vulvatagoyle— expectorates yeast onto the haughty fanged woman.

When one surgically enhanced Imp jumps the cordon and begs to put her hands on him—

WHAM!

—a Conscript brings down his mallet and squashes her against the street.

"Back! Back!"

Even Howard seems awed when the glittering Privilato and his entourage pass by and enter the classy shop.

"The guy looks like a long-haired Liberace," you complain. "Why is he so important? And what the hell is a Fetal Aperitif?"

"Something I've never partaken in—I'm not *privileged* enough, though I did have cotton candy once at Coney Island," and then Howard smiles at you in the oddest manner. "Mongrel fetuses exist as quite a resource in Hell, Mr. Foster. Akin to ore, akin to cash crops."

The notion—the mere way he said it—makes you queasy.

"Economic diversification, by any other classification."

"Baby farms?" you practically gag.

"Yes! Well put, sir, well put. And we'll be seeing one such 'farm' posthaste... But this facility here is one such utility. Like choice grapes selected for the finest wineries, choice *fetuses* are harvested for this four-star Aperitif bar." Howard's finger directs your gaze to the rearmost anteroom of the establishment, where you see a great tub made from wooden slats.

No no no no no, you think.

Worker Demons empty bushel baskets full of live fetuses into the tub...

"I was always amused by the French cliché," Howard goes on. "The idea that our shifty enemies in the Indian Wars would pile grapes into tubs and crush them barefoot..."

When the tub has been filled with squirming newborn Demons, a 9-foot-tall Golem steps in and begins to ponderously walk on them. Eventually the contents of the tub is sufficiently crushed, and a tap drains the precious liquid into kegs which are then rolled aside to ferment.

Howard looks forlorn. "It's supposedly delectable, not that I'll ever receive the opportunity to sample it, not on my pitiful stipend. Lucifer has seen to it that the poverty which mocked me in life will continue to do so in death..."

Inside, as his Soubrettes take turns fellating him beneath the table, the Privilato eyes trays of bizarre food placed before him by licentious servers. Wicked versions of shrimp and lobster (lobsters, of course, with horns), braised roasts of shimmering meat, steaming vegetables in arcane sauces. In spite of its alienness, it all looks delicious.

"You see, Mr. Foster, the *elite* in Hell gorge on delicacies the likes of which would sink the banquets of Locullus to tameness, and the wine? Splendid enough to green Bacchus with envy."

You watch now as the Privilato raises a tiny glass of the evil wine and shoots it back neat. The occult rush sets a wide smile on his face, and he looks past the table, right through the window...

At you.

The Privilato nods.

You're sure that if you actually had hands you would grab Howard by the collar and shake him. "Why are you showing me this stuff? And what the *fuck* is the big deal with that guy in there? He's got the best-looking girls in Hell for groupies, he flies around in a *Nectoport,* and he gets to drink wine that costs a million bucks a glass. Why?"

"Because," Howard answers, "and I'll iterate, the gentleman's name is Dowski Swikaj, formerly a friar from Guzow, Poland."

"Yeah?" you yell. "So what?!"

"In the frightful year of 1342 A.D., Mr. Swikaj won the Senary..."

«« — »»

The hollow sound in your head follows as the Turnstile's evil formulae are triggered and you and your guide are pressed yet again through the gauze of distance-collapsing sorcery. When the vertigo passes, you jerk your gaze to Howard.

"So that's it? The winners of the Senary get to become Privilatos?"

"Ah, I see your observations have at last heightened the acuity of your powers of deductive reckoning. I gratefully affirm."

You frown.

"However, our chancing upon Mr. Swikaj and his comely harem came quite by happenstance. We're on our way to behold more facets of the abyss that should deliver a more formidable impact."

THE SENARY

Shylock Square is long behind you now, though curious occult graftwork is still visible among passersby. One stunning woman in hot pants and a bra of the finest leaden fabric has no face at all but only smooth white skin and a bellybutton where her nose would be. Her face has been transplanted upon her abdomen, and when that fact finally registers, you notice that she is smiling at you. A buff man, Human save for elaborate horns, walks confidently into an enterprise called CRIPPENDALE'S; he's wearing a vest of penises, and onto his earlobes have been sewn scrotums. Lastly, a slyly smiling She-Imp passes, her majora replaced by what appears to be a baby's buttocks.

"I can perceive that you're finally acclimating," Howard remarks. "Your revulsion appears to be growing staid—quite a good sign."

Finally you're able to blurt, "You want me to accept the Senary, which means I'll become a Privilato after I die. Is that it?"

"Yes," Howard says. "And now you are weighing that possibility against the possibility of an eternity in Heaven, are you not?"

You nod very slowly.

"A good sign as well. But you needn't choose just yet. Let's take in more sights before we arrive at the clincher."

"The *clincher?* I can't imagine."

"No, I'm certain you cannot. No one can…"

Your senses reel as you cross a footbridge over a mucus-filled creek. Several destitute Trolls nod as they stand on the rail, fishing. One Troll has eyeballs in his bait can, the other, tongues yanked from their seats.

In the distance, hulking Conscripts stand guard around a narrow, black building that must be a mile long. MATERNITY BARRACKS, a high sign reads. Even from the distance you can hear the wails of infants…

You open your demonic mouth to speak but pause, and don't bother. You agreed to come here and *see.*

And now you will be shown.

Macabre, cancerous horses whinny as a prison wagon (identical

124

to those you saw at the Punitary) stops before a guarded entrance. Now you stare.

"It's loaded up with...*hot* chicks," you mutter.

"The supernumerians of Human female stock, Mr. Foster," Howard augments. "The penultimate in all of Hell—indeed—the proverbial cream of the crop. They're hunted down with the zeal of children at an Easter egg hunt."

Naturally, you don't understand. So far you've seen unbelievable lifeforms, most hideous but some attractive, and Human women have comprised a fare share of the latter. This wagon, however, beggars superlative description. It is full to bursting with Human women who are among the most attractive you've ever seen anywhere.

"They could be runway models," you utter.

"It's part of the new Luciferic Initiative, and Lucifer—however plodding he can sometimes be—has grown fond of efficiency. Two birds with one stone, so to speak. You see, the inhabitants of these queer barracks make up the very finest, the very most attractive Human women in all of Hell. And in their stay, they will serve dual purposes."

"I don't know what you're talking about," you drone as you approach, and now you watch the wedge-faced Conscripts haul the women out of the wagon. They're all gagged, shackled, and stark naked. In single file, then, they're led at trident-point into the barracks.

"There must be forty or fifty women packed into that wagon," you exclaim.

"Sixty-six, if you're interested in exactitude," Howard redresses. "And there are exactly sixty-six Impoundment Wings in this Maternity Barrack."

The number staggers you, but then you ask, "What to you mean, dual purposes?"

"Pardon me while I get us in-processed," Howard says aside.

The two gate guards—a pair of pugnacious, phlegm-eyed creatures in scaled armor—stop at a spiked iron gate.

THE SENARY

"I'm with the Office of the Senary," Howard relays and holds up his palm. It's the first time that you've noticed it: a luminous 6 branded in his palm.

The Conscripts bow and step back, then the spiked gate rises. But before he takes you in, the chain-gang of sixty-six outrageously beautiful woman are led in first. Hopeless eyes stare back at you as they're hauled onward.

"Ah, and here comes the most recent Impoundment Block to expire," Howard points out.

Another chain-gang of women are being led in the opposite direction, preparing to exit. This consignment, however, differs from the first group in two ways.

One, they're emaciated, haggard, and bone-thin, and—

Two, they're headless.

"Out with the old in with the new as they say," Howard explains. "The production cycle of these unfortunates has expired, while its only about to begin for the group we just saw entering..."

"Production cycle," you say more than ask. The headless women are *worn out,* (as if having one's head removed wouldn't wear one out enough) and then you suddenly have an idea why. Their bellies hang like limp sacks streaked with stretchmarks, their breasts but emptied flaps of skin.

"This particular barrack, by the way, is the major supplier of fetuses to the Aperitif bar we visited upon earlier." Howard leads on down the reeking corridor of sheet-iron. "The women, once beheaded, are taken a Decampitant Camp. You'll recall the Luciferic Initiative I referred to earlier? It's officially titled the Beheadment Initiative—the law of the land now. Human women deemed attractive enough for Supernumerary classification must *all* be beheaded, and the process functions twofold. It's a constituent of their punishment, and while the wares of their wombs supply the lucrative gourmand market, their heads provide an exclusive construction component."

Again, you scarcely hear Howard, your attentions fixed instead on the troop of headless women shuffling out of the complex. Moments later, several hunched Imps in laborers' garb exit the complex as well, each pushing wheelbarrows *full* of Human female heads. As the barrows pass, the eyes on the heads all hold wide on you.

"Why, why, why?" you plead.

"It's elementary, Mr. Foster. Lucifer *loathes* the Human Damned, but this unadulterated hatred burns exponentially hotter for the Human *Female* Damned." Howard pauses at a trapdoor-like window in the iron wall. "This may afford you an acceptable view..."

He raises the square metal viewing port and holds your gourd-head up to look.

Beyond the Barracks stretches a region of barren land that must encompass several square miles. The parcel is circumscribed completely by a high fence laced with barbs and within they trod aimlessly in a vast circle: tens of thousands of headless women.

"The idea enthralls Lucifer, that they walk headless for eternity, while their heads live on elsewhere and with equal permanence."

You're too appalled to even react now, but you have the creeping impression that there are worse things waiting to be seen...

"The *Beheadment* Initiative?" you question, dazed from the sight. "A *law* that all beautiful women come here to be decapitated and..."

"All beautiful *Human* women, Mr. Foster. Lucifer is quite nonchalant about *Hellborn* females. His utter hatred for Human women in particular is plainly explicated. You see, it was a *Human* female who destroyed his original abode, the 666-story Mephisto Building. This cunning female—whose name it is forbidden to speak or even think—undermined Lucifer's most powerful defenses and turned his monumental edifice of evil into a pile of rubble, and she did so with *White* Magic, not black."

You gulp. "So now he takes it out on every drop-dead gorgeous Human in Hell?"

"Yes, and to quite an effect. Remember when I inferred: two birds with one stone." Howard smiles. "Be patient, Mr. Foster, and you'll learn more in due time."

Metal pots along the corridor sputter with burning pitch. You watch the shadow of your own hideous head bob as Howard leads you down a labyrinth of squalling hallways and, at last, into—

"This is the initial processing point. The consignment we just saw entering? Here's where they come first," Howard explains.

You peer in through the ragged metal doorway...

All sixty-six women have been lain on a wide conveyor belt, with hip and neck girds to keep them in place. Midway along the belt stand two Imps in white labcoats. One wields a pair of scissors the size of hedge clippers and perfunctorily cuts off a woman's head while the other places the severed head between the woman's legs for further transport. At the next work station two more demonic surgeons slip metal tubes into each of the woman's breasts and the breasts—amid a wailing motor noise—quickly deflate.

"As you can see, first the heads are removed and then vacuum-powered cannulae are inserted into the massive breasts, to draw out the valuable mammary glands which are sold to Surgical Salons for implanting—"

They chop off their heads and liposuck their tits, the grueling fact sinks in.

"—after which they're conveyed to the next available Impoundment Block," Howard finishes and re-embarks down the corridor.

Every so often, as you're taken deeper into this nefarious network, wheel barrows full of mongrel newborns are rolled briskly past by more Imp and Troll laborers. You don't have to ask where they're going.

"And here," Howard announces after a long spell of walking, "is a typical Block in full swing..."

Your now-numb eyes look in to behold the spectacle: a long, low-ceilinged room containing exactly sixty-six gynecological beds, complete with stirrups. Each bed is occupied by one squirming, decapitated woman, legs forced apart and ankles locked in the stirrups. Most of the occupants display varying stages of pregnancy, and the few who don't are being vigorously copulated with by a variety of sexually enhanced

Demons, Trolls, and Imps. Many possess genitals like veined batons of meat, while others brandished odd, ridged tubules of flesh with nozzle-like coronas. Several even had penises with faces on the end.

"Each Impoundee is subjected to fornication on a fastidious level, until pregnancy shows. Then they merely wait out their term until the process begins again. And as for their *heads,* well, I'm sure by now you've taken proper note..."

You have. The severed head of each "Impoundee" is evident, placed atop a pole set back several yards between the subject's spread legs.

"It simply wouldn't do to merely use their bodies as production vessels; it's very important to Lucifer that the conscious head of each woman be forced to *watch* the entire process; in fact, our Master *delights* in that particular effect. Not only is each woman forced for watch herself be raped by monsters, she is forced to watch herself *give birth* to monsters. Over and over and over again."

"How long...do they have...to stay here?"

"For sixty-six full terms," Howard enlightens.

One woman, bloated as if to pop, shuddered on her table, while her accommodating head screams in agony. The belly quakes, then collapses; a basket on the floor catches the squalling newborn and afterbirth. Not a minute passes before the viscid infant is tossed into a wheel barrow, and not another minute before a heavily genitaled Sex-Demon steps up to begin the fornication period anew. Meanwhile, the head of a woman several beds down is shrieking like a machine with bad bearings, the medicine-ball-sized belly tremoring. When a labcoated Imp with goggles comes to inspect, he calls out, "Herman! This one's not dilating. Come and do your thing," and then a fat slovenly Human male lopes over, grinning dopily. He's wearing an older style New York Yankees uniform. Then—

WHAP, WHAP, WHAP!

—he takes to beating the woman's belly with a ball bat until, finally, it gives up its goods, pushing a dizzy demonic fetus through the well-used birth canal.

"Take me the fuck out of here!" you yell.

Howard rolls his eyes, scratching at some tiny red pocks on his face that appear to be ingrown hairs. "I regret your distress, Mr. Foster, but it's necessary that you recognize the systematics that exist here. You must *perceive* Lucifer's ultimate ideal of pursuing an order of faith antithetical to God."

"Fuck that shit," you profane. "This sucks. None of this makes any sense—"

"Excellent! You're beginning to comprehend!" Howard enthuses, taking you out.

"It doesn't make any sense at all for Lucifer to go to all this effort to do all this evil shit!"

Howard continues to beam. "Exactly! Because, antithetically speaking, the absence of logic is the *perfect* logic in a domain that must exist contrary to God!"

Your confoundment dizzies you when Howard finally wends you back outside into the creeping scarlet daylight, and as you move away from the barracks, the wails of newborn Demons and the shrieks of women in labor follow you like an atrocious banner.

Still, details bother you, and now that the shock of your witness is past, you slowly observe, "They use their babies for the 'gourmand market,' and they use their mammary glands for demonic implants, and once they've had sixty-six babies, their headless bodies are sentenced to eternity in the Decapitant Camp. Have I got it right so far?"

"Quite," Howard confirms.

"So...what happens to their heads? Earlier, didn't you say something about—"

"An exclusive construction component!" Howard continues to be pleased by your attentiveness, but then—

The black static veil crackles and surges and—

Here we go again...

—you psychically plummet into the next stop on the tour...

"This, Mr. Foster, is the second bird from the stone," Howard intones.

You're not sure what you're looking at, but when your supernatural vision sharpens—

"It's like a mansion, except it's *got* to be over five hundred feet on each side..."

"Sixty hundred and sixty-six," Howard redresses, "*if* you're interested in exactitude, and six floors each precisely sixty-six feet in height. Six belfries and six towers per side, six spires and crockets per tower. Six windows per dormer section, sixty-six chimneys, sixty-six occuli, and six hundred and sixty-six crest-spikes along each of sixty-six cornices, not to belabor the evidence of sixty-six—"

"Enough of the fucking sixes! Please!" you wail. "I'm SICK of the sixes!"

Howard waits for you to settle down, a bemused smile subtly set into his sallow face. Then he announces:

"Mr. Foster, it is my doubtless pleasure and unreserved honor to introduce to you the new personal abode of the Prince of Darkness... Manse Lucifer."

By now, you've already noticed the most distinguishing characteristic of the colossal manse. Its walls are not constructed of brick, block, cement slab, nor wood, nor stucco.

They're built with female Human heads.

The heads face outward and—to no surprise—they're all still very much alive. They've been lain like mason-work, with mortar meticulously packed around each. Millions of heads, no doubt, had been used to construct the mansion's outer walls and immense mansard-style roof.

"The walls are double layered," Howard points out, "so that living female faces form the walls inside, as well—God *knows* what they're forced to witness. All the interior floors, too, are made from the heads, including buttresses and load-bearing walls."

A house of heads inside and out, you can only think. *A MANSION of living female heads...*

You sense yourself lowering, then perceive that Howard has set your "stick" into a bone- and tooth-fragment filled slab of sidewalk. He's slipping something from his pocket. "As you can imagine, an equally spectacular interior exists." Howard, next, holds a small stack of dim photographs before your face.

"Good old fashioned photographs," you remark. "I'm surprised you have stuff like that in Hell."

"Not photographs, *Hecto*graphs. Hell's version of the tintypes of my early days. A process of gold nitrate merged with tin salt. Hectographs are, again, only a luxury for the very wealthy here…"

Your eyes hold wide on each macabre snapshot.

"The Atrium," Howard defines.

You are shown an impossible room walled with heads. Columns that ought to be Doric or Corinthian stand at each side of the arched entrance, these, too, constructed of heads. On one wall hangs a painting of Demons peering in on the Last Supper while platters of chopped infants and goblets of sperm wait on the long table to be consumed; on another hangs the Messiah being Crucified upside-down in Hell.

Next, "Lucifer's master bed chamber…"

Not only are the walls made from heads but so is the high poster bed, yet each head of the mattress has its tongue permanently protruded via studs through the lips. Mirrors shaped like inverted crosses ring the room.

Next, "Lucifer's Great Hall…"

Columned peristyles stretch down the long vault-ceilinged room fitted with scroll-backed couches and chairs upholstered in Human skin. The banquet table—which you assume must be sixty-six feet long—occupies the center, with higher backed skeletal chairs around it. The faces in the floor, ceiling, and walls, here, appear more appalled than in other rooms, and you can only suspect the reason has something to do with what they are forced to watch the Prince of Darkness and his guests dine on.

Next, "And Lucifer's Grand Courtyard…"

Nauseating topiary has been meticulously clipped into the configuration of the number six. Noxious rose bushes bear heads of not petals but vaginas, while an ivy of severed penises crawls up a glimmering silver lattice. Human heads only comprise the outer walls and curtilage, but then you see their evidence in one more place: the circular swimming pool that exists at the center of the "six." The entire pool is lined with them, and the pool appears to be filled with urine ever so faintly tinted with blood.

Next, "Ah, and Lucifer's throne in the Central Nave..."

Not only is the room floored and walled with heads but the great throne itself is composed of them as well. The throne bears a similarity to a Victorian bishop's chair, with even side-stiles, headbacks, and armrests made of heads. The heads forming the center of the seat seem understandably more weary than the rest. To the right sits an ornate Grandfather clock, whose pendulum chains are no doubt arteries of more unfortunates; its face has no hands. To the left hangs a painting of a glorious conqueror in a shining breastplate engraved with sixes. He wields a sweep-bladed cutlass while he stands over the headless corpse of, apparently, Christ. The sword-wielder's face seems to glow to the point that detail cannot be discerned.

"And lastly, Lucifer's commode-chamber, which you in your modern parlance would call a bathroom..."

The head-formed walls here are circular, presumably so that all may watch the Morning Star's elimination. A beautifully cut mosaic of amethysts make up the actual toilet bowl but the rim of the seat is made of more Human heads. The oddest adornment here, though, is a gilded, flat-topped stand, and on top of it sits a lone Human head on its side. The head's not connected or mortared to anything; it's just sitting there. You squint at it. It's that of a blond woman, slightly chubby-faced, with an expression of utter revulsion.

"What's with the single head on the stand?" you ask.

"Surely you've noticed a disheartening *absence* of toilet paper, Mr. Foster," Howard says. "The unfortunate blond belle's *face* serves the purpose..."

Your facsimile for a stomach sinks, then sinks further when you suspect you've seen the face before. *Anna Nicole?* you wonder, but... No. It can't be.

Howard puts the Hectographs away and re-hoists your head-stick. "The main house has obviously been completed, but constant additions are in perpetual progress," and then he points down an empty street— MEPHISTO AVENUE—as a queue of clattering steam-trucks and monster-drawn wagons approach, all manned by various demonic workmen. Several wagons are heaped high with heads while others haul sacks of occult cement. At a certain point near the house, two hooded Bio-Wizards depart from the mansion's entrance. They touch a pair of crooked wands together, then draw them apart to a distance wide enough to permit passage of the construction crew. After said passage, the Wizards reverse the odd procedure, and return to the entrance.

"What was that all about?"

"They were opening and closing the mansion's impenetrable defense perimeter. Nothing may gain entrance without proper clearance."

"Perimeter? I don't see any *perimeter.*"

"It's a Hex, Mr. Foster. It's called an Exsanguination Bridle. Ah, and how convenient! Watch what befalls this gaggle of very *un*wise insurgent ruffians and ne're-do-wells..."

You look up and see a spectacular white Griffin flying urgently toward one of the mansion's towers. Saddled to its back are several very determined-looking Imps and Humans, each hefting a keg of explosives. But when the Griffin's swift wings take it past a certain point—

FFFFFFFFFFFWAP!

—white feathers fly as the beast and its riders are immediately stricken by an energy which causes their blood to fire out of their bodies through every orifice. Then the bodies, and a rain of blood, hits the street. The kegs burst harmlessly, poofing billows of something akin to gunpowder.

"Wow," you say, impressed. "That's some security system."

"The very latest Senarial Science. And anyone who *is* granted entrance is thoroughly screened by Prism Veils operated by Warlocks with the Psychical Detection Regiments. They're able to read any and all negative or anti-Luciferic thoughts."

Then you look back at the obscene house; even in the utter evil of its design, you have to be impressed. But your confusion couldn't be more intense. "So this is the clincher? This is the final sight that's supposed to make me accept the Senary—a house of *heads?*"

Howard unreels a high, nasally laugh. "Goodness *no,* Mr. Foster. This is the final sight that's intended to fully evolve your awareness of the totality of Lucifer's power and forethought. The clincher shall arrive later..." Howard pauses then, then adds, "But the tour *is* nearly at an end. I dare say a minor respite is in order...before our *final* debarkation."

You're taking a final glance at the ghastly manse, at the innumerable living heads facing you, all those lips mouthing silent horrors, and all those eyes shock-wide by the excruciating particulars of their Damnation; and the millions more heads which comprise this entire incalculable place when the black static sizzles yet again and then—

Coolness.

Quiet.

Your gourd-head clears, and you find yourself back in the Turnstile. Its black, uneven, flat walls emit the faintest indescribable luminescence.

"Ah," Howard utters. He sits down on a squat, companulated protrusion made of the same material of the Turnstile itself. He loosens his frayed gray tie and smiles at you.

"Just as sleep is Nature's balm, I dare say *quietude* is its sedative."

You've been leaned against a corner whose angles are precisely sixty-six degrees. Within the polygon's inner vault, you're finally able to relax. The only sound you're aware of arrives as the most distant hum which is somehow organic, not electronic. That and an occasional *tick* of the steam-car's cooling engine.

THE SENARY

Howard unwraps a napkin and removes a cookie of some sort. "I'd offer you a Uneeda biscuit but, lo, your Auric Carrier doesn't allow you to consume food."

"Thanks just the same..." You try to collect your thoughts but aren't sure how to; you're not even sure what to think. But you know that Howard is merely giving you time to either consider or recover from all the detestable things you've seen.

You jerk your gaze at a sudden sound: a grunt, a shuffle. Torchlight sputters from a farther corner, then a shadow lengthens.

The Imperial Truncator—the watchman of this place—shuffles nonchalantly across the black floor, his cleaver-hands swinging, the Ghor-Hound helmet high on his head.

"I forgot all about him," you remark, but then: "Hey! What happened to the—"

"Ah, yes. Our lithe chauffeur, the Golemess..." Howard squints, then his shoulders slump. "Ostensibly not so lithe any longer."

Now another, less lively shuffle, and from the same corner, the Golemess appears. She seems winded, wearied now, and when she trudges into more torchlight, you see why.

She's pregnant.

"The dude with the meat cleavers for hands knocked her up!" you exclaim. The gray clay belly looks *stuffed*, the breasts doubled in volume, presumably full of Golem-milk now. *He put the blocks to her and then some...*

"I was unaware that our Golemess comes equipped with fertility features. No doubt before her clay was Hexegeninated, the Master Sculptors at the Edward Kelly Institute of Inanimate Enchantment implanted her with a reproductive tract and ovarian process. This is another Luciferic Law that's gradually activating: the Public Gravidity Initiative. Lucifer desires anything female—even things un-alive—to be fertile. More progeny, more fodder for the machinations of the Mephistopolis. God invented reproduction via Human passion, to bring forth more Children of God to one day enjoy the Firmament

136

of Heaven. Lucifer, therefore, *perverts* God's endeavor, to reduce Femalekind to repositories of lust, and bring forth more meat and building material."

You stare at the huge stomach as the fatigued Golemess lumbers to the steam-car. "But what...what's going to come out?"

"Immaterial," Howard answers. "Its purpose is served, and the Initiative is duly discharged."

Meat, you recite Howard's information. *Building material.*

"And now, Mr. Foster," Howard intones. "You've had this moment of respite. I'm curious as to the nature of your thoughts."

Your hideous head swivels to meet his gaze. "I'm thinking that everything here is illogical—"

"Which serves as the perfect logic within the confines of an antithetical demesne."

"—including my being here." You blink. "What, I win this *Senary* because I've tipped some scale of sin, some *fulcrum*, one percent in favor of Heaven? It makes more sense to go after some guy who's ten percent, or fifty, or eighty."

"Perhaps in your *own* purview of logic, but in Lucifer's purview bringing those closest to the edge is much more gratifying, and—I'll be honest—a much better bet."

You smirk. "Okay, fine. But in that case, your methods are *terrible*."

"Really?" Howard seems intrigued. "Be kind enough to articulate your impression."

You recite them thus far. "I'm just *good enough* a person that if I died right now, I'd go to Heaven, right?"

"Correct."

"But Lucifer wants me to give that up so that when I die, I come here instead. He wants me to *make that choice,* right?"

"Precisely."

"He wants me to give up Heaven, in favor of Hell, right?"

"Indubitably."

Your eyes lock open. "WELL THEN WHY WOULD I DO THAT? HELL SUCKS!"

Your outburst bounces off the vault's obsidian walls like bullets ricocheting. The Golemess flinches. Even the Imperial Truncator jolts from the start.

"My, Mr. Foster," Howard says after his own shock. "That's…quite an ejaculation…"

"You guys must be *out of your minds!*" you continue to rail at the senselessness of it all. "This place is the biggest pile of shit I've ever seen! Bridges made of *people?* Taverns where the kegs are *tits* with beer taps on the nipples, and bars that serve wine made from fermented babies? Towns made of guts and towns made of skin? And the guy who runs the whole shebang lives in a mansion made of *heads!* Who the FUCK would want to live here?"

"But certainly, sir, you can comprehend the unending bliss of one who enjoys Privilato status?" Howard questions.

"The Privilato? That asshole in the jewelly jacket?" You roll your demonic eyes. "He's a putz with a posse of hot chicks would wouldn't give a *shit* about him if he wasn't a Privilato in the first place. Big deal. He drives around town in a flying hole in the sky and gets a red carpet wherever he goes. You gotta do better than *that,* man."

"Ah, well, I see that you are underestimating the *entireness* of the Mephistopolis for those few granted privilege." Howard raises a finger. "Allow me to query. Seeing that the lion's share of your sins fall primarily into the *lust* category…if you could revel in the carnal pleasures of any woman in the world, who would that be?"

The question, absurd as it is, percolates in your mind. Angelina Jolie? Paris Hilton? Jessica Alba? Just as you think you've been stumped, the answers appears. "Well, I'm kind of Old School, but I'd still have to say Pamela Anderson."

Howard nods. "Bear in mind, of course, that since Mademoiselle Anderson is still a member of the Living World, it defies possibility for me to be familiar with her. However, I can assure you beyond all dubiety that the women awaiting you as a Privilato will be possessed of a desirability no less than sixty-six times that of your coveted Miss Anderson."

You try to picture that in your mind. *Women…sixty-six times HOTTER than Pam…*

Wow.

But still…the proposition is folly and you know it. "Doesn't matter if they're sixty-six *thousand* times hotter, Howard. This place is still Hell, and Hell sucks."

Howard seems quelled. "Your mind appears to be quite incontrovertibly made up."

"It is," you say without hesitation. "So get me out of this fucked up pumpkin so I can go back to my hum-drum little life like you promised."

"As you wish, if you're sure."

"Sure I'm sure, and this little tour of yours is the *reason* I'm sure. It proved to me that Lucifer's a Grade-A *moron*. He's a *putz*. All that power and all these resources and technologies, and look what he does with it. He could turn Hell into a great place, and you want to know why he doesn't?"

"I know why, Mr. Foster," Howard admits. "Because of his pride."

"Right. He's obsessed with being evil and disgusting and cruel because God's the opposite of that, and Lucifer's pissed off at God for throwing him out of Heaven. He's like a little kid having a tantrum because mommy spanked him. I don't want anything to do with this place, *or* him. Lucifer's a *dick*."

Howard's brow rises in a defeated surprise. "Why not let me at least encourage you to take the final leg of the tour."

"No reason to. My mind's made up."

"Then what harm can there be?"

You huff. "Well, what's the final leg? Believe me, I don't need to see any more piss pumps, baby factories, or Decapitant Camps."

THE SENARY

"The final leg is the Privilato Chateau that you would occupy if you accept the Senary. At least go and behold all the pleasures you'll be missing."

You pause. *Hmm.* Suddenly it begins to sound interesting again. But, "No. Why tempt myself to do the wrong thing when I've already decided to do the right thing?"

"Right and wrong are relative, Mr. Foster, and in Hell they're interchangeable. You find trepidation in the prospect of temptation? So did Jesus during His forty days in the wilderness. Why not test your resolve as He did? Need I remind you that Christ took a similar tour after He died on Calvary? Lucifer offered Jesus Privilato status, by the way, and he obviously turned it down. See all that Christ saw; face the *same* temptations He faced, in which case, if you still decide to turn the Senary down, you will have done what *Christ* did as well."

Your thoughts stretch like taffy. *He's got a point. I'll become an even better Christian by seeing every temptation and STILL turning them all down...*

You think a moment more, then say, "All right."

Howard stands up. He seems relieved.

"Still think you can get me to change my mind?" you ask, a bit prideful yourself now.

"Irrelative time will tell," Howard says. He pats sweat off his brow with a handkerchief embroidered, HPL. *This guy's really sweating bullets,* you think.

Howard picks up your head-stick and approaches the circle of geometric etchings in the black wall. "And the tour goes on," he murmurs.

For a reason you can't define—and just before the Turnstile powers up—you look behind you and see the Golemess lying back on the floor, her knees pulled back to her sleek shoulders. Her back arches. Evil water breaks and gushes, then the enormous belly tremors, hitches, and collapses as it disgorges a slick mongrel fetus with an accordioned face and arms where its legs should be. Puff-eyed, the demonic thing bawls as nub-like horns appear on its bald-head. It's almost cute.

Almost.

Between its chubby arm-legs dangles a penis and scrotum the size of an adult Human's.

The Golemess labors to her feet. Her elegant clay hands scoop the fetus up, afterbirth and all. The last thing you see before the Turnstile's black static shifts you into another phase is the new mother calmly sliding her newborn into the fuel-hatch of the steam-car's boiler housing. Just as calmly she pushes the hatch shut…

…and you fall through that now-familiar combustion of morbid energy amid the crackling vertigo of scintillescent black static, and just as the mongrel baby was pushed forth from the Golemess' womb, you and Howard are pushed through space and some wicked substitute for time until…

You're there.

Your head spins like a proverbial top as your senses first alight and you think you hear…

A deep incessant *throb,* like crickets in a vast field only much more intense. Before you can even contemplate the nature of the sound, it brings an immediate smile to your face.

It's then that your vision turns crisp; you find that you are indeed standing in a vast, sweeping field of verdant grass a yard high.

It's beautiful.

And the sounds throb on.

"Cicadas," you dreamily mutter. "The seventeen-year kind. It's one of my earliest childhood memories—that sound. It's always been my favorite sound…"

"The powers that be are aware of that," Howard tells you, your head-stick in hand as he walks along through the gorgeous, blight-free grass. The scent of the grass is intoxicating. "As a Privilato, every-thing you are endeared to, everything that brings you jubilancy and exultation will be provided to you to the very best of our abilities. And, mind you, *forever.*"

Then Howard turns and you see the castle.

"Noticing a familiarity?" Howard asked.

The castle's great buff-colored blocks gleam atop the grass-swept hill, with five massive bastions rimmed with turrets, merlons, and arrow-slits, a moat surrounding all. And come to think of it: *It DOES look familiar,* you recall.

"You were quite an aficionado of the Middle Ages when you were in middle school—"

Then the memory sweeps into your head. "Chateau-Gaillard..."

"Correct, the famed bastion of Richard the Lionhart, in Les Andelys, France. Of course, the real one is a ruin now, but Lucifer's Master Builders have constructed this duplicate, down to excruciating detail. It appears as it did, in every conceivable way, in 1192 A.D. In your early teens, castles, knights, and the like had a tendency to fascinate you."

And he's right; you remember now.

"While the interior has been modified to a scheme you're sure to be delighted in," Howard added.

Incredible, you think. As Howard approaches the draw-bridge you notice ten other magnificent castles on ten other hills in the dim distance. "Who lives in those?"

"Your neighbors. The other men—er, I should say, nine men and one woman who've won the Senary since it began in 4652 B.C."

"Nine men but just one woman?" you question.

"Yes. Women seem to be more concrete about their notions of sin versus redemption. Our only female winner is a quite attractive Judean named Archela, a concubine of Pontius Pilate. You're certain to make her acquaintance, along with all the winners," but then Howard cleared his throat. "That is, *if* you decide to accept your winnings."

"But I've already decided not to," you remind your guide. "This castle looks like really cool digs...but it's not worth my soul."

EDWARD LEE

"Of course, of course, but...wait till you view the interior."

Your gourd-head sways along on the stick as Howard carries it across the magnificent draw-bridge and through a barbican and iron portcullis. Next, up a stone spiral staircase, and suddenly the air feels cool as if climate-controlled. Through a spectacular archway, you're startled by a brilliant shine, then—

"Oh, wow," you utter.

"This is the Hall of Gold."

You're standing in long room that's completely walled in pure gold.

"Stunning, eh? The decorative effect seems to awe Humans. Six hundred and sixty-six tons of gold have been used to wall this room," Howard tells you as he walks on, through another arch, "While six hundred and sixty-six tons of diamonds wall this one—the foyer."

The sight is dizzying. You're now in the middle of another chamber walled similarly with diamonds. The effect is impossible to describe. "This really is beautiful," you admit.

"Indeed."

"But it's still not worth my soul. Come on, be serious. I get to spend eternity in a neat castle full of gold and diamonds? Big deal. I'm still in Hell."

"Um-hmm," Howard consents. "But you haven't met your house staff—sixty-six of them, by the way." Howard snaps his fingers, and then a diamond panel raises, and through it saunter dozens of the most beautiful women—Humans and Demons alike—that you can imagine.

The drove of smiling women don't make a sound as they enter, stand in rank, and bow.

The most gorgeous Human women you've ever seen, but now you must confess, that some of the Hybrids and Demons are even *more* gorgeous. Fellatitrines, Vulvatagoyles, Succubi. Lycanymphs and Mammaresses, and even a Golemess that puts your sultry chauffeur to shame.

"The sins of the flesh, Mr. Foster, but not a bad thing in a domain where sin has no consequences," Howard's voice echoes in the glittering hall.

You gulp. "Yeah, but I couldn't get it on with all these women in a hundred years."

"But of course you could, and a hundred after that and a hundred after that. Forever. And when you weary of these, *more* will be afforded you."

Now you stare at them. *That's an awful lot of nookie...*

"But now, we're off to your bed chamber, where your very *personal* harem awaits," and then Howard takes you up more steps, down a torch-studded corridor, and into a long room adorned with all manner of jewels and precious metals.

"Holy shit!" you exclaim when you spy the bed. "I'll bet you didn't get *that* at Mattress Discounters."

The bed is circular, twenty feet in diameter, but the mattress itself is somehow a mass of Human breasts.

"The Breast-Beds are Hexegenically manufactured, for Privilatos only," Howard informs. "I was never possessed of much of a sexual drive—much to my wife's ire, and I'd bet my precious Remington she was committing infidelities in Cleveland." Howard paused amid the digression. "Er, anyway, even I must admit, I wouldn't mind stretching out on such a Breast-Bed."

A bed made of tits, you tell yourself. *And not just any tits— GREAT tits.*

"But didn't you also say something about—"

"You're *personal* harem," Howard went on. "Oh, yes." Again, Howard snapped his fingers.

A door clicked open and in walked a very perfect and very buck-naked—

"It's Pam Anderson!" you wail.

And so it is. The woman curtsies for you, then stands in a displaying pose.

"She's even better looking than she was in *Barb Wire*," you observe, but then your eyes bulge when *five more* identical Pam Andersons enter the bedroom and stand in formation.

Your gaze snaps to Howard. "Six Pam Andersons? All for me?"

"All for you, Mr. Foster, should of course you accept the Senary."

You stare at the impossible line of spectacular women. "But how did you..."

"They're products of quite an impressive occult invention, called Hex-Cloning," Howard explains. "They look—and feel—exactly like the genuine woman in the Living World you so desire, but they'll do anything you tell them. Any time you want."

You gulp again, looking at those six pairs of legendary breasts...

"And I suspect you'll enjoy the next prospect: the Bath," Howard says and takes you into what you guess is the bathroom.

Solid gold toilet. Solid gold sink. A claw-foot tub made of still more gold sits on the immaculate floor.

"Pretty nice bathroom," you say.

"You're welcome to partake in baths with pure water, or, if you prefer," and then Howard snaps his fingers one more time.

Several large-bosomed and sultry She-Demons enter next, their bodies nearly as provocative as the half dozen Pam Andersons in the bedroom, only these women have petite horns and various colored skin.

"What's the big deal with these chicks?"

"They're your Bath Girls, in the event that you don't want to take a normal bath."

You blink at Howard. "Huh?"

"Girls?" Howard addresses them. "Be so good as to show Mr. Foster your surgical augmentation."

All at once, then, the She-Demons open their mouths and stuck out their tongues.

"Woe-boy!" you exclaim.

Each woman extrudes a tongue the size of a beef liver.

"Their tongues are *huge!*"

THE SENARY

"Of course, they need to be. They're Bath Girls. Only Privilatos, Exalted Dukes, and District Emirs are afforded this very expensive luxury—along with Satan himself, of course. Their sole purpose is to administer to you what's known as a tongue-bath."

You stare at the women's tongue as much as you stare at the consideration. *Tongue-baths. Wow...*

"Any time you so desire," Howard says. "For eternity. It's my understanding that the sensation is *most* stimulating."

I'll bet it is... I've got shitload of hot chicks here, that I can get it on with anytime I want...IF I accept the Senary... But then the reality sets in. "Sure, but you know, a guy can only do it so many times before he gets worn out."

"Ah, yes, refraction, the bane of all masculinity, but let us convene now on the north rampart, and I will show you yet one more otherworldly benefit of Privilato status."

The Bath Girls all wriggle their giant wet tongues as Howard moves you out of the bed chamber and onto a lofty balcony. From here you see the entire castle grounds, the inner wards, various stone buildings, intermediate towers. "There," Howard points over the parapet, "The Satanic Chapel. You *will* have to attend Black Mass on occasion, but I would think that little to ask in view of what you'll be receiving, hmm?"

The black church sits in the corner, past the courtyard proper, almost quaintly were it not for the high upside-down cross erected on its steeple. Several bosomy nuns busied themselves about the small building.

"But returning to my original promise, Privilato status entitles you to your very own personal aphrodisial farm. Note the garden, Mr. Foster."

You see the area of space, a great square of flower beds tended to by sultry women in white cloaks and hoods. Only their breasts could be seen through apertures in the cloaks.

"The women are Bio-Sorceresses, and they will suffice for your grounds-keeping staff. Every Privilato gets his one rod of Orgia Extremus Root. The Bio-Sorceresses are occult chemists who pick the root at harvest time, extract the Inhuman Growth hormones from it, and then further process a priceless Gonadotropic Elixir that not only abolishes sexual refraction between climaxes, but allows for massive ejaculatory volume and orgasms that last for not seconds but the equivalent of a full hour."

Your demonic mouth hangs open at the information.

"It should go without discourse that Privilatos spend most of their time engaged in one manner or other of licentious congress."

Hour-long orgasms, you think, *and a full-time boner...*

"And for such occasions when you *do* long for diversity of a non-sexual mode...there, in the corner opposite."

You follow Howard's finger to said corner, and see a troop of well-armed Conscripts surrounding one of those glowing green holes you saw the Privilato disembarking before he took his entourage into the Fetal Aperitifs bar.

"The Conscripts of the famed Diocletian Brigade will serve as your bodyguards when you wish to travel, and for traveling, you have at your constant disposal your very own Nectoport," Howard said.

For when I want to go out on the town, you think.

You must admit now...the possibility is sounding better and better.

"But wouldn't I need money?"

"Ah. The filthy lucre!" Howard takes you back inside, and turns into another room.

Jesus! The room's ceiling causes you to involuntarily look up.

"The Unholy Coffer-Vault," Howard says.

The room must be a hundred feet high and hundreds deep. It is filled with pallet after pallet of banded paper money.

"There must be a billion dollars here!"

"*Six* billion, Mr. Foster, though not dollars. Hellnotes." Howard's focus drifts off. "I once wrote a longish tale entitled 'Dreams in the

THE SENARY

Witch-House.' I thought it was most abysmal, but my friend August submitted it to Wright and got for me the unheard-of sum of $140.00. I've often wondered what that would be worth in Hellnotes."

As usual, you don't hear Howard; your attention, instead, has been hijacked by the airplane-hanger-sized vault of cash.

That's...A LOT of MONEY!

"You also need to be apprised, sir, that once you've expended the entirety of this vault, Satan's Treasurers will simply fill it up again."

Now you're getting dizzy looking at all of it...

"In spite of all of Hell's horrors, there's quite a bit for a *wealthy* man to do," Howard goads on. "Especially one who will know wealth for *eternity*..."

"Take me out of here," you ask suddenly. "I've got to think..."

Howard smiles.

He walks you back onto the parapet facing the inner wards and courtyard. Soft, fragrant breezes blow. You take in the 'scape of the fortress and beyond, more and more awed. *This place makes Bill Gates' house look like an out-house...and it could all be mine...*

But—

"Wait a minute. What good's all this money and luxury when I don't have friends to share it with?"

"Ah, there goes your good side shining through once more," Howard replies. "But I'll remind you that you had no abundance of friends in the Living World, and were quite content with that."

"Yeah, sure, but— Even a loner like me needs *some* friends."

Howard shrugs. "I'd like to think that *I'm* your friend, Mr. Foster. I've *delighted* in your company, and I truly admire your earthy resolve and unsophisticated good will."

The comment makes you look at him. "You're right, Howard. You are my friend. You're actually a pretty cool guy."

"I'm grateful and touched," and then Howard leans closer. "And not to portray myself too *terribly* mercenary...were you to accept the Senary, you'd easily have the power to relieve me of my laborious

148

duties at the Hall of Automatic Writers and have me re-assigned as, say, your personal archivist and biographer? And during any free time you saw fit to afford me…" Howard sighed dreamily. "I could forge on with my *serious* work."

"If I accept the Senary, Howard, then I'd do that—"

"Great Pegana!"

"But," you add with an odd stammer. "I-I-I… I don't think I'm going to accept…," yet even as the words leave your lips, you can't stop thinking about all this luxury, all this money, and all these women at your disposal.

"Alas, our time is nearly done," Howard tells you. He turns his pallid face back to the courtyards. "But I seem to have digressed yet again, with regard to your previous concerns. Besides myself, you *would* have some direct friends and acquaintances. See?"

Suddenly you smelled a simple, yet delectable aroma:

Burgers on the grill?

And once again your unnatural eyes follow Howard's gesture where a small congregation mingles. Several women and two men chatted happily about a barbeque, and sure enough, they were cooking hamburgers and hot dogs.

"Wait a minute," you object. "How can there be hamburgers and hot dogs in Hell? They must be fucked up, like *dick*-burgers or some shit, right?"

"Quite the contrary, Mr. Foster. It's true, there are no cattle nor swine in Hell, at least none that would taste the same as what you're accustomed to, yet through the marvel of Hexegenic Engineering, our Archlocks can produce foodstuffs that taste identical to any food on Earth." Howard's brow rises. "*If* one is so privileged."

"Privileged as in a Privilato, you mean."

"Quite. But, please. Be more attentive."

Next, you take closer note of the actual *people* at the barbeque, and the recognition jolts you.

You *know* everyone there.

"My father and mother!" you rejoice. "My sister, too!" They had all died years ago but now you deduce the direction of their Afterlife. Manning the grill itself is Randal, who glances upward and waves.

"And Randal! My best friend where I live, but…wait. He couldn't be here. He's not dead."

"Regrettably, he is, Mr. Foster," Howard tells you. "He was killed by an unstable intruder at his convenience store, very recently, apparently a quite obese homeless loafer. And the two women, whom I'm sure you'll recognize as well. They were killed last night, in something referred to as a 'drive-by.'"

You blink, and see them.

The two trashily attractive women turn and wave as well. Tight T-shirts cling to impressive bosoms, and they read: DO ME TILL I PUKE and NO GAG REFLEX.

"The hookers from the bar!" you exclaim.

"Indeed, and, look, there's one more."

Across the yard a beautiful girl-next-door type strides toward the congregation, pushing a wheelbarrow full of iced-down bottles of beer.

"Marcie! My very first girlfriend!" you instantly recognize. "And…man. She could suck a rock through a muffler! I didn't even know she was dead."

"I'm told she suffered a calamitous mishap involving a steamroller, but that's neither here nor there. What matters is that she's here, now, in the flesh. She as well as the other Human Damned who mean the most to you." Howard offers you a stern look. "And you'd be doing them all an *immeasurable* service by accepting the Senary, Mr. Foster."

"How's that?"

"Because there's no purpose in Lucifer keeping them here if you chose not to take up residence in the castle. I'm afraid your friends and family would be re-delegated back into Hell's mainstream, where they wouldn't fare well at all, I'm afraid."

Your gaze at him shifts. "So it's blackmail?"

"Lucifer has no qualms in revealing his motives. He wants something from you very badly, and he will go to great pains to coerce you into giving it to him. By offering you the prize of all your dreams and all your fantasies, which you will be able to enjoy forever."

"Sex, money, and luxury," you state rather than ask.

"Yes, and let us not forget *envy,* for you will be envied, by everyone in Hell. The gift Lucifer wishes to bestow upon you—in exchange for the gift you will give to him—represents the distillation of what all Humans desire most."

Now your eyes drift back to the red sky. "I still don't see what Lucifer gets out of the deal. Another soul? From what I can see, he's got plenty of those."

"Plenty, yes, but, lo, not yours. Not the Soul of one who willingly says no to God's promise of Salvation. For someone on the Fulcrum, to cast God aside in favor of Lucifer—*that,* Mr. Foster, is the only satisfaction Lucifer can ever truly enjoy."

Your vision reels again in the sight of the castle and its spectacular grounds, your friends and family, as well as the sheer carnal pleasure that awaits.

Howard turns around, with you on the stick. Suddenly you're facing all sixty-six of your personal concubines, standing beautiful and nude, in formation, the six Pamela Andersons right up front.

My God, you think. *I can't believe what I'm about to do...*

"Well, Mr. Foster?" Howard asks.

You don't even hesitate now. "I accept the Senary."

Howard's pale face seems to flush with relief. "Great Pegana! For a while I truly feared you would turn it down."

You sigh. "So what happens now?"

"Well, I hope you'll pardon the cliché, keeping in mind, however, that clichés are actually quite powerful totems of classicism here."

"Cliché?"

Howard nods. "You'll have to sign a formal contract."

"In blood, I suppose," you scoff.

"Yes. Your own."

Then it strikes you: "I can't sign a contract! I'm a pumpkin! I've got no hands!"

"Not *here,* Mr. Foster. Remember, right now you are still in fact an inhabitant of the Living World. Once I displace you back to the Larken House, The Senarial Messenger will have your contract prepared."

The Deaconess, you remember. "So *then* what? I sign and then kill myself?"

"Goodness no! You still have the rest of your life to enjoy, and you will be able to do so in grand style."

"I don't get it," you tell him.

"Upon putting your commitment into writing, Lucifer will grant a so-called 'signing bonus,' in the sum of six million dollars—"

"Six million! In cash?"

"Cash money, sir, this for you to suitably finance yourself until your physical life does, in fact, end. You will die painlessly in your sleep, Mr. Foster, six days after your sixty-sixth birthday."

Your demonic eyes bloom. *And I'm only thirty-three now! I've still got HALF MY LIFE left to live! And with six million bucks to boot!*

"There's only one point I need to make, though, Mr. Foster, and I cannot over-emphasize its pertinency." Howard looks at you quite seriously. "Once you've signed the contract, no amount of repentance can reverse its terms. *Once you've signed the contract...* You've abandoned God forever."

The words sink deep.

Howard shrugs. "But with all you'll be given here, in a lock-solid guarantee? What real man would ever *want* to repent?"

As you stare once more at all those beautiful women and demons, you can think of nothing—absolutely *nothing*—to counter what he's just said.

"You've got a deal, Howard," you say.

"And so do you, Mr. Foster. You have Lucifer's untold gratitude for the victory you're allowing him to score over God." Howard takes your Snot-Gourd off the stick. "We'll all be waiting for you thirty-three years from now. And I look forward to an eternity of friendship with you."

"Ditto," you say.

"And now? Until that wondrous time…" and Howard removes the pulpy plug in the back of the gourd, and the gas of your Ethereal Spirit slips out like air from a popped balloon…

(VII)

Foster's eyes snapped open like someone who'd just wakened from a nightmare of falling. He remained sweat-drenched in the attic chair, stewing in the insufferable heat. The hole in the wall met his direct line of sight, and through it all he could see was the straggly backyard tinted by moonlight.

The candles guttered all around him.

"You're back," whispered the Deaconess, "from a journey only eleven people in history have taken…"

Fostered nodded and drew in long breath. "It wasn't a dream, was it?"

"No. It was the greatest of all privileges." She stepped from the dark corner, her nude body shellacked in sweat itself. The macabre crucible of the baby's skullcap remained below the hole in the wall, but the Sterno had long gone out.

"I can tell by your aura," said the Deaconess. "You've accepted the Senary."

"Yes."

"Praise Lucifer," she sighed. "You will one day be a Privilato, the greatest thing to be in Hell save for Lucifer himself."

"Thirty-three years from now, I was told."

THE SENARY

The robust woman handed Foster a towel. He felt winded yet also content when he dried the sweat off his body and put his clothes back on. "I was also told something about six million dollars in cash…" The Deaconess grinned. "Such greed! How wonderful! But…first things first." She handed him a piece of paper…and an ice-pick.

"I guess this is self-explanatory," Foster commented. He didn't like pain but considering…

MEMORANDUM OF AGREEMENT, read the contract, along with a simplification of everything he'd been promised. *A lock-solid guarantee,* he recalled Howard's words. *And all I have to trade for it is my soul…*

He winced as he punctured his forearm with the awl, saw blood well up, then he ran the point along the blood.

Signing his name was harder than he thought.

"There."

The Deaconess looked awed at the sheet of paper. "You're so, so privileged…" Suddenly she fell to her knees, hugging Foster's hips. "Please, I beg you. In my own Damnation, recruit *me* into your harem! I would be so honored to serve a Privilato! Please!"

"Sure," Foster agreed, "but…where's that six million?"

Her smile seemed drunken now from what he'd just granted her. She kissed his crotch, and pointed behind him.

Two Samsonite suitcases sat on the other side of the room. *This can't be possible,* he thought, but when he opened them all he could do was stare for full minutes. Each hefty suitcase had been *filled* with banded $100 bills.

"The are six hundred bands, $10,000 per band," the Deaconess told him.

Foster grunted when he hefted each case. "It's a good thing these suitcases have wheels," but then another thought came to him. "Wait a minute. I can't roll two big-ass suitcases to a bus stop in a ghetto, at *night*. I'd get mugged in two seconds."

The Deaconess' bare skin glittered in the candlelight. "Lucifer guarantees your safety, not just in Hell but here also. From this point on, nothing can ever hurt you."

"Really?" Foster replied, not terribly confident.

"Oh, yes. In fact, you'll be protected by not one but two Warding Incantations, which are quite similar to the occult bridle which protects Manse Lucifer from any anti-Satanic endeavor."

"That's hardcore..."

"I'll demonstrate," and then the Deaconess wielded the ice-pick.

Foster's heart skipped a beat.

"Any object turned on you as a weapon will be repulsed—" The Deaconess threw the ice-pick hard as she could right at Foster—

"Shit!"

—but as it flew directly for his face, it veered harmlessly off and stuck in the bare-wood wall.

"Wow!"

"And any *person* who might attempt to assault you with his bare hands"—the nude woman smiled more mischievously—"will instantly have his blood removed from his body."

Foster recalled the bold but luckless insurgents' attempt to bomb the Manse, and how their blood had been magically sucked out of every orifice.

He looked at her, at the contract in her hand, then at the suitcases. "I guess...all there is for me to do now is—"

"Go home, and enjoy the rest of your life here with your riches, knowing that many more riches await when you die and rise to the glory of Lucifer."

So. That's it, I guess. Foster scratched his head. "What are your plans?"

"I will rise to that glory now, Mr. Foster," she said. "As your Senarial Messenger, I have but one more duty to perform: the execution of your contract."

Contract in hand, the Deaconess walked demurely to the chair, then stood on it.

"Hey! You're not going to—"

"But I must, Mr. Foster." From a rafter she pulled down a previously prepared noose and calmly put it around her neck. "I'll see you at your castle, in thirty-three years."

Foster froze.

The Deaconess rolled the contract into a ball, put it in her mouth, and stepped off the chair…

THUNK…

Jesus, Foster thought. He watched her hang there, the nude body agleam, swaying ever so gently. The rope creaked several times, then tightened to silence.

The suitcases thunked as he clumsily got them down the stairs. For some reason he was not the least bit at odds with the prospect of walking out of an abandoned house with two suitcases full of cash. He bumped the front door open with his rump, then wheeled the suitcases out into the teaming night. Moonlight cooly painted his face; crickets throbbed dense as electronic music. Foster felt enlivened even after this ultimate sin: his complete betrayal of God on High. Nor was he afraid of the fact that he was standing in a ghetto with six million dollars in cash.

A tiny light beamed above the bus stop just down the street the street. Foster looked at his watch, then chuckled and shook his head when he saw that the bus would be coming by six minutes from now.

"Yo!" shot the subtle voice. Dollar-store sandals slapped the cement. Then another darker voice—a man's.

"Shee-it…"

Bags in hand, Foster turned to face them, unworried.

"This the fuck askin' 'bout the Larken House," said the familiar prostitute whom Foster recognized at once: the woman who'd shown him where the house was, in the zebra-striped tube-top. Her white teeth gleamed when she smiled.

Two more figures stood on either side, a slouchy black male with his hair stuffed in a stocking that looked like Jiffy Pop, and a stocky high-chinned white guy in jeans cut off at mid-calf, a ten-sizes-too-large t-shirt, and a whitewall. He had snakes tattooed on the sides of his neck.

The black guy took one step. "What's in the suitcases, my man?"

Foster stalled, then laughed. "You wouldn't believe me if I told you."

The white guy bulled forward: "What's in the suitcases, white boy!" his voice boomed, and from nowhere he'd produced a very large buck knife.

"Six million dollars. If you want it, you'll have to take it."

The black guy nodded to the white one. "Just another poo-putt white muv-fuck."

"Shee-it," chuckled the white guy, and then he lunged with the knife.

"Cut dat boy!" the girl cheered on, "Cut him!" but it was only a second later when she shrieked. Plumes of blood launched from the attacker's eyes, mouth, nose, and ears. His crotch, too, expelled a copious volume which saturated the ludicrous pants. Then the knife clattered to the sidewalk and he collapsed.

"Ambrose!" shrieked the girl, fingertips to face. "What he do?"

"Don't know," crackled the voice of the black guy. There was a *click!* when he cocked a small pistol. "But he got somethin' in them cases, so's I'll just bust a cap in his face."

Here was the proof of Foster's new-found faith. "Go ahead," he said. "Bust all the 'caps' you want."

The tiny pistol's report sounded more like a loud hand-clap. A muzzle-flash bloomed in a way that Foster found spectacular. More spectacular, though, was the way the bullet was instantly repelled by the otherworldly ward surrounding him, and bounced immediately back into the black man's Adam's apple.

The man gargled, pop-eyed, and actually hopped about in the nearest weedy yard, hand clamped to his throat. He thrashed into some bushes and collapsed.

THE SENARY

Foster looked at the girl. "I'm protected by Lucifer, the Morning Star. That's what I did in the Larken House tonight. I *sold my soul*...to Lucifer."

The girl ran away.

"Hmm."

Foster wheeled the suitcases down the sidewalk and across the street. Exactly sixty-six steps later, he arrived at the glass-shattered bus shelter where he detected the ember of a cigarette brighten, then lessen.

"Oh, you," a ragged voice greeted. "How's it going?"

It was the bum from the Deaconess' church. "Hi, Forbes. I'm fine."

The bum sucked the cigarette down to the filter, then flicked it away with begrimed fingers. His body odor seemed thick as heavy fog. "You goin' on a trip?" he asked, noticing the suitcases. "Shit, man, the Greyhound station's the other way."

Am I...going on a trip? Foster could've laughed. "No, I'm just going home."

The bum, Forbes, showed a toothless grin. "I'll suck the nut out'a your cock for twenty bucks."

"Oh, no thanks," Foster said.

"Or you can jerk off in my mouth. Lotta guys like to do that for some reason, and I can always use the extra calories."

"Uh, no. No thanks." Foster pulled some twenties out of his pocket and passed them to the bum. "But here's some food money for you."

Even in the dark, the bum's face beamed. "Hey, man! Thanks! God bless ya!"

Not God. Not anymore...

"Yeah, I'm takin' the bus to the Bayway Bridge to sleep. Ain't sleepin' in the Deaconess' church no more."

"Yes, I remember you telling me. Bad dreams."

"But I sure miss her. Somethin' happened to her, somethin' fucked her up." Now the bum looked beseeching. "You seen her tonight?"

Foster stared down at him. "Do you really want to know, Forbes?"

158

"Well...sure. You seen her?"

"Yes. About ten minutes ago—or, more likely, *six* minutes ago—I saw her commit suicide in a house across the street—the Larken House."

Forbes' pose stiffened. "No way, man!"

"I'm afraid so. She killed herself as a means of executing a contract I had just signed."

"Fuck! A contract?"

"I sold my soul to the Devil tonight, Forbes. Sounds crazy, doesn't it?"

"Shit yeah, man! The Devil? Really?"

"Yes," Foster calmly stated. "The Devil. I'm protected by the Devil. I am now a *disciple*...of the Devil."

"Aw, you're full'a shit," then—

SCHULP

Foster never saw the knife in Forbes' mangy hand, until that same hand was already pulling it out of Foster's lower abdomen.

Holy— You gotta be—

Shock—and also *outrage*—made Foster's face feel twice its size. Blood like hot soup poured through his fingers; he also smelled his own feces, as the knife had clearly punctured intestines. He began to convulse as he slumped to the other corner of the shelter.

"Fuckin' people always tellin' me bullshit 'cos they just think I'm a retarded bum, man," Forbes complained. "Well, fuck them and fuck you."

"Forbes," Foster croaked. "Call an ambu—"

"Here's your fuckin' protection, fucker," and then the bum stuck the knife in again, several more times.

What Foster felt more than the pain was simply outrage.

"I could use some new clothes, ya shit," Forbes said, but he just stared and stared when he opened one of the suitcases. He scratched his beard, begetting dandruff. Then:

"What a fuckin' great day!" He slapped the case closed. "Thank you, God!"

THE SENARY

Foster watched through hemorrhaged eyes as Forbes grabbed the suitcases and ambled away in the dark.

What a ripoff…

Each time Foster coughed, blood sprayed into the air and more innards uncoiled in his hands. He died exactly six minutes later.

EPILOGUE

Was it a dream?

You hear a *THUNK!* as in the sound of a cleaver striking a cutting board, and then comes the impression of rising—up a circular staircase?—and you hear footsteps. Then—open air.

Finally your eyelids prize apart.

"'Let not thy hand be stretched out to receive, and shut when thou shouldest pay,'" comes a high-pitched, New England accent.

Your vision re-forms and then you know that—

This…is no dream.

You are back at the Privilato castle, and the first thing you see is the grand courtyard and inner wards.

It's Howard who looks back at you; he seems elated, but there's also a tinge of scorn in his eyes. "It's a line from the Bible," his voice piped, "which I foolhardily never believed in. The *Book of Ecclesiasticus,* parablizing the sin of greed. I'd have been wiser to have heeded that book, rather than in obsessing over the creation of my own."

"You promised me thirty-three years! You promised me supernatural protection!" you wail at him.

"I, personally, forged no such promise, Mr. Foster. It was, instead—as you're well aware—*Lucifer's* promise."

"I sold my soul for a price!" you scream.

"Consider the author of the terms," Howard lamented. "It's so very regrettable: that resonant and universal power known as avarice.

You were a very, very easy victim, Mr. Foster. But, honestly! Why do you think they call him the Lord of Lies, the Great Deceiver?"

"This is bullshit!" but then only now do you realize something crucial, because when you try to look around, your head will not obey the commands of your brain. "What-what—"

"—happened to you?" Howard finishes. "It's elementary. You died, you went to Hell, and immediately upon the commencement of your eternal Damnation, you were decapitated." Howard, then, holds up a mirror that reflects back your severed head which has been neatly propped upright within a stone sconce. "And, as you have hopefully cogitated, we are back at the Chateau-Gaillard—"

"*My* castle!" you spit in outrage, "where I'm supposed to spend eternity living in luxury as a Privilato! But I can't be a Privilato with my fuckin' HEAD cut off!"

Howard's voice, in spite of its elevated pitch, seems to turn foreboding, "Not your castle, Mr. Foster. Mine."

Only now do your eyes lower to scan the rest of Howard's form. He's no longer dressed in the shabby 1920's-styled shirt and slacks...

He's wearing a surplice of multifaceted jewels of every color conceivable and inconceivable. An ornate "P" has been mysteriously imbued on his forehead. More jewels glitter when Howard smiles: the most illustrious dental implants. "You haven't won the Senary, Mr. Foster. I have. Lucifer is not only notoriously dishonest, he's also *industriously* dishonest. And I'd say your current circumstance demonstrates the extent of his machinations. By effectively causing you to believe that you won the Senary, that ever-important soul-saving one-percent of your free-will was corrupted, and since I caused your tide to turn, so to speak, the Senary has been awarded to *me*."

"This is a pile of shit!" you bellow. "You screwed me!"

"Indeed—"

"I could've gone to Heaven!"

"Quite right, but here you are instead," and then Howard picks your head up by the hair and carries you along, holding it over the ramparts. "Enjoy the view while you can. You'll not see my beautiful castle again."

"It's supposed to be *my* beautiful castle!" you're sobbing now. "That was the deal!"

"That was the deal that your greed allowed you to perceive. So intoxicated were you, Mr. Foster, by the prospect of having all of this, that you never once considered the unreliability of the monarch here. Love is blind, they say, which is true, but it's truer still that greed is so much *more* blind." Howard looks forlorn for a moment. "The *genuine* deal is that I won the Senary and its sequent Privilato status by convincing you of the opposite, for enticing you to give your salvation to Lucifer of your own free will. It really is quite a prize for my master and I might add, my master rewards those who do him service."

"I won, damn it! Not you! *I* won!"

"You've won nothing but what your greed and betrayal of faith have earned you."

The sound of a breeze stretches over the vast landscape.

"Where's my body?" you moan now, tears running.

"There," and Howard holds your head between two merlons where you see the revelers in the courtyard: your mother, father, and sister; Randal, and the two rowdy prostitutes; Marcie, your first girlfriend; and the six Pamela Andersons. They're all chatting happily as they busy themselves around the barbeque. Racks of ribs have already been lain across the grill, while Randal and Marcie are systematically sawing or cleaving steaks off of the headless body stretched across a long butcher block table. *Your* body.

You begin to cry like a baby.

"There, there," Howard consoles, and after a few more steps that familiar black static crackles, you scream, and—

WHAM!

—you're someplace else, and it only takes you a moment to realize that you've seen this place before as well, not in reality but in the Hectographs Howard showed you earlier. Thousands and thousands of heads look at *your* head as Howard walks you through Lucifer's Atrium, Great Hall, Dining Room, and, lastly, the Bed Chamber.

Wall after wall after wall of living female heads.

Many of them smile when you pass by.

"So behold now, Mr. Foster, the *true* seat of your destiny. You will remain here forever, and though I can fathom your disappointment in now acknowledging the ruse played on you, you may at least take some solace in knowing that you have inherited a unique privilege…"

Oh no, your thoughts croak when Howard takes you into Lucifer's circular-walled commode-chamber, where more, *more* female heads look at you with the most satisfied smiles. The head smiling the most, however, is that of the lone chubby-faced blond lying cheek-down on the gilded toilet-stand.

"Oh please!" she exclaims in a trashy Southern accent. "Please let it be true!"

"And so it is, my dear," Howard tells the head as he lifts it off the stand and flings it to the floor.

And what he puts in its place on the stand is *your* head.

"You are now the first male head to become a permanent fixture at Manse Lucifer," Howard says.

"Howard!" you scream. "I'm begging you, man! Don't do this to me!"

"Ah, but really, you've done it to yourself, haven't you?" and then Howard turns to make his exit.

"Don't leave me here! This isn't fair! You tricked me! I don't deserve to be the Devil's toilet paper for eternity, do I? My sins weren't *that* bad!"

"Sin is relative, Mr. Foster," pipes Howard's voice a final time. "And with those words I'm afraid I must take my leave and enjoy the privileges I've duly inherited." Howard sighs dreamily, and smiles with his jewels for teeth. "At last, I'll finally be able to write *The Lurker at the Threshold!* And thank you, Mr. Foster, very much. I could never have won the Senary without you…"

"NOOOOOOOOOOO!"

Howard leaves the commode-chamber and closes the head-paneled door behind him.

All the heads which form the walls, floor, and ceiling of the room begin to laugh.

And all you can do now is sit there in dread, wondering how often the master of Manse Lucifer moves his bowels...

HEAD, HUNTED

JOHN SHIRLEY

"They want me? You're sure? They don't care about the whole stock options thing?"

"The guy said he was only interested in your production record, Gus. He says to me, 'I understand Gus Taft maximizes production. That's where we're coming from.' I mean, you probably won't get prosecuted for the back-dating thing, Gus—Steve Jobs got off, and lots of the others. You will too, man. And they know that. Shit, guys from AIG are getting work out there in the marketplace."

Gus and Morrie were having a late afternoon cocktail in The Cubicle, a literally cubical building of plas-glass, tinted in places, the sides mostly transparent, restaurant, bar and, on the third floor, an art gallery. You could see the people walking by on the windy Chicago sidewalk, looking kind of ghostly—everything was bloodless through the glass—and they could see you. They can see you scratch your nuts or pick your damn nose, Gus thought, with disgust. He missed the old days of insular, windowless bars, with plenty of dark wood, gloomy booths, places with some real atmosphere where you could smoke a cigar and get some work done without feeling like strangers were at your elbow, listening, looking over your shoulder. And this place—an art gallery too, for Chris'sakes. How faggy could you be. Faggy as that waiter...

It was early autumn, and a newly fallen maple leaf, damp and crinkled at the edges, blew against the glass and stuck there. The pale young waiter with the spiky haircut glared at the leaf, pursing his lips.

"I mean, come on," Morrie was saying, between nibbles on the olive from his martini, "backdating executive options, big whoop. They were making an example of you… Everybody had to give the agency a few sacrificial lambs. Howard Gaines told me they were sorry as all Hell to let you go—you got those plants running at twenty-five percent higher capacity with twenty-five per cent less staff! That's magic, pal! Believe me, they'd never have let you go if it wasn't a choice between you and the CFO. Everyone knows it, Gus—you're the Man!"

Morrie grinned at him, his long cadaverous face looking even more so in the electric-blue light shining up from inside the transparent bar, a fan of blue and green, refracted from the martini glass, across his right cheek. Gus tried not to stare at that one crooked front tooth; he'd always wondered why Morrie didn't get it fixed. He was a successful head hunter, ran his own agency filling executive spots, he could afford it.

Gus picked up his own glass and toasted Morrie, one middle-aged white guy to another. "We gotta stick together, guys like us. A dying breed. Thanks for thinking of me, man."

"You aren't listening, Gus—they came and *asked* for you. They said they tried to find you directly but you were out of town…after you got, uh, laid off over that little rule bust, you were gone." He sipped his drink. "Where'd you go anyway?"

"Hm? Oh, I took some time. Thailand. Why not. Corrina left me last year. So…"

Morrie leaned toward him so Gus could smell some rotting bit of breakfast stuck in that crooked tooth, and it wasn't pleasant. "You go to one of those special Bangkok, uh…you know…"

Gus raised a hand to signify Don't Go There. He didn't want to talk about those girls. Not one of them over fourteen. Doing was one thing, when you were wasted and you had three Viagra in you. But talking about it made his stomach flip-flop. Corrina had been so self-righteous…

"Hey what goes on there stays there, right, Morrie? So—how do I meet the guy doing the hiring?"

«« —»»

"Howdy—this Central Power?" Gus asked.

The reception area of Room 3223, a leased room in a downtown skyscraper, was a stifling concoction of cork walls, no furniture but the boxlike counter with its single red phone which didn't seem to be plugged into anything. The woman behind the reception counter in the overlit, almost featureless waiting room looked at him in startlement, and seemed to squeak out, "Mmph please mmph?" in response.

She was a mousy little woman with stiff brown hair and large eyes, dark blue but so dilated they might've been black. A single curling hair grew out of a large mole on her right cheek. And she seemed short, too short for the counter. But what struck Gus about her was the almost tangible reek of fear she gave off.

"I'm Gus Taft? I had an appointment with Mr. Overgrin…if this is Central Power."

He looked around and once more thought it strange there was no logo, no decorative paintings, no carpet—the floor, he saw now, was concrete, and smelled like it had just dried.

"Yes," she said suddenly, as if prodded to speak. Her voice squeaky, tremulous. "Yes, Mr. Taft. Mr. Overgrin is…is expecting you."

"I guess you folks just moved in, eh? Interior decorator still at it?"

"Yes. Mr. Overgrin is…Ow!" She winced. "Yes the Decorator is still at it. Yes he is. The interior decorator. I mean. Not Mr…Mr. Overgrin…"

"Are you okay, miss?" Gus said impulsively. He imagined coming to her aid, somehow—maybe she'd just gotten a bad papercut she didn't want to show him—and maybe picking up on her. She might be better looking from the neck down.

"Yes, I'm…the interior decorator is…Ow! I'm fine."

He stepped closer, as casually as he could manage, and glanced down over the edge of the counter, wondering was she a midget or what, the counter up to her collarbone, and then he froze, seeing …

"Mr. Taft! Can I call you Gus? I'm Dick Overgrin!"

Gus turned, dazed, to the big man in the suit, a red-faced man with a large rubbery nose and a wide, wide smile and blocky teeth that looked faintly pink. Unusually large shoes. Nice shoes, Italian looked like, but almost as big as clown feet. He barely took this in—his mind was still on the receptionist; how she was plugged into what looked like a rough flat stone table, on the other side of the counter. He must have seen that wrong. Must've been an illusion of…of…

It was like she was growing out of the hole in the stone, from the waist up, blue business dress-suit and all, like she was a potted plant…

But he made himself advance to Dick Overgrin—what wide, jiggly cheeks the man had, what tiny black pupils in his eyes—and shake his hand. How odd the guy's hand felt, like cellophane. His suit was the color of dried blood, with wide shoulders—they must be padded—and wide lapels. Gus had the odd feeling that Overgrin's height kept changing. When he came closer, Overgrin seemed to shrink a little; when he stood back he felt as if he were looking up a sequoia.

And there was a heat…a heat that seemed to emanate from the man…

I must be coming down with something, Gus thought. Fever. Too much stress. Hope I didn't catch anything in Thailand.

Overgrin let go of his hand—Gus's palm stung, ever so slightly, after the contact—and gestured toward a door behind him. "Right this way. We'll show you the power plant."

Gus blinked in surprise. They were in the middle of downtown Chicago—how could there be a power plant right here, to show? Must be talking about a model or a video of the facility. *Get a grip, Gus.*

He heard the receptionist squeak, saw Overgrin narrow his eyes and look at her. Heard a hissing sound, a faint moan of despair. Turned to look at her...and she was gone.

How had she gone anywhere? Now that he looked a little closer at the counter, he could see no way for her to get out from behind it. There was no door behind her, no break in the counter...

"Mr. Taft? This way..."

"Oh sure. Call me Gus," he added mechanically, following Overgrin through the door, down a hallway as featureless as the reception room, and into what seemed to be a conference room without a conference table. There was a window, but it was curtained. It was just a big empty room with fluorescent lighting. Gus was aware that his heart was pounding. Had he been set up? Was Overgrin actually some kind of federal agent? Was he about to be arrested for his part in the stock options scandal? His lawyer had said he was in the clear...

There was a door on the left, now—and Gus was pretty sure there hadn't been one there before.

Seriously, he thought, I must have a fever. Delirium. Picked up something in Bangkok...

Overgrin stepped to the door, put his hand on the knob, and said, "We've got a new inter-plane transportation system for mortals..."

Mortals? Had he actually said *mortals*?

"...got control of the Nectoports back," Overgrin was saying, "and this is a modification of that technology. Interworld Nectoport. Take my arm, please. It'll be a bit dizzying..."

Gus found himself putting his hand on the crook of Overgrin's arm and the door opened...but it didn't open with the doorknob. The door simply dimpled inward, then vanished, replaced by a green blob of light—and then (he wasn't sure if this was something he was seeing in his mind, since it seemed transparent, tenuous) there was a gigantic mouth on the other side—with a crooked front tooth. Gus heard himself screaming wordlessly, the sound cut off as his body melted away, the mouth inhaling so that they were sucked into it on a plume of hot fetid air, sucked like smoke through a crack pipe; he and Overgrin had become all vaporous like pipesmoke, were slurped through a roaring white noise, Gus's gaseous body twisting around and around like a dishrag being squeezed of water, and then…

Then they were solid again, reconstituted, standing on a platform overlooking a blood-red sea. Far below, unspeakable things oozed to the surface, churned, and withdrew grumbling. Overgrin was saying something about how you got used to the inter-plane transport. In time…

This place was hot, like a cauldron, the sky not some infinite reach—like an Earthly sky would have— but a kind of lid over the world. But it wasn't exactly a heat he felt on his body—it was more a psychic feeling of dislike from someone. The time he'd met that prosecutor, he'd known the guy despised him; he could feel it. It was as if this whole world despised you and you felt it as a heat that wanted to consume you inside…and never quite did.

"That's the Sea of Cagliostro—you see, over there, the cabanas on the shore? When you need to stay in Hell for a while you'll get a free home there…"

"Did you say…"

"Well yes. That's the term you prefer, isn't it? Hell? Hades? You can just make out the River Styx over there…and there's Mephistopolis…quite the thriving place…"

Overgrin's appearance seemed to waver around the edges and Gus had a definite sense that the man's appearance was a camouflage, a disguise, and his real self was trying to break out.

"I…I'm in…" Gus thought: I'm dreaming. But it doesn't feel like a dream. Only, it kind of does. And yet…round and round…dream and real, real and dream…

"Now, if you'll come right through this Nectoport…" Gus let himself be whooshed to several more locations. He stared at each of them with mute incomprehension. St. Iscariot Abbey. Boniface Square. ("You'll get your entertainment here, after a long cycle of work at the plant, if you take the job…I see Robert Johnson's playing at the nightclub, tonight...") Rockefeller Mint. ("A businessman likes to know where the money is, eh? Am I right?") Osiris Heights. ("Beautiful, isn't it? The screams of the slaves, here, are so melodious. Like birdsong. You may well earn a nice residence in Osiris. After. You know...") The Mephisto Building. "And here's the Department of Raw Materials—"

At the Department of Raw Materials Gus was stricken from his numbness by the monumental, purulent heaps of dead bodies, and stripped, wet bones, slated for "recycling". All the bodies showing the most appalling signs of torture, maiming, expressions of physical contempt.

"And here's the Office of Transfiguration..."

They paused inside a great work room, to gaze at a row of decapitated heads, men and women of various races, the heads with rolling eyes, lolling, snapping tongues, shouting hoarsely—with what voice boxes?—begging to be killed, begging for death. While a thing...an enormous multiarmed *thing,* its limbs seemingly endlessly stretchable...attached the heads, one by one, to all the wrong bodies in the wrong places, sealing them in place with specialized instruments; and beyond them bodies were crushed under a great roller, yet seemed to live on anyway, though squashed flat and squealing.

"I just wanted you to know, Gus," said Overgrin, absently kicking one of the waiting heads into a pile of reeking offal, "that this facility is at your disposal. I know you're innovative and you might want to use this facility to alter the plant workers, increase efficiency..."

"Uck..." was all Gus could get out, swaying. "I...cuh...cuh..."

"Having adaptation shock, I see. Quite normal. I thought it best to simply bring you—you'd not have believed me if I'd tried to prepare you. And of course it's not as, er, uncomfortable here as people make out, depending on your position in the, ah, hierarchy. As an independent contractor here you'd be essentially a Hierarchal, in status at least, and as such not treated like a mortal. Were it not for our pre-arrangements, of course, you'd have been torn limb from limb by now..."

HEAD, HUNTED

"Uck..."

"...or possibly skinned alive...and I mean alive, very alive..."

"Uck..."

"And then slow roasted. And then...but it's irrelevant, delicious as it might be to contemplate. You're in a special position here. You've already, of course, earned a place in Hell—but as a Special Contractor you'll be protected."

"Uck..."

"Oh if you're going to vomit, don't waste it, we do want to make a good impression on...on those who are monitoring us from afar. Here, vomit in this head's mouth...good, good... Oh, do you recognize him, by the way? An important person in Enron, I believe, before he died. Died not long ago, as human time is measured... Right, I'll chuck him in the offal and we're off... Right through here."

Through a blue blur, and then they were standing on a catwalk overlooking what appeared to be an ordinary industrial complex. But looking closer he saw things scuttling around at the bases of the metal towers, dragging shrieking souls behind them.

"The Industrial Complex. A nice view from here. There's the Central Power Plant where you'll work if you take the job."

"I...uh...cuh..."

"One more jump through this handy Nectoport...and here we are, the main power generation room of the Central Power Plant. Now, if you take the job, what we're looking for is simple: an increase of efficiency along the lines of what you accomplished in energy plants in the USA. We want more power, faster. The trouble is, our power derives from Agonicity, obtained from the suffering of souls, and there's a spacial saturation point for souls in this facility, we can't get too many in here, since souls each have their own life-force fields. Of course you can compress them hugely but there's only so many sardines you can crowd into a can, am I right? So we're looking for a greater efficiency, and someone to keep an eye on it once that's accomplished, keep it running smoothly. The Ushers are prone to getting caught up in the torture

176

and losing sight of the bigger picture, not shifting from victim to victim fast enough, and so on. Being mere low class scum, of course, they probably never saw the bigger picture at all."

"Uck," Gus said, not sure how he was managing to stay standing as he stared around at the power plant.

An intricate array of devices linked the tortured souls—which looked very much like solid, living people, to Gus. Many of them were being compressed, slowly crushed, and he could see the energy released from their pain glimmering as it was sucked up in the intake mechanisms operated by demons; leering, gleeful demons. The looks on the faces of the tortured souls—the looks on the faces of the demons...The contrast between the two sets of expressions constituted some kind of archetypal existential equation...

It had to be a nightmare, Gus decided. And it was. And it was real at the same time. It was both. It was a real nightmare, it was nightmarishly real.

"I wonder," Overgrin said, "if you'd mind if I changed out of this mortal shell—it really is quite uncomfortable..."

He stuck his finger deep in one nostril and started digging around in there—and then ripped his own face from his skull...only it wasn't his face, it was his outer face, it was his mortal mask. He removed it, and then quickly stripped off the suit and false human body, to reveal his real form: a looming, hooved being, his face classically diabolic, his massive head topped with magnificent curling horns.

Gus screamed and turned to run, to run blindly...and tripped over a transparent pipe through which ran semi-vaporized human souls, screaming silently as they were compressed through it.

Overgrin helped him to his feet and put a drink in his hand. "This'll brace you up," he said, chuckling, as Gus automatically drank it down, desperate for any escape from the horror. "You're suffering from instinctive reaction, I guess—and perhaps you have some shred of empathy left. Most humans only suppress it, few actually get rid of it completely. You will, though, in time, if you work for us...unless you don't want to. Some feel it enhances the pleasure of tormenting, to keep some empathy... Feeling better? It's a special sort of whiskey... Tastes slightly of piss, I know, and there's a reason for that, but it has all the kick you need..."

Gus was feeling better, in fact. He felt slightly drunk, numb around the edges, a trifle energized. The demon Overgrin was saying something about how the drink was mostly alcohol and cocaine distilled from the piss of drug addicts, but Gus, at that moment, didn't care where it came from. Overgrin took him into an observation booth, where the screaming of tortured souls was muffled, making it easier to talk.

"And really, old boy," said the demon Overgrin, slapping him on the back, making him stagger, "none of this should upset you terribly. Think back! We admire all the vices here but there's a time and place for everything and this is no time for hypocrisy, old boy! After all, you were a big man in Midwest Energy, which owned dozens of coal mines. You started out in public relations, back in the '70s, convincing people that black lung and the toxic-gas in the mines were things of the past—but of course they aren't. You didn't mind. Not our man Gus! Later on, you knew perfectly well that the coal-fired power plants were causing lung cancer and emphysema, deaths from asthma. You knew they were spreading mercury pollution around the world. You didn't mind! And the lobbyists you ran for the company—getting those troublesome regulations eliminated. Millions suffered for it— and you didn't mind that either! And we admired that! But what really impressed us was when you worked out how to get rid of twenty-five percent of the workers at the plants, to increase profitability and kick the stock up, while at the same time getting twenty-five percent more efficiency! Of course you did some of it with outsourcing the billing and accounting staff—you are a kind of outsourcing for us, Gus old boy!—and quietly removing people who were in charge of keeping the pollution down to a dull roar, but a great deal of it you did by simply putting a fuck of a lot more pressure on the employees you had left! Getting them to work longer hours for less pay, undercutting unions, union busting where you could, so they had to work harder in more dangerous circumstances, it was just...diabolic! Just so admirably diabolic! We didn't want to wait till you died—we wanted you right now! You'll be allowed plenty of leave in the upper world, with lots of *very* young girls who—as usual—will be forced to pretend they like you touching them when in fact—" He paused to chuckle appreciatively. "—when in fact they want to scream with disgust whenever you touch them! *Exquisite!* You'll be paid a million dollars a year—oh believe me, we have an appreciation of the *value of money* down here!—and you'll live for hundreds more mortal years, so long as you keep things hopping in the Plant, and then, when you are allowed to shuffle off the ol' mortal coil, why, you'll have earned a special position in the Hierarchy of the afterlife... It's all in your contract. Contract is over here, on this desk, written on the skin of those innocents you've helped kill with your work at Midwest Energy... Gus? You're not going to faint are you?"

The piss whiskey had all but worn off—and Gus found himself looking through the window of the booth, at the damned souls and the demons; found himself looking back and forth between those two sets of expressions...those two sets of eyes...the eyes of those being tortured to provide energy, and the eyes of the torturers...and it was all too terrifyingly familiar. From where? From some dark closet in the back of his conscience where he'd looked, just once, after seeing a bit of news footage about a child dying of cancer near one of their power plants...

He felt a horrible inner wrench, an indescribable wave of self disgust rolling over him, like a tsunami of diarrhea, and he covered his eyes and said, "For God's sake—kill me and start punishing me! Or...or send me back to Earth if you're willing! I can't take this!"

"So you don't want the job?" Overgrin sighed. "Very disappointing indeed. I'm going to be punished for this. For at least a century. Oh well. I just thought you might enjoy the glorious challenge of it all. I mean, a man of your instincts. I guess, though, with your history, a mere million a year and all those whoring little girls isn't enough to tempt you… I was willing to make it three million a year but…well…if you feel you're not able to bear it…"

Three million a year. Teenaged girls…

"Just step through here, Mr. Taft, and I'll return you to your own world…"

Gus opened his eyes as a thought struck him. Those faces in the pipes. The machine with the spikes coming down. The slow, slow meat grinder…

The blue blob of light awaited him. Beyond it he could see that reception room and the door out to the corridor of the office building; a corridor that would lead to the elevator, that would lead to the entry hall, that would lead to the street, that would put him back on the sidewalk of Chicago, good old, familiar Chicago. Where he was aging and out of work and without any real prospects.

A man could get used to all kinds of things. He'd proven that himself.

Gus cleared his throat and said, hoarsely, "Suppose you redirected those pipes there, into the grinders, directly, mixing in the, ah, slurry-souls and the physicalized souls. That might increase the overall torment a great deal, in itself. The two together would torment one another, it seems to me. Then if you replaced some of these demons with mortal souls, souls who used to work for certain American companies, people I know who're basically psychopathic, they could be counted on not to get distracted by the, what you call it, delights of cruelty, they're really more practical than that… I could supervise them personally… Now over here…"

"Gus? Before we go on with our plans, would you like to sign the contract now? I've upped the price to three million. Apart from that, it's not really negotiable, so…"

"Well…why the Hell not. Here you go. Done. You got any more of that piss whiskey?"

"Certainly. I'll have a case sent over to your cabana… And I have a bottle right here." Overgrin poured them each a drink. "We'll drink to the beginning of a beautiful relationship. But then, in a way, we've always worked together. Here's to unregulated free enterprise—and the prospect of *infinite* profitability!"

THEN SHALL THE REIGN OF LUCIFER END...

JOHN EVERSON

R hi kissed the dust on the wooden floor and tasted the rancid spice of age. Brett and Charlie had brought her here to dispose of. She had no illusions about their motives. After they'd drugged her, tied her up, beaten and then raped her repeatedly, she had known hours ago why, after a week in hell on earth, they had finally driven her out to the most remote location in the county. They were frightened by what they'd done to her over the past few days in that locked room, and knew they would never get away with it if she went free. She was used up now, and they wanted her to die. Only trouble was, from what she could tell, they were too scared to actually take care of the deed themselves.

For days they'd kept her locked in a room in the city. They'd chained her, abused her and used her like an animal. She had swallowed their sour cum and even more sour piss, as they had laughed and pulled her hair to force her to nod yes every time they asked "mmm, you like it?" But through all of the degradation and torture, they had always fucked her with condoms, as if afraid that they might get her pregnant. They had been very intent on learning her cycle when they had first picked her up and brought her to the torture room. She had taken that as a good sign that they intended to let her go eventually.

THEN SHALL THE REIGN...

So when they both used her on the dirty planks of the abandoned house and, for the first time, both rode her bareback, Rhi knew it was over for her.

End of the line.

This time she just laid there, without protest, as they filled her up with so much hot spunk that it oozed back out over her swollen distended labial lips. Their orgasms burned like rough sandpaper on a fresh wound as their sperm coated the bruised and bleeding flesh inside her. The rash on her thighs burned from the chafing of their hairy, anxious legs and a smell like dead fish filled the room as they pummeled her again and again, knocking her head on the boards. She hadn't showered in a week, and Rhi cried as she smelled the rank scent of herself and their stale sweat mingle while the pain spread again all across her belly and legs.

Afterwards, they punched her in the gut and kicked her in the back and laughed until she had staggered away from them and then fallen over to lie trembling on the bare floor like a drunk with the tremens.

She figured they had originally lugged her to the old farmhouse thinking she was dead—she'd blacked out at some point back in the city, in the torture room. They probably had thought she was gone for good. From the red, searing pain in her back and neck, she wished they had been right. But instead, after they muscled her from the trunk and tossed her here on the floor of the abandoned old house, she had started to moan. She supposed that only then had they realized she was not dead. Not even close. That's when they decided to take advantage of the situation to plant one more fuck in her. Actually two, for the price of one. It was no bargain as far as Rhi was concerned.

Fuck it hurt. The pain rolled over her brain in waves of awful surf. She could taste the iron of her blood and the acid of her pain and defeat with every swallow. She'd done nothing to deserve this but exist...sometimes existing was a condemnation in and of itself.

After they'd done their business, they'd left her there, bleeding and dying on the floor of the old house. Rhi kept her eyes closed and relished the quiet. The house was silent as death without her rapists in the room. She could feel the warmth of her blood and their foul sperm leaking out of her to stain the floor beneath, but she didn't dare try to move. The room may have been still, but everything screamed too loud inside. Maybe she *would* finally die here, she hoped. She'd never wanted to live anyway. Not because anything unusual had happened to her. She'd been dumped last month, again, by another shiftless loser who'd fucked her and then run. And her mom had met her match this summer in the big C. The docs'd tried to saw off mom's boobs to save her, but it didn't do any good. In just a few months, Rhi had watched the poor woman go from a robust, brassy, take-no-shit-from-anyone woman to a carved-up shell of zombie without any fat, hair or spirit.

But Rhi knew her mom's death and her own chronic disease of getting dumped were not reasons to give up; everyone goes through shit like that. The problem was, Rhi had never felt all that committed to life anyway. She never had her mom's spirit, and couldn't just fuck and be happy like so many of the guys she met…and lost. Maybe she just didn't have the energy to keep them. Lately, she hadn't had the energy to care whether she lived or died. Why else would she have been stupid enough to answer an ad that had read simply, *"Female test subject wanted. Must be over 18, and willing to pose nude. E-mail photo and bra size to demonx@inferno.com."*

Their voices were returning. They were chanting and the odor of something like October burning leaves filled the air. Rhi had a flash of Easter mass at church when she was a girl, and it occurred to her what the smell was. Not autumn leaves.

Incense.

The strange words grew closer. More intense. Rhi's toes clenched as she waited for the inevitable. And then it happened. Charlie's hairy fingers clenched her shoulder and pulled Rhi up to her knees. Something shiny glinted in Brett's hand.

That's when the pain really began.

THEN SHALL THE REIGN...

«« — »»

When Rhi came to again, it was night. Blackness blanketed her body. Muscles screamed in agony when she lifted her head. The memory of why replayed in vivid agony behind her eyes. Charlie and Brett had walked around her in a circle chanting strange words and spreading incense; then they had knelt and begun to carve her alive with a flimsy serrated steak knife, there on the floor. When the cutting began, she'd found one last burst of energy she didn't know she even had. Maybe she didn't totally want to die after all? She had punched and kicked and tried to escape, but was too weak from a week of fighting ropes and beatings. Charlie subdued her easily with a couple hard fists to the jaw and a tight chokehold around the neck.

Through the haze of pain, Rhi thought that they still did not seem intent on killing her…they hurt like a bitch, but none of the blades bit deep. They stung more than stabbed, crossing and crisscrossing the surface of her back, drawing lines of pain in her shoulders and ribs and then, when they flipped her bloody body to face them, they carved her breasts and belly. Maybe they were trying to draw her pain out? These were not the shrieking buffoons who had raped her and laughed at her for days. Charlie and Brett looked deadly serious, as they held her down and drew designs on her in permanent ink; blood.

She felt every cut now, and stared at her naked chest—her chest whose nipples and breasts those apes had pawed and twisted and sucked for hours—to see what horrible words they had finally decided to etch into her indelibly, flesh graffiti. They had to be words, she thought. Their knives had cut her for hours it seemed, slowly and deliberately, in curls and straight lines. They had skipped space and sliced again, splitting the skin dozens of times to free rivers of liquid fire that left her hoarse from screaming. She couldn't move through it all, as one of them always pinned her hard to the floor while the other

190

drew bloody notes in her skin. Her throat now felt too swollen to speak. As she stared through the shadows at herself, desperately afraid of what scars they had forced her to wear for life, she realized that it was not all black around her. She could make out the curves and twists of ornate tattoos of blood that connected her nipples to her bellybutton and arrowed down to that crusted thatch between her legs. Everything wept tears of blood, and the air itself seemed to cry with her. The faint glow in the room was of red, horrible light.

When Rhi tried to move, her back threatened to explode. And her left leg felt numb…probably from where they had kicked it, again and again, like a soccer ball.

Why? Rhi whispered…*what did I do…*

Fuck you! A voice answered from the darkness. Taunting. *What did any of us do? Yet here we are. Just fucking deal with it, like everyone else. So your daddy fucked you? Well, you're a big girl now, kick him in the balls. So your boyfriend dropped you for someone else? You're a big girl now, fuckin' cut out his heart and eat it. Don't you know, eating your pain gives you strength?*

Rhi tried to swallow the hot iron leaking in her mouth and choked.

Would you rather go to hell with me? Huh? The voice taunted. *Follow me to the Mephistopolis…the city of the dead. Try petting a Ghor-Hound and we'll see how much you whine about a little beating.*

Rhi could see the owner of the voice now, a shadowy imp in what seemed to be a doorway. The crimson light bled through its oval border, and she raised a hand toward the figure, pleading for help.

Wait a minute… the thing said, scratching its chin. It laughed nervously, just before it turned and ran away.

…you're not dead…

《《 — 》》

THEN SHALL THE REIGN...

This is gonna sound stupid, but the thing I love about hell, is the chairs. You go into a restaurant, order some soul soup, and more often than not, you prop your burnin' ass down in a literal throne of a chair carved with intricate barbs and spines and inlaid with dozens of silently screaming skulls. Think about it—every time you sit down, you're planting your ass cheeks on some poor fuck's brainpan, some schmuck who screwed up so bad he didn't even succeed in hell! Screaming skulls are a dime a billion here in hell, but I still love the artistry. What else is there to do in eternity, but carve horrible beauty from bone, artful utility from death?

I was sipping a virgin Bloody Mary—which had as much virgin in it as vodka, thanks to Satan and the pulping stations—when she came through for the first time. The wall behind the bar just exploded, bone and gluey blood spraying everywhere. Through the breach she came, hair a wild spray of brambles and weed, face a smooth complexion of creamy death, body etched in bloody symbols and writhed in the weeds of the cemetery, only her bluish white belly button poking obscenely through the cover. Her feet disappeared in a skein of twisted muddy roots.

As she fell in a muddy, crimson heap to the ground just in front of the bar, the sky opened up outside, and rain coated the windows in sheets of red. The air in the bar thickened, and in moments the floor of the tiny oasis was overrun with crimson foam, as some new slaughter from above overflowed the sewers below.

The woman rose from a crumple of limbs on the floor and shook the dirt from her hair. The roots, however, still wreathed her in organic clothes. She opened a dark, terrified mouth and screamed until the glasses rattled dangerously behind the bar, and then she ran for the door into the bloodstorm like a banshee.

"What in eternity was that?" I whispered.

"What difference does it make?" someone else griped. "If we don't hit the road, it's gonna drown us..."

He was right. The blood had risen several inches already. You hardly noticed it at first because it was warm and relaxing—a hot salt bath. But spend a long enough bath in a bloodrain, and you'll die forever regretting it. The shit was like acid on souls—it ate away at your skin until you were nothing but bleached bone. And unlike most punishments in hell, you didn't automatically grow your skin back after a bloodbath. Sometimes it took long, painful years. Sometimes, I'd heard, your body never grew back at all...but the pain—akin to having your flesh continually, repeatedly scoured with a dull cheese grater—never dulled.

We covered our heads with whatever we could grab—flesh napkins, newsrapers, Zap-heads who'd passed out on the floor—and ran out of the bar with our shields into the blood. All around us a siren wail of the less fortunate, burning dead went off. The blood raged like fire as it ate into your post mortem body, eager to dissolve the spirit beneath, and I raised my voice to join the chorus. My condo was only blocks away, but I could feel the rain eat into my skin like the growing warmth of an acid burn.

I nearly broke the lock off my door and dove through my bedroom and into my bath to rinse the acid rain away as fast as possible, but I could tell that I'd be feeling the destruction of this desecration for days to come. My skin burned like the very real fires of hell.

But I'd get over it. I hadn't been caught in awhile, but I'd lived through bloodrain before.

What bothered me more than the pain though, was what had started it all. Aside from the usual genital-rending shrieks from the johns near the wall of flesh in the red light district, it had been a quiet night until she was suddenly, violently burst from the bar's wall. And then, to coin a bad phrase, all hell had broken loose. Who was she, and why was she here?

《《—》》

Rhi stood naked on the street, a rain of rust lathering her body like pig's blood at a prom gone cruel. She'd pulled the roots away from her skin after falling to the floor from...she had no idea where. One minute, she'd been following the shadowy form of a taunting imp, and the next she was lying on the floor of a strange, hellish place with strange, hellish people and pulling out the barbs of roots and vines and stems she'd gotten entangled in during her fall.

The sky screamed at her in vicious wet curses. She ran.

Everywhere she went, the blood followed.

«« — »»

The word spread quickly. How could it not...after the girl fell into our bar, the blood rain continued for 6 days and nights. The helevision declared that this much pain and suffering had not descended on the Mephistopolis since before the last visit of the Etheress. After her last incendiary attack on Lucifer's citadel had reduced his prized armies and plans to rubble, the Morning Star had retreated deep inside the ruins of the Mephisto Building, his warren of suffering. As Lucifer licked his wounds in silence, the atrocity level in hell had actually dropped. Oh make no mistake—it was still hell. But it seemed as if some of the heart had gone out of the suffering. Some theorized that the travelling rain of blood was Lucifer's latest strategy for releasing the power of the damned to use for his own ends.

But I knew better. I'd seen the girl's eyes as she fell through into the realm. She'd been shocked and scared and lost. And I'd seen the warmth of her aura...she was no lost soul. She was an offering of the River Gods sent through to hell in a sieve from earth. A creature of blood and bone that would soon find her end here in the place where such things could never, ever exist.

At least that's what I thought at the time. But then the blood rain came near again, and I realized that the girl was still here, some-where...and on the move. This time, instead of hiding in my apartment, I decided to find her. It hasn't hard…I just followed the weather (and stayed out of it).

I stopped at a scalper's and bought the skin of some poor pathetic lover who'd lost it during a sexual encounter in the Ampitheatre and set out into the epicenter of the storm. You could smell the iron everywhere…it was like breathing a menstrual cycle; the air was humid and spoiled with the endless stream of dying blood.

No one else lurked about; even the Constabs and Bonecrushers stayed in from the rain. I wondered what Lucifer thought; surely even in the depths of his despair, he was aware of the spreading stain.

"Who are you?" I asked, when I found her. She stood in the center of the Slaughterhouse Square like a waif in invisible thrall. Her eyes shone bright with vacancy. She wasn't fully here. Maybe the enormity of the atrocities of the Mephistopolis had left her in denial.

"It won't stop," she said. Her belly swelled like a blue-white gourd. I realized in a horrible flash that she was pregnant with death.

"You brought through the blood of fertility with you," I said. "But there is not fertility in hell."

"They were beating me," she said. "they beat me to death…"

I reached out to touch her, and couldn't quite connect. My hand passed through her skin and she flinched. My skin crawled.

"You're not dead," I pronounced.

"Then why am I here?" she asked.

"Because you always wanted to visit the city of the dead?

She shook her head.

Something screeched nearby. The telltale gleam of death steel shone from the alley just beyond. "Come on," I said. "They've had enough of you."

"And you haven't?"

"I'm curious."

"I'm dead."

"Tell me a better one. I'm the one without a corporeal body here."

THEN SHALL THE REIGN...

I dragged her into a stairwell and forced the door to the storeroom beyond.

The Cockomite grinned salaciously at us when we slipped inside. The thing guarded the door with its large sacks of flesh and opened a dark maw wide. A glint of jism drooled to the ground. The room smelled like salty seaweed and piss. The cockomite gurgled expectantly.

"Come to cum?" it gasped. Instantly its fat blue-veined torso began to grow, a grotesque mushroom threatening to drown us in a coming eruption of its diseased clumps of rotting sperm.

Rhi's mouth dropped as she watched the cockomite elongate to its full 12-foot length. The cankers on its belly glistened with pus and the rhythmic throb of the veins in its concave, glans-like chest were audible in the small room.

"What's a' matter?" the thing laughed. More saliva dripped like pearly, yellowed handcream to the ground. "Haven't you ever seen a dickhead before?"

"Yeah," she said. "One killed me. Two, actually."

"You're not dead. You just haven't been laid right. Come closer and let me help."

The girl squealed and I pushed her ahead, and away from the cockomite. The damned things were a pestilence in an ocean of foul. And like any plague, their numbers seemed to be growing exponentially. One heckled you from almost every dark corner. They couldn't stand the firelight of hell in the outdoors—shriveled up and dissolved—but lately no shadow seemed safe from the wretched things. I'd heard speculation that they were the souls of human child molesters, but I never stuck around one long enough to ask.

When we found an empty spot deep within the basement of the building, I grabbed her shoulder and forced her to stop. "Enough." I said. "Why are you here? Who sent you?"

The black beneath her eyes rippled like waves. "I don't know why. They tied me down, and fucked me, both of them. They kicked me a lot, and then cut all these designs into my skin." She gestured at the intricate pattern of cuts that crisscrossed her body, some gashes still weeping pale plasma and pus, some scabbed over. She looked as if she'd run into a very deliberate barbed wire fence. "They filled the room with incense and said all sorts of weird things..."

"What kind of things?"

"Some of it I couldn't understand... But I heard them talking about making me the mother of hell...and fucking me to the other side."

A cold spot grew in my gut as I stared at the unnatural blue tinge to her belly. "Did they say anything else about hell?"

"They said a lot of shit. I couldn't understand most of it. For awhile one would chant something while the other one got between my legs and...you know. They traded off."

"What kind of chanting?"

"It sounded like another language. Then Charlie cut me, and everything got blurry. The next thing I knew, I woke up in this hot, shadowy place where some little gargoyle was making fun of me. When I tried to follow him, I fell through all this dirt and mud and roots—like I was slipping through a tunnel. When I hit the floor, I was here. But there was blood everywhere, and horrible creatures. I ran, but no matter where I went there was blood. So much blood."

"Deadpass," I said. I knew now how she'd gotten here. And I had a suspicion of why.

"Huh?"

"They performed a ritual over you, and then dropped you on a deadpass."

"What's that?"

"A place where the walls between hell and earth are thin. They beat you to within an inch of your life, performed a ritual, and prayed that you were close enough to death to slip through the deadpass to hell."

Her mouth wrinkled up, as if she was going to burst out crying. I gripped her shoulder tight. Crying here would only make matters worse. It would lead all manner of pain sycophants here.

"Why?" she whispered. "I didn't do anything to them."

I placed a hand over her belly and sensed the angry, twisting infant within. "Were you pregnant before they raped you?"

"No," she said, confirming my suspicion.

"I think I know why. Though it was a huge longshot. I'm not sure what they hope to gain."

From the other room, I heard footsteps. Things clinking and rattling...as if someone was searching for something...or someone.

"We have to go," I hissed.

She held my arm, refusing to move. "Why did they do this to me, tell me?"

I leaned close and whispered my suspicion in her ear. "Because if a living woman conceives and bears a child in hell, she becomes the Mother of Hell. And her offspring, the prince. She would unseat Satan himself."

"Then I need to get home and have my baby there," she said.

"That's even worse," I said. "Then you will unleash Hell on earth."

Something crashed at the doorway and I scooped her up like a doll and began to run deeper into the dark labyrinth. "We have to go, now!"

The noise behind us grew as we ran through the building, knocking over chairs and glasses and who knows what.

I pushed through a set of doors and entered a milking room, and cursed myself for not realizing where we were sooner.

"Shit," I moaned, as I ran through the long lab and the heads of a score of demons turned to take us in. In the center of the room, an insanely bloated woman lay prone upon a table. She was naked, and the well-used flesh of her gut and thighs hung over the edges of the table like great gobs of melted cheese, but her enormous breasts were encased and held in place atop her in sucker-like cups. Tubes of bubbling liquid ran from those suckers to a hissing, vibrating machine nearby. The juice seemed to flicker and swirl in the tubes in ribbons of both snow cream and cherry red. The woman's screams echoed and rebounded through the room like the amplified cries of a cornered mountain cat.

Some of the demons monitored the equipment while others brought additional tubes around from an octopus of a machine to connect to her mouth and sex.

"What are they doing to her?" Rhi gasped.

"The same thing that will happen to you if I don't get you out of here. She came here through a deadpass too, and now they're milking the blood of human kindness from her. As long as they can feed her, and titillate her and keep her alive in hell, they can extract gallons of it from her every day. Enough to heal half the wounds of hell."

"She's alive?" Rhi asked.

I nodded. "You two may be the only living humans in hell right now. It's a very rare thing for a living soul to get sucked through a deadpass. But when it happens...well, hell has its uses for humans. You're more valuable here than any fortune you've ever imagined."

As the demons pressed the tubes to the woman's mouth and vagina, she shuddered. Silver-strong tendrils slipped like hungry snakes inside the fat woman's soft wet, pink parts, and a jarringly mechanical whirring sound filled the room as a dark fluid flowed through the tubes to pump liquid inside her. Whatever it was, it rendered her euphoric. In seconds her screams from the suction of milking had quieted and we could hear ecstatic moans shuddering through the tube.

Five demons flexed and adjusted their dark leathery wings menacingly, and began walking toward us.

"They can see your aura," I hissed, and lofted her to my shoulder again to run. When I found a door back to the street, I took it. As soon as we stepped outside, my feet went ankle-deep in puddles of steaming blood. The bloodrain had not stopped while we were inside.

Shaking it off, I dragged her up a flight of stairs and found our way blocked. An army of Constabs waited across the street. They stood stock still, long scimitars and violet eyes waiting for their quarry.

THEN SHALL THE REIGN...

Us.

"Let's end this now, before it goes any further," a demon captain demanded. It stepped forward from the mob, approaching the curtain of bloodrain that surrounded Rhi like a hideous umbrella. It ran down the outside of the stolen flesh I wore, and even with the protective curing agent I'd applied to the skin, it was still dissolving my "raincoat" layer by layer, a poison death to the dead. A poison that threatened annihilation just centimeters from my own skin.

It was the only thing that kept the army of lost souls from charging us right now. No one wanted to spend the next two months regrowing their flesh from the seeds of bone. They waited for her to make a mistake. We were all cowards here. Sadists and cowards.

"Let us pass," I demanded, and pressed her to step sideways down the street. As the curtain of bloodrain moved, so did the line of Ushers ripple and retreat, anvil-like heads bobbing in a still breeze.

"She brings us all down," the demon leader yelled. "Why are you sheltering her?"

"She's done nothing to you," I answered. "Stay away from her, and your skin stays intact. What is easier than that?"

"That's enough," one of the others bellowed, and marched into the rain of blood, scimitar in hand. But no sooner had he entered Bri's umbra of acid rain than he fell screaming to the pavement, clawing at the burning skin that sloughed off his body like warm wax. As he scratched, skin and sinew separated and fell to dissolve on the road to hell—the road *of* hell. In seconds nothing remained of the demon's obsidian angst but dull yellow ribs and femurs, clacking and smacking together like ghastly maracas. His remains would be ground to bonedust for gravebread by morning while he might already have been reborn as an Excre-worm.

None of the other soldiers in hell's army followed. What was the benefit of dying again, and again and again? None of us would ever leave here to go to heaven. So why would we die for hell?

"Come on," I whispered, and led Bri through the barricade. For

200

awhile, some stragglers followed us, but soon, the steady patter of red rain was broken only by our footfalls.

I took her to a place I knew far from the center of the Mephistopolis. A place in the country, if boiling craters of molten rock could be called pastoral. I knew of a small passage across the Sea of Obsession that led to an island long abandoned. Once it had housed two sisters, whose mutual hatred had not only destroyed their mortal lives with knives and hatchets, but had led them to be isolated even in hell.

For eons they tortured each other, cutting off arms and heads and puncturing eyeballs with skewers of burning lead. They always recovered—this was hell after all. But then Satan himself pressed them from isolation into servitude in his war against the Etheress and her sister, and months ago their island of brutal isolation had been abandoned, a refuge for those who could weather the fiery Sea of Obsession to harbor there.

I knew of the island…why, I won't say. But it was a refuge in a hell of hells. I led Rhi to the hidden dock, tied her arms and legs together hogstyle and took the boat across the boiling chum-capped waves of the Sea of Obsession to the tiny rock landing. She shivered and screamed beneath the gag as the temptations of the water drew her soul out to hover and shimmer, shrieking above us…but I'd tied the ropes tight for a reason. And when we had set our shelter in the two-room shack there, I eased her down on a wooden chair, untied the last of her binds and told her of the scriptures.

> *"When the mother of hell descends from the fertile valley of mortals and gives birth to a child conceived in hell, not by demons but by mortal man, then shall the reign of Lucifer end, and the dominion of man begin. A child born in hell will rise to rule, and whether his throne sits in hell or on earth, his kingdom shall rival the Lord God Almighty's. The Morning Star will bow to his glory and his power*

THEN SHALL THE REIGN...

shall shake the heavens. The kingdom of man will fall
under his terrible scepter and the kingdom of hell will
bow to his dominion."

She shook her head. "I wasn't pregnant on earth."

"That's the problem," I said. "They fucked you, and before their sperm could do the deed in the mortal realm, they sent you through the deadpass to arrive here. When their seed took root within you, it was after you fell through to live in hell...and that means that your child is neither alive nor dead, human nor demon. And it will be the worst of all."

She rubbed her belly, which protruded beyond the line of her pants. "How can this be?" she moaned. "When they killed me, I wasn't pregnant. And already I'm showing like it's my time?"

"This is hell," I said. It's a lame answer, but that pretty much answers everything here.

It rained blood for 7 days. We stayed in the tiny shack at the island's center, and ate all of the cobwebbed provisions the sisters had left behind. We slept a lot, when the screams from the mainland didn't keep us awake. And when we were alert, I told her of the horrors of eternity, and she reminded me of the indignities and pain of life.

It was the best time I've ever had in hell.

"How did you end up here?" she asked one day, as I ran a long black nail through the flow of her hair. My touch passed through her when I wasn't careful, so I was very careful. I wanted to feel her, to capture her in my memory for eternity. I knew she would not be here to savor long. I laughed softly at her question and hummed a stupid song for a moment.

"Why?" she asked again.

"Because the music didn't move me?"

She looked confused, and shook me with her hands on both shoulders. "Why are you in hell?"

I sighed. "You can sing about the power of love, but that only ends up making you realize how you will never have it. You can talk about passion and possibilities," I said. It was an old, tired explanation for me. "But the songs were lies and the talk got old. You couldn't make me want to live."

She looked genuinely confused.

"They write songs about the power of love and of finding yourself and your soulmate. But the sad fact of the matter is, you can't find yourself in someone else. And no matter how much love someone gives you, if you don't have it already for yourself... forget about it. Nobody can make you want to live, but you. I was happy to take a pass on living. Just wasn't in me. So I ended it. And now I'm here."

And in that moment, as I looked into Rhi's eyes, I heard a song from my past that I had always mocked. Something in my chest ached then, something that had never ached before and in a wave of bitter irony, I understood.

I looked into Rhi's hopeful eyes and understood that I was truly damned.

In that week, Rhi's belly continued to swell at an alarming rate. And the bloodrain accused her presence, and ran in crimson rivulets down the tiny windows of our shack, it soon found an exit point inside our refuge as well. When Rhi pulled herself off the human hair-stuffed cushion of the couch on the seventh night of our escape, the burlap beneath her was stained in a dark purplish butterfly. The poor girl had only been in hell for 13 days, and already she was full term with the scourge of Satan.

"Oh shit," she cried. "The baby's coming, isn't it?"

"The prince of hell," I corrected. "He won't be a baby for long."

From outside, a horrible keening wail rose up above the splatter of gore. I went to the window and stared at the bubbling reek of the Sea of Obsession. Now it was my turn:

"Oh shit," I said.

"What is it?" she gasped, while bending over and holding her gut. Outside, the waters of the Sea had risen higher and higher, fed by the endless bloodrain, until the waves lapped just yards away from our doorway. But atop that roiling sea of nightmare and desire, rocked a thousand black boats.

"They're coming for you," I said. Then I shook my head and corrected myself. "They're coming for your child."

"It will go easier for you if you let them take the thing from you," I suggested.

She reacted as I expected. I rubbed the sore spot on my arm, rather than punching her back.

"They'll kill me, and then my baby," she yelled. "You've got to help me get away from here. Send me back home. Do you think I'm fuckin' nuts?"

I shook my head. "No," I said. "But consider this. If you actually make it through the deadpass back to Earth, you will be pursued in the shadows of every night by evil. Satan will not tolerate you suckling his undoing in a place he can barely reach. And make no mistake. It may be hard for him...but he *will* find you. His reach is long. And he will kill your child sooner or later. If he doesn't...well, the result may be even worse."

"How could it be worse?" she screamed.

"Because your child is no human baby," I hissed. I took her by the shoulders, forcing her to look at me. To listen. "Think about it...what baby gestates in 13 days? What baby gathers Satan's most loyal legion to the march to destroy it? You are not harboring a *baby* in your womb Rhi, you are carrying the sword of darkness, the future king of hell."

"Not if I raise him right," she declared, holding both hands across her middle and crying out bravely. "I can teach him to use his power for good."

"And Lucifer could begin healing the sick and sending lost souls to heaven." I shook my head. "He *could*...but it's not bloody likely."

Her eyes were red and she balled up her fists to wipe them free. Then she beat them against my chest, pounding to be free of my grip. "Tell me," she demanded. "Tell me how to go home."

"How badly do you want it?" I asked quietly. Behind me, the walls began to rattle, as the host of hell trudged through the bloody swamp to our tiny hideaway.

"More than anything," she whispered.

I looked at the figures coming towards us through the front windows, and then stared at the empty, angry sea through the pane in the back.

"Then maybe, just maybe, I brought you to the right place."

When they broke through the door and crashed into the room, Lucifer's army found me alone.

"Where is she?" their leader demanded, and I shrugged.

"Who?"

"The girl you brought here," the Usher snarled. The points of its teeth looked none too friendly, and the horns on its skull shivered with the thirst to impale.

"As you can see, she's gone," I said.

"The bloodrain centers here. She can't have gone far."

"Mehitobel!!," screamed a serpentine creature from outside the doorway. "The rain has stopped. The blood is…gone."

A black blade slid across my neck, drawing instant heat in its wake. I felt skin flap like a new mouth against my throat.

"Where?" the demon said again. "Don't toy with us."

I shrugged and pointed towards the back door of the cottage. Towards the water.

"She's gone to find her obsession."

《《 — 》》

205

Rhi slid into the warm water like a bath, feet sinking into the liquefied flesh of a million crumbled lives that lined the red sea's bottom. But rather than think about the fingers and rancid, curdled flesh that rippled and tickled her soles as she marched away from the army behind, Rhi only thought about one thing: Planting a shiv right in the balls of that fucking prick Brett and yanking upwards until his balls met his bellybutton. And then she could repeat the trick with his creepy thug friend Charlie. She imagined opening them both up for the crows, and as she let her chin touch and slip under the water, her sole thought was of the joy it would bring her to step back through the muddy hole of the deadpass and into the lost farmhouse. Oh, the bloodrain she would bring *there*...

Inside her, a baby writhed in preternatural excitement at the thought.

«« — »»

The room lay deadly silent, but inside, both a mother and a newborn child breathed. Neither stirred. But the baby stared at two men with its dark, intelligent eyes.

Charlie looked up at Brett and shook his head. They'd been standing in the doorway now for several minutes arguing in whispers.

"C'mon, that's ridiculous. She goes to hell for a couple weeks and comes back nine months pregnant...and delivers?"

Charlie stared at the infant, but Brett didn't answer the question. Instead, he pointed. "Hey man, your nose is bleeding."

Charlie wiped his face with a sleeve and gasped when he saw the stain.

"What the fuck?"

Brett laughed. "Shhh...don't swear in front of our baby."

"Yeah, real funny. Damn thing's kinda creepy, isn't it? Hasn't blinked since we walked in here."

Brett stared at the bloody naked creature himself, and then

Charlie reached out to touch the side of Brett's head, and returned the observational favor: "Hey man, your ear's bleeding."

"What the fuck?

Sure enough, when Brett brought his hand up to his ear, it came away red as fire engine paint.

"Something's not right here, man."

"No shit. There's a woman on the floor who just gave birth to a baby she wasn't pregnant with two weeks ago, it's staring us down like the fuckin' devil, and we're bleeding for no reason. Time to go, maybe?"

They both began to back away. The infant never took its eyes off them.

"Yeah, I..." Brett doubled over.

"What's the matter man?"

He gasped. "Hurts...in my ...gut." He crumpled to the floor. "Oh fuck, fuck fuck!" he cried. "I'm not liking this, Brett."

"I'm... not either..." Brett started to say, but instead of "Either," what came out was a throaty gurgle, followed quickly by a spontaneous stream of blackish red bile. He gasped and choked in surprise. Then Brett heaved, again and again, each spasm coming faster, harder and more painful. Between each loud grunt and liquidy cough, he swore. Then he cried, as his mouth splattered the floor with chunks of something that did not look like food.

The baby, and its cold, black eyes, did not look away.

But Charlie did. Because suddenly his eyes felt like a swarm of bees had just honed in on him to attack. His pupils burned with pain and he rubbed them...only to find his palms lathered in crimson tears.

"Oh Jesus Christ," he swore, and the baby, for the first time in its earthly life, opened its lungs to cry.

"This...is...not...good," gasped Brett weakly from nearby.

That's when Brett felt the knifing pressure in his guts increase. He started to unhitch his belt, still spewing bloody meat from his mouth, but it was already too late. His pants filled with something hot and acidy as his bowels let go, and he slipped in the mess of his insides and fell for the last time to the floor.

It was just seconds later that Charlie joined him, coughing and crying and feeling the warmth of his own boiling guts streaming down his leg like hot piss. But he knew it wasn't piss, or even shit for that matter. He was dissolving from within. His shoes were already drenched in gore when he fell to the floor next to his gagging friend, a shuddering skeleton wreathed in boiling, desiccating flesh.

«« — »»

Rhi opened her eyes and stared into the baby's elfin black orbs. They were bottomless, achingly open. A blank slate to build a world in. She gently hugged the infant close and felt her heart surge.

"We did it," she whispered, and struggled to sit up with the baby. That's when she saw the bodies of Charlie and Brett.

"All of it," she grinned. "They got what they deserved. And now we can start a new life. I kinda fucked up mine, but the whole world is open to you."

She kissed the tiny wet pink mouth of the child.

"I'll help you be whatever you want to be."

The baby's dark eyes never left the bodies on the floor. They never blinked at all.

SHUNNED

CHARLEE JACOB

Well, fuck. What did they mean no one could've seen it coming? What Broodren ever had enough brain cells working together all at once and the luck to stay alive to get anything accomplished—much less have a number one rap hit for the Mephistopolis street culture?

His name was Kibideaux and the song was AVE.

"Extreme unction
got no function...
all debunkshun.
Do you believe
an angel on your sleeve,
the devil make her grieve?
Doin' the bow-wow up her ow-ow
with a little zap-zow."
And the male chorus goes, "Phht phht phht puh puh mmm hmm
puh puh mmm hmm..."
And the female chorus goes, "Weeeeeeeeeeeeeeeeeeeee!"
"That ain't no feather
he be stickin' up her nether,
his wings like leather.
He cums all black

SHUNNED

and that's a fact,
smearin' Heaven's crack
'til you can't see dawn
'cause salvation's gone,
sniffin' up some mummy's lawn."
And the male chorus goes, "Phht phht phht puh puh mmm hmm
puh puh mmm hmm…"
And the female chorus goes, "Weeeeeeeeeeeeeeeeeeee…"
"Now it's damnation's show,
gonna screw us real slow
'til the Hershey squirts blow.
Devil sure loves ass
with his big dick of brass,
but that Player's lost his gas.
It ain't no fire,
and he'll never get no higher
no matter his desire.
It's a lake of shit,
flushed from Heaven's conduit…
so get used to it."

Broodren crouched everywhere, mumbling necro-nonsense, muttering fragments of the lowest trailer park magic, chewing on the scraps of demons wasted in the holocaust which ensued after that Etherean geek Walter suicided, blowing out his brains in the Bastille of Otherwise Souls.

Clouds of crimson and roaring winds. Was this anything radically different from Evil's usual mecca-mechanican shenanigans?

More intense, maybe, than the storm of repercussions devised for the damned. More excruciating than the torment of the Mutilation Squads delivered in nerve-shredding bits and bytes of almost poetically nuclear rendering. Filling Mephistopolis with a burning no worse than God's exile, no better than radiation.

"We outnumber them!" Kibideaux told his audience. "Even with the millions butchered at the Atrocidome…"

Some numbnuts grinding a Grand Duchess's crispy nipple between his back molars sang, "Squish squash, I was havin' a wash, all alone on Saturday night. Rub-a-dub, I was jerkin' in her grub, cummin', everything was all right!"

Kibideaux ignored him. He understood that, as a rule Broodren were not a bright bunch. This was only because they were young, destined never to get much older. Half-castes, they were the frequent victims of every devil to stalk through Hell's capital.

Yet recently, slogans had been found scrawled on buildings and the train cars running from the Outer Sectors into the stinking bowels of the central city. On the sign to the Tiberius Depot Outer Sector South was a blasphemous GOD LOVES YOU! Then, discovered on the great suspension bridge where the tracks spanned a mile-wide waterway of monstrous excrement, some bravely-foolish, soulless gargoyle-human hybrid had inched upward on the obscenely-wrought intricacies of steel to spray paint in neon pink the goading JESUS LIVES! PACK UP YOUR SHIT, SHLOMO! WE'S A'GOIN' WAY NORTH A'HERE!

Kibideaux had himself orchestrated a daring group of his followers to release Madonna-clit pink banners and balloons over no less than the mighty edifice of bullshit tyranny—the Mephisto Building (prior to its destruction, of course) which read:

IT'S NEVER TOO LATE TO BE SAVED.

But Lucifer didn't even appear on his balcony or send Ushers to cut the rebellious kids to pieces. It seemed he had bigger problems, like the First Saint of Hell—what was her name?—Cassie—who also had an interest (a foretold one at that, well isn't that special?) in overthrowing the Angel of Light.

Now some whore-shifter cackled. "You don't have souls. You ain't nothin' but the boogers of Sin City."

SHUNNED

Kibideaux grinned to think that he'd brought them together, free of Zap and the usual in-fighting these in-bred Heinz 666 mongrel hellions indulged in.

Kibideaux raised his fist in answer to this furry-cunted bitch. The minions howled, best bones and weapons plucked from the edges of the Holocaust.

He was charismatic. Had been since his birth, fathered by a Grand Duke who in his life on earth had been Shaka Zulu and borne of a human female soul, Joan D'Arc.

Now many fine upstanding Christians might wonder what St. Joan was doing consigned to Hell. Well, she'd been excommunicated, accused of witchcraft, tried and found guilty of such, then burned at the stake. At one point she had lied, recanting to save her life, which essentially meant turning her back on the angels who had appeared to her. True, in the end, she was back on course. But the fact remained that she'd lost faith and turned away from God, for whatever reason and however briefly.

Fairness had nothing to do with it. Never had, never would. In a perfect universe, Kibideaux believed a loving god wouldn't have judged so many so harshly. God would have forgiven His angels. There would have been no fall from grace, for (New Testament, not Old) according to the writ, such a fall from grace wasn't really possible. Jesus, supposedly, bore the sins of transgressors.

Kibideaux preached a new messiah who would free the tried and tribulated Broodren and, ultimately, Hell's entirety. MAYBE. He didn't know if he cared about Trolls, Imps, Ushers, etc.

Right now he felt like Peter Pan, and the other Broodren were his Lost Boys. He was likewise—and this was downright heresy in Mephistopolis—an evangelist.

It turned out Kibideaux'd had a dream. In it was somebody important, who would join his cause and change all this motley damnation crap around.

CHARLEE JACOB

«« — »»

Shunned sat in her cell, having no interaction with anyone, contemplating the lightless. A food tray would be pushed through a slot once every turn of the obsidian moon, filled with abominably reeking slop she was grateful she couldn't see. It smelled and tasted like the bloody snot of Caco-ticks.

Every now and then a voice—discorporeal, discarnate, discombobulated—floated around her, taunting, "You are nothing, nobody. Even your crack whore of a mother, stuffed with semen curds and gargling skidmark soup didn't want you. Even Hell doesn't want you. It's why you're here...alone. Nasty, shunned thing."

Except Shunned knew there were others on the opposite sides of her four walls. Also above and below, like in chicken coops too short to stand up in, not wide enough to stretch out in. She heard as they wailed and beat their heads, damaged. She'd tried calling to them but none answered save for occasionally scratching on a wall. Up to their necks, as was she, in their own waste.

Shunned understood things she ought not to have.

For who had taught her language? How to speak?

Why did she recall a mother she'd never seen?

How could she see her future and that of these other prisoners?

The most arcane of abominable crimes was that in which the tiny (at first anyway) victim remains forever a victim.

Where was God at this point? Displaying attitude far darker than a playfully wry sense of humor.

Her few nano-seconds of life: umbilical tinsel dragged out, bitten through with half-rotted teeth. Salty! No vocal prayers nor silent curses. Left in a shit-smeared, urine puddled toilet in lieu of the manger 'some' received, wrapped in cheap brown paper towels and stuffed in the box for used sanitary napkins.

(Others had been buried under Dumpster slop, slowly or discov-

217

ered by rats and flies. Or had been thrown out of cars racing down a highway as tarantulas made their midnight crossing—not bearing gold, frankincense, and myrrh. Or had been killed by coat hangers twisting in the uterus until they were scrambled eggs and spam. Or kicked to death until they rolled from the womb like ejecta from the pinched hole a little farther back between the cheeks.)

Lamentations and the gnashing of groins.

Something no amount of carefully constructed Latin could console.

And then suddenly…the doors swung open!

Why? Were they going to be hosed down again?

No. A young woman only a few years older than Shunned was passing by the Purghole. She had bright yellow hair that hurt the abortion's eyes, black clothes like the shapelessly, shamelessly shadowmoon. Flip-flop shoes.

And the mere fact that this woman walked so close to their prison opened it up. Just like that. Steaming filth flowed from each doorway. But only Shunned crawled from her cell.

"Come out," she hearkened to the others. "It's a sign. Jesus loves us…"

None even raised their heads. They shut their soft-boiled eyes against even the barest illumination, drooling mustard-yellow sludge from their mouth holes. Some were only toddlers, others ancient…so wrinkled their gender wasn't apparent.

Idiots, all. Shunned wept for them, tears cleaning two trails of muck from her face.

«« — »»

Kibideaux came awake from yet another dream. He and thousands of his followers slept in an underground subway tunnel. Millions of other Broodren dozed or stood guard on trains which had stopped running when the Etherean Walter caused the mass explosion.

The Etheress ran things since Lucifer's second fall. This sort of irritated Kibideaux because he hadn't been able to get in to see her. Black knights, legions of fallen angels like Ezoriel, guarded her as she attempted to deal with the destroyed areas of the city and its survivors. Kibideaux planned tomorrow to march all his people to her HQ and demand a hearing.

But now: yeah, another dream. He jumped up and ran, leaping over gurgling, snoring, farting brethren. He didn't even know which direction he was moving in. That meant he was being led. Prodigious!

He exited the tunnel, crossed through four trains still on the tracks, their doors open, and ran up a flight of stairs to the street.

A girl slowly made her way down the steaming roadway. She had so much filth on her that at first he couldn't even tell she was naked. Long greasy black hair hung in her face.

She was maybe two hundred feet from him, yet he heard her soft murmurs as if she whispered directly against his ear.

"Projectile prawns out of living bronze, empty of wonderment in the fall of spirituality. Eat fuck kill, kill what you fuck, then eat it. Mutable nightmare transcendent. What is the shadow pooling, wet dreaming at my feet? This music is smoke; I am the mirror. Together a magic to fool the masses.

"Convulsions adrift on seas of wormwood, Lucifer surfs on a beam of light, a finger laser, tentacle of morning star. He does NOT walk upon the water but commands to be carried on the wave by minions luminous. Beautiful as the perfect combination of pale and garnet."

"Girl, are you okay? Who are you?" Kibideaux asked as she approached.

Now, he was accustomed to rotten stenches because he'd been born in Hell but, damnation, she stank!

She might have turned her eyes to him, he wasn't certain, with all that stringy dark hair on her face.

She said, "You deserve darkness, thin as razor dolls, chic with bones edged like thresholds. I PROMISE!"

SHUNNED

"So…is this something I'm supposed to comprehend?" he asked.
She shook her head. "I dreamed you. I'm supposed to go with you."
"Yeah?" Kibideaux's thistly eyebrows turned up. "To where?"
"Heaven."

«« — »»

Question: How many battles does it take to rattle suicide's skinny hips?
Answer: Trick question. Suicide's hips don't rattle. They rock of ages.

«« — »»

Deep Purple. "Hush, hush. I thought I heard her calling my name now…"

«« — »»

When you give up everything, why are you surprised there's nothing left?

«« — »»

Question: How is it the stars run through this tube of universe, from birth to entropy?
Answer: Like shit through a goose.

«« — »»

Kibideaux was both ecstatic and terrified. He knew this girl was the one from his first dream.
Get it? She was the ONE, man! The cosmic!

220

He'd borrowed the use of a flophouse from a Broodren harlot pal. Leading the girl in, every Bapho-roach and Polter-rat in sight skittered, shrieking. He even saw the lice levitate off the venereal bed and out the broken window. And the bump-uglies in the rooms to either side got real quiet.

He bathed her, took several hours to shower her all squeaky. She had red hair after all the excrement washed out. And suprisingly sparkling skin, unblemished except for a sprinkling of freckles across the bridge of her nose that glittered like the stars no one could see in Mephistopolis.

(Which he knew about because he'd dreamed them, too.)

Aside from her sputtered stream of possibly profound/likely psychotic gobbledeegook, all she was later able to tell him was her name.

Shunned.

Then, once she was clean and actually beautiful, she wept, tears singing hymns down her cheekbones. He sighed, knowing now for the first time in his miserable existence the full import of the word 'radiant'.

Now I know I'm superior and fated for an exaltation above my humble beginning, Kibideaux thought to himself as he gently put his arm around her and let her cry on his shoulder. He further thought, Because I'm in love and that shit just does not happen in Hell.

"We'll get there, honey," he told her. "Don't worry. We'll get to Heaven."

《《 — 》》

Broodren danced in the street, up from sewers and from wrecks of cars, flapping elbows like demon chickens, goose-necking and goose-stepping.

Amazing that none had even heard of the Purghole. It had been Lucifer's best-kept secret. Where certain infants who'd ended up aborted or otherwise died unbaptised were kept in total freakdom darkness.

SHUNNED

Question: Is it Purgatory or Limbo in-between Heaven and Hell?

Answer: The dancing Broodren cry Hellwillfuckya as they limbo lower now.

«« — »»

Cassie shook herself out of her own sleep, finding herself in a lounge chair beside a scented pool. In it: lilies. Nearby…hibiscus.

Had she dreamed it all: the horrors, Hell, her twin sister Lissa and their father both dead? Like on *Dallas* when an entire season was dumped as a nightmare?

Why had she fallen asleep anyway—other than from absolute exhaustion?

It was because of that infernal music, very distant, and sickening.

No, NOT infernal.

Celestial.

Spectral sounds rebounding. Harps? Not that she was sure what one sounded like. She'd watched old Marx Brothers flicks. One of them had played this instrument. Which one?

Oh, *Harpo*. Duh.

Wind chimes, and the noise a crystal goblet made with a little wine in it and your finger wet, running around the rim.

A very tall, impossibly handsome—man?—approached her across the garden.

Not a man. It was the Fallen Angel of Repentance, Ezoriel, leader of the Contumacy. But what happened to the revolution now that Lucifer and his major fucklings were gone?

"Your Holiness," he said, "the book discovered hidden by Satan has proved to be correct. The broodren leader, Kibideaux, has arrived at my estate with several million of his followers. And he's brought a girl called Shunned."

Cassie jumped to her feet. "Oh, I wish I could go!"

Ezoriel bowed his head. "I am sorry that is not in the cards. But, if she *is* the one—and this we will know soon enough—then the three of us, the Broodren leader, the girl, and I will enter Heaven to petition for forgiveness. It will be the beginning of a new era."

Ezoriel couldn't hide his hopeful smile as Kibideaux and Shunned were led in by black knights.

There had been vague messages. The barest of suggestions. Whispers. Just enough that a few words could be understood drifting from the heights.

Salvation.

Redemption.

Return.

"You'll say hello if you see Angelese?" Cassie asked, referring to the Caliginaut celestial who'd suffered so much to help Hell's first saint achieve her full power and destiny. When Cassie had last seen her angelic friend, Lucifer had been overthrown, literally, to fall forever. And Angelese was finally going home to Heaven.

«« — »»

Broodren had never collected in such numbers before. This being Hell, they probably didn't have the right to assemble (or any other rights for that matter). Kibideaux had been able to summon them because he was the strangest, smartest half-caste ever, even if he was also at times a sarcastic, antithetical little sonofabitch. Even as he'd crawled from his poor mother's womb, shreds of gray-green placenta between his teeth and under his claws. It didn't damage her that much. Her pubic hair was always aflame, so he liked to joke that he was lucky because he'd already passed through the fire.

Yet he'd still been but an innocent thing, as were all the infants created out of rape and monstrous lust in Mephistopolis. Not that it took long for them to be corrupted—or slaughtered—but at least they began blameless, which nothing else in Hell could boast. And there was *so* much rape and *so* much monstrous lust that once Kibideaux began traversing the humungous city and counting, he discovered that Broodren outnumbered all other classes...excluding human souls who'd fallen to eternal strife.

Fragile little maniacs-in-the-making, taking into consideration where they grew up, however their alotted years (months, weeks, days, hours, even minutes). Nature or nurture? Ah, the endless bickering on how one progressed from a total zero-waif into a heinous atrocity-perpetrator.

Kibideaux had given this a great deal of thought and tended to vote for nurture. Not that Broodren received any nurturing. But Nature, to him, represented a goddess figure, benevolent of her growing charges, tending every leaf, flower, and ugly poisonous toadstool. Serpents whose bites drove mad, spiders whose venom disfigured and necrotized. She loved everything created under her gentle jurisdiction.

Which was precisely why Kibideaux didn't believe in Nature. Besides, there could be no such in Hell. All that arrived there did so to suffer the most humiliating ordeals.

"So many Broodren," he said to Shunned as they marched toward Ezoriel's palatial grounds. "All born blameless. The only ones..."

"Not the only ones," Shunned corrected him. "Those of us in the Purghole are innocently born here, too."

"Oh, yeah," he muttered, lowering his head. "But I only just learned about you guys. Besides, we'll change things for everybody."

"They wouldn't come out," Shunned said sadly. "I don't know why."

"They're sick, baby. That's all," he told her, brushing her rosy red hair from her eyes. "We'll get 'em healed. It'll be in the petition, see?"

But inside he harbored doubts, fears, and resentment as the beautiful home and Nether Sphere of the fallen angel Ezoriel came into view, not a stone's throw from where black-garbed knights boiled the minced corpses of demons to create the steam that helped supply the chateau with pure water.

The Nether-Sphere had been a secret until recently. But after the explosion, there weren't many secrets left in a place which thrived on bearing souls to the bone and beyond.

The Zen of Zed.

Zoom!

What was the sound of sin? Pounding heart or faint of heart?

(Deep, rhythmic, thrusting.)

The crumbling of worlds and babies' skulls into powdery dust so fine that a single singeing breath into it went Huuuuuuush.

(Hush. I thought I heard her calling my name now.)

The percussive sarcasm of locusts crunching continents to nothing.

Shrieks—well...

Yet in degrees of pitch.

From: Pitch black soprano...

To: Pitch black basso-profundo.

"We'll heal them," he repeated to Shunned. "But you should already know that. Because you're the messiah I dreamed was coming to us. I heard that all messiahs emerge from wastelands and there's no greater wasteland than Hell itself."

Shunned smiled and kissed him on the cheek.

A cheer rose up from the Broodren, so loud it rattled Ezoriel's fortress turrets and minarets. The water in the moat sloshed.

«« — »»

Cassie hugged Shunned who could only shyly smile.

"Do we get them a Nectoport? Do we need necromancers? Or does she just click her heels and say 'There's no place like home, no place like home'?" the Etheress asked Ezoriel.

SHUNNED

"According to the book Lucifer had hidden, she need only utter one word," replied the fallen angel, watching the Purghole refugee with anticipation and the Broodren rapper-evangelist with mistrust. "Shunned, do you know what that word is?"

Because it wasn't in Lucifer's book on the Purghole captives.

"Don't feel nervous," Cassie tried to reassure her, knowing what it felt like to have so much pressure on delicate, unsuspecting shoulders.

Shunned looked up. It was perhaps a theoretical UP. From the accidental occident to the Disorient, most thought of UP when they contemplated Heaven.

Cassie wondered why, as Hell's first saint, this hadn't been a job allotted her. It embarrassed her a bit, Etheress virginal as steaming stone. A straight-up world amid the morgue was her realm...and her prison.

What shadows lengthened, funereal and damned? Pathology, depression, suicidal scars livid beneath crimson skies, chasing a black moon, swords and bones of rebellion. The science of sin was for ancient children to number unto the God who forgot them instead of forgiving as promised.

It sometimes made her consider, just exactly who did get accepted into Heaven? One thing was certain. Cassie would not be there.

"Are you okay, Shunned? Maybe you need time. This is all new to you," Cassie said. "None of us even knew about the Purghole."

"Neither did we—and Broodren know all the shit on the street," Kibideaux huffed as he stood protectively closer to his girl.

"I am quite sure that is a mild exaggeration," Ezoriel told him drily.

"How would you know? Living up here in a fuckin' palace like your sin wasn't what started all this misery for the rest of us?" Kibideaux snapped. At almost half the angel's height, the Broodren evangelist took several steps forward, prepared to get all up in his face.

226

Then Shunned glided between them, taking each by the hand.

"Father?" she asked in a voice so sweet, Cassie felt her own heart break a little.

And she thought she'd grown so tough.

The three vanished, leaving Hell's First Saint alone.

《《 — 》》

Where was everything?

A few haunting whispers bent around geometrically impossible corners, saying nothing particularly sensical. Thrones and couches of gold, gone, stolen, power gems plucked out like eyes, leaving hollows perceiving naught. A fine dust, glittering, covered all ragged curves and broken angles.

They had floated through a gate but it wasn't a pearly one. Millennia of misted clouds had rusted it.

《《 — 》》

Question: If Jesus died for our sins, where did they go?

Answer: Below! Below below—yo ho! Ding dong the bitch is red...

《《 — 》》

Shunned saw blood on her wrists and feet. There was a wound in her side. The gouges of invisible thorns ringed her scalp.

Ezoriel commented, "Stigmata."

"But where is everybody," Kibideaux wanted to know. "And there, just for a second, before we arrived...did you see those people?"

The angel shook his head.

"Well, I did," the Broodren told him. "They were the Otherwise

227

SHUNNED

Souls, released from the Bastille when that dork Etherean busted a cap on himself. They were supposed to be ascending and transcending. And, man, that's what they were doing all right—ascending and transcending to NOWHERE."

"That is impossible," Ezoriel said, turning around. Out of the corner of his eye he caught a flash of turquoise vestment and heard sighs, not in a white noise but a static of fire opals.

APPARITIONS: Here and there a feather, or only the feather's dander. As if miles away a million dandelions simultaneously loosed fluffy seeds to the wind. A solitary eye blinked, quicksilver. Ozone, cherry blossoms, wine lightly scented with blood freely given.

MAGNETISM: Occasional soft lightning, out-of-focus and with thunder as a choir in slightly off-key harmony. For there was no true harmony in this haunted place. Rains of rose petals, yes. Butterfly storms. Blinding diamond fogs. But no harmony.

POSSESSION, TELEPATHY, POLTERGEIST: Instances of psychokinesis. A genuine entity could attach itself to individuals and cause 'incidents'.

RECORDING: Perhaps a ghostly replaying of a long-past tragedy. Literally photographed upon its surroundings, pictures which repeat actions, music and voices programmed to transfigure for those sufficiently sensitive or bound in some way to the haunting.

"I do not understand," Ezoriel said. "There have been messages from God that some have clearly received."

"What if they didn't come from Heaven?" asked Shunned.

"Are we sure this here is Heaven?" Kibideaux furthered.

"Yes," Ezoriel stressed. "I used to live here."

"Could they have gone somewhere else?" Shunned murmured to herself, walking around the blasted white infinity. "Perhaps they wander, like the stars."

"This place has obviously been empty a long time," Kibideaux offered. "Over a hundred years ago, on earth, a human named Nietzsche proclaimed God was dead."

228

Shunned cried out, "No! Father..."

The Broodren put his arm around her shoulder. "I'm sorry. I didn't mean it. I mean, you should know—right?"

"There could be no spirit stronger than the Holy Spirit," Ezoriel said to no one in particular. He seemed thoroughly bewildered, crushed. After all these thousands of years, hoping for forgiveness and reinstatement, only to find...what?

Sight/insight.

Blindness/zero attenuation.

Devotion/hysteria.

Was there some insight to be gleaned through devotion to hysterical blindness?

An egocentric God who had become skeptical of His own spirituality, a schism which drained away both His Vengeance and His Love.

Perhaps even the fate of Gods and Demons wasn't immutable after all.

Ezoriel shook his head. Science's trivial vibrations and the mystic's tempest that swirled them to superficial planes. An actualized pragmatic threshold, beyond which nothing answered.

"Come here," they heard a soft voice say.

Ezoriel, Kibideaux, and Shunned turned.

"It is the Caliginaut, Angelese," Ezoriel told the other two.

"Yeah? Is she real?" the Broodren wanted to know. "She doesn't look too well."

"She returned to Heaven after a long time working on earth and in Hell. What it must have done to her to find Heaven thus. She has gone mad," Ezoriel replied.

"Come here," she said to Shunned. "I want to tell you secrets."

Shunned backed away as the Caliginaut approached through a gauze of mist.

"Wait! I need to tell you secrets..."

Angelese ran toward Shunned who was frightened by the sight of her. Shunned saw a terrible shadow twisting up from the angel's ankles.

SHUNNED

Angelese was in a rapture of torment as the shadow raked claws into celestial flesh. She was ecstatic in masochism as she shouted at Shunned, "You are of the bloodline...it shows on you now!"

Angelese's orgasmic grin was rictal as the Umbra-Specter's talons sliced her torso open from crotch to breastbone, then across both breasts vertically, bisecting nipples and forming a gory cross. She shrieked, gasped as she ran fingers through the bloody furrows, "Holy DNA twists through your genes!"

Shunned crouched, cringing, no longer able to move. All her life—as she'd known it in Hell—she'd constantly had drilled into her YOU ARE NOTHING; YOU ARE LESS THAN THE SHIT THAT THE FLIES DINING ON THE DUNG HEAP EXCRETE. YOU DIDN'T DESERVE THE WORLD SO YOUR MOTHER KILLED YOU. NOTHING! WORTHLESS! SHUNNED EVEN BY THE DAMNED!

Angelese shuddered violently, spastically as the Umbra-Specter darkened her entire form with its shadow. Her eyes fluttered up to fanatic whites, begging for more atrocity to be done to her, reveling in the horror as she revealed another taboo secret. "You are descended from Jesus himself through his carnal and spiritual love for his apostle, Mary Magdalene! They always claimed he was a virgin but he was a man before he ascended to Heaven. It made God furious..."

Angelese laughed, carved stem to stern, gushing blood in sparkling scarlet fountains.

"...it's why He made Christ suffer so during the crucifixion until Jesus cried out, 'Lord, why has Thou forsaken me?' It's why God didn't really forgive anyone as he'd promised..."

Her beating heart was visible through the cross's intersection between her breasts, enough of Angelese's skull broken (with delicate scalp and fine baby hair fluttering as a banner from the first of all holy crusades and sanctioned Inquisitions) that Shunned could see brain as a rosy-gold cotton candy.

Angelese, insane celestial, high on combustible destructable sex, gibbered and giggled and snorted damson plum-colored snot. Shunned covered her squeezed-shut eyes with her hands, yet still saw everything.

Kibideaux hurried to take Shunned in his arms. He growled at Angelese, "Shut up, you crazy bitch. Why do you want to go and hurt this poor girl like that? I thought you guys were supposed to be compassionate."

He saw Shunned's blood transfer onto him, leaking sideways, staining his owns wrists, his face...

"All of the shunned in the Purghole are descended from Jesus and Magdalene. There are those alive on earth," Angelese continued, words whistling through a partially severed windpipe. She sounded like a mutilated nightingale. "The ones in the Purghole are those aborted by their mothers or born dead or having died shortly after birth, before they could be baptised."

Shunned whispered, "It isn't true."

"I am afraid it is, Child," Ezoriel said. "This is why only you could get us here, through your bloodline and youth. The others in the Purghole are powerless, too old or too braindead. Beyond caring."

Ezoriel stared across the pale wasteland that Paradise had become. "Although we did not know about this. How could we?"

Angelese pointed at Kibideaux, her teeth chattering together. "YOU! I have the greatest secret of all for you..."

"Shut up, you little gossip," Ezoriel warned her. "Can you not see what your penchant for babble and pain has brought you?"

But she told the Broodren slyly, "Come! Come here."

The Umbra-Specter spasmed and engulfed her, itself turning from black to darkest red. Then Angelese and the shadow burst into a million droplets of blood.

Shunned crawled forward and touched a single drop. It spread from her fingers to the stains of her own stigmata. She gazed up at the Broodren, confused.

"I'm sorry, Kibi," she said. Then she vanished.

SHUNNED

Kibideaux screamed. Even as he knew that she'd returned herself to Hell and the dark Purghole. Shunned and her cousins—tapping at the walls, hands pressed to the oozing cracks, forever to be reaching for a contact they would never know.

The final two to enter empty Heaven watched a figure slowly come their way. A fluttering mirage like a running watercolor rainbow, trapped on a baking horizon.

"I tried to get God to forgive the fallen angels who were steadfastly, resolutely combatting Lucifer," they heard him say. "And to free the Otherwise Souls in the Bastille. To free all the sinful I had supposedly died for. Otherwise, what was the point of the Gospel?"

Ezoriel dropped to his knees and bowed his head. "Lord," he managed in a cracked, awed voice.

Kibideaux knelt but continued to look the man straight in the eye, his expression defiant, insisting on answers.

"My Father would not listen," the man continued. "Eventually I lost all hope of helping anyone. I could not even help my own children, my descendants."

"Because Lucifer built the Purghole for them as his great affront to you. Kept secret. But we found his book," Ezoriel remarked.

Jesus sighed. "Not Lucifer. It was my Father's book. He built the Purghole. He had always claimed to be a Jealous God... Not even Lucifer knew it was there—in his own kingdom. Eventually I got tired of begging and did an exorcism. For what else was The Word if not possessed? And not by demonic forces—no offense intended..."

"None taken, Lord," Ezoriel replied.

"If not possessed by demonic forces, then possessed by arrogance and absolute power's corruption," Jesus concluded. He placed his hand on Ezoriel's head. "You and all the others are forgiven. It never should have taken this long. I am sorry."

New, brilliantly-patterned wings sprouted out from Ezoriel's charred remnants.

"Return and tell everyone."

And Ezoriel was gone, leaving only Kibideaux and Heaven's Exorcist.

Jesus took the Broodren's hand and announced, "Together you and I will start over."

"Us?" The Broodren was shocked. "Why me? I'm just a half-caste hellion trying to free millions of kids like me."

Jesus smiled. "Because you are Heaven's last saint."

DEMONLEE DEVILISH

L.H. MAYNARD
AND M.P.N SIMS

The black moon howled.

In the fetid streets of the city a battalion of Ushers stopped their imaginative evisceration of a dozen recently dead human souls and raised curved horned heads, the anvil shape accentuating the canine-like teeth of the long jaws, and howled in unison.

The full moon had been a year in the creation. Its howling had a sweet cadence that was unknown in Mephistopolis. Because the sound was so pure it infuriated the residents of Hell. Things were done differently here, and for such innocent riffs to emanate from such a familiar part of their landscape, well, it was enough to send them into a frenzy of madness.

The Ushers knew the howling was a rare event. It meant something of significance was going to happen. Being an evolution of the natural order, the moon was one of the few occupants of the city that was not directly controlled by Satan. Lucifer was a bit OCD where control was concerned. His way or the hellway was the usual rule. For years he had orders in place for scientists to capture and manipulate the moon, but despite regular torture and beheadings, the perpetual blackness continued as devilishly as nature didn't intend.

What did the moon foretell that night?

Octo-Dogs roamed this part of the city. Canines as large as ponies but with eight legs instead of the normal four. They had evolved over the years to give them more chance of escape from the numerous predators that existed in fun city. In truth, the mutation had been deliberately created by scientists back in the early days when they wanted to try all kinds of genetic engineering as a means for more food varieties. Hot, dog leg was a specialty in the southern parts of the sprawling cesspit.

Two cadaverous Skele-Men strolled past, each holding a severed head on a stake.

"Tickets for tonight," one of the heads crooned.

"Front row for tonight's performance."

From their concealment behind a pile of corpses on the dockside Regan and Carter watched and waited.

"What's the concert?" Regan asked, pushing a shiny lock of blonde hair behind a multi-studded ear.

Carter scratched an itch on his stubbled chin. "It'll be the 'Greatest Rock 'N' Roll Band In The World'," he mimicked a barker shouting out an introduction, only he whispered very quietly. The last thing they needed so soon after arriving in Hell was to be caught.

"Only we're not in the 'world'," Regan reasoned.

Indicating for her to keep close to him, Carter unfolded his long legs and slipped into the shadows fronting the dock. Both of them ignored the slimy hands and other appendages that grabbed at their ankles as they made their way around the dock of the bay. They didn't have time to sit or waste time. They had a finite amount of time to do what they had to do and get back to their boat. A minute too long, a delay they couldn't control, and their way back to human life would be lost, probably forever.

Behind the first row of tall buildings once they got away from the waterfront was a large area that had been cleared. It had become a vast amphitheatre where daily concerts were put on as a distraction.

Regan and Carter slipped into a back row and crouched down.

"You'll see what I mean," Carter whispered in her ear, marveling as always at the sweet smell of her hair, even here where sweetness was ugly and pleasant aromas were banned.

A Demon appeared on the vast stage, the blue lighting accentuating the pus-filled wounds on its legs. Pieces of flesh dripped from the shoulders, whether from its own body or stolen from another it was impossible to say.

"Fellow denizens of Hell," The Demon boomed, using a hollowed out human leg bone as amplification. "Tonight we have a special treat. A newly departed from earth member of the band. Joining our favorites tonight is a very important addition, one we've been trying to get hold of for years but the foolhardy little human just wouldn't die."

There were strange grunts and mumblings from the audience that might have been laughter, or a parody of it.

"I'll introduce them one by one but first of all please shout it up and give an extra special Hellish welcome for The Greatest Rock 'N' Roll Band In The World...

...echoing...

The Greatest Rock 'N' Roll Band In The World...

...echo...

... Greatest Rock 'N' Roll Band In The World...

... Rock 'N' Roll Band In The World...

... Roll Band In The World...

... In The World...

...echo fades...

On the stage, instruments and mikes already set up, the musicians gave no indication of awareness where they were.

"On lead vocals, endlessly singing The End, beginning again every time the last note is uttered, thus never reaching The End for all eternity, Jim Morrison, who can never find the exit Doors.

"On lead guitar, playing a medley of Voodoo Chile, and Watchtower, and never stopping even though his fingers were worn away years ago, Mr. Jimi Hendrix, quite an Experience.

DEMONLEE DEVILISH

"On drums, his arms never once stopping their movement even when off stage, fresh from his hedonistic Zeppelin days, John Bonham. And joining him tonight, as he does every night, the twin drum sound crazily played with eternal manic madness by Keith Moon, just don't say Who?

"On bass, fingers fluttering without stopping, day after day after day, after...you get the idea...Who else but craggy John Entwhistle.

"And tonight, for his debut in Hell, the one we have been after for years, the resilient but now quite dead, in fact you could say Stone cold dead, yes, it's the one and only Keith Richards, and he won't get no Satisfaction down here.

"Without further ado, they've started already, all playing different songs, all locked into their own personal riff of destruction, I give you...

...Rock 'N' Roll Band In The World...

...Roll Band In The World...

...In The World...

The music started and within seconds Regan realized there was no music in Hell, just sounds. Familiar sounds, lyrics she knew, but played simultaneously it was a discordant cacophony. The audience loved it.

"I sound like my mother," Regan whispered in Carter's ear. "But is this what you call music?"

"You might sound like your mother, and mine, but neither of them speaking in my ear like you just did would give me a hard-on. At least not as immediate as you do."

Regan playfully punched his arm. "You help me find who we're looking for and I'll give you plenty of boners."

"And help me do something about it?"

"When Hell freezes over..."

Moving away from the stadium, they shifted into the cramped streets of the area known as Hitler Ville. Trolls congregated on street corners, pushing anything that passed by them into the road, hoping a passing vehicle would crush them.

L.H. MAYNARD AND M.P.N SIMS

Ahead of them at a crossroads, Carter suddenly saw two hooded figures in long white cloaks. "Extipicists from the Sacred College of Anthropomancy."

"What are they?"

"Lucifer's personal Diviners."

Regan let herself be pulled by Carter into a side alley. "What do they do?"

Carter sighed. "Everything down here is dead. Except us. Because of that our life force, energy, whatever you want to call it, gives off a glow. The Extipicists can see the glow and so they can find us."

Regan looked behind her. "This alley stinks."

Carter glanced up, at the steep walls of the apartment blocks above them. He saw what he expected. Hesitating for just an instant, as it wasn't something he really wanted her to see, yet realizing that Regan had to be tough if they were going to achieve what they came for. "Look up there."

Chained in layers on the walls was row after row of humans. Not quite dead and still in their human form. The lower rows were filled with obscenely obese humans, fat dripping off them like butter from corn on the cob. As the rows got higher so the people got thinner. Those at the very top were bare skeletons, almost completely devoid of flesh.

Each of them was fed a diet that guaranteed they would have continual diarrhea. For years on end they would defecate ceaselessly, the product of their bowels raining down on the row beneath. Those at the top had been there for over a century and were at the end of production.

The waste matter, the excrement, the by-product of the continual straining and grunting was collected in huge metal containers at street level. At regular intervals demons with squashed nose-less faces would appear and wheel away the filled containers, while new and empty ones were put in place. This went on without end.

"That is gross," Regan said, her pert nose wrinkling with disgust.

243

"They use the contents for making the roads. They mix it with crushed bones and it makes a solid enough surface. When it rains it gets a bit sticky but mostly it works."

Regan stood from her crouching position. "So we're standing on…"

"Nothing less." He grabbed her hand. "Come on, let's get out of here."

Regan's sister had been killed, murdered by a sex killer who had raped her, vaginally and anally, as well as forcing her to perform orally, before cutting her body over a hundred times so she slowly bled to death. He drank her blood and was wearing her panties when he was caught. Before he could be tried, he committed suicide in prison. Carter knew some girl in New Orleans who knew some stuff and word got to him that the killer was in Hell. He had been trying to impress Regan for months but she pretended to be disinterested which drove him nuts. The way to her heart was going to come by taking her to her sister's killer…even if it meant the most dangerous trip either of them had ever considered.

They were close to Attila Avenue, a wide boulevard of prestige shops and dungeons. The shopping was amongst the best in the city; rare human parts perfectly preserved, souls that had only been turned once after their original owner had died, food delicacies from mutated and interbred species—like the human-lion loins, or the whale-woman thigh bones.

The black moon continued to howl for another few minutes before it stopped.

"The concert is over," Carter said. "That means there will be crowds everywhere. So long as we keep a low profile that should work in our favor. We can use them as cover."

Regan looked at her reflection in a greasy puddle. The bootleg jeans, ripped and torn artfully, the inches of flat flesh beneath her white embroidered top, the brown high-heeled boots. "We don't look much like your typical citizen of Hell."

Carter never needed an excuse to stare at her but he had to admit she was right. They stood out for their clothes, their aura, their healthy glow. They were alive amongst the dead and the created, and they stood out as if they were shouting to be found.

"We'll have to change our clothes."

"I forgot my credit card," Regan said, her hands held palm upwards. "And I have no idea what this century's fashion is here."

"Wait here," Carter shoved her gently into a shop doorway. She turned and nearly shrieked when she saw what the shop was selling.

Carter disappeared down a dark alley. Things moved in the shadows, things that babbled and grunted. These were Shadow-Poes, small monkey-like creatures that had been bred as servants years ago but which developed a taste for human flesh that meant they ate as many as they served. They were banished to the Outer Sectors but gradually colonies of them began to filter back into the city and lived off the waste matter in the streets. They were expert muggers.

Two approached Carter as he walked slowly along the alley. One in front and the second just behind. While the one in front made a move to hit him, the second would swipe his legs away and once on the floor their razor-sharp talons and teeth would strip him of anything worth taking, including his skin.

As the first rushed at him Carter turned and plunged two fingers into the eyes of the second SP. It fell screeching to the floor. Diverted by the obvious pain of its companion the first one hesitated. Long enough for Carter to brush the blade of his knife across its throat, cutting so deep without much effort so that the head lolled backwards and almost facing down its back.

Without wasting a moment, Carter quickly ripped off the greasy clothing they wore.

When he got back to the main street, Regan was trying to fend off the unwanted attentions of a naked demon, its extended and mis-shapen penis waving in the air as if it had a life of its own. Carter threatened to cut it off and the thing soon scuttled away.

DEMONLEE DEVILISH

"It was offering you the experience of a lifetime," he said.

"I'd rather wait for a normal-sized one."

"You can wait for…"

"Don't even be so gross as to say it."

Carter handed her one of the outfits. "Here put this on."

"It's foul. Can I put it over my own clothes?"

"Much as I'd love to see you strip off, yes we'd better wear these just for now. They make us blend in a little bit."

"There's blood on this one."

"Don't ask. But can I ask you something? It's kind of personal."

"34B, and yes I'm wearing a thong."

"That's interesting to know, but what I wanted to ask was what you said about waiting for a normal…what I mean is, have you waited?"

Dressed in the stinking rags she still looked gorgeous to him. "Do you mean am I still a virgin? Yes, is that a problem for you?"

Carter took her hand. "The opposite. Nothing is pure down here. Everything is tainted, evil. You're alive, you're essentially a good person, and to top it all you're truly innocent. Those thoughts you have about my body don't count…Anyway that makes you extremely powerful. Trouble is it also makes you very valuable. If you were captured, Lucifer or his top executives would be able to make an awful lot of money from you."

They began to walk along the street. Keeping to the edges, the darkness, trying to be as invisible as possible.

They passed by public eviscerations, where some poor soul was tethered between two poles and people who were lucky winners of a raffle type competition were able to have thirty seconds tearing and cutting at the skin of the stomach to get at the precious entrails inside.

Rushed past also were crowd rape events where twenty or more freshly departed human women were tied spread-eagled to specially adapted trolleys where every orifice was open and made available. When the normal channels were torn and of little use, specially cre-

246

ated tools were used to cut new openings in different parts of their bodies.

Eventually they came to the part of the city that Carter had heard about.

There were many sectors to the city and most had begun to be mapped out on a new grid system Lucifer had approved. The part they were in was still not spoken about. Most things were the opposite of what they should be in this city. Most things were exaggerated and distorted. Horror was manifest. Terror was an everyday currency. Fear and loathing wasn't a fancy title, it was an ambition.

In this part of the city things were different. They were quieter. There was darkness but it brooded rather than screamed. There were shadows but they drifted like mist on a moor rather than slunk like mangy dogs.

Hell had evolved over 5,000 years on a diet of horror. Blood and gore were the currencies here. There was no place for suggestion, just eyeball gouging; no room for quiet development, merely all guns blazing. But here in this part of the city things were different.

The part of the city they were in was called James Town. Other areas of the district were Blackwood, Wakefield County, Hope Hodgson Heights, and some newer subdivisions such as Wright Acres.

The quiet infiltration of this softer approach to life in Hell was frowned upon in high places. There were rumors of ethnic cleansing to come. Talk was of colonies of Ushers being forcibly housed in the Aickman district. Maybe some Trolls and Demons being appointed to the Council. Talk was quiet as appropriate, but it was insistent.

Carter had a fascination for ghost stories over horror stories, although sometimes the edges got blurred. While he was here, if there was anything he could do to help then he would.

"Is this where he'll be?" Regan asked, her voice hushed in the darkness.

There was a huge Ash Tree in the center of a black marble square. Hanging from its pendulous branches were headless corpses, twitching in a perpetual death dance. The heads were impaled on metal stakes that formed into a pentagram around the tree. Each head was wailing in endless misery.

"There's a house around here—Red Lodge. He'll be there."

"How do you know?"

Carter smiled. "That's where all the criminal suicides are taken once they've passed over. It was a coup for the sector. They wanted to disprove the known theory that there are no such things as ghosts. It is widely believed that ghosts are merely soulless projections—just images left over. People here believe in ghosts as being more material than that. By using the recently dead bodies of criminals, especially killers and rapists, they want to prove they're right. He'll be here."

This entire part of the city was covered like a sheet by pale gray mist. It meant everything was continually damp. The mist swirled like a scene from an early Hammer film, a Ripper Victorian street, horses clip-clopping on cobbles.

The Red Lodge was a couple of streets along from the square. It was obvious how it got its name, and how it maintained it. Rows of humans were fixed on the roof, their legs amputated and the bleeding stumps positioned so that the blood flowed evenly down the previously white washed walls.

Regan stared at the house. This was where her sister's killer was, and she itched to get at him. She hadn't been satisfied with the life sentence the judge had passed but that was nothing to the frustration she'd felt when he killed himself before a year of his time had been spent.

"How will we get in?" She asked.

Carter stripped off the Shadow-Poes clothes. "By using our life force to surprise them. Come on get your clothes off—the borrowed ones at least."

"So we just walk up to the front door and they let us in?"

"They won't be expecting anyone to walk right in off the street. They won't be anticipating live humans. They won't be able to resist a real live virgin. The combination will be irresistible."

"What if it isn't?"

Carter hefted his long knife in one hand and an Uzi in the other. "Then we use subtle persuasion."

The heavy oak door of the Lodge was carved with intricate and ancient artwork. Snakes, gods, creatures with strange forms. As Carter pushed the door, and as it creaked slowly open, a cloud of ectoplasm wafted from the hallway. It was cold in the entrance hall, their breath misted in front of them. A winding staircase from a house in an Agatha Christie novel towered above them.

Carter took Regan's hand. He pointed to a door, and they moved over to it. Regan strained to hear any sounds from behind the door but there was nothing. Carter felt the door handle, and it turned in his hand.

He pushed the door with his shoulder and it opened into a room lit by candles.

As the door closed behind her, and her eyes got accustomed to the gloom, Regan looked at Carter and saw he was smiling.

Carter moved away from her and shook the hand of the man sitting in an overstuffed maroon armchair. There were other people in the room but it was the seated man that held Regan's attention. This was Wexford, her sister's killer.

"You did well, Carter," Wexford said, as Carter took his position behind the armchair. "And so we meet again Regan. This time I'm not the prisoner in the dock and you're not spitting your venom at me from the viewing gallery."

"I'm sorry, Regan," Carter said quietly.

"I'll bet you are."

"They've got my family. I had no choice."

Wexford clapped his hands slowly and sarcastically. "Very touching, ladies. Now to business. You've come to get me, Regan. To make sure justice is done. Couldn't be satisfied with my death, you wanted to follow me beyond the grave."

"I wanted to make you suffer properly for what you did to my sister."

Wexford stood from the chair. He was skinny, death didn't agree with him. "The only one that's going to suffer is you. A virgin? Not for long..." He motioned to the other figures in the room and they began to converge on Regan.

She screamed, not in fear but in rage. Pushing Wexford out of the way as if he was a limp rag, she launched herself at Carter. Shock was written on his face as he fell to the floor, Regan on top of him, punching and scratching at his face.

As hands pulled her away, none of them except Carter knew that she held the knife and the Uzi in either hand. Shrugging her arms free she scrambled to her knees and began to dispense her own brand of justice.

BABY NUKES IN HELL

GERARD HOUARNER

"You're, like, the smallest gang in Hell," Skyve said, stretching her arms in the courtyard crater just enough to reinforce how much bigger she was than Scar and Teeth. "I mean, is this it? The four of you? And, like, you're all so short."

Teeth, near the crater rim, rolled her eyes and looked down to Scar with an I-told-you-so expression. Her secondary ridge of dentata, below the jaw-line and along her throat, glistened as flesh-seams parted. Her third and fourth sets, Scar knew from experience, were open and ready underneath the Troll-skin bustier. The fifth, well, that one was less effective on females.

Here it comes, Scar thought, sinking lower into the hole to avoid detection. Their target had just rounded the remains of a stone wall. It was almost time. But it seemed as if Skyve was already giving them the shuffle before the break away, getting ready to back out and leave them dancing with a pissed-off Golem. Lucifer's Biowizards had learned a lot since they'd made Scar and his crew: Skyve was a piece of work, more Spirit Body than demon, long, lean, and from what they'd seen of her during her Dead Girls' initiation, very mean. She was Chernobyl vat born, like the rest of them, but that didn't make her one of the gang. She'd talked a good game, but maybe that was all she was really good at.

BABY NUKES IN HELL

"That's why we're called the Baby Nukes," answered Scar, ignoring Teeth, but passing a finger along the ridges that had earned him his street name, the price of eternal rumbling and illicit teratologists.

He knew Match was tracking their conversation from his lookout post atop the nearby ruined bell-tower on their right flank—the boy could smell Nectoports precious moments before they materialized. Once, he even spotted a bi-face trying to pass itself off as a Grand Duke recruiting them for a break-in job at the Academy of Teratology.

Considering that job had given Scar and the rest of the gang the shakes.

Down time in a bone-grinding station promised more thrills. Biowizard spells still sang through their demonic DNA, echoed through their earliest vat memories, burst with star-killing fury through the helter-skelter panic of their escape from childhood. Any hint of Lucifer's bright light made them shrivel. They'd stopped playing with Hell's hierarchy for money and kicks after that one, and lost themselves in the mean streets of Mephistopolis where the odds for skipping out of tight spots and on to ravage and play another day were significantly higher.

Though still a fool's bet.

Match was good. He knew to keep his guard up, trust what his sensory organs told him even through the suppuration and poorly stitched protective flaps. Enchantment Dust didn't dazzle him. Neither would a raw but fetching Broodren recruit like Skyve, full of pride and arrogance because she happened to have been well made and escaped her vat before she was scrapped or programmed. Match didn't need Scar's signal, he'd catch the bad before it broke surface.

But Fetch, in position behind an upper-tier flying vault holding up the remains of the rest of the old Satanic cathedral on their right, was all speed and bounce and swift-cut motion, a balled-up manic muscle aching to stretch and flex. He couldn't catch subtle cues, he just ran into, through, around and over whatever was in his way. He actually enjoyed Golem-baiting, but even with his demonic gift, there was no need to goad a Golem if it wasn't necessary.

Scar stiffened, caught up in a thought thread he knew better than to indulge in. But he couldn't help himself. His demon blood boiled, touched off by the possibility of Skyve's punking.

They were the badasss Baby Nukes, demon gangbanging Broodren born in the College of Spells and Discantations' Chernobyl vats. Graffiti that on the Mephisto Building, angel fucker. Carve that into the Flesh Warrens, baby. Mephistopolis' inner city had forged them to be tough and mean and fast on the treacherous ruins of its streets. Yeah, they weren't as slick as Outer Sector Broodren with their shabby grifts and pathetic begging, feeding on Hell's fringes like leeches, without pride or joy. The Baby Nukes weren't slick. No, man, but they were savage. And they weren't morons, like so many demons. Fun was fun, but they hadn't survived this long in Hell together by taking stupid risks. There always had to be a plan. And a purpose.

Not necessarily a sensible plan, nor a useful purpose. They were demons, after all. But purpose and plan, nonetheless. Because that's how they rolled.

Scar sniffed the bracing sulfur stench rising from a rent at his feet at the bottom of the crater. He focused on stroking his face, tracing the raised lines of flesh that would spell out a warning if Fetch was watching, one short finger motion away from an abort.

Pay attention, Scar thought, aiming the words straight at Fetch.

The Golem was closing into range, but Skyve didn't seem to notice. Instead of studying her target's gait, looking for hitches in its step, as well as searching the uneven terrain for treacherous footing and places to duck into, she continued to fidget and undulate as if caught between a cramp and a seduction.

Bad sign. Scar couldn't really blame recruits for backing out. Golem-tipping wasn't for amateurs.

The gang might break even for the time wasted in testing her by passing her parts on to the bone market. Maybe there was an illegal teratologist in the market for some of her shapelier parts. There was always a market for sex grafts.

Hell, maybe they'd just eat her. Scar could tell Teeth was ready for that.

"I was expecting a good-sized district gang, a few hundred at least," Skyve started up again, glancing back and forth between Scar and Teeth as if expecting one of them to offer her sympathy. "I mean, the Papa Docs and the Zombie Nation just started around here and they already have 10,000 members each. And the Coyotes, they've gone city-wide. They're down with the Mongols. Even the Mob's paying attention to them. You know, I got an offer from the Fallen Papists. They really want me with them." She wasn't looking at the Golem entering the tip-zone they'd established in the rubble-filled alley.

"We've aligned ourselves with the bigger gangs," he explained. "The Yancy Street Ghouls, The Newsboy Legion of Hell, the Dead End Kids. Even messed with the Dead Boys."

"Bunch of pussies," Teeth muttered. "Even before I got through with them."

Skyve stared hard a Scar. "What happened, you got kicked out?"

Here it was. Scar licked his lips, tongue thorns ready to bristle. "No, we quit. They were all a bunch of angels. Like those Dead Girls you were so hot to hook up with."

"You ever join the Contumacy?"

Scar flinched. Teeth's eyes widened, and she quickly turned to watch the approaching Golem.

Damnation. Hadn't seen that one coming. Could they have been set up? Was she Constabulary working an undercover operation? He glanced up at Match's position searching for a sign from him confirming the depths of Skyve's betrayal.

But no, nothing. No warning.

There was just an instant of distrust, a moment filled with conjecture about Match selling them out, making a deal so he could be with his Chernobyl vat twin sister, the angel-whore serving a grand Duke in his Templar Gate condo penthouse.

Fucking bitch whore who does he think he is fucking us over for a vat sister like that ever meant anything little miss perfect—

But the moment passed, flushed by vivid memories of Match's rage, always burning at the thought of his sister behaving with such intense kindness and generosity, initially refusing to join their plot to escape from the College's vats. The idea of being genetically linked to a demon designed and conditioned for angelic performance for the amusement of one of the wealthier Grand Dukes, who'd found the true, and cheaper, angels too easy to corrupt, tortured Match and his need for primal bonds with exquisite precision.

He might sell them out to kill her, as revenge for the betrayal that forced him to join Scar's escape plot or be consigned to the shit heaps. But he'd never join her in service. And no Grand Duke would ever sacrifice such a rare and wonderful possession for the capture of irrelevant street thugs.

The spirit of Lucifer lived even in Hell's smallest damnations.

Scar settled back against the crater wall. Skyve was asking more stupid questions, babbling on about babies. Apparently, that was another of her habits. So maybe there was no hidden layer of danger. This was just about another nervous recruit realizing just how bad a situation she'd talked herself into, looking for a way out.

Well, at least the Baby Nukes knew where lunch was coming from.

"And, I mean, you're all so young," Skyve said, bubbling with uncertainty. "Babies."

"You said that," Teeth said.

Scar wasn't sure from which orifice the words had emerged. If they'd had time, he would have told Skyve about the time Teeth ate her siblings and a Biowizard's arm while on the operating table undergoing modifications.

"Here it comes," Scar said, catching sight of the Golem and bracing himself for a jump out of the crater and into the next tunnel mouth. His finger touched the scar that would bring the exercise to a halt.

"You ready?" Teeth asked, grinning.

"Like fishing in the Styx," Skyve said, and she was gone.

Startled, Scar gave the abort sign, but it was too late. Fetch was arcing through the air in a perfect trajectory ending at the point where Skyve was leading the Golem by jumping out in front of the creature, sneaking in a weak jab, then darting back and away.

The Golem stood its ground, stared at her, as if it didn't know what it was supposed to do.

"What the Heaven," Teeth muttered, then jumped out to support Skyve.

Scar followed, flanking the Golem, daring to prance in and out of its reach, carving its earthen flesh with razor finger nails and heel palm quills. Teeth snapped at its fingers, even managed a nip of the neck.

Fetch adjusted his descent. Skyve came back, threw herself at the Golem, tapping its head and heart and groin as if counting coup.

"Cut that tribal shit," Scar shouted, again looking to Fetch and finding no warning. But something was wrong. Golems always chased. They couldn't help themselves.

"I don't need your advice," Skyve said, and proved herself right because, at last, the Golem was focusing on her, reaching out as it staggered after her. She back-flipped out of its grasp, kicking at its wrist, flinging rock and dust into its chiseled eyes.

Scar retreated, signaled for Teeth to do the same. They both watched the windows and doorways in the surrounding structures, all abandoned leftovers from the city's Medieval era, while Skyve proved her daring.

And as Fetch swooped down and landed a surprise blow on the Golem's left rear hip, Skyve proved she had the balls of a Baby Nuke by throwing herself at the creature's feet, stretching her body out in blind faith. Or complete confidence.

It tottered under Fetch's blow, tripped over Skyve. Fell.

Landed flat on its blank face with a satisfying, ground-shaking thud.

Flailed, kicked, and otherwise made pointless attempts at getting back up. Golems were a far cry from the stronger and more agile Ushers.

The thing moaned.

Scar had never heard a Golem moan, before.

But the Golem was upended. Their task was done. Each Baby Nuke scrambled to his or her previously identified safe corner, a separate entrance to the labyrinth of old tunnels running through the ancient neighborhood. Time to find cover before the Nectoports brought in the Mutilation Squads.

But the squads never came.

And, more frightening to Scar, the Golem got up on its own.

«« — »»

"Did I make it?" Skyve asked, beaming with pride. "Can we do it again?"

They were going to have to work on that pride. And the enthusiasm.

Scar looked to Match, who scrambled into their underground rendezvous, an old, low and wide dungeon from a long-gone castle. Brimstone veins provided dim but fiery illumination. The stench was reminiscent of a Troll Womb ripped open by a ravenous Griffin. "What the hell was that?" Scar asked, nearly grabbing hold of his look-out with both hands before pulling back, instinctively recalling the occasionally acidic fluids that leaked from his open sores.

But before he could answer, Fetch jumped into the dungeon and the conversation. "A good show, that's what I call it. I was perfect. You saw? Made adjustments on the fly, saw where Skyve was heading, tapped that chunk of clay right over her. Great team work, there, Skyvie, I vote for her, I want her, I—"

"Annoying," Teeth acknowledged, arms crossed. "But good."

"The Golem," Scar reminded them. "It got up. They don't do that. Not without help."

"Remember the time we tipped one into that oven we rigged?" Match asked. "It was a real shake and bake, and then we broke it into a million pieces. Wish I had a piece right now."

Scar kicked Match on the shin, and the demon shivered and sat down. Whatever past he was running from had suddenly, if momentarily, emerged to run alongside him, and he needed a rest. Scar remembered once being curious about what had happened to Match in his vat. But only once.

"Maybe the Constabulary is redesigning the Golems," Teeth suggested, while her other sets of teeth clicked with worry.

"Why the hell would they bother?" Skyve asked.

"They wouldn't," Scar said. "And where was the Mutilation Squad follow-up? They always come when we hit a Golem."

"Not a trace," Match confirmed. "You want me to go out and check again?"

Scar waved Match down.

"So what's going on?" Skyve stretched and rolled, her feet and hands nearly touching opposite walls.

They might have to find bigger safe holes.

"Anything?" Scar asked Fetch.

"It smelled just like a Golem," Fetch said, scratching a lesion on his arm.

Teeth *tsked* from multiple mouths.

"But it didn't sound like one," he continued. "Not from the inside. Too many things going on in the clay. Clicky-things. And organics. It's been customized. Nothing standard or mass-produced."

"There was demon meat in it?" It was a perversion that caught Scar by surprise.

"What does any of that even mean?" Match mumbled from a gloomy corner.

"Are we going to take it apart?" Skyve said, then sat up suddenly. "Hey, did you guys vote? Am I a Baby Nuke? Do I get a say on what we're going to do? I say let's take it apart and find out what makes it tick."

"Probationary Baby Nuke," Scar announced.

"We can still eat you," Teeth added.

"Maybe we're making a mistake," Fetch said, thumbing in Match's direction. "She sounds a little like him."

"I'm nothing like him," Skyve said, cocking her head and thrusting her chin out as she turned on Fetch. "I'm bigger and stronger—"

"But not as sensitive," Match said.

"— and smarter, and I could tip a Golem all on my own, now that I see how you guys do it, and then I'd make you do it too so you could belong to my gang—"

"What would you call it?" Fetch said.

"The Golem Tippers, of course—"

"Nice," Fetch said, making a bug-eyed face.

"Great. The Constabulary will never figure out who's responsible for their Golem-tipping problem," Teeth said.

"She's smarter, all right," added Fetch, laying on the sarcasm thick.

"We need to follow it," Scar said, and everyone became so still the primeval fires around and below them could be heard roaring. "Maybe the Constabulary got tired of their Golems being knocked down and sent in a special one to mess with us. Or maybe something else is going on nearby, something we can score on. Carve another bone notch for doing what nobody else can."

"Is that what you guys do?" Skyve asked. "Carve notches into your own bones?"

Scar said, "Yes." And then, "Any Ushers out there?"

"No squads, not even another Golem," Match said. "There's a party of Young Mongols a few blocks away scaring up Plague Squatters—"

"Pussies," Teeth said.

"—and a Caco-Dragon rousing itself for a little meal in the catacombs under the old Colosseum. The usual Were-Jackals and Polter-Rats. Someone's got DemonVision on and watching My Favorite Sin—"

"Wish The Horror Show was on," Fetch said. "Or the Cemetery Dancers."

"—and there's a group of Ministration Monks leading a prayer vigil in the name of Ezoriel for demons to repent."

Scar shook his head. "And there's not a trace of Nectoports?"

"Nothing. Oh, and there's quite a few baby demons being made. Want to hear?"

"No," Teeth said.

"Yes," said Fetch, rousing.

"Is this a vote?" Skyve asked.

"We're going back topside," Scar said, leading the way back up the tunnel to the surface. "Things are way too quiet. It almost sounds like a little piece of Purgatory landed in the middle of Hell."

"And you know that can't be right," said Teeth.

«« — »»

The signs of Hell's disorder did not lessen as they followed the Golem through the old district. They passed under crumbling lavaducts, through ancient magma baths, and over a broken theater stage and the remains of stalls that had once comprised a market. In these forgotten ruins in the heart of Mephistopolis, Lucifer's first city-building efforts based on the earliest Living World urban centers could still be glimpsed. The millennia of reconstruction and rebuilding had missed the area, as if Lucifer intended a tiny part of the heart of his domain to remain pure and pristine in its particular form of corruption. It was a museum demon schools never took their charges to visit, a historical site guides never pointed out to their demon tourists.

The district was inconsequential, a repository of demonic failures and a stalking ground for predators lost in the city's immensity. Mutilation Squads came here for training. Wizards tried out new spells on structures still standing. Gangs used the area to settle their turf wars so their own territories wouldn't suffer damage, and because the authorities rarely intervened. They didn't want to interfere with the cycle of evil and damnation that gave Mephistopolis its unique character.

It was the only place in which the Baby Nukes felt safe.

And here they were following a mystery, Scar thought, with growing trepidation. Following a mystery wrapped up in a Golem now clearly making its way to the district's heart, only eight blocks square, where not even the Ushers, not even the Caco-Dragon, ever ventured. They were heading for Blackheart, the Devil's Playground, Lucifer's Asshole, the Dark, on the rare occasions anyone wanted to mention it in conversation. Most times, the place was left unmentioned, a blank spot in Hell.

The place nothing ever came out of.

"Scar," Match said.

"I see," Scar answered.

"We're going in?" Teeth asked.

"I need a nap," Match answered.

"Is it going to be bad?" Skyve asked, excited.

Scar said, "Yes."

"We need a Diviner," Match said. "When are we ever going to recruit a Diviner?"

《《 — 》》

They went in and nothing happened to them. The streets narrowed, twisted, rose and fell over uneven ground just as they did in the surrounding blocks. Hell's heat and stench wasn't any worse.

What was different was the silence. The screams of the tormented were as distant as Scar had ever heard them. It was as if they had discovered the quiet eye of Hell's eternal storm.

"I heard Ezoriel tried to hide his forces here early in the Contumacy," Teeth said, watching the roof lines. "Sent in scouts. They never came out."

"I heard the Academy of Teratology dumps new hybrids down here," Fetch said, as he went back and forth ahead of them checking doors and ground floor windows.

"I heard they dropped one they called a picleeketchum down here and it survived, but didn't want to come out," Match said, seemingly attending to Skyve. "It liked it here."

Scar had faith Match's survival instincts were keeping his finer senses tuned to the faintest hint of danger as well as the Golem's progress. "When did any of you start believing in Hell's lies?"

"Hey, nobody's lived in these buildings for ages," Skyve said as she climbed part way up a pile of rubble to poke her head in a second storey window. "Most of these are nothing but shells."

"Good way to lose your head," Teeth pointed out.

"Nectoport," said Match.

Everyone froze. Scar glanced at every one of them. They'd all recognized the futility of running. Like a bunch of freshly damned, they'd been lured into a trap.

"I told you we should have found ourselves a Diviner," said Match. "We'd have seen this coming."

"They don't see everything," Scar said. "They never saw us leaving, or where we're going to be."

"Is that what you do?" Skyve asked. "Some kind of anti-Diviner?"

Scar felt a moment of distrust trying to break through his concentration. What was she, another BioWizard manipulating his insides, testing and probing him, trying to find out if something useful had emerged from the random collision of uncountable trillions of evil atoms that made up Lucifer's realm? Whatthefuckdidshethinkgshewas—

"What he does isn't any of your business," said Teeth.

—arroganttearheranewcuntbitchwhoreangelsuckingpieceofshit fromLucifer'sass—

"But," Skyve blurted, her full lips pouting, "I'm a member of your gang, aren't I?"

Bad things were coming. He couldn't lose himself in the rage, couldn't succumb to blind, raw demonic nature. He was more than that. The Biowizards had designed him for much more. The pricks. Tearing at his soul, the blackened, stunted heart of what he'd become writhed and screamed, trapped in eternal damnation. Easier to destroy her, send her to the Emaciation Detail, rip her limb from limb and sell her parts for another trip to the teratologist—

Fetch interrupted. "Why aren't we Excre-Worms yet?"

Kill her now, kill them all, the whole fucking lot, screw the Baby Nukes, betray them all, get whatever he could get, and maybe then he'd have the resources to transform himself into what he wanted to be, instead of a thing others made him—

"The Nectoport appeared ahead of us," Match answered. "Where the Golem stopped."

Stop, Scar told himself. Please, stop. Just like the Golem. Be still.

The others looked to him. Skyve bit her lip and chewed on a piece of her own flesh. Her lips still seemed full. "Careful," said Scar, motioning them forward. Hell's song of damnation faded into the background noise in his mind, the sounds of his whining and screaming and moaning always flowing in a sub-current through his thoughts, the noise of drills and saws and machinery operated by Biowizards and teratologists echoing on and on inside him, both woven together into his own personal psychic scar.

The Baby Nukes blended into the terrain, hugging the walls and building shells, stepping gingerly through rubble, crossing dividing walls and alleys like flitting Umbra Specters among the clouds, until Match held up a hand.

They crawled to a low wall, peeked through holes. Figures had gathered in the center of a desolate, circular depression, flat and black, the glassy surface veined with cracks. Crater, Scar thought. Another damned crater. Mephistopolis was filled with them, signatures of Contumacy incursions and Satanic wrath, and this district in particular had more than its share. But this crater hadn't flattened the ancient buildings that surrounded it.

The structures had been constructed around the rim.

He looked to the others for confirmation of his suspicion, but their collective attention had been captured by the activity surrounding the Golem. A wiser leader would have pulled the gang back, but they were demons and this was Hell, and wisdom was a sin they only occasionally indulged in.

When Scar followed their gaze, it was as if Hell had concentrated its essence, reflecting and magnifying everything they were and could ever be in the spectacle of the damned unfolding before them. It took everything he had to refrain from jumping up and running to his annihilation so he could experience fully for just a moment the intense, intoxicating energy of malevolence radiating from the crater's heart.

A Nectoport had unloaded a clutch of Ushers, built for Extermination, but they remained uncharacteristically docile, claws held close to their genitalia and fangs pressed against their own jaws and chins, as if intimidated into submission by a higher evil. Scar twitched at the sight of Biowizards and Arch-Locks, Warlocks and Teratologists, who ringed the Golem performing rituals, studying instruments, frantically inspecting the creature's surface and inserting rods and needle-like instruments into tiny holes for which they hunted with fanatical intensity. Time-bomb memories from his own Chernobyl vat caused Scar to black out for an instant. But he recovered quickly, his hunger for a closer experience sated by past torments.

Further off, clerks from the Kafka Bureau of the Office of Departmental Agencies Authority, holding forms and notepads in two of their six appendages, attended Upper Hierarchal demons bearing the stigmata of service to various Industrial Zone centers as well as

GERARD HOUARNER

the Constabulary, Colleges, and other elite Mephistopolis institutions. A few Grand Dukes stood off to the side, out of the way, watching a portable Demonvision broadcast of a Demonocracy Debate between District Representative candidates whose mouths had been surgically sewn shut while a voice-over announcer reported the news: a rise in anti-Satanic criminality due to increased consignments of hypocritical religious fanatics still denying their evil essence; the arrest of a clerk in the Department of Development Hell for refusing to take bribes and initiating a new film production; and the continued search for the lone voter who cast his ballot in the recent Luciferin election for Luficer's opponent. Extipicists huddled together as if desperately piecing together a single clear vision of the future. Unsacred Cardinals prayed, counting off their demon beads.

A Troll Clown stood away from all the others, shifting nervously from one huge jingling foot to another.

Another Nectoport materialized, and a Conscript gang spilled out bearing a pedestal and a statue of Lucifer, part of the special project Scar had heard was being run by a consortium of former despotic rulers from the Living World who'd prevailed upon Lucifer to put up statues of himself throughout Mephistopolis. They'd presented a nameless artist bearing a talent so great she could capture Lucifer's unbearably beautiful likeness, resulting in works in which his visage could not be perceived. It had been rumored that the despots hoped to be rewarded with their own statues, even if the works were relegated to offal piles in the Outer Districts, and Scar knew of a good number of Hell's denizens who enjoyed the idea of their old torturers suffering the pain of hope in Hell.

Entranced by the activity, Scar felt something grow inside him that he couldn't identify at first, as well as a shrinking of every organ in his body. It occurred to him that they had voluntarily walked into the very worst place they could have found in Hell.

Well, maybe Mephisto Tower would have been worse.

"Guys—" Fetch whispered.

269

BABY NUKES IN HELL

"What are all those—" Skyve started.

"Lucifer's court," Teeth said.

Cold. Scar put the word to what he felt: cold.

"That Golem," Match said.

"Oh, my," Skyve said.

"That Golem has a hard-on," Match said.

"But they don't have dicks," Teeth protested.

"Tell that to the tent pole," Skyve said.

Cold. He'd felt cold in the vats.

He'd been afraid.

Conscripts scurried away from the bustling cluster erecting Lucifer's statue, away from the Baby Nukes' hiding place, to the side of an old magma mill that hadn't collapsed. They began a graffiti tableau Scar recognized as tags he'd seen recently pop up throughout the city: "Be true to your nature: sink to your worst." and "If you can't be evil, be stupid."

"So those are Satanic propaganda messages," said Teeth, sounding disappointed. "And here I thought my old gang, the Pseudo Punks were making a comeback."

"If that's the big guy's court—" Match started to say.

"Just part of it," Teeth added.

"—then where's the big guy himself?"

"He never leaves Mephisto House," Scar said.

"Never's a long time," said Skyve, "especially in Hell. He must be coming."

Teeth got it first, looked to Scar. Match next. They would have had to wait a while for Fetch and Skyve to catch up.

"He's already here," Scar said. The cold inside him hurt.

Scar tapped Match, then wiped his fingers off on himself. "Can you zero in on what's being said around the—"

A grinding, metallic, ululating moan rose from the circle of BioWizards and Archlocks. The Ushers burst into frenetic motion, morphing into lightning-fast columns that disemboweled all the

Conscripts and left the statue of Lucifer smashed to pieces on the blackened ground.

The Ushers returned to their stations, assuming their submissive stance. On their way back, a detachment swarmed over the Troll Clown and killed it, with sudden and violent jingling, in what perhaps was not an entirely random act of violence.

The Kafka clerks marched excitedly in place, as if eager to scurry for cover. All conversation stopped, and all attention focused on the Golem.

"No way," Fetch said, with awe.

Skyve answered, hardly loud enough to be heard: "Way."

"How?" they both said, a stunned chorus of wonder.

"It's too dangerous for Lucifer to leave the Mephisto House," Scar said. "Physically. But his spirit could, in theory, with the proper technology, spell casting, and a suitable host, discorporate and travel—"

"He possessed the Golem," Skyve said.

"A specially designed Golem, tailored for him," Scar continued, "filled with the necessary demonic organic matter able to contain enough of his spirit to accomplish whatever he needs to do here—"

"Why not come with the others in a Nectoport?" Fetch asked.

"Too obvious," Match replied. "Spies see him leaving through a Nectoport, find out he's out in the open, and who knows how fast Ezoriel or another enemy could strike."

"Okay, then why did he walk half-way across his own city in that stupid Golem?" Fetch continued. "I mean, I like to get out and about, but the Nectoport—"

"A Golem traveling with that crowd would raise suspicions," Scar said. "Like bringing a toothpick to Armageddon." He turned to Match and tapped his own ear, pointed at the Golem. "Nobody pays attention to a Golem on its own."

"I tipped Lucifer," Fetch whispered, his voice catching over the magnitude of what he'd done.

"Why is he here?" Skyve asked.

Scar was impressed. She'd cut to the essence of the issue. Maybe there was hope of her survival as a Baby Nuke, after all. If she could only stop making him paranoid.

Match croaked, the sound a Bapho-Roach made when crushed under a Griffin's paw.

The sound was louder than Scar would have wanted, but the Ushers remained in place. The court was preoccupied with the Golem, pulling out the needles and tubes while joining in a complex chant whose purpose was not immediately apparent.

Match spoke, channeling the words he heard coming from the crater: "If you're through desecrating the birthplace of my never-ending punishment, open the gate."

The chanting grew louder while the Kafka clerks scurried to the crater's exact center and threw off loose rubble, uncovering a deeper indentation surrounded by finely fractured crystallized earth. A pair of shapes could be seen imbedded in the ground after the clerks left, and before the Court formed a loose circle around the depression.

"Are those burnt wings?" Teeth asked.

No one else answered, so Scar said, "Yes."

"Angel wings."

"Yes."

It was Skyve who dared to say, "Lucifer's."

"This is where he landed when he was thrown out of Heaven."

A beam of light shot up from the depression, thin and pale white, before flickering out. The chanting stopped, and Match grumbled someone saying, "The Way is open."

And continued, in someone else's voice, "About fucking time."

As the Golem advanced to the hole, Scar nodded. "That really is a gate."

"To what?" Skyve asked.

"The Living World?" Fetch asked, rising slightly, as if preparing to sprint through Lucifer's court and dive into the hole.

"No," Scar answered, rolling an eye. "To another Plane. It has to be. The impact of His landing was so great, it cracked the reality of this existence, opened a doorway to another place."

Skyve nodded her head, her mouth hanging open. "That's so awesome."

"Big deal," said Fetch, dismissing the scene with a wave of his hand, phasing through half-a-dozen rude gestures. "What do we need with another Plane? There's all kinds of traffic between the Planes. There's nothing here for us. Let's throw some rocks at them and get out of here. Everybody'll really be scared of the Baby Nukes once they find out what we saw, and did."

"We can't run as fast as you can," Skyve said.

Scar shook his head. "We need to stay. Find out more about what's going on. Obviously this is no ordinary Plane. They can't all be reached. Look how far off Heaven is. No, this is one of the mystery Planes. Imagine what this place might be worth to Ezoriel. Or a lot of others."

Skyve whispered, "Maybe it's a way to Heaven."

"Death should be so easy," Teeth answered.

Match, back in his own voice, spoke haltingly while oozing nervously from several sores. "We could just sneak back the way we came, try not to run into the picleeketchum or anything else dangerous. Just knowing this much should worth something."

"But then we wouldn't be the Baby Nukes," Scar replied, relying on the tried-and-true sin of pride to convince the gang to try something demonically foolhardy. Sinning warmed him against the coldness of his fear.

Skyve moved suddenly between them, pushed her face against a crack in the wall for a better view. "Oh," she said.

The Golem was down on its hands and knees, positioning its cock over the hole in the center's crater.

"Don't think that thing's going to fit," said Fetch.

But it did, with the help of gels and foams sprayed on by a pair of attending Warlocks, and a great deal of mystical chanting and encouraging grunts. And when the Golem had penetrated the hole between Planes to its satisfaction, gently testing the fit by slowly raising and lowering its hips, it began to thrust deeper, and then harder, and finally faster, until the Golem had become a pumping machine as powerful as the engines running the bone crushers and flesh processors in the Industrial Sector.

Despite the attention of its attendants, who poured on additional lubricants, the Golem's clay form reddened with the heat of its efforts. Smoke rose from the hole, and cracks shot out from the impact point like webs spun by mad spiders, multiplying the original markings on the glazed crater surface. The Ushers looked on, drooling, while technicians approached the Golem gingerly, instruments held out, hurriedly taking measurements and readings.

Lucifer's Extipicists paused in their consultations to watch.

"Wonder what that feels like," Skyve said, rolling her shoulders and hips.

Scar was moved to demonstrate for her.

"I think I'd like to try that," Fetch said, hands over whatever might have grown between his legs in the vats.

Scar had made it a rule never to inquire about a gang member's personal habits. Too bad they never had a chance to demonstrate to Skyve all the things that weren't allowed in the gang.

The Golem cried out, kicking and flailing, squirming as much as its stiff, clumsy body could, maw wide open with dust falling from its gaping emptiness like black snow. And then it collapsed, rolled over, threw its arms up and legs wide. Its cock, a tower as mighty as any in Mephistopolis, sagged, curled, and finally cracked and fell off to the side.

The Kafka clerks hurried forward to collect the broken Satanic implement.

Fetch turned away with a frown. "I take that back…"

Scar prodded Match. "What are they saying?"

Match babbled in a series of voices, including a Grand Duke's that made Skyve clamp her hands over his mouth to silence the resonating sound. After she pulled her hands away, with a look of disgust, Match continued, passing through the clicks of the Kafka clerks and the meaningless jargon of technicians until he found the Golem's grating words.

"...can't go again, this vessel won't last. We'll just have to keep trying with the hybrids and work on building up their tolerance and stamina. Yes, I will contribute my own Demonic DNA, but I'll be supervising all experiments directly in the Mephisto Tower. No, you will not carry any samples to the College. Do you wish to question me again? That is correct. We will continue until we find a proper offering that will be accepted. Allow me the privilege of weighing the risk of spreading my seed to another Plane, while I allow you the privilege of serving as concubine to a nest of Bapho-Roaches."

"It's a Power Exchange," said Scar, feeling cold again. He didn't know how he could be sure, but all the pieces of what they'd seen and heard seemed to fall into place. "Lucifer's trying to initiate a Power Exchange with whatever's on the other side."

The value of the precious information still couldn't warm him.

"Do you think I would do that?" the Golem asked, answering an unheard question.

The Ushers turned on the court. A scramble escalated into a fiery display of spells and a thunderous storm of chants and cries. The ground shook and rumbled from the impact of blows and bolts, the air simmered with the heat of protective charms crumbling under overwhelming force. Roasting demon meat reminded Scar that he was hungry, but his instinct to flee was much stronger.

When the unleashed energies had subsided, a Grand Duke had been reduced to ashes and a number of attendants lay in various states of injury, from disembowelment to lolling heads, open wounds with bones protruding to holes clear through body parts.

Scar thought they'd just experienced what the locals called a picleeketchum lurking in their district's forbidden ruins.

"Take the injured to the nearest hospital," the Golem said, rising to its feet, pushing off attempts to aid its effort. "Camouflage the gate. Prepare to return to Mephisto Tower."

Another Nectoport appeared, and the injured were carried in while the rest of the court filed into the other waiting transports.

Match groaned, holding his belly and his head. He was bleeding from the ears and his skin was a deeper shade of mottled gray than usual.

"We have what we need," Scar said, and motioned for Fetch and Teeth to help Match. Let's go find out what the market value of a secret I'm sure even Divination hasn't revealed—"

Skyve stood up, exposing herself to the party below.

Scar watched her, stunned. Teeth hissed, and both she and Match jumped to bring her down. But Skyve hopped out of their reach, over the wall, and walked toward the dwindling knot of Luciferin courtiers.

A part of Scar wanted to be carried off by betrayal's blind rage so he could chase her down and tear her apart before the Ushers had their chance. But another part recognized that she was only acting on an impulse he'd been guarding against, a need they probably all had in one way or another.

They were in Lucifer's presence. They'd all been resisting the tidal pull to the source of their essence. How could they walk away from their Maker?

Scar suddenly understood Skyve's odd, quirky power to lead them places where he never could. If he was their street general, insuring the Baby Nukes' daily survival, she might well be their spiritual guide.

The combination might have worked, if they'd had a chance at existence beyond the next few moments.

Several of Lucifer's entourage noticed Skyve's appearance. The Golem turned to observe her advance. The Ushers sprang forward, but heeled after a few leaping steps when the Golem uttered a painful, metallic recall.

Scar, seeing they were not going to be instantly recycled, followed Skyve on to the crater floor. Teeth whined like an Ogre crippled by Karyolysis, but she came up behind Scar, her hand brushing against his, almost by accident. It seemed like most of her teeth were chattering. Match staggered out next, pulling up loose flaps of flesh and shaking off excess pus dripping from his face, as if making himself presentable. Fetch waited until they'd almost reached the line of Ushers to make his appearance, showing off his speed. He barely dodged a startled Usher's attempt to grab him.

"Come along, my children," the Golem said, gesturing for them to come to him with a stiff arm and hand. "Don't be afraid. Every Citizen has a part to play in Hell's grand drama."

Officials parted, a number of them taking readings of the Baby Nukes with their instruments and retreating to converse excitedly among themselves. An Extipicist stepped forward, dabbed her fingers in Match's wounds, and sampled the viscous, greenish-white matter she'd retrieved. She was immediately seized by spasms, throwing her head back and screeching before falling to the ground in a twitching seizure. Her peers fluttered over her before placing her in one of the Nectoports bound for Mephisto Tower instead of a hospital.

"I wonder if he's going to grow another dick and fuck us with it," Teeth said.

Skyve was the first to reach the Golem, and it embraced her with both arms. She slid out of its grasp after nuzzling the clay, and stood by the creature's side, eyes fluttering, a stunned expression on her face, as if she'd just awakened from a dream and found herself in a nightmare.

Scar stopped just beyond the Golem's reach. The rest of the Baby Nukes gathered at his back. He was beyond cold, numb to fear. And yet he had the presence of mind to check the spacing between the Ushers, the distance to the gateway at the crater's center, the number of attendants close enough to give them any trouble if he decided to make a run for it. Or attack the Golem.

BABY NUKES IN HELL

As if they had a chance in Hell.

He knew any plan was suicidal, but he was sure he was already on his way to the dung heaps and there was nothing to lose. Besides, he wanted to go out a Baby Nuke. He was grateful he didn't have to endure the full glory of Lucifer's true face. Though the sight might have fulfilled a good number of his secret demonic drives and needs, his own demon identity would have been diminished, if not completely extinguished, by the Father of Evil. And that would have been a pitiful end for the Baby Nukes.

"My children, I'm so glad you decided to come forward," the Golem said. "And I was just wondering if I could find a use for you or feed you to the Caco-Dragon nesting just outside these ruins."

Skyve's distress was evident on her face, and Scar wished she could hold herself together. He didn't want to look back at the rest of the Baby Nukes, but hoped they were all at least frozen in terror. Posture was everything for a gang caught in the open. "You knew?"

"This is my realm. Even if my Extipicists cannot always confirm details, I have an idea of what has and will happen. Besides, you really are my children, another experiment in my search for the shapes my domain takes in creating its torments. I commissioned the demonic DNA lines, the very Chernobyl vats, which created you. You are tiny fragments of my will. My nature. Along with everything else here."

Scar felt Lucifer's revelation tug at his concentration. He only had one other question in mind: "Why did you let us follow you?"

"You never know what will come in handy."

And then he had nothing. Scar was at a loss for words. To know that Lucifer was personally responsible for the trauma of his creation was both an honor his mind could barely encompass and a horrific affront that made him want to chew through the Golem's clay body to rip out, with his sharpened teeth, whatever soft, tasty chunk of demonic meat quivering at its core that served as host for Lucifer's spirit.

If he'd known anything about exorcisms, he would have started one even knowing he'd be struck down before getting out more than a few words.

"I'm glad we're not going to be punished," Skyve said. She moved away from the Golem, walked toward the Baby Nukes.

Scar was startled back to the immediate reality of their situation by her ability to break from Lucifer's aura and rejoin the gang.

He stared at her as she stood by his side, ignoring Teeth's restless shifting behind him. She really was a Baby Nuke. He found comfort in the thought.

"Punishment?" the Golem said. "Being self-aware in Hell is the minimal punishment I require. Today, there's no need for additional penalties. Today, I have only opportunities to hand out. Though if you hadn't had the courage to step forward as you did, you'd be eating shit right now."

Scar wouldn't look back, but he was sure the rest of the gang was giving Skyve the same look he'd just given her.

Nearly all of Lucifer's traveling entourage had boarded the Nectoport. The hospital carrier vanished, then the one that had borne the Conscripts destroyed by the Ushers. A few attendants were securing lines around the Golem to haul him up to the remaining Nectoport, floating overhead, while one of the surviving Grand Dukes supervised a scribbling Kafka clerk.

Scar's all-pervading sense of doom collapsed into the concrete reality of what was happening.

Contracts were being drawn. The clerk was finalizing the document specifying a non-negotiable binding agreement for all participants with the Grand Duke as a witness, a perfectly legal practice in Hell. As if to confirm Scar's perceptions, the clerk darted forward and stabbed each of the Baby Nukes with the point of a bone pen, the organic matter at the end of the pen used immediately to sign their names to the contract.

They didn't have to do a thing. Lucifer had designed Hell to make falling deeper into damnation as easy as possible.

"Our deal is done," the Golem said as it was pulled, with the slightest swing and sway, into the Nectoport overhead. "A Grand Dukeship to anyone who comes back and tells me what's on the other side of the gate."

"You don't know?" Skyve asked.

Teeth found curses Scar had never heard before.

Fetch and Match passed internal organs.

Scar nearly laughed at the obscenity of their impending doom.

But to Scar's surprise, their reality remained unchanged. For the moment.

"My knowledge ends with the borders of my realm, child," the Golem said from above, like a father explaining the obvious to a child. "I've heard whispers from that Plane, and I've done my best to interpret them over the millennia. Generations of Anthropomancers and Extipicists have channeled all of their skills and talents into discovering the meaning of what waits beyond that small hole. I've had offerings delivered. Even found a way to make them, myself. But as you saw, we've had nothing but failures in our attempts at true communication."

"Why do you care?" Skyve asked.

Scar braced himself for instant recycling to lower forms, wishing for annihilation. He didn't want to know. He was certain the rest of the Baby Nukes had other concerns on their minds.

But Skyve was pushing to discover Lucifer's need to connect with whatever lay beyond the gate. And suddenly, it seemed as if that knowledge might hold the key to their survival.

"What a bracing young demon you are," the Golem said, from the lip of the last Nectoport. "Did our experiments finally yield a path to deeper and more subtle forms of torment? I hope so."

"You didn't answer the question," said Skyve, inspiring gasps from the remnants of Lucifer's attendants.

"Dancing with the Devil? We'll have to do this again someday when I'm in my true form. But you want an answer?"

"He's going to do something bad to us," Teeth whispered. "Just shut up, don't make it worse."

"I landed there after my Fall, thundering accusations and recriminations following me the way down along with the flames. It was all tedious. But the impact of my landing was spectacular. Heaven is far off. I breached the wall between this Plane and another. Through the chaos, I heard something from the hole. Felt something. Whatever is on the other side, it gave me a moment's solace that allowed me to receive the vision of what I was sent here to do.

"For that, I'm grateful."

"So you want to thank whatever's on the other side?" Skyve asked.

"Of course not. I want whatever else it can give me. Think of the power. I want to rip that damned hole wide open and take whatever I can get from the other side."

Scar surprised himself by asking: "Where do we come in?"

"Actually, you're leaving. Down the hole. Which my host's work has temporarily widened."

"But we can't fit—"

"Of course you can. You're demons. Your Lord commands that you fit, and you will."

The Ushers closed around them, but Scar didn't wait to be dragged away. He led the Baby Nukes to the breach, and as they ringed the hole the Nectoport hovered closer so they could be dowsed with lubricants. The Ushers assembled at their backs, prepared to prod.

"You'll get more if you come back with terms for a Power Exchange," the Golem said. "And can you even imagine what gifts I'll lavish on you if you discover how to breach the wall between the Planes so I can take what I want?" The Golem's mechanical laughter erupted from several sudden cracks in its body, and glistening meat pushed out from its orifices. "Bring me the keys to Heaven, dear children, and I'll give you Hell itself."

"He's so full of shit he can't keep it inside, anymore," said Teeth.

Match and Fetch snickered, and even Teeth broke down and smiled. Scar matched her, and nodded to Skyve, who winked.

"Baby Nukes to the end," she said.

She went for the hole first, but Scar held her back and motioned for Match to go first. "More lubrication," he said, indicating his open sores.

Match opened up and let himself ooze, then squirmed into the hole feet first. "It feels kind of cold," he said, and looked off in the direction of Templar gate, as if saying goodbye to his sister. Then he was through.

Skyve couldn't be held back any longer, but before she went in she turned to the rest of them and asked, "Do we get to carve notches on our bones on the other side for what we did here?"

"Sure thing," Scar said.

Skyve dove in head first.

Fetch went in without a word, gone in a blink, but Teeth took her time, pausing to give Scar a quick kiss before crawling through head first.

The Golem raised a hand, perhaps in triumph, maybe in farewell, as Scar worked his way down. He went feet first, not because he was scared, but so he could give Lucifer the finger just before his hand went down.

«« — »»

Scar didn't feel too badly about the deal with the devil and leaving Hell. He thought that, for once, they might even have gotten the better of the deal and beaten the devil, actually escaping their damnation. Whatever waited for them on the other side, it wouldn't be Hell, so none of them would come back as a rat or a roach or a worm or a maggot. At best, they might be slipping into oblivion. At worst, they'd experience something different from Hell. How could they lose?

«« — »»

Where they went was nothing like Hell.

It was also worse, in ways that made them all beg for the day when they could, at last, return to face their Maker.

But they took it all like Baby Nukes.

HELL
AIN'T A
BAD PLACE
TO BE

BRYAN SMITH

The last day of John Marlowe's mortal life began with a hangover. He woke up, opened his bleary eyes, took a good look around, shuddered at the disarray in the bedroom, and went back to sleep for a few more hours. When he got up again, he shrugged into the clothes he'd worn the day before, stumbled into the kitchen, and opened the fridge.

It was still there.

The severed head sat in an aluminum pie tray, the ragged stump of its neck buried in a layer of cookie dough. Strands of blood-flecked blond hair dangled through the shelf slats, brushing the plastic lid of a bowl of tuna salad.

"Fuck. I really did it."

John Marlowe was forty-two. He hadn't killed anyone since his early twenties. In those days, he'd had some level of ambition, as well as a young man's elevated sense of his own importance in the grand scheme of things. He'd wanted to make his mark in the world. Do something big and become famous. As a teenager he learned to play guitar and tried starting a band. The rock star life seemed like a good gig. Groupies and all the drugs you could handle. Problems set in when he discovered he couldn't sing or write even one half-decent song. So he gave that up and decided to become a novelist. A cele-

HELL AIN'T A BAD PLACE TO BE

brated man of letters. He imagined a different kind of fame and fortune. National Book Awards and interviews on NPR. The bigger literary names even had their own kind of groupies. Brainy women who would pin their hair back and wear owl's-eye glasses, hide their sleek and wanton bodies in modest clothes. The sexy librarian type. But in the bedroom they'd be foul-mouthed, dominating hellcats. If anything, it was an even more appealing prospect than the abandoned dream of busty, miniskirt-wearing rock star groupies, all of whom would have been empty-headed bottle-blond bimbos straight out of an '80s Poison video. Not that there was anything wrong with empty-headed bottle-blond bimbos. It was just a question of whether you more enjoyed the refined taste of an expensive wine or the simpler taste of a cheap domestic beer. There was a time and place for both, and at that point in his young existence John had decided he was going to be the kind of man who preferred the finer things in life. All he had to do to make this happen was sit down and write the Great American Novel, and perhaps follow it up with maybe half a dozen lesser novels over the course of the next thirty years or so to keep the cash and lit-slut groupies rolling in.

He sat down to write the novel.

Wrote one page.

Read through it a dozen times or so.

And decided it was again time to reevaluate his goals in life.

Still thinking in terms of groupies and fame and fortune, he toyed with the idea of becoming an actor. He went so far as to take a few acting classes. Three classes, to be exact, each of them a study in awkwardness and boredom.

By then he was close to accepting he had no ability whatever in any of the creative fields. He could maybe go into politics. He was young and good-looking, and possessed more than enough personal charisma to get by. He could be a congressman. A senator. Hell, he could be president. The job clearly didn't require brains. If anything, he was overqualified.

But politics bored him even more than acting, so fuck that.

The reality that banging bimbos could be something of a potential liability in the political arena was somewhat of a deciding factor, as well.

And then it happened, the moment that changed his life.

The goddamn epiphany.

He could be a serial killer.

And not just any ordinary dumb bastard of a serial killer. The usual guys in that field were greasy dullards. Ugly bastards who wore over-sized glasses with thick lenses. Sexual predators driven by anger and frustration, who killed because no woman in her right mind would ever voluntarily give up the goods to a guy like that. Those guys, they didn't exactly stir the imagination. Sure, every once in a while someone more interesting came along, someone like Ted Bundy. Now there was a guy who was legitimately a legend in the annals of serial killing. Some guys had killed more women than Ted, but few had ever done it with the pizazz of the Deliberate Stranger. But even he had botched it all in the end. John decided he would follow in Bundy's footsteps only to a degree. He would do everything his new hero had done right, avoid his missteps, and elevate the killing game to a whole new level. And by the time he was done, he meant to be the world's most prolific and creative serial killer ever. Books would be written about him. Movies made. He would finally be a celebrity of a sort. And, hell, some of the more interesting and charismatic serial killers, Ted included, even had their own groupies.

Yep, on paper it all looked very positive.

That summer, at the age of twenty-two, he killed three women. He did his homework so well beforehand that he was never a suspect in any of the ensuing investigations. He was never questioned. None of the suspect sketches the police circulated ever looked remotely like him. And yet, the killings had been public and spectacularly grue-some. The corpses were decapitated and mutilated in myriad creative ways. None of this strangling the lass and ditching her body in a remote patch of wilderness never to be discovered jazz. This was to be a very open campaign of shock and awe horror. And it worked. The local media went apoplectic after the first killing. The national press got in on the act after the third victim was discovered. He was dubbed The Little Rock Madman, not a bad serial killer name. All was going very much according to plan.

Except for one little thing.

John just wasn't enjoying the work very much.

Oh, he'd gotten a real high from successfully pulling off the first job. In those first moments of his new existence as a murderer, he'd been certain he'd at last found his true calling in life. But the high faded faster than he expected and his sleep that night was disrupted by nightmares. He chalked it up to first time pangs of conscience. Not even that, really. This was just social conditioning, a mental and chemical reflex, something that would surely fade as the work became more routine. So he pressed ahead with his plan. But the nightmares and sleep disruptions got exponentially worse after he offed the second and third girls. After the third one, he got blind drunk and wound up in a pool of his own piss and vomit in an alley behind a Little Rock dive bar. He woke up screaming and crying every night for months. Turned out he had a real conscience after all. The faces of the dead women haunted him day and night. His day job suffered. He dropped out of grad school. And his life continued on a grim downward spiral until the night he got down on his knees in yet another backstreet alley and begged God and his victims for forgiveness.

His life changed after that night. He did everything he could think of to atone, short of turning himself in and signing a confession. He went back to school and graduated with honors. He became a very successful man. A wealthy man. He donated tons of money to victims groups and death penalty advocates. He went to church twice a week and continued to pray every day for forgiveness. Years went by. Decades. Enough time that the killings he'd done that long ago summer began to seem like something he must have imagined, something that couldn't possibly be real. Except that every once in a while, even all these years later, the local media would dredge the whole thing up again, reminding the public that the Little Rock Madman had never been caught. Even so, the passage of time and his acts of contrition combined to convince him that he had truly transformed himself. He wasn't really a monster. That bloody summer had ultimately been nothing more than a blip in an otherwise exemplary life, a wrong path he'd been wise enough to quickly abandon.

An impression that had lasted until roughly one week prior to today.

John stared at his wife's severed head and said, "You fucking bitch."

He'd come home early from work that day and caught her in bed with a much younger man. A large black man with a bodybuilder's physique and a model's chiseled face. Later he learned the man was an expensive male prostitute. Which explained Linda's reaction upon seeing him in the bedroom doorway. There had been no shame. No quick, startled disengagement of the two sleek, sweaty bodies. Instead she'd yelled at him to get out of the room so she could finish. Turned out she'd just wanted to get her money's worth. John had retreated to his study down the hall, where he cracked the seal on a bottle of very fine old scotch and settled into his leather executive's chair to listen to his wife's orgasmic screams. The screams interested him. They were high and shrill, not entirely dissimilar to the screams made by the victims of the Little Rock Madman. The thought made him frown. Linda never sounded like that when he was putting it to her.

He started thinking about killing her after that first sip of scotch. The thought seemed to come from nowhere and sent a shudder of revulsion rippling through his whole body. He'd had no conscious, active thoughts about killing anyone in twenty years. The scotch turned sour in his stomach and he felt bile at the back of his throat.

At some point the screams from the bedroom faded and stopped. A little later he heard muted conversation in the hallway. Then male laughter and feminine giggling. They were laughing at him. The insight did nothing to lighten his thoughts. Then she came into the study, a robe cinched tight around her shapely body, and made several declarations. They were not going to get divorced. Of course not. She enjoyed her position in the community too much. He was never going to breathe a word of this to anyone. She would continue to screw the thousand-dollar-a-pop prostitute twice a week, and she would continue to sample any other strange flesh that caught her fancy, including John's young lesbian niece, who she'd apparently been corrupting for months. And furthermore, he was never going to have sex with her again, because he was just no good at it. Not only that, but he was not allowed to have affairs of his own. She would not have anyone in town talking about her behind her back. Then she pried the bottle of scotch from his shaking fingers and told him he was not allowed to drink anymore. Still more ultimatums followed, each more galling than the last.

He was initially defiant. "You realize this is ludicrous, right? What makes you think I'll be a good little doggie and do everything you say?"

She smirked and looked down her regal nose at him. "Because you talk in your sleep. Mr. Madman. Why, you're practically verbose."

John just stared at her, suddenly cold and dead inside.

"There are things you don't want people to know."

He stayed silent, struggled to breathe.

"Nasty things."

His fingers dug into his knees, made the bones grind.

"So, yes, I do think I have the leverage I need here." Her smirk deepened, became a look of utter, smug certainty. "I own you now, John. You're my little wind-up toy. Finish up whatever you're doing in here and come out to the kitchen. I'm going to write up a list of new chores for you."

She turned her back on him and sashayed back through the door, making a show of how little she feared the infamous Little Rock Madman.

John slumped in his chair.

His thoughts turned to murder again.

But that sense of revulsion was still there. He'd worked so hard to redeem himself. He just couldn't let himself succumb to the old demons. Not even at the cost of his own manhood and dignity. The dark thoughts nonetheless stayed with him in the days that followed, though he struggled hard against them, even in the face of so much deep humiliation. And it got worse. She kept doing things to deepen his shame. The worst was yesterday, when she made him watch her fuck the prostitute. They tied him to a chair in the bedroom, and then they did it all. Missionary position. Girl on top. From behind, with both anal and vaginal penetration. Reverse cowgirl and face-sitting. Jesus, but it just went on and fucking on. By the time the prostitute left, John had been reduced to a trembling lump of insensible flesh. Linda didn't free him from the chair until hours later. She then slapped him out of his stupor and ordered him to take out the trash and wash the dishes.

John did take out the trash.

Then he got into his Mercedes and drove far, far away from there. He stayed out for hours, drinking himself senseless in a succession of low-rent dives in the worst part of town. He didn't remember coming home. Didn't remember going to bed. But his sleep was tortured with nightmare visions of bloody murder. The images were so vivid and real. His wife dying horribly at his hands, tortured first, then chopped and diced into little pieces.

Turned out there was a reason the images were so damn vivid.

They were fucking real, man. Not nightmares at all, but memories.

John threw the refrigerator door shut.

He thought, *Well, that's it.*

There was no denying the truth of it. There was no coming back from this. It was the thing he'd told himself he couldn't live with if it happened again, and John had always been a man true to his word. He would honor this vow.

But first he would bear witness to the rest of his shame.

He shuffled out of the kitchen and made his way to the dining room. Here was where most of the action had occurred. John's knees went weak at the sight of the carnage. There were pieces of Linda on the dinner table. Her breasts on a ceramic plate. One looked to have been partially devoured. He saw fingers protruding from candle holders, each fingernail adorned with the shade of deep scarlet polish Linda favored. The lower half of her body was arranged with its legs spread in the center of the table. He supposed he'd climbed onto the table and defiled it at least once during the evening. What remained of her torso sat in a chair, a large knife protruding from the space between her missing breasts. And of course there was a simply amazing amount of blood splashed all over the room.

Feeling numb, John drank it all in.

It was incredible.

The Little Rock Madman had clearly not lost his gift for creative slaughter during his long period of inactivity. He even felt a strange sort of pride beneath the overwhelming sense of horror and failure.

The numbness faded.

A wash of nausea swept through him and he vomited profusely, the force of it sending him to his hands and knees. He heaved and heaved, spewing bile all over a severed big toe that had found its way to the floor. The spasms continued long after his stomach had emptied its contents. His joints and muscles ached with the pain of it, pain so overwhelming he actually welcomed it, because for a time it blocked out the reality of what he had done. But eventually the sickness gripping him faded and he was again forced to face the awful truth.

He got to his feet and staggered out of the room. His body reeled as he made his way through the big house, pitching side to side, hands held out to his sides in order to bounce off the walls and remain upright. Stumbling through the door to his study, he spied his leather chair and fell toward it with his arms extended, seeking it with the desperation of a shipwreck survivor grasping for the only life-preserver in sight. He made it to the chair, sat there slumped and panting for several minutes.

Many minutes passed. He began to regain some measure of physical and mental control. Then he set about doing the things he needed to do. He found a pad of paper and a pen, and he began to write the untold story of The Little Rock Madman. The rambling confession contained more than enough details about the murders to convince authorities the real killer had at last been unmasked, albeit posthumously. The letter also contained heartfelt apologies to the families of his victims, and proclaimed that he would not ask for their forgiveness because he did not deserve it. Any of them were welcome to come to his grave to piss on it. He concluded by stating that while his wife had undeniably been a heartless bitch of truly epic proportions, she had not deserved to die. He apologized to her family and said that they, too, were welcome to piss on his grave.

He read the confession through two times, then signed it.

He reached for the bottle of old scotch Linda had pried from his fingers a week ago, but didn't pick it up, deciding he didn't deserve even this one last fleeting pleasure. Instead he opened the bottom drawer of his desk, removed the .44 Magnum from the lock box at the back, put the gun's barrel in his mouth, and squeezed the trigger. He didn't hear the gun's report or even really feel what the large-caliber bullet did to his head. The awesome destructive power of the weapon did its work too fast and too efficiently for that, triggering a brief geyser of blood and brains that splattered shelves of leather-bound books behind his desk.

The next thing he was aware of was music.

Crunchy, distorted guitar chords and a thumping drum beat.

In a moment he recognized the song as "Highway To Hell" by AC/DC. He had loved them as a teenager, but hearing this particular song now was not exactly the most reassuring thing he had ever experienced.

John opened his eyes and realized at once that he was in Hell.

HELL AIN'T A BAD PLACE TO BE

At first blush it looked like any large metropolitan city. Buildings, the rumble of traffic, honking horns, and the buzz of nearby voices. He was standing on a sidewalk. A standard issue city sidewalk. This could have been a street in Manhattan. Maybe Greenwich Village. But then there were the obvious big differences. The street vendor selling fried human eyeballs from a cart across the street. The sign on a utility pole which read CITY MUTILATION ZONE. And the many creatures that could only be demons of various sorts in the mix of milling pedestrians. He looked up and saw the roiling red sky and the sickle-shaped black moon that hung there.

He pinched himself and said, "Ouch."

He patted his face and the top of his head, which was somehow intact, and that was quite a remarkable thing indeed, given that he'd just fired a bullet through it. But there was no denying the physical reality. He was alive again. In Hell, but alive.

He shook his head. "I'll be damned."

A hooker in miniskirt, high heels, and red fishnets paused in the process of strutting past him, turning a face toward him that looked like it had been boiled in acid. "We're all Damned. You want a blowjob?"

John decided her face probably had actually been boiled in acid. "Um…no. Thanks anyway."

The hooker's face twisted, forming an expression that might have been a sneer. It was hard to tell through all the scarring. "You sure? You don't know what you're missing. Ask anybody, they'll tell you. I give the best head of any whore in Hell."

Against his will, an image of his erect cock wedged in the scary black slit that was the hooker's mouth formed in John's head. He grimaced. "No, sorry. I, uh, no offense or anything, but…"

The hooker reached into the little handbag slung over her shoulder and removed something. He heard a click of a button and saw a shiny blade pop open. The hooker brandished the switchblade and said, "We're going into that alley behind you. I'm gonna blow you and then I'm gonna cut your dick off for a trophy." Her face twisted again, the scarred flesh arranging itself into something that could theoretically have been a smile. "And there ain't shit you can do about it."

John swallowed hard. "Um..."

Run, he thought. *Just run.*

Another second and he might have bolted, but the soft, sultry voice to his right stopped him. "Get lost, whore. This one's mine."

Great.

The whores of Hell were arguing over him, and he hadn't been here five minutes yet. Not an auspicious start. He was feeling a bit like a piece of meat. It was not a feeling he enjoyed. "Look—"

He turned to address the second whore, but the words died in his throat with a gurgle. He went cold inside and again felt the urge to bolt. The second woman was not another cheap streetwalker. She was gorgeous, with long, lustrous blond hair and an exquisite face worthy of the cover of *Vogue*. The body was just as stunning, sleek and slender but with lush curves and ample breasts. It was the kind of body meant for modeling swimsuits. The dress she wore looked stylish and sexy, not at all like anything a whore would have in her wardrobe. It looked expensive. He knew nothing of the current fashion trends in Hell, but instinct told him this woman would always stand at its cutting edge. The backless black dress looked molded to her figure, a supple second skin that would be a pleasure and privilege to peel away from her creamy, unblemished flesh.

John felt the same instant, reflexive lust he'd felt the first time he'd seen her.

Which had been at a nightclub in Little Rock twenty years ago, the night before he hacked her into seemingly a million little pieces in that public park.

Her smile broadened, became truly radiant. "Hello, John. I knew you were coming. I can't tell you how good it is to see you again."

Beyond any shadow of a doubt, it was her.

HELL AIN'T A BAD PLACE TO BE

Angela Willis.

A memory came to him. Angela's mother on the news, crying for the cameras, begging the police to do anything to catch the monster who had taken her baby.

John turned and ran.

He shoved his way through the crowd on the sidewalk with heedless abandon, knocking a fat man into a demon's back in the process. The demon turned, snarling as its black wings unfurled. Its mouth widened, the flesh displaying a shocking level of elasticity as the black maw grew to a size large enough to swallow the fat man's head, which it promptly did. John kept moving, turning his back on the demon as its flashing, razor-sharp teeth clamped together.

He glanced back twice to see if Angela was pursuing him, but he seemed to have lost her in the foot traffic. He slowed his pace and eventually came to a panting stop outside the open door of a rock club. Live music blared through the open door, filling this section of the street with its concussive beat. It was yet another AC/DC song. "Night Prowler." John frowned. It was obvious he was hearing live music and not a recording. But that voice…

Nah, couldn't be…

Curiosity and the need to find a place to hide and collect his wits drew him into the club. The place wasn't very big, a dark and grimy dive. There was a bar and a stage. Between them was a scattering of tables. The people sitting at the tables were drinking and watching the band, who were not AC/DC. The singer, though, was Bon Scott. No mistaking that guy for anyone else, and no mistaking that whiskey-drenched Scottish yowl. Some of the musicians in his backing band looked kind of familiar, too. A younger John Marlowe would likely have recognized them all on the spot.

"Night Prowler" ended and Scott interacted with the crowd, cracking jokes and engaging in witty and ribald banter with a large-breasted female in a miniskirt. The female was humanoid, but not human, with red eyes and tusks protruding from the corners of her mouth. Two small black wings, unnoticeable at first, were folded tight against the broad expanse of her back. John cringed at an impossible-sounding proposition made by the she-thing, then wandered over to the bar, slid onto a stool, and ordered a beer.

The bald and burly bartender crossed his massive tattooed forearms and sneered. "Ain't got no Guinness."

"Newcastle?"

"Nope."

"Spaten?"

"You ain't in Germany, dickhole."

"Harpoon IPA?"

"You really aren't getting the picture, are you?"

John rattled off a long list of other favorite brews, none of which were stocked at the Dirty Halo, which was the name of the place. "Look, can I just get a menu?"

The bartender picked up a glass and placed it under a tap. "Shut up, asshole." He flipped the taphead down and filled the glass with a rich, dark brew. He set the glass in front of John. "Drink that. You'll like it."

John picked up the glass, sniffed at it, and took a tentative sip. The sensation of the liquid on his tongue was exquisite. He showed the bartender an astonished expression. "Dear God, that is the best fucking beer I have ever fucking had."

The bartender smirked. "That's Gein's Mean Imperial Stout. Most popular beer in the Bathory district." The big man's brow creased. "You're new to the Mephistopolis, aren't you?"

John sampled some more beer and shivered at the heady taste. "Yeah. How did you know?"

The man laughed. "The freshly Damned are always fuckin' clueless, man."

John wasn't offended by the remark. "Makes sense. Listen, I just got here. Any idea where I should go from here? I mean…" He waved a hand at the club's open entrance, a vague gesture meant to encompass the whole of Hell itself. "…this is all sort of overwhelming. Hell is just this giant fucking city. There's all kinds of insane shit out there, but people have jobs. They go to clubs to see bands. So how do I fit in? Where will I live? Do I go to some kind of infernal temp agency?"

"This has all been arranged for you, John."

John jumped at the sound of her voice. The pint glass popped out of his grip and tumbled over, spilling stout all over the bar.

The bartender didn't look happy. In fact, he looked furious. But then his face turned pale. He unclenched his fists and bowed his head, mumbling words of terrified contrition, alternately referring to Angela as "My Lady" and "Your Highness."

John puzzled over the bartender's obsequious reaction, then looked at Angela. "I'm just not going to get away from you, am I?"

She sat on the stool next to him and placed a hand in his lap. "No, you won't." She laughed, and the sound was as he remembered it from that long ago night in the park before he revealed his true intentions. Soft and musical, like a feather tickling the pleasure centers of his brain. She massaged his crotch, stirring him to full arousal with an ease that belied the circumstances. "And believe me, John, you won't want to. I'm the personal concubine of a Grand Duke. I have an exalted position in this part of the Mephistopolis, with privileges that aren't available to most humans. I always get what I want, John. And what I want now is you."

He frowned. "I chopped your head off and had sex with your dead body. If what you say is true, you're probably taking me back to your unholy castle or whatever to torture me for the rest of eternity. Right?"

She smiled as she tugged at his zipper tab. "Has it not occurred to you to wonder why I'm in Hell, John? After all, I was just an innocent victim of a horrible crime, right?"

John's frown deepened. "Huh. Well, now that you mention it…"

"My name joined the endless list of the Eternally Damned the day I smothered my sick and elderly grandmother with a pillow. I was eight, John." Her hand was inside his pants now. He gasped at the feel of her fingers curling around his stiff member. "The 'accidental drowning' of my little brother on our beach vacation a few years later was just icing on the Damnation cake. And for weeks I'd been imagining how I might get away with killing a pregnant co-worker when you came along and did what you did." There was a strangely wistful note in her tone now. "Which was the best thing that ever happened to me."

John gasped and gripped the edge of the bar as she continued to stroke him.

He looked at her and managed to speak between gasps. "Are you...fucking...kidding...me?

Another of those incredible laughs. "Oh, darling, I would never kid you. Life on the other side bored me so. All those repressed notions of right and wrong. It was stultifying. When you sent me here, you set me free."

John whimpered. "I sent you to...Hell."

She smiled and licked her lips. "Yes, and here I've flourished. Suddenly I found myself in a place where I was free to indulge all my darkest passions. Absolutely free to commit acts of atrocity I would never have dared imagining before. And I reveled in it, darling. I crushed the skulls of little children with bricks. Broiled a baby in an oven and fed it to its mother. Sawed off a man's penis, cooked it, and fed it to him."

John gasped again and slapped the top of the bar. "Holy shit, you are one sick bitch."

She giggled, the little girlish quality of which was quite disturbing juxtaposed against the recitation of purest evil spilling from her lovely mouth. "Yes, I am. I quickly became a rather notorious character, John, and soon caught the attention of District Commissioner of Torture Kennedy. From there I slept and murdered my way up the power hierarchy, eventually arriving at my current position as personal concubine to Grand Duke Dracul. I have riches beyond imagining at my disposal. I have a lover willing and able to give me everything I could ever want. Including you, John."

HELL AIN'T A BAD PLACE TO BE

A corner of John's mouth quirked. "Me?"

She stopped stroking him and wrapped her fingers tighter around his cock, making him whimper again and slide toward the edge of the stool. "Yes. The Grand Duke's sources were able to pinpoint the precise moment and location of your arrival in Hell, and as a gift to me a document was filed with Luciferic bureaucracy allowing me to claim you as my own personal property."

She squeezed him harder and John's fingernails dug into the bar. "You mean...like...your slave?"

"Technically, yes."

John thought of his last week of mortal life and marriage with Linda.

So this was going to be his existence in Hell—an eternity of the same torment.

Well, he couldn't say he didn't deserve it, at least.

She giggled again. "Oh, relax. You're going to love it, seeing as I'll be fucking you half-blind a lot of the time. Do you know, John, that when you held me down in that park and showed me the meat cleaver, I knew I'd at last found a kindred soul? Oh, I was scared half to fucking death, but in that moment I knew you were like me inside. I wanted to tell you, but..." She shrugged, and there was something almost sad in her smile now. "Anyway, I don't think you would have listened. You were too focused on your work."

She relinquished her grip on his cock and John came explosively all over the front of the bar. He collapsed against the top of the bar and lay there in a shuddering, whimpering heap for several moments while Angela stroked his hair. The band launched into another song while she leaned close and cooed reassurances in his ear. When it was over, Angela took John by the hand and pulled him off the barstool.

He still felt woozy and staggered along beside her as they left the Dirty Halo. "Where are we going?"

She smiled again as they came to a stop out on the sidewalk. "Home, John. I'm taking you to your new home. And there'll be a special surprise for you once we get there."

Surprise?

She saw his concerned expression and gave his arm a gentle squeeze. "You will love it. I promise."

"Okay. Whatever."

He looked up and saw huge winged creatures moving across the scarlet sky. His took another good look around. He saw thick clusters of black and impossibly tall skyscrapers in the distance. They dominated the skyline. He also saw the thick smokestacks of factories belching great billowing clouds of black, diseased smoke at the sky. The stench of decay permeated everything.

John looked at Angela. "What does 'City Mutilation Zone' mean?"

She laughed. "An institutionalized method of random slaughter. Nothing for you to worry about." She winked. "When you're with me, that is."

"I offed myself with a .44 caliber bullet. Probably took off the top of my head. So where's the giant fucking hole in my skull?"

"That was your mortal flesh, John. You have a new body now. Your *spirit* body."

John nodded. "Uh huh. *Or*...and let me just throw this out there...alternate theory kind of thing...maybe this is all a hallucination. I'm in a coma, being kept alive by machines, dreaming of a new and strange life in an impossible place because I'm too far gone to ever come back all the way. The Brits had a show like that, long after you died. Was pretty good."

"Do you really believe that, John?"

John's gaze was drawn upward again, where he saw two more winged things flapping across the roiling red sky, each of them grinning and clutching the leg of a screaming nude woman. The woman dangled upside down, her giant white breasts jiggling as her face twisted in an expression of endless horror.

He looked at Angela again. "No. I don't believe it."

The corners of her mouth twitched, trembling on the edge of amusement. "And why is that?"

HELL AIN'T A BAD PLACE TO BE

"Because in a lot of truly fucked up ways, this place feels far more real than the place I left behind."

Her smile broadened. "Like a place where society's polite veneer has been stripped away, exposing and reveling in the grandly terrible truth behind the lie?"

"Um. Sure, something like that."

A big black boat of a car rolled up to the curb and stopped. A rotting severed head was impaled on a large spike on the hood. He wondered if rotting head hood ornaments came standard with limos in hell. A door opened and a man in chauffeur's livery popped out. The chauffeur called out a greeting to Angela and came quickly around to their side, where he opened one of the rear doors and stood aside for his passengers to enter. Angela touched the man lightly on the arm as she entered the car and said, "Thank you, David."

John looked at the man again, a thunderstruck expression on his face. Holy shit.

It was him all right.

He followed Angela into the car, a question freezing on the tip of his tongue as he slid onto the slick leather seat. The streetwalker who'd accosted him upon his arrival in Hell lay hog-tied across the seat opposite them. She turned her head toward them at their arrival, her eyes wet and imploring as she recognized him. The hooker gurgled at him, spittle flying from the corners of her crimson-stained slit-mouth.

John squinted at her as the chauffeur threw the door shut. "What?"

She gurgled at him again.

It was then that he noticed the pink flap of bloody flesh impaled on one of her stiletto heels.

Her fucking tongue.

John grimaced. "Whoa."

Angela giggled. "You like? She did threaten you, after all."

John looked at her. "Yeah. She did." He frowned. "Is this the surprise you were talking about?"

"No, John. She's merely an appetizer. And I'll not spoil the surprise. You'll just have to wait until we've arrived at your new home."

"Which is where again?"

She beamed at him. "With me, John! In the court of Grand Duke Dracul. You'll be my manservant and trusted aide." Yet another of those girlish giggles that made her sound like a demented teeny-bopper. "As well as my indefatigable fuck toy."

John gritted his teeth. He wasn't sure how he felt about a life in shackles. It'd been a long, long time since he'd been subservient to anyone, with the glaring exception of the miserable week as Linda's whipped puppy. But he clearly wasn't in a position to argue or rebel. Besides, the life she described sounded as if it would be a dream come true for most residents of the Mephistopolis. He supposed many here would resent his easy ascension to so coveted a position. Which posed another matter of some personal significance. Though he had worked hard to redeem himself through the bulk of his adult life, there was no doubt the likes of John Marlowe deserved to spend eternity in Hell. But he would apparently spend that eternity living in luxury and circulating amongst Hell's power elite. He was no expert on matters spiritual, but he was pretty sure this was not the sort of fate envisioned by the fire and brimstone preachers back on earth for especially egregious sinners. Surely one so vile as The Little Rock Madman should boil forever in a lake of fire.

Angela slid open a cabinet to reveal a fully stocked bar. "Drink, John?"

"If you've got something like bourbon in there, I'll have a double." He eyed the gleaming bottles and reconsidered. "No, make that a triple. And while you're at it, could you please tell me how in the name of blue fucking hell David Hasselhoff could be your chauffeur. The man's not dead yet."

Angela filled two glasses with amber liquid from a smoky black bottle and passed one to John. "Cheers."

They clinked glasses.

HELL AIN'T A BAD PLACE TO BE

"Cheers."

John shivered. The booze had a bite, but was also smooth going down, like liquid nirvana.

Angela closed the bar and settled back into the seat. "Oh, David's been dead since the '80s, John. Before me, even. That thing on earth is a magickal construct, a thing fashioned by skilled Bio-Wizards in Lucifer's most secret laboratories. It bides its time. A moment will come. All the world will be watching. And then..."

John let the implied question hang. Whatever diabolical design Hell had in mind for the Hoff's ringer on earth was something he could live without knowing. Things were weird enough already. Something else had occurred to him while watching Angela shift around in the seat and noted the exquisitely supple way the fabric of the dress adhered to her flesh. Ripples and eddies of white radiance swirled across the dress whenever light hit it in just the right way.

"Your dress. It looks..."

She sipped more of the smoky booze and scooted closer to him, placed a hand on his knee. "You like? It's a one of a kind design. Skin, of course. Human skin. Specially treated and enchanted. An anniversary gift from the Grand Duke."

"Okay."

They finished their drinks and had one more. By then the limo had reached its destination. The door to John's right opened. He stepped past the Hoff and gaped at the huge mansion. It stood like a hulking black beast against the scarlet sky, and it looked like the kind of place Donald Trump would want to call home after his own inevitable arrival in Hell.

John looked at Angela. "Is this..." He gulped. "It couldn't be..."

She took him by the arm again. "It's your new home, darling."

John tried to say something else, but only a wheeze emerged.

Angela laughed. "Come. I'll give you the tour."

The tour was a blur of endless hallways and rooms. Dracul's mansion consisted of seemingly a thousand different wings. The place was awash in decadence. He saw things having frenzied sex with other things. Some of it may even have been consensual. They passed through a kitchen, where a bloated human body was roasting slowly over an open pit. At one point he peered through the open doorway of a bedroom and saw a bound man having his nuts chewed off by a woman in a Nun's habit. After a time that felt like two, maybe three years, they arrived at a spacious set of living quarters, impeccably appointed adjoining rooms. One of the rooms was technically John's, but Angela insisted this was a formality. He would spend nearly all his time with her. When she wasn't attending to the Grand Duke's needs and passions, anyway.

John sat on the edge of a plush bed the size of a houseboat and watched the Hoff dump the still-bound hooker on the floor. Angela dismissed the dead B-lister and the man quietly departed, closing the door behind him.

Angela grinned. "Alone at last." Her gaze flicked briefly to the hooker. "Except for our toy here. Oh..." She put a finger to her red lips. "I almost forgot. Your surprise."

She took him by the hand and pulled him to his feet, then into the other bedroom and on through to a small anteroom.

John gasped.

He didn't say anything for a long time, but Angela was beaming at him again.

Then he began to smile, too.

He walked toward her, bent at the waist to look into her eyes. "Hello, Linda. I can't tell you how happy I am to see you again."

Angela came forward, wound a length of Linda's sweat-stained hair in her hand, and lifted her head up. "John, did Linda ever tell you about the thing she did as a teenager? The thing that Damned her?"

"Probably not."

"She and some friends came across a young black child in their neighborhood. He was lost, wasn't supposed to be there. They took him to an empty house and did nasty things to him, things she confessed to me last night after some hours on the rack. She laughed at his cries when she put a cigarette out in his eye."

John arched an eyebrow. "Huh. No. That's news to me."

Linda tried to tell him something, but he couldn't make it out. Her mouth had been sewn shut. She was locked in a pillory. Nude. Her pendulous breasts and sleek, lithe body shiny with fear-sweat. He unzipped his pants and stepped behind her, did the thing she'd told him he would never do with her again. And while he did it, he noted with pleasure the vast array of torture implements hanging from hooks on the walls. When he was done, he tried out a few of them on her.

But he didn't let himself go too far. Not this time. Not yet.

He had plenty of time to creatively hurt her.

Eternity, in fact.

When he was done playing, he let Angela guide him back to the main room. There he swept Angela into his arms and kissed her with a romantic abandon he hadn't felt since the early days of his courtship of Linda.

She eased out of the embrace after a time and said, "You'll be happy here."

John experienced one last pang of something like conscience, a final dying echo of remorse. Then he thought of Linda in the pillory. Licked his lips and savored the sweet taste of Angela's lips. Looked at the bound hooker and thought of some things that might be fun.

He looked into Angela's sparkling eyes again. "Had a beer at that place. Something called Gein's Mean Imperial Stout."

"You can have it perpetually on tap in your room, if you like."

"That singer. Bon Scott. Could he come over some time, maybe entertain us?"

"He'll have a standing invitation."

John's smile was bemused. "I've been thinking I deserve to be here. You know what I mean."

She angled her body against his, slid against his crotch. "Yes. And you do deserve to be here. Right here. With me. With anything you want as yours for the asking."

He pulled her close, kissed her again, breathing the words into her mouth. "I think you're right. I really do."

They kissed some more.

Made love.

Did some interesting things to the hooker.

Did other, even more interesting things to Linda.

And at some point in the festivities, John came to a conclusion. He was right where some secret part of his heart had always known was his destiny.

His true home, the one that had waited for him with such patience.

And possibly he was even falling in love.

Hell, things couldn't be better.

THE HOUSE OF USHERS

OF USHERS

BRIAN KEENE

"**W**hat's the worst thing you've ever done?"

Michaels didn't answer. He, Adam, and Terrell were hunkered down in an alley behind a stack of corpses. Raw sewage bubbled up from the cracked pavement, soaking their knees and feet with filth. The black sky boiled and spit. Instead of hail, decapitated heads fell from the clouds. Michaels hoped the storm would end soon. He much preferred rains of blood or shit—they didn't hurt when they struck you.

Terrell tapped Adam on the shoulder.

"What?" Adam whispered.

"Check this out."

Terrell buried his face between the rotting breasts of a particularly obese corpse and made motorboat sounds. The mounds of flesh jiggled, disturbing a nest of beetles that had burrowed inside them. Terrell came up for air and picked insects and decaying flesh from his chin. He and Adam giggled.

Ignoring them, Michaels peeked over the carrion pile and stared at the barracks. Nothing had changed. Two Ushers still stood out front, guarding the door. Their chisel-slit eyes remained alert, and their nostrils flared. They did not move. Shivering, Michaels ducked down again and glared at Adam.

"What did you ask me?"

Adam repeated it. "What's the worst thing you've ever done?"

"The worst thing I ever did was let you assholes talk me into doing this."

Terrell grinned. It was not a flattering look for him. Every day, the Mephistopolis blossomed with new diseases, and Terrell always caught them. It had been the same way when he was alive. Anytime a new venereal disease came along, Terrell got it. As above, so below. This week, the flesh was sloughing off his face in waxy, glistening sheets.

"Come on, Michaels," he slurred. "You want out of here as bad as we do. So don't even front."

"Of course I do. But there's got to be a better way."

Even as he said it, Michaels knew it wasn't true. This was the only way, unless they wanted to wait for another Deadpass to open somewhere else. Who knew how long that could take? A week, a decade, an eternity? Of course, here in Hell, every day was an eternity. Terrified as he was, Michaels knew this was their only shot at escaping—right through the very bowels of Hell—into the House of Ushers. Deadpasses—holes between the living world and the Hellplanes—were few and far between. The only other ways out were through the Labyrinth, ascendancy to demon-hood, or divine intervention. As slim as the chances were of finding another Deadpass, those options were even less viable. Adam's plan was their only opportunity to escape.

A head splattered against the pavement, showering them with brains and interrupting Michaels' thoughts.

"Seriously," Adam asked a third time. "What's the worst thing you've ever done? Humor me."

Michaels sighed. "First of all, you're ripping off Peter Straub. That's the opening sentence to *Ghost Story*. You're a writer. That's theft—a sin."

Adam shrugged. "Have you taken a look around? Given our current situation, I don't think that matters. It's one small sin among a sea of great ones. The end result is the same. And you're right. It is the opening sentence to *Ghost Story*. But it's a good sentence. It has presence and weight. It fucking resonates, man. If you hit it with a hammer, you'd hear a resounding gong. So I'm stealing it."

Michaels grinned. "Is that the worst thing you've ever done?"

"No…"

Adam fell silent, suddenly afraid. Each man felt it. In Hell, the obsidian sky never changed. There were no moons or sun. Daylight was a memory from their previous existence. But now, against that churning blackness, a shadow soared overhead—predatory and horrifying. For something to inspire fear in this place, it had to be exceptional, and the shadow was. It glided over the city, blotting out the falling heads.

A dead cat hissed at the far end of the alley. The cat had seen better days. Apparently, it had been mummified at some point during its existence. Dirty, tattered bandages hung from its skeletal frame. Without warning, the shadow swept down from the sky. It made no sound as it attacked. Something black and shapeless seized the howling cat and the shadow took flight again, leaving coldness in its wake.

All three men shivered.

"Yo," Terrell whispered, "we can't keep hiding behind this pile of dead bodies. If that thing—whatever it was—don't get us, then the damn garbage trolls will."

"He's right," Michaels said. "They'll be along to load these corpses into a Meat Truck anytime now."

Terrell nodded. "We need to get the fuck inside those barracks."

"Not yet," Adam cautioned. "We can't do shit until they send a squad out. If we go in there before the Ushers leave, we'll be outnumbered—toast."

Three more heads exploded across the pavement. Michaels wished for an umbrella.

"We're going to be toast anyway," he said. "So why don't you fucking answer your own question while we wait, Adam? What's the worst thing *you've* ever done?"

Adam paused. When he spoke again, they had to strain to hear him over the constant wails of the damned. His eyes were wet and red.

"I killed my wife. She was pregnant. The kid…wasn't mine. I lost my mind. Made it look like an accident, pushed her out of the attic window. That's what got me here."

"Jesus Christ…"

Terrell flinched. "Michaels! You know you ain't supposed to say that name here. The fuck is wrong with you? Want to lead them right to us? You'll bring all of Hell down on us."

"Sorry."

Adam wiped away his tears. "How about you guys? What did you do to wind up here?"

"I shot a baby," Terrell said. "My crew was at the zoo, tracking down this bitch that ripped us off. Found her with this baby. Boss-man told me to shoot the baby. I hesitated, but you know how it is. Peer pressure and shit. If I hadn't done it, that would have been it for my ass. So I did. And then the bitch we were chasing shot me and I woke up here."

Michaels shook his head, disgusted and speechless.

"What?" Terrell glared at him. "You too good to be here, Michaels? You an innocent man? You here by mistake?"

"I don't *know* why I'm here," Michaels said, "but it's certainly not because I killed somebody. I just lived my life. I'm not an evil person."

Adam started to respond, but a wailing siren cut him off. All three men risked another peek at the Usher barracks. Red lights flashed inside as the alarm continued to blare. Sulfurous smoke belched from the tall, crooked chimney on top of the building. In the alley, the pavement rumbled beneath their feet.

Michaels gasped. "Feel that?"

"Fuck," Terrell whispered, "it's a stampede."

"It's not a stampede," Adam said. "It's our chance. Cross your fingers."

Frightened, Terrell grabbed Michaels' hand and squeezed. Michaels returned the gesture. Terrell's ulcerated skin burst, squirting pus between Michael's fingers, but Michaels didn't mind. In truth, he barely noticed. His attention was focused on the House of Ushers. Even though he didn't need to anymore, he forgot to breathe.

Adam leaned forward, watching intently. "Here we go. They're sending out a squad. Soon as they leave, the barracks will be empty—just a few Ushers and a skeleton crew. All we have to do is make it past them, find the basement, and go through the Deadpass. Then we're home free."

Michaels rolled his eyes. "Oh, yeah, no problem—easy as pie."

"Do you want to back out? Because now is the time."

"No. But these are fucking Ushers, Adam. They fuck and they kill and they fuck what they kill. That's what they're bred for—pain and mutilation and rape. It's like trying to kill a bull with a toothpick."

Adam shook his head. "They're not invincible."

"Shit," Terrell said, "they're damn close. Can't kill the fuckers on Earth."

"No, we can't," Adam agreed, "but we *can* kill them here. Ushers can die in Hell. Blow their heads off, chop them up, cut out their hearts—and the benevolent damned can cast spells on them here, too."

"Except," Michaels reminded him, "that none of us are benevolent damned."

"No," Adam said, "we aren't. But we do have weapons. And they'll work."

"They better," Terrell said. "I had to suck the pus out of a thousand infected clits just to score these things."

"You'd have done that anyway."

"Fuck you, Adam. I didn't like eating pussy when I was alive, and I sure as shit don't like it now."

Ignoring him, Adam lifted the legs of a corpse and pulled out a large sack. He'd stashed it beneath the bodies when they arrived, safeguarding it from discovery in case they were captured. He opened the sack and reached inside. Michaels and Terrell crowded around him. The first thing Adam pulled out was a sword. The blade was long and thin and very sharp—forged in the Mephistopolis. The metal held a reddish tint, and glinted in the firelight. The hilt was fashioned to depict a mockery of the crucifixion; Christ hung upside down, nailed through the eyes as well as the wrists and feet, his face leering with a madman's grin, his manhood replaced with a crude gaping vagina. Michaels shuddered as he accepted the weapon from Adam. It felt unclean.

Adam produced a second weapon from the sack; a pistol, remarkably similar to a Wilson Combat 1911, but it was manufactured from the black bones of a Great Wyrm. The magazine held ghoul talons instead of bullets. The deadly projectiles had hollow centers, and each one contained a corrosive, acidic center. Terrell held the pistol sideways, so that the sights were pointing to the left.

"That's what I'm talking about." He nodded in satisfaction.

"You're holding it wrong," Michaels told him.

"That's how they do it in the movies."

"Fire it like that and the acid's gonna splash back on you."

"Shit." Terrell sneered, and more of his face fell off. "Ain't no brass flying out of this thing. Acid gonna go out the front. And besides, you see my motherfucking skin? Acid burns would be an improvement on that shit."

Michaels shrugged. "Suit yourself."

Adam pulled out a collapsible shotgun, the twin barrels folded over the stock. He snapped it into place and locked the hinge with a cotter pin carved from the fang of a Vamphyr. Then he reached into his coat pocket and smiled.

"What kind of ammo does that thing take?" Terrell asked.

Still smiling, Adam pulled his hand from his pocket and opened his fingers. Rough lumps of melted silver lay in his palm. Michaels and Terrell both gasped in surprise. Adam dropped the loads down both barrels.

"Yo," Terrell asked, "where the fuck did you get silver?"

"You don't want to know. Let's just say I paid a price and leave it at that."

Michaels studied the weapon. "How's it going to fire? Don't you need some kind of primer or powder?"

"Nope," Adam said. "Trust me, it'll work just fine. Remember that angel they captured last month? Before it died, I snuck into the dungeons and had the angel bless the shotgun. It shoots spells, and never runs out of ammo. The silver is just an extra measure."

Michaels whistled with appreciation. "You thought ahead."

"That's right," Adam said. "Every step of the way. Soon as I found out there was a Deadpass inside the House of Ushers' basement, I started planning. So relax. I'm telling you, this will work."

"It better."

"What you got back on Earth, anyway?" Terrell asked. "What's so important, Michaels?"

"You mean escaping from Hell isn't reason enough?"

"For me and Adam, sure. But you're different. Could be you don't belong here, like you say. But whether you do or don't, I ain't never met a man that wanted out of here more than you do. I can tell. I read people like books."

"Is that so?" Michaels raised his middle finger. "Here. Can you read sign language?"

The barracks' doors flew open and an Usher battalion poured out into the street. Adam, Terrell, and Michaels hugged the pavement, biting their lips and praying to the God who'd condemned them here that they wouldn't be spotted. The Ushers were dressed for urban riot control—studded leather armor with blood-stained, razor-sharp spikes and edges; great, curved weapons with sigils etched into the blades; firearms that could disintegrate a body with one fiery blast; massive clubs that could pulp the heads of a dozen men with one blow. But the armament was more for psychological use than practical. The Ushers didn't even need it. Their inhuman design was one of Hell's most enduring and efficient legacies. An Usher's claws could rend steel and their jaws and teeth were powerful enough to chew through bedrock. They would lay waste at random, decimating a city block and slaying all who dwelled there. They would rape, dismember, torture, and kill— then do it all over again to anything that was left, regardless of whether it was still recognizable or even intact, all in the name of civil obedience and of keeping the populace on its toes.

All to retain the status quo.

Trembling, Michaels dared to peek over the corpses and watched the battalion march out of sight. The Ushers moved like a column of ants. There were hundreds of them and their stench was terrible. Cloven feet pounded the pavement. The buildings swayed from the vibration. The damned stopped wailing, terrified into silence.

Michaels didn't notice that both Adam and Terrell had pissed themselves because he was too busy doing the same.

After the column had marched out of sight, the three men stood up. Still concealed in the alley, they peered out at the House of Ushers. The barracks were silent. The two guards were still positioned at the door, but their attention was focused farther down the street, where a baby vendor was serving up roasted infants on hot buns and loading them with ketchup, mustard, onions and relish. The vendor handed the treats to three minor demons, who greedily devoured them. Watching, the Ushers drooled, but did not leave their post.

"They're distracted." Adam readied the shotgun, holding it slightly upright so the silver wouldn't slip out of the barrels. "You guys ready?"

"Let's do this shit," Terrell said.

Michaels gripped the sword and nodded. He was too afraid to speak.

Adam strode out of the alley and quickly crossed the street. After a moment's hesitation, Michaels and Terrell followed. As they drew closer, one of the Ushers turned towards them, broad nostrils flaring, catching their scent. It grunted, more out of annoyance than surprise. Snorting, it took a single step in their direction. The pavement grew black where it trod. Adam faltered. Behind him, Michaels and Terrell prepared to run.

Then Adam shot the Usher in the face.

The shotgun belched greenish-white flame. The creature reared backward, clawing at its eyes. Crackling energy clung to its head. Its mottled flesh sizzled, sloughing off in sheets. Michaels sniffed the air. Above the stench of sulfur and shit and his own piss, he smelled cooked meat. His stomach grumbled. He hadn't eaten in a year.

Bellowing, the wounded Usher collapsed to its knees, and then tottered forward, dead. Its flesh continued to bubble and fizz. The other guard rushed towards them. It made no sound, but its eyes said all they needed to know. Michaels raised his sword with trembling hands and braced himself for the charge. He shut his eyes and whimpered. Adam's shotgun rang out again. Michael's heard the second Usher fall. He opened his eyes and stared in disbelief. Both creatures had been dispatched.

"Holy shit."

"Indeed," Adam said. "Now let's keep moving."

They dashed up the steps and halted in front of the closed door. This close to the barracks, the building's aura made them nauseous. Michaels fought to keep from puking. He didn't need to, of course. There was nothing in his stomach *to* puke up. But the old habits of living died hard.

"What the fuck we waiting for?" Terrell reached for the handle.

"Don't," Adam warned him, but it was too late.

Terrell's hand wrapped around the door handle. Immediately, the brass twisted, coming to life. Metallic tendrils coiled around his fingers and squeezed. His bones snapped. Terrell screamed. The tendrils climbed higher, racing up his wrist and forearm, pulling him closer.

"The sword," Adam yelled. "Michaels, cut him loose."

"I can't just—"

"Do it, motherfucker," Terrell shrieked. His eyes rolled into the back of his head and his teeth chattered with pain and shock. "It ain't like the shit ain't gonna grow back again. Cut it off, man!"

Michaels raised the sword, hesitating.

Adam shoved him. "What are you waiting for?"

Terrell moaned. The coils had reached his elbow. More bones snapped. Blood flowed. Cursing, Michaels brought the sword down, cleaving Terrell's arm just above the elbow. The hilt grew warm in his hands, and the carved figure of Christ sighed against his palm. Disgusted, Michaels almost dropped the sword.

Terrell stared at his stump. Blood jetted from the wound. The tentacles crushed the severed appendage into paste. Then they slowly reformed into a doorknob.

"I'm sorry, man," Michaels apologized. "There wasn't anything else we could do."

Terrell grinned. "Shit, it don't matter. Like I said, it'll grow back. They always do in this place. Long as I can still hold this pistol, it ain't no thing."

He demonstrated, posing like Wesley Snipes in *New Jack City*.

"You're still holding it wrong," Michaels told him. "You're gonna fuck yourself up."

Terrell nodded at his stump. "Can't be no worse than this."

"We're wasting time," Adam said, glancing down the deserted street. "The head storm's over. No telling when the street will get busy again."

"Well," Terrell said, his voice indignant. "Let's see you open the fucking thing."

Nodding, Adam stepped closer to the door. Then he whispered in a language the others had never heard. When he was finished, he stepped backward. Slowly, the door creaked open. The stench that wafted out was revolting—a charnel miasma that seemed to cling to them.

Michaels gaped. "Where did you learn to do that?"

"Same place I got the weapons. The language is Sumerian."

"But what did it mean? Those words you said?"

"I don't know. It's the Ushers' password. Probably something nasty."

"We gonna stand here all night?" Terrell asked. "Thought you said time's a wasting."

Adam swept his arm out and bowed. "Lead the way."

"Shit. Don't look at me."

"Then get out of the way." Adam pushed past Terrell and entered the House of Ushers. Michaels crept along behind him. Terrell hesitated, and then followed.

They passed through a foyer carved from black marble and stepped into a large room, obviously bigger inside than the barrack's outside dimensions. The high, vaulted ceilings stretched hundreds of feet over their heads, and the walls were barely visible on the horizon. Endless rows of bunk beds ran the length of the room, stacked three high. The frames were constructed from stone and the pillows and mattresses were stuffed with human hair. Blonde locks spilled from a torn pillow. The mattresses and pillowcases were made out of human skin.

"My God," Michaels gasped. His voice echoed in the vast chamber.

God… God… God…

"Dude!" Adam punched his shoulder in anger. "Don't fucking say that name here. They'll be on us quicker thank you can blink."

"Sorry. It's just…so big. It's kind of hard to wrap my brain around, you know?"

Adam nodded. "It's bigger on the inside than it is on the outside — some kind of interspatial dimension thing."

"Are you sure all the Ushers are gone? Can this place really be deserted?"

"No. Like I said before, there's still the skeleton crew to deal with.

That's why we need to keep moving. Find the Deadpass before they find us."

"True that," Terrell said. His stump had stopped bleeding. "Let's get the fuck out of here."

"We're going home," Michaels whispered, trying to convince himself that it was true.

"According to my sources," Adam said, pointing to their left, "the basement stairs should be over that way."

Michaels balked. "How far?"

"About a quarter of a mile."

"My Go…"

Adam and Terrell tensed, but Michaels stopped himself from finishing the word in time.

"Sorry."

They walked on, side by side, weapons at the ready. Their footsteps rang out. Otherwise, the barracks were silent. They passed by what looked like a bath of some kind—a stone circle surrounding a depression in the floor. Words and figures were carved in the masonry, but none of them could read it. The pool was filled with black, stagnant liquid.

"What's that?" Michaels whispered.

Adam shook his head. "I don't know. An Usher foot bath, maybe?"

"I'm serious."

"So am I. I don't know what it is, but that water looks pretty nasty."

Terrell reached into his pocket and pulled out a coin. Hitler's face was engraved on one side. Reverend Jim Baker's face decorated the other.

"What are you doing?" Adam asked.

"Making a wish."

Balancing the coin on the ball of his thumb, Terrell flicked it into the pool. It made no sound as it broke the surface, but small concentric rings spread out across the water, lapping at the stones. Then the rings began to run backwards, drawing into the center of the pool. As they watched, the liquid began to congeal. A small pseudo-pod formed in the middle of the water and then rose into the air, growing in size.

"I got a bad feeling about this," Terrell moaned.

"Move!" Adam shoved them both forward.

They ran past the bath. Behind them, the black tentacle waved about in the air like a snake. Then it collapsed back into the pool.

Adam glared at Terrell. "Quit fucking around."

"Yo, how was I supposed to know that shit was alive?"

Michaels glanced back the way they'd come. "What was that thing, anyway?"

"I don't know," Adam said. "Something bad, obviously. There's nothing good in here. All the more reason for us to get out. Now, let's keep moving, and for fuck's sake, Terrell, don't touch anything else."

They moved on, searching for the basement stairs, trying to ignore the horrors around them. Obscene tapestries and paintings adorned the walls. One of them depicted the Virgin Mary in a bukkake scene with the twelve Disciples. Another showed the prophet Mohammed receiving anal from a particularly well-endowed demon. A third was of the Whore of Babylon riding astride a multi-headed beast. Each of the creature's faces was that of a world leader. American Presidents, British Prime Ministers, and military despots leered down at them. The tip of the beast's penis—which was small in comparison to the rest of its size—also had a face.

Gawking, Michaels pointed. "Isn't that Bush?"

"Sure is." Adam grinned. "Always knew he was a dickhead."

All three of them laughed. The sound echoed throughout the barracks, and they fell silent again. Then they continued on their way.

"Do you guys really want to know the worst thing I've ever done?" Michael asked.

They nodded.

"I was married. My wife, Linda, was my world. I loved her like you wouldn't believe. You ever love somebody so much that your stomach hurts?"

"Yeah," Adam whispered. "I have."

"Well, that was how I felt about Linda. But I ignored her. Not on purpose. I bought her nice things. Gave her security—a nice home, nice car. But I didn't pay attention to her needs. I worked for an online brokerage. Long hours. Climbing the corporate ladder. Same old story. I focused on my career. Dedicated myself to achieving my goals—becoming what I'd always wanted to be. I was following my dreams, and I expected Linda to follow them with me. She was my wife, after all. She should support me."

"Damn straight," Terrell said. "Bitches ain't shit but hoes and tricks."

"Shut up," Michaels grumbled. "It's not like that at all. Linda had dreams, too. She wanted to have kids. That's all. Just two kids—a boy and a girl. But I kept putting it off. Told her I needed to focus on my career. And then, five years later, Linda got ovarian cancer."

Adam paused. "Shit."

"Yeah," Michaels said, leading them forward. "She survived, but the doctors said she'd never be able to have kids. If we'd started trying earlier—if I hadn't made her wait. But I ignored her desires. That's why I'm here."

"That ain't so bad," Terrell said. "You must have done worse shit than that."

Michaels shook his head. "No. That's my greatest sin. She's getting married again. Next week, in fact. The demons have been taunting me with it, torturing me by showing me scenes of her new life. She looks happy."

"Sorry," Adam said. "That must be tough to watch."

Michaels shrugged. "I pretend it is. I scream and wail and do everything the demons expect me to do. But the truth is, I'm happy for her. Seeing Linda like that and knowing that she's happy makes Hell

BRIAN KEENE

a little more bearable. She's got a second chance, you know? Maybe Linda and her new husband can adopt. Maybe he'll pay more attention to her."

Adam stared at him in comprehension. "You're going to the wedding, aren't you? That's why you want out of here."

"Yeah," Michaels admitted. "That's my plan. I want to see her happy. Want to say I'm sorry. I never got the chance before."

"Maybe you will," Adam said.

"God, I hope so."

God... God... God...

"Damn it, Michaels!" Adam glanced around, alarmed.

A dry rasping sound echoed across the chamber.

"The fuck is that?" Terrell aimed the pistol at nothing.

"Oh shit," Adam moaned. "It's the skeleton crew."

The rasping sounds drew closer. Michaels spotted movement from several different areas, all closing in on their location. As the figures drew closer, he heard clicking, like wooden wind chimes. Then the creatures emerged into the light.

They were skeletons, bare of flesh or clothing—just white bones, polished till they gleamed. Their eyes were black holes, devoid of light. They carried an assortment of weapons—swords, maces, guns, axes, and knives. Spying the three intruders, the skeletons charged. They did not speak or shout. The only sound was the clatter of their bodies. They moved in creaking spasms.

"Fuck this." Still holding the handgun to one side, Terrell opened fire. He squeezed the trigger three times. The corrosive bullets tore into the skeletons, shattering their bones. At the same time, the ghoul talon jackets sprang from the side of the pistol—directly into Terrell's disease-ravaged face. Flinching, he dropped the pistol and screamed. Welts appeared on his flesh. They turned from red to black. His skin split open and began to bubble. Tendrils of smoke curled from his face. The welts grew wider, revealing bone and gristle. Then the acid began eating its way through that, as well.

331

THE HOUSE OF USHERS

"It burns," he screamed. "Oh motherfucker, it's eating my fucking skin off!"

His cries turned into gurgles as the acid dissolved his tongue. Terrell fell to the floor, thrashing in agony. His melted flesh spread out in a steaming pool.

The skeletons drew closer. Adam's shotgun rang out, firing spells at point blank range. Michaels swung the sword, cleaving through bones like they were butter. Jesus laughed gleefully beneath his palms. When an opening appeared, Adam grabbed Michaels' arm and pulled him along.

"Come on!"

They ran, almost slipping in Terrell's liquefied remains. There was nothing they could do for him. It would be at least a full day before he reformed. Dodging the skeletons, they fled down an aisle of bunks.

"The staircase!" Adam pointed. "I see it over there."

Michaels didn't respond. His lungs felt like bursting. His head throbbed.

They dashed down the black marble stairs, ignoring the carved-bone handrail, and emerged into the basement. The Deadpass glowed in the center, crackling with eldritch energies. Although it made no noise, they heard it humming inside their heads.

"That's it," Adam shouted. "We're home free, Michaels."

He ran towards the portal. Michaels followed him, but slid to a halt as a huge, dark form lumbered out from behind a vat of eyeballs and blocked their path. It was an Usher—the biggest Michaels had ever seen. Its eyes were as large as dinner plates. When it breathed, Michaels cringed. It was like standing next to a blast furnace filled with feces. The creature wore a necklace of human skulls and a loin-cloth made from human skin.

Adam didn't even have time to scream.

The Usher's massive hands shot out and seized him by the neck. It picked him up and turned him around. Adam's feet dangled above

332

the floor. The shotgun fell from his hands. Grunting, the Usher turned him around. Then, still holding him aloft with one hand, it ran a talon along his backside, slicing his pants open.

Quivering, Adam pleaded with Michaels to help him. Instead, Michaels stepped backward. He heard the skeletons at the top of the stairs.

The Usher's penis sprang forward, swaying and bobbing like a snake. The thick, slimy organ pulsated in the dim light, covered with warts and sores. It laughed. The sound was like sandpaper.

Moving carefully. Michaels crept around them. Adam reached for him, but Michaels looked away.

The Usher positioned its throbbing cock and pulled Adam closer.

"Michaels! Help me you bastard!"

"I'm sorry, Adam. I've got a wedding to attend. Got to get to the church on time."

The last thing Michaels heard before he leapt through the Deadpass was the condemned man's screams. Michaels considered praying for Adam, but he knew from experience that prayers for the damned were an exercise in futility.

He abandoned his friend and didn't look back.

It was the second worst thing he'd ever done.